Peaches

and Lace

Joy Ross Davis

This is a work of fiction. Names, characters, places, and incidents are products of the author's imagination or are used fictitiously and are not to be construed as real. Any resemblance to actual events, locations, organizations, or persons, living or dead, is entirely coincidental.

World Castle Publishing, LLC
Pensacola, Florida
Copyright © Joy Ross Davis 2019
Paperback ISBN: 9781950890361
eBook ISBN: 9781950890378
First Edition World Castle Publishing, LLC, August 12, 2019
http://www.worldcastlepublishing.com

Cover: Karen Fuller
Editor: Maxine Bringenberg

This book is dedicated with love and gratitude to my dear friend and gifted writer, Parris Afton Bonds.

Chapter 1

At 6:00 a.m., a large truck pulled up in front of the Salvation Army collection site in the heart of Atlanta. A woman wearing ragged jeans and a blue hoodie climbed out of the driver's side and headed straight for the manager. He waved at her, and as she came closer, he grabbed her in a bear hug.

"It's been a while. How've you been?"

"Fine, Marcus, just fine. Hope I didn't get you up too early."

"Are you kidding? For one of your donations, I'd stay up all night! And I want to thank you for helping my family. Everything's so much better now thanks to you."

"Come and see what I've brought for the girls at Harmony House." The men had already started unloading the precious cargo. "Be careful," she said to them. "Those are special gowns for special women."

"What do we have here?" Marcus asked.

"Let's see. I think there are four wedding gowns with detachable trains, never worn, four pairs of heels, all the necessary undergarments, including a few hoop skirts in case they're needed. There are four veils and some girlie things. But please, keep it quiet."

"As per our agreement," he said. "Though I still don't know why you don't want the whole of Atlanta knowing how much you give to Harmony House."

The woman shook her head. "The important thing is that the

girls know. You and I know. That's enough, right?"

Marcus shrugged. "I guess so. The girls are always so delighted with the dresses. Never in their lives would they be able to afford one of your wedding gowns. But every time you come, they spend hours and hours trying on the dresses, modeling them for each other, choosing the one they like best. Your dresses lift their spirits and give them a sense of pride and hope. Even if they're not getting married, they still love those dresses. It's the bright spot of their month whenever you come."

"You still have your seamstress in case the gowns need alterations?"

"Oh, yes, we do. In fact, one of the new girls at Harmony House is a whiz on the sewing machine. She's had a terrible life, but she seems to be getting better. Her eyes will light up when she sees these dresses."

"Oh," she said. "I cleared out an apartment near the studio, so I've brought a couple of beds, an old TV, a few bureaus. Just odds and ends that might be of use."

"It's far too much, as usual."

"Not nearly enough as I see it. They're almost finished unloading." She gave him a swift kiss on the cheek. "Take care of my girls," she said. "And remember...."

He nodded. "It's a secret, just between the two of us."

She winked at him. "All of these are only partially paid for. A down payment was made, but the bride never showed up again. I really don't understand, but I've had these four gowns for over a year taking up space in the workshop. I've tried to get in touch with the girls, but I can't seem to find them. The numbers have been changed or no one claims to know them. I don't have the answers, but there's no point in keeping them when they're just taking up space."

"Stuff happens. Lives take a spin when we least expect it."

"That's for sure. Hey, I need to run now, Marcus. Send me photos if you can. I loved the last ones."

"Are you sure you don't want that cup of coffee?"

"I can't today. Maybe next time. The show's tonight, and I'm nervous as a cat, but I have plenty to do to keep me busy. Will Andrew be able to help usher? I have a tuxedo for him, just like last year."

Marcus shook his head. "That oldest of mine. He's in and out all the time, but I managed to remind him. He said he'd be glad to do it. I think he's looking forward to doing something that he gets paid for, and hobnobbing with the rich and famous."

The woman giggled. "Just make sure he's at the auditorium at 6:30 night. This is the big one, Marcus, and it's very important that Andrew show up. Will he do it?"

"I'll drive him myself and threaten him within an inch of his life."

She laughed. "No need to go that far. He's a good boy, and he did a fine job last year."

Marcus rubbed his arms. "It's cold out here. Come in where it's warm and have some coffee."

"Next time. I promise." She climbed into the truck, seated herself, and waved. "Take care of my girls," she said, "and call me if you need anything." Then she put her finger to her mouth. "Shhh."

Marcus pretended to zip his lips. Then he gave her a thumbs up.

The woman waved as she drove away, but when she checked the side mirror, she thought she saw a man leaning on the wall of the building, a very tall man wearing a dark blue frock coat, his arms crossed over his broad chest. She slammed on the brakes and opened the door, but when she looked back, there was no one there.

"What's wrong?" Marcus asked.

"Nothing," she said. "Did you happen to see a tall man leaning against the wall over there? He had on an old-fashioned blue coat."

7

"I haven't seen anyone else. Are you sure you saw him?"

"No, I'm not sure," she said. "Probably my mind playing tricks on me."

Marcus looked worried.

"It's okay," she said. "Just my overactive imagination. See you next time."

She waved again and drove away.

Chapter 2

Peaches Malone unzipped the hoodie and tossed it on the chair in her office. She slipped on a pair of heels, studied her face and hair in the mirror, put on a fresh blouse, and then went out into the darkened auditorium.

"Ugh," she said. "We need lights."

She walked to the side hall and flipped the switches. The auditorium lit up. Then she noticed that the lights didn't come on in the back of the auditorium.

She thought for a minute. "Where are those switches?" she mumbled. "Ah, other side."

Once she'd flipped those, the back of the auditorium was bathed in light.

Peaches walked back to the middle of the room where she kept her microphone, but as she bent to pick it up and test it, she froze.

The man she'd seen earlier stood at the back of the auditorium leaning against the wall.

Peaches bolted toward the back of the building as fast as her stilettos could carry her. "You there, who are you? I saw you at the Salvation Army just a little while ago."

"I think you might have dropped these," he said and handed her a two pairs of white heels.

"Oh," she said, and took the shoes. "These are for the girls at the Salvation Army. They must have dropped from the bag. You followed and came here to bring these?"

"I asked the manager where I could find you. He trusted me enough to tell me."

"You know him?"

The tall man nodded. "Yes," he said. "I didn't mind bringing them."

"You should have just left them there. Didn't he tell you they were donations?"

"No. He said he thought they might be, but he wasn't sure and it was best to ask you."

"Well, thank you for bringing them."

"It was no problem," he said. "I'll be going now."

"Do you need a job? Do you model?" Her hands began trembling. "I want to talk to you," she said, and put the shoes into one of the seats, but as she looked again, the man had simply vanished.

Gone.

"Where *is* he?" she asked aloud, and held out her hands. "How could he have disappeared right before my eyes?"

The side door made a swishing sound as it closed. Peaches studied the double doors and the side door. *But how could he have gotten so quickly to the side door without my seeing him?*

"Peaches," Aileen called from the stage. "What's wrong?"

Peaches sucked in a breath. Her heart pounded. Her hands trembled wildly.

"Peaches, you okay back there?"

Peaches turned around and headed back down the center aisle, and plopped down into a chair.

"We've thirty minutes until rehearsal," Aileen said. "I'm early, but I just wanted to make sure everything was okay."

"You're a jewel, Aileen," Peaches said. "As long as everyone shows up, we'll be fine."

"Everyone except Rand is here already. They're all in the back. I'm sure Rand will be here. You know him. He's always late."

Peaches sighed and surveyed her still-trembling hands. "This show is so important," she said. "We just can't have any mistakes. Rand needs to try to be on time. I think my nerves are a total mess."

Peaches rifled through her purse, found her compact, and flipped it open. She smoothed her long blonde hair and checked her makeup, and used her pinky finger to straighten the corners of her red lipstick, then ran a finger over each dark brow. Lifting her head to ensure she'd left no make-up lines, she glanced at the thickness of the mascara that framed her cerulean blue eyes, and then puckered her lips. She smoothed on a bit of lip gloss.

"You look stunning as always, Peaches. Your makeup is already perfect. No need to fiddle with it."

Peaches smiled at Aileen. "Flattery will get you just about anywhere in this business," she said. Then she turned to look to the back of the small auditorium.

"Peaches, were you looking for someone back there near the doors?"

Peaches shook her head. "It was no one, some guy who brought — well, never mind."

"Hmm, was he good looking?"

Peaches chuckled. "Yes, very," she said.

"I'll go back and see if Rand is here," Aileen said. "You sure you're okay? Be right back."

Peaches shooed her away and watched as her assistant disappeared into the studio space. Then she turned and looked toward the double doors again.

And there he stood, arms crossed, staring straight at her.

"Hello?" she called to him. "You, in the back. Will you please answer me?"

He pointed to himself.

"Yes, you," she said, and stood up. "Would you please come down here?"

"Uh, Peaches," Aileen said. "Who are you talking to? I don't see anyone."

Peaches turned and gave her a quizzical look. "He's standing right there by the double doors."

Aileen leaned forward. "I still can't see anyone," she said.

Suddenly, the double doors flew open, and in rushed a young man with long brown hair, dressed in shorts and a T-shirt.

"Sorry, Peaches," he said, obviously winded. "My car."

"It's okay, Rand. Just get dressed and get on stage. We've only twenty minutes until rehearsal."

"Will do," he said.

When she looked toward the double doors, the man had disappeared again. Peaches frowned. "What is up with this guy?" she asked.

"What guy?" Aileen responded.

"The one I told you about. He was standing in the back by the double doors. Tall guy wearing a blue frock coat. He looked right at me but wouldn't say anything."

Peaches sat back down and ran a hand through her thick blonde hair.

There was something about him, something wonderfully mysterious that she found very attractive. Or perhaps it was the shimmer of the back lights that cast an eerie glow all around him. Maybe it was his Victorian costume. He stood like a giant, his head high above the door frame—he must have been around 6'7" tall—and that coat, that blue frock coat. By the way the light played off it, she knew the material must be rich blue velvet. His stark white ruffled shirt befitted the period of the upcoming runway show, a throwback to the late 1880s, and his tight black pants with those leather boots…she imagined him to be quite handsome, though she'd never really seen his face in the light.

"Peaches, are you ready for me?"

Peaches blinked to clear away the visions swirling in her mind. "You look great, Rand. Now, where is the bride?"

A young girl in a satin wedding gown stood center stage. "Here," she called.

Peaches walked to the stage and examined the dress, a long-sleeved Victorian-style gown made of ecru satin and trimmed in the finest lace. Peaches ran her hand along the satin bodice and felt instant joy. The satin cascaded down the bodice and into the skirt in silky waves. She thrived on the feel of these satin gowns. Satin, the fabric of royalty. When her fingers lit on the material, without fail, she felt like a beloved queen ruling over her court. Sometimes she felt as if the satin talked back to her, and thanked her for the opportunity for its royal elegance to be displayed.

She closed her eyes and listened for a moment. Yes, there it was. A barely audible "Thank you, Peaches." When she opened her eyes again, she trained her thoughts on the bodice, then examined the pearl beading and lace insets that ran the length of the sleeves, stopping at the girl's thin wrists.

"Hold your arms out, honey," she said. Peaches examined every detail of the fitted sleeves, all the while chewing on her bottom lip. "Yes, those are good," she said with a smile. "Now, just let me make a final check of the bodice." Peaches smoothed the satin bodice and made slight adjustments to the lace dotted with pearls that lay snuggly across the girl's small chest. "Now, give us a twirl."

As the girl twirled around, Peaches' eyes widened. Then she gasped and put her hand to her mouth. "What's this? Look at this," Peaches said. "Look."

Aileen stared at the two-inch rip in the edge of the corset lacing for the back of the gown.

"Oh mercy," Peaches said. "How in the world did that happen?"

Aileen shook her head. "I swear, Peaches. I didn't see it." Aileen ran her hands along the back of the gown. "I went over every inch of it this morning as we put it on her. Honest to God, that rip wasn't there. I'm sorry, Peaches," Aileen said. She brushed a stray dark lock from her cheek and leaned in to inspect the tear.

"Margaret-Ann, can you come out here?" Peaches asked. "Please, come quickly."

A rather tall but slightly overweight woman, with curly gray hair and huge round black-rimmed glasses, bustled in, wearing a flowing floral caftan and rubber-soled shoes. Peaches held out a hand to her.

Margaret-Ann stroked her hands. "You're trembling. Whatever is wrong, Peaches?"

"Look at this. There's a two-inch tear right here in the back of this gown. The runway show is tomorrow night. Everything has to be perfect."

"Calm yourself, Peaches," Margaret-Ann said, her voice as soft and bright as a melody. "Let's have a look."

Peaches pointed to the tear. "How could that have happened?" she asked.

Margaret-Ann touched the small tear. "This is fine satin, very fine," she said. "It takes a deft hand to handle it. The lace at the edge of the bodice is fragile as butterfly wings. Now, it doesn't matter at this point how it happened. It matters whether or not I have time to fix it."

"I have every faith that you can get this fixed, so don't get stressed about it. Okay?"

"I'll do it," Margaret Ann said, "and don't you go worrying about me. I'm perfectly capable of fixing a little tear in the fabric."

Peaches smiled. "Worried? Me? Don't be silly. Peaches Malone doesn't worry," she said, and winked.

"Well," Margaret-Ann said. "Tomorrow night is THE show, Peaches. We've got a full, sold-out house. People from all over the world are coming. This one show will give them what they all want: an exclusive look at the new creations of Peaches and Lace."

Peaches nodded but didn't smile. "Yes," she said, and wrung

her trembling hands.

"I'll take care of it. Don't you worry yourself. Now, come with me, girl," she said to the model, "and let's see what I can do."

The young model carefully picked up the billowing satin and lace skirt of the wedding gown and followed Margaret-Ann.

"This dress is the crowning jewel of the collection. Please do your very best," Peaches said softly.

Margaret-Ann nodded. "You know I will, Peaches."

Peaches hugged her then, and stroked the side of her face. "I know you will," she said. "You're the best seamstress in all of Atlanta."

Margaret-Ann chuckled and leaned in close. "You do yourself a favor. Go outside to your private garden and soak up the glory of nature. It'll do you good. This show will go off without a single hitch, and tomorrow night, you'll have more orders than we can handle, so we can't have the star of the show feeling poorly."

Peaches felt her eyes tear. "This one is so important, Margaret-Ann. So very important. Our whole futures might depend on this one show."

Margaret-Ann patted her arm. "Now, dry those eyes. Don't ruin your mascara," she chuckled. "We've got this. Your audience will be astounded by these beautiful new gowns."

"You think so?"

Margaret-Ann winked. "Oh, I know so," she said, and walked toward the sewing rooms. "No worries, Peaches. No worries... except for those shoes of yours."

"My shoes? What's wrong with these shoes?"

"You'd think the nation's top fashion designer could put on a pair of matching stilettos," Margaret-Ann said, and chuckled as she walked away.

Peaches looked down. One black heel, one navy blue heel.

"I can't believe I did that," she said, and laughed out loud and remembered her early morning stop at Harmony House.

"Too much of a hurry, I guess."

Chapter 3

Peaches gazed back to the double doors of the auditorium. The man wasn't there.

Her heart felt heavy, her hands trembled. So much depended on this show, the Grand Winter Show, the one so eagerly anticipated by the public — her public. And now, her international public.

She swallowed hard.

Success at this show would give her the money she needed, the money to achieve a long-held dream, one she'd had since she was a little girl. Even as a small child, she had spent hours poring over fashion magazines, magazines that had been thrown into the trash bin at the apartment building where she lived. Every few days she'd go through the bins looking for discarded magazines. By the time she was eight, she had a huge stack that had been donated by the proprietor of the building. And every night, after she'd spent the day helping out in the restaurant downstairs, she'd spend hours until bedtime looking through every page. By the time she was ten, she was creating her own designs on white paper napkins that she got from the owner of the restaurant.

His customers were French and Spanish, and the magazines they left behind showed her worlds beyond her own in the dismal, impoverished neighborhood of east Atlanta. Her room in the apartment wasn't filled with toys but with fashion magazines, stacks of them, everywhere there was a couple of inches of space.

She smiled at the memories. Those magazines created the world she longed for now, had longed for since she was but a tiny girl.

A shop in the United States and a shop in Europe. Yes, that would mean success!

Suddenly, she saw the man appear again beside the double doors of the auditorium. She was determined to talk to him, but as she left the stage, a gasp and a squeal came from Margaret-Ann.

"Peaches," she said. "Come here quickly."

Peaches looked toward the doors again, but the man had utterly disappeared…again.

"How does he do that?" she asked. "How?"

"Peaches, come quickly!"

Peaches turned and went down the long hallway. "What is it, Margaret-Ann?" she said as she hurried to the dressing room. "Are you ill? Do I need to call a doctor?"

Tears streamed down Margaret-Ann's face. Peaches felt as if her heart had plunged into her stomach. She wrapped her arms around Margaret-Ann.

"Please tell me what's wrong. I promise we'll fix it, whatever it is."

Margaret-Ann snuffled. "It's gone," she said.

"What's gone?"

"The two-inch tear. I can't find it anywhere, and I marked it with my pins. But see for yourself, Peaches. There's no tear anywhere."

Peaches ran her fingers between the pins, pulled gently, lifted the edge of the bodice. "There's nothing there," she whispered. "Nothing. How did this happen?"

"We'll call it a miracle of the universe," Margaret-Ann said.

Peaches smiled and shook her head. "There must be an explanation. Rips don't fix themselves, especially on a fine satin gown like this one."

18

"Well, it's fixed, and without any of my help. I'm going to inspect carefully again."

Peaches let out a big sigh. It seemed a burden had been lifted off her shoulders, and she leaned against the door frame. "It's such a relief," she said.

"But isn't it time for — ?"

"Oh, the inspection!" Peaches clapped her hands. "Roll call," she announced. "Is everyone here?"

Several of the models nodded. "All present and accounted for," one of them said.

"Please get with your partners. We need to inspect each outfit carefully to make sure there are no imperfections."

Peaches heard the soft grumbling from the models. Inspections like these were time-consuming and boring, but perfection was a hallmark of Peaches and Lace.

Margaret-Ann smoothed the front of her apron and walked to the couple nearest her. She ran her hands over the bodice of the sheath gown, checking each seam.

"Aileen?" Peaches called. "We could use some help here. Inspect the trains on each gown to make sure there are no tears, no seams pulled apart."

Aileen appeared in a flash and took her place beside Margaret-Ann. Peaches smiled at her.

"We all must remember," she announced to the group, "that with each show, our reputation is on the line. Together, we can pull off a great show, but it takes all of us. Our public demands not only beauty, but perfection, and we're the ones who can give it to them. Right?"

"Right," the group said in unison.

Peaches smiled at them, but she grimaced as she watched her hands tremble when she inspected another gown.

An hour later, inspection finished, a collective sigh came from the models.

"Okay," Peaches said. "You've all done a marvelous job.

Now, go and get changed. Let either Margaret-Ann or Aileen make sure the garments are hung correctly in your stations, since we'll be doing a final steaming before the show tomorrow night. Is everyone okay? Any questions?"

The models shook their heads in unison.

"Time to relax now," Peaches said. "I'm very proud of you all. Let's give ourselves a round of applause."

There were whoops and hollers and the almost deafening sounds of twenty pairs of hands clapping.

"Now, go away and relax," Peaches said. "Please stay for an hour in case we find any imperfections. I want everything perfect, absolutely perfect for the show tomorrow night."

The models chuckled and each walked toward the lounge area.

Peaches turned away from them and walked toward the long hallway that housed her office, her mismatched stilettos clicking against the tile floor. Her stomach had settled down. Now if she could just stop those trembling hands. But she knew that wouldn't happen just yet. Her audience would be packed with dignitaries from all over the world: France, Spain, Portugal, Italy, and the U.S. She couldn't begin to fathom the impact of this one. Here she was, a designer from Atlanta, about to present her work to the international set—to royalty—and she owed it all to her best friend Lily.

Chapter 4

The next evening, the auditorium began to fill with clients, potential clients, hopeful young women with their mothers, curious reporters from papers all across the South, and journalists from other countries. From behind the drapes, Peaches watched the faces of the incoming guests. Right away she saw the internationals come in. They were high society, most of them with brightly colored banners draped from their shoulders and secured at their waists. Prime ministers, members of royal families, ambassadors, and noble dignitaries—all accompanied by aides—came in and took their marked seats.

After a few minutes, when she thought her heart might just hammer its way out of her chest, she escaped through a side door and headed for her sanctuary, a walled private English-style garden replete with a variety of hostas, two large magnolia trees, and an assortment of rose bushes. Two bird feeders hung from the magnolia trees and a stone pathway made for easy refills. Four white wrought iron benches sat at various places throughout, and in the very center between the two magnolias, an antique turquoise fluted bird bath almost four feet tall carved with figures of garden goddesses provided water for her thirsty birds.

She sat on the closest bench and sipped her favorite gourmet coffee, tipped with a hint of Bailey's Irish Cream.

"Mmm," she whispered as she took another sip. It was

the moment she'd been waiting for all day—alone, safe in her sanctuary, and with her coffee and Bailey's. Just a moment to herself to savor the exquisite aroma and taste of her favorite drink.

"Meow," she heard, and grinned.

"Ah, there you are, Missy. I wondered where you'd gone."

Peaches picked up the white Persian and hugged her close. She'd never had a pet before, but for the last two years, she'd been feeding and housing the cat. Reaching into her pants pocket, she drew out a few treats. Missy gobbled them up as if she hadn't eaten in a month.

Peaches chuckled. "Now, I know you're not that hungry," she said, and ran her hands along the soft fur of the cat's back. She put another handful of treats down, set Missy on the bench, and let her nibble away. "It's almost time to go inside. Plenty of food and water in there, and your cozy bed is waiting."

"May I sit?" came a deep male voice.

Peaches jumped and turned swiftly toward the voice, drops of her cherished coffee spilling out onto her white pants. Missy paid no attention. She finished the treats and curled into a ball on the bench.

"Ouch," Peaches said, and stood up. "That's hot, and look at my pants! My silk pants might be ruined."

"Forgive me," the man said.

"This is a *private* garden. How did you get in here, anyway?" Peaches said as she scrubbed at the dark spots. "And just who are you?"

"The gate was open. It looked so welcoming that I decided to come in. I'm sorry I frightened you. My name is TuckerD."

"What kind of name is that?" she asked, still scrubbing at the stain.

He shrugged and then pulled a small white cloth from his blue frock coat and handed it to her. "Try this. It's very good at removing any stains."

Peaches took it from his large hand. "Thank you, but I really think it's hopeless. Silk doesn't lend itself to…." Peaches stopped talking and her mouth dropped open. "They're gone," she said. "The stains are gone. It's like they were never there."

The man smiled. "My grandma's cleaning rag," he said. "Works like magic every time."

Peaches handed the rag back to him.

"Keep it," he said. "Consider it a gift."

Reluctantly, Peaches folded the cloth and stuffed it into her pants pocket.

"The runway show starts in an hour, and I have to change clothes," she said. "You're one of the new models, aren't you? I saw you yesterday in the back of the auditorium. I assume you're representing our Victorian line."

The tall man didn't respond.

"Did you sign the sheet?" she asked. "Each model signs the sheet to verify attendance."

The man shook his head.

"Why not?"

"I'm not really a model," he said. Then he turned to walk away.

"Wait!" Peaches scrambled after him and grabbed his arm. She stepped in front of him, and when she did, she smelled a pleasant aroma, a mixture of citrus and…something else.

Cedar? She thought. *Yes, it's cedar. Oranges and cedar wood.*

Standing in front of him, she took his hand and ran her hand along the cuff of his shirt. "Where did you get this lace? It's not what I use in men's shirts."

"Ireland," he said, "another gift from my grandma."

Peaches examined the stitches and the delicate pattern of the lace. "This is Carrickmacross lace," she said, her voice filled with wonder.

The tall man nodded once.

"You're very fortunate," she said, her fingers still working the lace. "This is highly sought after all over the world. And you say your grandmother gave it to you?"

Peaches stared up at him, craning her neck to see his face. She noticed his features for the first time — the brilliant sea-blue eyes, the sharp nose, high cheekbones, long black hair with highlights of gold streaked through it, pulled back at his neck and hanging to the middle of his back.

"Well," he said, and moved the latch on the gate. "She made the shirt for me."

"What was she like, your grandmother?"

TuckerD chuckled. "She's...she was a doozy. Sharp as a tack, a talker for sure. And a great cook, especially when it came to apple tarts. Mmm, those were good."

"Did she hug you a lot?"

"All the time," he said.

"It must have been nice to have a loving grandmother."

"Well, she was pretty good with a switch too if I remember correctly. Not that I got into trouble, mind you."

Peaches laughed. "I can only imagine," she said.

TuckerD withdrew his pocket watch and flipped it open. "It's almost time," he said, and stepped around her to open the gate. He walked through and closed it back almost immediately.

"Stop!" Peaches called. "Please, I want to talk to you."

She struggled with the latch, finally loosening it and opening the gate. When she stepped out of her private sanctuary, she saw no one.

The man had disappeared.

Peaches stood and stared at the emptiness. Her stomach churned and her hands shook even worse. "He disappeared," she whispered to no one. "Vanished."

A sick feeling overwhelmed her and she stumbled to the bench. Missy climbed onto her lap.

"It's not possible for him to walk that fast," she said to herself, her trembling fingers automatically rubbing the cat's soft fur.

"Not possible. Who is he?"

Chapter 5

Inside her dressing room, Peaches stood in front of the full-length mirrors lining each wall and surveyed her appearance. She smiled at her shiny voluminous blonde hair. Almost immediately, she bent over, used her hands to ruffle the hair, then straightened up once again. She liked for her long hair to appear a bit messy, as if it were done casually and without much effort.

She turned back and forth in front of the mirrors, checking the snug fit of the bodice of her gown, a peach colored sleeveless confection, which fell softly to below her knees in front but to ankle length in back—the new high-low style, it was called. With a high round neck that dropped to a deep V in back, the sleek, form-fitting silk gown enhanced her figure and made her feel vibrant. She stood straight as an arrow, reaching her full height of five feet three inches, her narrow shoulders back and stomach flat. She'd chosen her signature peach stilettos, which not only gave her added height but complemented the gown perfectly. Her ears were adorned with thick gold hoop earrings, and a thick gold cuff bracelet encircled her wrist. Embroidered on the hem of the gown in front was a small gold P done in old-world calligraphy: her signature mark, sewn by hand onto each garment she created.

She reapplied her lipstick, held out her fingers to check her nail polish, dabbed a bit of perfume behind each ear and an extra dab at her throat. She wore only Joy by Jean Patou, a gift from a former admirer who had proven to have more money than sense. She inhaled the floral fragrance and smiled.

Peaches repeated her beloved description of the perfume: "Over twenty-eight dozen May roses and 10,600 jasmine flowers are used to make one ounce of this classic parfum, which is still coveted by women around the world."

How well she knew it!

Satisfied with her looks, she took a deep breath and checked her Rolex. Thirty minutes until show time. Then she leaned in close to the mirror.

"You've still got it, babe, even at almost forty," she whispered, a slight smile forming on her face. And then she heard that nagging voice from her childhood.

No one likes an ugly woman. Make sure you're beautiful at all times. Otherwise, no one will want you around.

Her hands shook even more. Peaches blinked her eyes and rubbed her forehead. "Go away, voice," she whispered. "You've tormented me all my life. Just go away."

She took a deep breath and stepped to the back door. "Missy," she called. "Time to come in."

The fluffy cat appeared almost at once and went directly to her soft, cushioned bed in one corner of Peaches' office.

"That's my girl," Peaches said, and bent down to give her a rub. "You're such a good girl. You'd like me no matter how I looked, wouldn't you? Now, go to sleep, and I'll check on you when I'm finished."

She stood back up, checked herself in the mirror one more time, then headed backstage.

"Margaret-Ann," she called as she walked down the hall. "Is everyone ready?" And when she saw the look on Margaret-Ann's face, her heart skipped a beat. "What's wrong?"

"Peaches, we're short a model. Rand left an hour ago and hasn't come back, and he's our lead escort. He didn't say where he was going. One of our girls won't have a partner."

Peaches wrung her still-trembling hands. "Where's Mark, our replacement model?"

"He left earlier when he saw that all the models were present."

"I could call him, but he's probably at work now." Peaches furrowed her brow and paced.

"Are your hands trembling, Peaches?" Margaret-Ann asked.

Peaches stopped and smiled at Margaret-Ann. "No worries," she said, and put a hand on her shoulder. "I think it's just nervous jitters." After another minute of pacing, she stopped. "Wait, what about the man who was here earlier, the one in the blue coat?"

"I never saw a man in a blue coat," Margaret-Ann said.

Peaches looked toward the back of the auditorium, but he wasn't there. "I'll be right back," she said. "Hold down the fort."

Peaches made her way quickly around the building to the garden, careful not to dirty her heels or her gown. When she opened the gate, she saw him sitting on one of the benches.

"What are you doing back here?"

He turned around and smiled at her.

"We need you as an escort in the show. One of our brides is without a groom. Please, will you be an escort?

He got up from the bench and leaned down to her. "I can't," he said. "It's not my…my job to be one of your models."

"Maybe it isn't," Peaches said. "But tonight, I could use your help. You've got the right look, and I'm in an emergency situation. Please? Will you please be our model?"

TuckerD sighed. "Very well," he said. "Just this once."

Peaches beamed. "Thank you," she said with a sigh. "Now, it's almost show time. Will you follow me and I'll get you set up?" Peaches took a few steps and looked back to make sure he was following her.

When they reached the back stage entrance, she stopped, stood on her tiptoes, and straightened the collar of his blue velvet coat, smelling once again the strange but pleasant aroma of oranges and cedar. Then she tugged at the lace sleeves of his white shirt until they were perfectly aligned.

"Perfect," she said. "Come, and I'll introduce you to your bride. Her name is Jennifer. She's almost six feet tall, so the two of you will be perfect together."

"I...this is not—"

"I'm desperate," she said. "Please help me, just this once."

The man nodded.

Peaches let out the breath she was holding and tried to calm the trembling that traveled from her hands throughout her whole body. She pointed to a beautiful young woman dressed in a flowing, billowy wedding gown.

"Jennifer?"

The young girl looked toward her. "Yes, ma'am?"

"This is...what is your name again?"

The tall man stammered. "TuckerD."

"Jennifer, this is TuckerD. He'll be your escort tonight."

Jennifer's eyes widened. "But where's Rand? We practiced all afternoon. He knows what to do, when to pause, when to walk. Where is he?"

Peaches moved close to her. "Rand has left us, so this man will be your escort. The two of you will be stunning as a couple. But I'm afraid you'll have to lead him around, show him when to pause, when to walk."

Jennifer gazed at the man, then held out her hand. "I'm Jennifer. I'll show you exactly what to do."

The tall man bowed. "Thank you," he said. "I've never done this before."

"Well," Peaches said. "Have no fear. Jennifer is my top model. She's been with me for five years, and she knows runway etiquette better than anyone else."

Jennifer smiled. "You're an angel, Peaches," Jennifer said. "It's no wonder that you won Fashion Designer of the Year! No one else can compete with you. And never fear, Mr. TuckerD. Just follow my lead, and everything will be fine. It will be nice to have a tall escort. Rand is a bit shorter than I am, but you're just fine."

"It's time," Peaches said, and clapped her hands. "Places everyone. The show is about to begin. And remember, no smiling. Keep the looks on your faces serious. Straighten those backs and hold your heads high. Peaches and Lace doesn't tolerate sloppy posture."

Chapter 6

Peaches walked out onto the stage amidst thunderous applause, which continued until she picked up the microphone. She hesitated for a moment and looked out over the audience. From what she could see, every seat was taken and there were people lining the walls of the auditorium. Even all of the folding chairs were occupied.

"Thank you," she said, and smiled. "I'd like to welcome you to our Peaches and Lace Grand Winter Show. Tonight, we will premier ten stunning new wedding gowns, some a bit avant-garde, and some featuring a decidedly Victorian flare. And of course, once again, we offer a very special peach-colored confection that is sure to please the most discriminating bride. I trust that you have your brochures, which feature all of our beautiful new designs and any contact information you need. And be sure to sign up for our next show, a mere six months away. Now please, sit back, relax, and enjoy the show."

Peaches took the microphone and stepped far to the side of the stage and runway.

"Our first creation is worn by the gorgeous Jennifer Blake. She's wearing a Victorian-style white satin ball gown with peach tulle under slips, and long satin sleeves with pearled buttons that run to the wrist. The bodice is satin trimmed in fine Irish lace, and as she turns, you can see the detachable ten-foot satin and lace train."

The oohs and aahs from the crowd delighted her.

"Her escort is wearing a decidedly Victorian velvet coat with white shirt, cuffed again in fine Irish lace to match that of the bride. Black pants and a black top hat complete the look."

When the bride and groom stopped center stage, the bride stepped forward, and with her arms outstretched, did a slow turn to show off the gorgeous cut and fit of the gown. The groom politely held her long train, then let it fall to the floor as she finished the turn. The two of them glided to the front of the stage and stood together, the bride turning to the side with one hand resting on the groom's arm so that the full beauty of the gown and train could be admired. Arm in arm, they stepped carefully onto the short runway, walked the length of it in slow steps, stopped at the end for a moment, then maneuvered a flawless turn to get back to the stage.

"They make a striking couple, don't you think?" Peaches asked the audience. "The gown is number one in your brochure. It's called Victorian Elegance."

Applause echoed throughout the auditorium, and amidst the clapping, Peaches had her eyes trained on her audience, looking for all of those who might be marking their brochures, potential clients. She saw several young girls leaning over and speaking to their mothers, while their fathers made notes on the brochures.

Peaches smiled.

Two and a half hours later, she was still smiling as the audience rose to their feet, the sound of their applause almost deafening. Her bride and groom couples stood together at the front of the stage and took their bows. At that, the crowd seemed to grow even louder, with some hoots and hollers and even some whistles, unusual for a group of elite citizens, the only ones who could afford her designs.

With the microphone again, Peaches stepped in front of the couples. "Thank you," she said, and gave a slight bow to the couples. Then she turned to the audience. "I hope you've enjoyed my new creations tonight, and I hope that the young women I see among you will consider Peaches and Lace as the creators of their wedding fashions."

The audience again roared with delight.

"Thank you so much for coming," Peaches said. "And girls, don't forget about us. We're here for you. I wish you all a good night."

Then Peaches grabbed her clipboard from a shelf in the podium, stepped off the stage, and walked out into the crowd. People gathered around her, making sure she had their brochures, on which they'd written their contact information. One particular family—mother, father, grandmother, and beautiful daughter—pulled her aside.

"Oh, Daddy, I must have it," the daughter said. "It's everything I've dreamed of in a wedding gown."

"Well, sweetie," he said. "If it makes you happy, then it's yours."

"Oh, Daddy, thank you. Won't it be beautiful?"

Daddy nodded his head. "You'll be beautiful," he said as Mother looked on, a huge smile on her face. "Miss Malone—" he said.

"Please, call me Peaches."

The man nodded. "Peaches," he said. "My daughter here wants to place an order for that very first gown, the one with the peach skirt underneath. Seems she thinks it's perfect for her August wedding."

Peaches smiled and hugged the pretty girl. "You'll be stunning in it," she said to her. "Just stunning."

"Can you have it ready by August?"

"Oh, most certainly," Peaches said. "It's only October now, so we've plenty of time. You'll need to come by very soon for the first of your fittings. Can you do that?"

The girl looked up at her father. "Can we buy it, Daddy?

Please?"

The father glanced down at the brochure again.

"Half down and half when it's finished," Peaches said. "Cash only, if that's agreeable."

"Yes, I'd heard that. You deal in cash. Here you go," he said, and handed her a thick envelope. "Twenty now and twenty when it's done?"

Peaches nodded and slipped the envelope under the metal clasp on her clipboard. Then she pulled a receipt book from her back pocket and wrote out a receipt, gently tore it off, and handed it to her newest customer.

"She'll be a stunning bride in a Peaches and Lace original. And the one she's chosen is our most spectacular gown. There's not another like it."

The young girl let out a little yelp. "Thank you, Daddy," she said. "I'll have the most beautiful wedding in the whole state."

"Don't forget to call soon to set up your first fitting," Peaches said.

The family walked away, the young girl still gigging with delight, and by the time the auditorium had emptied, Peaches had twenty-five orders.

She looked at her clipboard and smiled.

Chapter 7

It was 1:00 a.m. when Peaches walked through the door of her small apartment.

Once she'd changed out of her gown and hung it on the shower rod, she reached for the steamer and waited for it to heat, but when she pressed the button, nothing came out. She banged it a couple of times on the side of the tub, then pressed the button again. That time, the steam came pouring out. She ran it carefully over every inch of the outfit, making sure there were no stains, no dirty spots, but before she had time to turn it off, the steam stopped.

Peaches sighed.

Her high heels went on the second shelf in the linen closet, and her one pair of fancy earrings and cuff bracelet went into her makeup drawer under the sink. Satisfied that everything was in its place, she put the old steamer away, slipped into her worn but comfy pajamas, and padded barefoot into the kitchen.

As she warmed the cocoa and milk in the old microwave, she reached to an upper cabinet and took down a battered metal box. With a key from her key ring, she opened it carefully then went to her purse and removed twenty thousand dollars in cash. The money went directly into the box, now locked and secured once again. She smiled when she felt the weight of the box. Soon, she'd have enough.

By the time she'd replaced it onto the shelf, the microwave

had dinged its third and final time.

Peaches reached in and grabbed her cup, blew on its contents several times, then squeezed around the small table for two and sat in the corner chair, her favorite because it was opposite the only window in the kitchen. Here she could sit, drink her cocoa, and listen to the sounds of the great horned owl as it called "who who who" to the night.

Who are you, Peaches Malone? she thought. *Would your clients still adore you if they knew the real you? If they could see this apartment, would they trust you to create a magnificent gown that would cost them forty to a hundred thousand dollars?*

Peaches sipped her cocoa.

It was a constant worry—that one of her clients would delve deep into her past and her present and discover anything personal about her. It was the reason she never allowed anyone to know her address. She'd set up her life so that her personal side would be forever removed from her public. Her public cherished and admired her as Peaches Malone, the best wedding gown designer in the world. Among her clientele were movie stars, congressmen, secretaries to the elite, world-famous dignitaries, and even a president or two. Only the wealthiest could afford her gowns.

But it wasn't always so.

Once, in her late teens, she'd been engaged to a wonderful, encouraging man who gave her all he could afford. His death, a mere month before their wedding, had shaken her to the core. And though she told herself that she'd never let any man have her heart again, only a year later, she did. This time she went for looks, not money, but she failed to get to know him properly, and after two years of severe physical abuse, she'd fought back, almost killing him with a cast iron skillet.

She'd run away then, getting as far from him as possible. A few months later, she received the divorce papers. How he found her, she didn't know. Nor did she know if he'd come after her and try to exact revenge. But she moved on and eventually tucked those memories deep down in the memory bank.

When she was in her late twenties and had spent years as an assistant to a little known designer, she sketched an idea for a wedding gown on a white paper napkin in an old diner where she ate lunch alone most of the time. As she rose to leave, the napkin slid onto the floor. Another woman's hands reached for it before hers did. The woman stared at the sketch for a moment before she spoke.

"That's my napkin," Peaches said. "May I have it back?"

The woman looked at the short, slim blonde with the glorious mane of hair that hung down her back in beautiful waves. "Did you design this gown?"

Peaches nodded.

"Do you need a job?" the woman asked.

"What sort of job?"

"I'm looking for a new designer for wedding gowns. I own a company that specializes in wedding finery.

"Then you should already have a designer," Peaches said. "I don't want to be second fiddle."

"Our designer left over a month ago. We haven't found a replacement as yet."

And that was the beginning of her career. It seemed like a lifetime ago.

Now at the table, Peaches caught a glimpse of the runway night's brochure. She thumbed through it and smiled, the tiniest bit of pride in her work making its way to the surface. Peaches was especially fond of the ball gown with the peach underskirt, the hem of it peeking out just enough to reveal its beautiful color. In her mind it the most beautiful gown she'd ever created, perfect for just the right bride. Then, she glanced at the names and phone numbers written so precisely beside each gown in the brochure. Four names were written beside the beautiful ball gown. She'd have to see each of these four brides and persuade three of them to choose another color for the underskirt. A future bride with a slim upper body with slim arms, not too busty. Yes, that would be perfect for the peach confection, her favorite of all her creations.

Twenty other names were inked beside other gowns in the collection, gowns that could be fitted to practically any size bride. Twenty-five orders would be difficult to fill in four months, but Peaches would see that all of them were made perfectly and suited her brides to a T. And these twenty-five orders would give her what she longed for the most: money. They might even give her enough, even with the high cost of her exquisite materials and expert labor.

The thoughts overwhelmed her, and as she sipped the last of her cocoa, her eyes grew scratchy and her lids heavy. She stretched out an arm over the table and laid her head down. As she drifted off to sleep, a voice startled her awake again.

"Peaches, you'll not get any proper sleep at this table."

Peaches opened her eyes and looked toward the voice. "What are you doing up at this hour, Margaret-Ann?"

"You know I can't sleep until you're in safe and sound."

Peaches chuckled. "I'm perfectly capable of taking care of myself, but I appreciate your concern. A few more sips and I'll be ready for bed."

Margaret-Ann left her to it.

A few minutes later, Peaches trudged off to her room. She sneaked a look in Margaret-Ann's room and found her, as usual, propped in bed reading her equine handbook. If there was one thing that woman loved besides sewing, it was horses. She'd been raised on a horse ranch, and she and Peaches owned one for a while until money ran out and they had to sell. Peaches had developed a love for the magnificent beasts herself.

Margaret-Ann motioned her forward and pointed to a full-color photo. "Remember what it's called?"

Peaches smiled. "I think it's a Gypsy Vanner."

Margaret-Ann smiled. "And this one?"

"Fresian."

"You've not forgotten, have you?"

Peaches smiled. "I remember," she said. "Good night."

"Good night, Peaches. Oh, and Peaches?"

Peaches turned back to her.

"Don't you worry about not having any other relatives besides your tired old mom. If you had them, you probably wouldn't like them."

"Where did that come from?" Peaches asked.

Margaret-Ann shrugged. "I know it stays with you, that maybe you feel abandoned, but you have me."

Peaches smiled. "You're right...on both counts. And I appreciate you, M...Mama. Sleep well."

Chapter 8

The cellphone rang before she'd even opened her eyes the next morning. She fumbled on her nightstand until she found the beast. "Yes, what is it?"

"Peaches, did I wake you? It's almost seven. I thought you'd be here by now."

"Aileen?"

"Yes, it's me. Are you sick?"

"No, I'm not sick. I'm tired, Aileen. Worn out. I hardly slept at all. I think I must have drifted off about five, so I've been up all night…for the third night in a row. I'm exhausted."

"Oh, I'm sorry, then. But I didn't really know what to do. We have a minor situation here. Can you come in for just a little while?"

"What sort of situation?"

Aileen hesitated for a few seconds. "This guy's been hanging around. When I asked him what he wanted, he said he was waiting for you."

"What guy? I have no appointments this morning."

"Can you just come in for a little while?

Peaches sighed. "I'll be there in a few minutes," she said, and hung up. She shivered as she got out of bed. "We need some heat in this place," she said, and turned up the thermostat to sixty-five degrees. She took a quick shower, being careful not to wet her hair, threw on some faded jeans and a well-worn sweatshirt, stepped into her ankle boots, then fluffed her hair with her hands. She didn't bother with makeup, just some lightly bronzed moisturizer for her face and neck. She glanced at her perfume, hesitated, then made one small spritz on her wrist. She rubbed her wrists together, then closed her eyes and inhaled the wondrous aroma of her favorite JOY.

Then a sudden twinge of guilt overtook her. *It's too expensive to use every day,* she thought. *Conserve, conserve, conserve.*

Donning her favorite denim jacket, she was out of the house within minutes, anticipating the half-mile walk to the studio. The walk always made her feel full of life, energetic, ready to take on the world, and the faster she walked, the better she felt. Four and a half minutes later, she stood — winded — at the door to the studio. Though winter had come, the cold didn't bother her at all as long as she walked quickly. She took several deep breaths, shook out her arms and legs, and closed her eyes long enough for her body to relax.

"You're here," Aileen said as she opened the door. "That was fast. He's over there," she said, and pointed.

Peaches looked down the hall toward her office, and yes, there was a man standing there. "How is Missy this morning? Did you let her out so that she could roam the garden?"

"She's fine," Aileen said. "She's the sweetest cat in the world, and I'd swear she understands everything I say to her."

Peaches smiled. "She's an angel," she said. "And she refuses to leave the garden. Isn't that amazing?"

"Maybe she thinks it's hers," Aileen said, and laughed. "Pretty swanky for a cat, eh? Her own private garden."

"Maybe so," Peaches said and, took another look at the man. Her face lit up. "That's TuckerD, one of our models, Aileen. Didn't you recognize him? He was here all day yesterday, and was in the runway show dressed exactly as he is now."

"Peaches, I told you," Aileen said, and put her hands on her hips. "I never saw him. You saw him, obviously, but I didn't. And as far as the runway show goes, I was in the back the whole time with the models, adjusting their wedding gowns, as usual. But if you tell me that you know him and that he is okay, then that's fine with me."

Peaches said in a softer voice, "I'll go find out what he wants." As she walked off, she turned back to Aileen. "You're a good watchdog, Aileen. I like that."

Aileen smiled, lowered her head, and went back toward the fitting room.

"Aileen," Peaches called. "Don't forget these."

Aileen stopped and walked back to where Peaches stood. "What are they?"

Peaches handed her four white paper table napkins. Sketched on each was a new design, two with long sweeping lace trains, and two without a train at all, only a long veil trimmed in lace.

"Oh my," Aileen said. "I adore this one here without the train. It's so simple, so chic, so...so modern. And the lace, it's exquisite. What kind of lace is it? I don't see this much."

"From Ireland," Peaches said. "Carrickmacross lace, the finest available—still handmade, but only in a few patterns. The original patterns haven't been made since the early 1900s. Make a copy of each and put the originals on Margaret-Ann's desk for me."

"But how would we get it?" Aileen asked.

Peaches winked. "Well, I suppose one of us would have to go to Ireland again."

"How you come up with these designs so fast is beyond me," Aileen said. "You're a wedding gown genius."

"I told you. I stay up most nights trying to get the images onto paper. Whenever the image for the design comes, I become a sort of slave to it until I transfer the image to paper. Now, let me go take care of our model," Peaches said. "I'll find out why he's here."

And with that, Peaches walked toward the man. As she neared, he brought out his hands. In each was a Styrofoam cup of steaming liquid.

"Good morning," he said. "Might I interest you in a cup of hot coffee, preferably in the private garden?"

Peaches cocked her head. "You came here to have a cup of coffee in the garden with me? It's cold out there."

The tall man shrugged. "The coffee's hot. It will keep you warm."

"Follow me, then," Peaches said. "And if this is about your pay, you'll get it in one week."

"My pay?"

Peaches turned back to him. "For being our stand-in groom," she said. "You'll be paid for your part in the runway show."

He chuckled. "Paid for walking with a beautiful young lady on my arm? Now, that's a good job!"

In the private garden, they sat on a stone bench as he handed her a cup. "It's very hot," he said. "Careful."

Missy hopped up on the bench. "There you are, my sweet girl," Peaches said as she took the cup.

TuckerD reached into his coat pocket and brought out a brown paper bag, slipped his large hand inside, and offered her a hot biscuit, napkinned just right so as not to burn her fingers. He brought out another for himself.

"Models get paid pretty well," Peaches said as she blew on her coffee. "Didn't you know that?" Peaches took a small bite of the biscuit and gave a bite to Missy, who devoured it and promptly crawled into TuckerD's lap.

"I guess I knew it," TuckerD said, "but since I've never done it, it didn't register that it was a job. I thought I was just helping out." He rubbed the cat and she purred. "Animals seem to like me."

"Yes, I see that. This is a good biscuit," Peaches said. "Thank you."

The man smiled and stroked Missy.

"We called you TuckerD for the fashion show. I'd never heard that name before."

"It's an old, strong name. It means 'bringer of light.'"

"Hmm," Peaches said, and took a sip of coffee. "So, I should call you TuckerD?"

He put down his cup and ate most of his biscuit, giving Missy the last of it. "I'd be honored to have you call me TuckerD—quite honored, indeed."

"And you may call me Peaches," she said.

"Is that a family name? I've never known anyone named Peaches before. It suits you."

"No, not a family name. I'm a drifter, so to speak, in the world of genealogy. I don't know who any of my family is besides Margaret-Ann."

"What? No pesky brothers or sisters, cousins, sainted uncles?"

Peaches shook her head. "No one. May I ask you another question?"

He nodded.

"Are you homeless? Do you need a place to stay for a while until you get—"

"My home is far away from the city," he said. "Very far away. I'm here on a sort of mission. Perhaps that's what you would call it."

"So, you're a missionary then?" Peaches asked as her heart sank. "You're a minister here on a mission?"

"No, no," he said, and shook his head vigorously. "No, I'm no minister. What's a better word? I am here to complete a task I was given by my superiors."

"Oh," Peaches said, and smiled. She studied his face, and was struck once again by the intensity in his eyes, the fine cut of his jaw, the smooth unlined skin, the dark brows. Peaches couldn't remember ever seeing a man so handsome. She felt a twinge in her heart.

I'm attracted to him, she thought. *No, that won't do. No.*

"What's wrong?" TuckerD asked. "You seem to have drifted into another world."

Peaches shook her head and brushed crumbs from her jeans. "It's nothing. I'm fine, really," she said, and fluffed her hair. "So, I asked if you needed a place to stay while you complete your work. There's an apartment behind the studio. It's small and in rough shape, but it's livable, and it's got a great fireplace if you want it."

"Thank you," TuckerD said as he put his cup and napkin back in the bag. "But...."

"But what? You're homeless. I know it just from the look of you. You're wearing the same clothes you wore yesterday and last night. People don't wear the same clothes all the time if they have other things to choose from."

He cocked his head to the side. "Is it important to you that I stay there?"

Peaches chuckled, then surprised even herself with a big yawn. "Important to me? No, certainly not," she lied. "What you do is your business. It's just that if you're going to stay on here, you need a place to live. It's just common sense."

TuckerD said nothing. Missy meowed. He ran his hand along her back, and she fell fast asleep in his lap.

"And, it's important if you don't want to freeze to death. Winter is upon us," she said as she pulled her jacket tighter around her. "I guess I'm offering you a job with us, and I'd like to know that you have a decent place to live." Peaches shivered and then yawned again. "I'm sorry," she said. "I don't sleep much."

"Are you cold?" TuckerD asked.

"No, no, I'm perfectly fine," she said.

He gently took her by the shoulders and turned her back to him.

"What are you doing?

"Shh," he said. "I won't hurt you."

TuckerD closed his eyes for a second. Then he took his index finger and touched her cold neck. Peaches stopped shivering almost immediately. He ran his finger slowly down her back, and as he did, Peaches felt a heavenly warmth spreading throughout her body, relaxing her and filling her not only with warmth, but with a hint of…what was it? Desire.

When his finger reached the middle of her back, she gasped with the pleasure of it. When she felt his finger touch the base of her spine, she took in a quick breath and held it. She was warm all over, and sleepy-eyed.

"Are you warmer now?" he said and bent close to her, his breath on her ear sending tingles through her body. Immediately, the familiar scent wafted over her. Oranges and cedar.

She nodded as she savored the warmth and the tingling sensation. She'd felt nothing like it before, nothing as pleasant or as stimulating. After a few seconds, the tingling disappeared but the heavenly warmth remained. She was sitting outside in the cold, yet she felt nothing but a gentle heat throughout every inch of her.

"Better?" he asked again.

Peaches took a deep breath and turned. "Yes, thank you for whatever you did just then. I feel much better, warm all over."

TuckerD smiled.

"I offered you a job," Peaches said. "Do you want it? It pays a good wage, it's only part-time, and you'd be able to use your costume there for all the Victorian designs. Oh, and the apartment is rent free, if you'll be working for me. I keep a lot of our clothing there, too, so you can find another outfit you might prefer. And best of all, it has a small kitchen that I renovated last year."

"I'm not much of a cook," TuckerD said.

"Well, what DO you do? You've told me virtually nothing about yourself."

TuckerD smiled. "I travel a lot," he said. "For the company I work for."

"And what company is that?"

"You've probably never heard of them," TuckerD said. "None of the offices are around here. But one of the regional managers is here this week and has called us to a meeting."

"That's what you're doing here?"

"That, and having coffee with you," he said.

"And?"

"Helping you and Missy stay warm on this very cold day."

Peaches blushed. "How did you do that?"

"Did it help?"

"I've never felt anything quite like it."

"But you're warm now, right?"

"Very much so. Thank you, TuckerD."

"Here," he said, and handed her a small flower bloom. "A small token of my gratitude."

"It's pretty," she said, and held it to her nose. "Smells like a rose, but with a more delicate scent."

"It's a miniature rose called Lipstick and Lace. See, the edges are red like lipstick, yet the center is white like lace."

Peaches smiled. "Lipstick and Lace."

She leaned toward him and rested her head on his chest. "I'm so tired," she whispered. "So very tired."

She saw Missy wake and jump down off the bench as if she were following a command.

"Sleep then," TuckerD said, and kissed her on the forehead. "Sleep."

Peaches felt his arms tighten around her, felt her body being lifted off the cold stone and into his lap, felt his warmth surrounding her. And then, she felt herself rising as TuckerD stood up.

"Sleep, my beauty," he whispered, placing another kiss on her forehead.

After that, after he whispered to her, Peaches heard nothing else, but in her sweet slumber, she had the sensation of being spirited away.

Chapter 9

"Peaches," Margaret-Ann said. "Wake up, hon. Your 12:00 appointment is here with both of her parents."

When Peaches opened her eyes and glanced around, she was sitting in her office chair surrounded by sketches of wedding gowns. She rubbed her eyes and swallowed. "I need some water," she said, her voice sounding quite scratchy.

"Aileen," Margaret-Ann called. "Bring Peaches a glass of water. She has clients to see."

Peaches squeezed her eyes shut, then opened them again and swiveled in her chair. "I had the strangest dream."

"Well, it must have been strange," Margaret-Ann said, "from the sound of it. You were talking in your sleep, mumbling words I couldn't understand. But I hated to wake you. You get so little sleep these days."

Peaches rubbed her eyes again. "How long have I been asleep?"

"Oh, thank you, Aileen," Margaret-Ann said, and handed the glass of water to Peaches. "This should help that scratchy throat. Aileen said that tall man with the blue coat was waiting to see you this morning when you came in about 7:00. She said you went out into the garden for a few minutes, so she went back into the fitting room. An hour later, she found you asleep in here."

"So, I've been sleeping for three hours, here at the desk?"

Margaret-Ann nodded. "You'd no business out in the garden

as cold as it is. Even with a cup of hot coffee, it's still too cold for you to be meeting some man out there. What did he want, anyway? He must not be much of a gentleman if he'd want you to sit outside in the cold."

"He just brought me coffee and a biscuit. And I wasn't cold at all. I can't explain it, but it was quite nice, really."

"You could have caught your death from a cold," Margaret-Ann said. "I'll be surprised if you don't come down with something. How many times have I warned you about hooking up with losers? But do you listen?"

Peaches just looked at her.

Margaret-Ann left and closed the door behind her, but opened it again straight away. "You're not superhuman, Peaches. You're a woman in her late thirties working like mad. Time waits for no one, and the sooner you realize it, the better off we'll both be. You take too many risks with your health."

"He's no loser. Now please, close the door. We'll talk about this later."

She looked at her large mahogany desk, one of the few luxury items she'd allowed herself to purchase. The little rose was gone. She checked the floor and around the desk, but nothing. She wondered just where it had gone.

Peaches got up out of the chair and walked into her spacious bathroom, the walls decorated in antique Victorian blue and gold wallpaper. A large gilded mirror hung above a sink with gold fixtures, the toilet, hidden by a pony wall, decorated with the same wallpaper, and there was an antique claw-foot tub with a hand-held shower. On the bathroom door was a full-length gilded mirror that matched the smaller one above the sink.

She loved her bathroom and had taken great care to decorate it in the Victorian style that appealed to her so, though she couldn't explain why. It was large enough to contain two closets, one for hanging clothes and shoes, the other for towels, make up, and other necessities, all organized so that nothing was out of place.

She gazed at herself in the full-length mirror and wondered if she should change clothes. She didn't remember scheduling any client meetings today. It was to be a day of sketching and straightening, working on new designs, making calls to prospective clients from the brochures that had been handed to her after the show.

After a spritz of Joy, she brushed her teeth, applied a bit of shimmery blush, and headed out to meet the client, surprised at how great she felt. After being sleep deprived for so many nights, she could hardly believe how the three-hour nap had revived her in body and in spirit.

Sleep, my beauty.

Peaches stopped and braced herself with a hand on the wall.

His voice. TuckerD's voice. She'd heard it only this morning, she thought, but she could barely remember the conversation. She tried to think back to their meeting in the garden, but all she could recall was feeling his index finger travel down her back, bringing with it the most pleasurable warmth she'd ever known.

It was so warm, she thought. *So cozy.*

She wondered if she'd dreamed the whole thing. If not, where had he gone? And how in the world had she ended up asleep at her desk? It must have been a dream.

Peaches shook her head, took a deep breath, let it out slowly, and walked on to the meeting room where, to her surprise, the people standing before her were the ones she remembered from the show, the man who'd handed her twenty thousand dollars in cash, his wife and daughter beside him. When she walked in, the man stood.

"Good to see you again," he said. "I hope we didn't come at a bad time. My daughter insisted we get in touch immediately. She loved the dress so much that she didn't want to wait."

"No, of course, it's the perfect time," she said with a broad smile. "I certainly don't blame her for wanting to have that

51

magnificent gown. I have many orders to fill, so the sooner we can get started, the better for all of us."

The daughter spoke up. "Will there be plenty of time to make the dress?"

Peaches smiled. "We'll make time," she said. "Do you have any questions?"

The mother spoke up. "I'm a little concerned about the fullness of the gown. We want our daughter to look her best. It's a huge affair with many dignitaries attending, and I'm afraid that such a full gown will make her appear…well, too plumpish."

"Mother!"

"Oh, sweetheart," her mother said. "It's not anything against you. It's just that women who wear ball gowns need to be super skinny. You're like me, shapely with lots of curves, and while you are a beautiful young girl, I'm afraid the dress might not be flattering."

"Have no fear," Peaches said, and laid a hand on the girl's arm. "Our dresses are all specifically tailored and fitted to bring out the very best attributes of all of our brides. The bodice is corseted, so that it can be adjusted to make the most of that small waist. The attached ball gown is also adjustable so that it will fit perfectly. In spite of what many people think, a full skirt doesn't add bulk to the bride. In fact, because of the precise fit of the bodice, she'll look quite thin, I think. The perfect complementary fit is our signature, our hallmark. My brides all look beautiful, so you'll be in good hands. I promise you that."

"Mother's afraid I'll look fat," the girl said.

"Oh, for shame," Peaches exclaimed. "At Peaches and Lace, every bride looks her very best. We have ways of making you look just perfect. The gown itself will be designed to give you the most flattering shape you could dream of."

The girl looked at her mother.

"She's right," the mother said. "You have such a fine reputation that I know I have nothing to worry about. Our girl will be stunning."

The young girl beamed.

"Now, one other thing is the hair and makeup. We can do that here, too, if you want, for a fee. We have an expert hair stylist and make-up artist who attends to any bride who chooses to use his services. You can let me know, but please do it as quickly as possible, as I have to book his services in advance."

"And at what cost?" the father asked.

"Daddy!" the daughter cried. "Don't you want me to look my best? Don't you want me to be beautiful for my wedding?"

"Of course, my little love. Of course. Add the hair and makeup to our order, please, Ms. Malone."

"Peaches," she said. "Just call me Peaches. Everyone does."

"Oh, Daddy! I'm going to look so beautiful," the daughter said. "With Peaches overseeing my wedding look, I might even be as gorgeous as she is."

"Oh mercy, child," Peaches said. "You're stunning, and you'll be exquisite on your wedding day. I'll make sure of it. Now, let's get you back to the fitting room so that Margaret-Ann can begin to work on your gown."

As they walked down the hall to the fitting room, the young girl blabbering away about her wedding, Peaches thought she caught a glimpse of TuckerD standing outside another small office. She stopped dead still.

"TuckerD?" she called.

But no answer came, and when she looked again, nothing was there except the body-form mannequin.

"Margaret-Ann," she called. "What's the red mannequin doing out here in the hallway? It should be with the rest of them in the sewing room."

When she got no answer, she went into the fitting room. Margaret-Ann sat at her sewing table.

"A new customer for you," Peaches said. "Will you make sure she's measured properly?"

Margaret-Ann looked up from her sewing. "Hello, dear. Please take a seat. I'll be just another moment."

"What is the red mannequin doing in the hallway?" Peaches asked softly.

"The red one?" Margaret-Ann asked. "I think Aileen moved it out there so that we could rearrange things, but I need it in here. I guess she just forgot to move it back. It's one of our few full mannequins, a necessity for measuring our new client."

"Buzz Aileen and tell her to bring it around, then. I need to discuss the arrangements with the parents." Peaches turned to the couple. "If you'll follow me, we can get the details. Please, take a seat, and let me get some specifics. Now tell me again when the wedding is set and which venue you'll be using."

"We'd really like to book The White Castle," the father said.

Peaches looked up at him. "The White Castle is very impressive. I hope they have an opening. They're usually booked up solid for at least a year. However, we have a gorgeous venue called The Dome. It's smaller, more intimate, but it can seat up to five hundred guests and a full wedding party. Would you like a brochure?"

"I'm afraid my little princess has her heart set on The White Castle."

"Oh, Daddy," the daughter cried, "do you think it will have an opening?"

"Perhaps our lovely Dome would serve you just as well," Peaches said.

"I'm calling The White Castle first. I'd like for my daughter to be married there. Her mother and I were married there."

Peaches nodded. "Why don't you give them a call, then? The number is on that sheet of paper in front of you. Step outside if you wish, and we girls will discuss the dress."

After a few moments, the father returned. "Peaches was right, honey," he said, and covered her hand with his. "The White Castle has no openings. They're booked solid through December of next year."

The young girl broke down and sobbed.

"Do you have any connections there at all?" the man said to Peaches.

Peaches shook her head. A knock on the door begged for her attention. "Excuse me," she said.

Margaret-Ann stood at the door.

"What is it?" Peaches asked.

"He's here again. That tall man."

"TuckerD?"

"Who else?" Margaret-Ann said. "He knows a gold mine when he's found one."

Peaches narrowed her eyes and leaned close to Margaret-Ann. "Please, don't say that."

"Well, it's true. Everyone knows you're loaded. But they don't know that we live like paupers so that you can stockpile money, though only God knows why."

"We agreed. Three years, Margaret-Ann. That was the deal. Three years of saving money any way we can. Only another few months to go. Then, everything will change. Now, where is TuckerD?"

"Standing outside your office."

Peaches put a hand on Margaret-Ann's shoulder and smiled. "We've only a few more months," Peaches said, "and then I promise you that all the sacrifices we've made will be well worth it."

"Go on, now," Margaret-Ann said. "Go see your TuckerD."

Chapter 10

TuckerD stood in front of the office, his arms crossed over his chest, feet slightly apart, sea-blue eyes staring up toward the ceiling.

"There must be something very interesting on that ceiling," Peaches said. "Can you point it out to me?"

"I...I'm afraid you caught me daydreaming."

"Ah," she said, "the artist's curse."

TuckerD chuckled. "I'm surely no artist."

"Is there something I can help you with?" Peaches asked. "I've an appointment with some very disappointed clients. The daughter was sobbing as I left. I can't be gone too long."

"Disappointed in you, your design?"

Peaches brushed at the front of her white blouse. "No, not really with me or the design. The bride to be had her heart set on a certain venue for her wedding, but sadly, the place is booked solid for at least a year. The poor girl is beside herself."

"Aren't there other venues?" TuckerD asked.

Peaches inched closer to him. "Of course. I recommended a beautiful one, my very own called The Dome. But you see, her parents were married at The White Castle, so it's a sentimental thing."

"The White Castle?"

"Oh, it's quite magnificent, and the favored choice of the rich and powerful all over the world. I think of it as my vision of Heaven, if there were such a place — which there isn't — but if there were...."

"Well, that's a shame for the clients, to be so disappointed before the wedding takes place."

"Of course," Peaches said, "and it doesn't bode well for Peaches and Lace either. I'm supposed to be the miracle worker of weddings. But I have no connections at The White Castle, so I've tried to steer them toward my own venue. It's just as beautiful and certainly just as sought after. I'm usually booked solid, but I do have one opening available."

"Did you tell her?"

Peaches shook her head. "That girl has her heart set. I'm not sure what to do about it."

"How about a short stroll through the garden?" TuckerD said, and put a hand on her shoulder. "Perhaps we can think of something."

Peaches didn't answer right away. Instead, she held up her index finger. "Give me a moment.

Margaret-Ann?" she called, and headed down the hall and into the sewing room.

"I'm busy," Margaret-Ann said.

"Please, I need your help for just a minute."

Margaret-Ann sighed and got up from her chair. The two of them went in to see the girl and her parents, and though the girl was no longer sobbing, she sniffed several times.

Peaches bent down. "Come along, honey. It's time for another fitting. It won't take long."

"You just come with me now, dear," Margaret-Ann said, "and don't you worry yourself one little bit. You'll have the most beautiful wedding...and wedding gown...that anyone's ever seen."

And as the two of them walked out, a faint smile played across the girl's lips.

"May I get you some tea or coffee while you wait?" Peaches

said to the parents.

They both shook their heads, neither of them looking the least bit happy, the father holding the mother's hand in his.

"Excuse me for just a moment," Peaches said.

They didn't look up.

She walked out into the garden, shivered, and saw TuckerD sitting on the bench with his head in his hands. He seemed to be mumbling, but she couldn't understand the words.

She backed quietly to the door and went back inside. Something about his countenance told her he needed privacy, so she left him to whatever it was he was doing out there. Then she stepped into her bathroom, fluffed her hair, smoothed on some fresh lipstick, and applied another layer of mascara. She turned her face this way and that to check for the appearance of any wrinkles. But what she noticed most of all were the dark bags under her eyes. So, with a trembling hand, she applied more concealer in a lighter shade, then some highly luminous powder on top of that. It gave her just the right glow.

"Better," she said.

She grabbed a coat and two large bird seed cakes, and headed outside again. She found TuckerD in the very same spot.

He smiled at her and patted the bench. "Sit with me," he said. "But only for a minute or two. You must be cold."

"I need to fill the feeders," she said.

TuckerD stood. "Here, let me help. I hadn't even noticed any feeders out here."

"They're toward the back. See the two magnolia trees at the end of the garden? The feeders are in the trees so that the birds have sanctuary if they need it."

They walked to the trees.

"Be prepared for a flurry of wings. They usually fly away when I come too near, even to feed them."

But as they got closer, all was quiet. Peaches looked up at TuckerD and shrugged. Then she opened the first feeder and dropped in the two-pound cake. TuckerD mimicked her actions and filled the second feeder.

"Close it up and that's it," she said.

As soon as the feeders were closed, several birds flew down and began to peck away at the seeds.

Peaches smiled. "I've never seen that before," she whispered, and tucked her trembling hands under her.

"Maybe they're just very hungry," TuckerD said.

"They get a new cake every three days," she said. "I don't think that's it."

"I like the little landings you've built for them," TuckerD said, noting the large square of wood that stood out from each feeder.

"Just in case they need a rest," she said. "A carpenter who helped me with the studio built them for me."

Between the two trees sat an enormous ornate turquoise bird bath full of water.

"The bird bath is beautiful," he said. "It looks quite… almost…."

"It's very old," she said, "and came from an antique store here in Georgia. When I found it, I just couldn't resist it. It was pricey, but so beautiful I just had to have it. It's larger than usual, so the birds have plenty of room to splash around and bathe, or just to perch on the thick edge and drink."

"You never cease to amaze me with your good taste, Peaches. This is the most elegant bird feeding station I've ever seen. You've gone to some trouble, haven't you?"

"No trouble," Peaches said. "You're actually the only one who's seen them so close up."

TuckerD bowed, took her hand, and kissed it. "I'm deeply honored, my lady."

Peaches smiled. "Well, you should be," she said, and giggled. *Did I just giggle?* "I do love the little birds, but someday, I'll have a place where I can feed the birds and also take care of a few horses. That's my dream."

"Horses, eh?"

Peaches nodded. "They're magnificent animals, smarter than most people would imagine, and so regal. Yes, I'd like to own a few."

"Do you ride?"

Peaches nodded. "I learned to ride almost before I could walk, but I haven't been on a horse in a long time." She checked her watch. "Oh, we should get back," she said. "And my little bird sanctuary is a secret, okay?"

TuckerD nodded. "As you wish," he said as he took her hand. "Thank you for showing it to me. I'm deeply moved by it, by the care and attention you've taken to care for and protect these tiny creatures."

"Now, back to the business of getting clients and designing gowns."

After they'd walked a few minutes, TuckerD turned to her. "Care to sit for just a moment?" TuckerD seated himself on the bench.

Peaches shrugged and sat next to him, her hands in a perpetual tremble now. "I was glad to see you this morning," she said.

"May I?" he asked.

When Peaches nodded, he put an arm around her and pulled her closer to him, then rested his chin on the top of her head. "And I was delighted to see you, Peaches. You're more beautiful every time I look at you."

Peaches slid her hand around his waist and inhaled his scent. "Thank you," she whispered. "By the way, what is the name of the cologne you wear? I've never smelled anything quite like it."

"Cologne?" he asked.

"Yes, I love the scent. It smells like oranges and cedar wood. I've never smelled it before."

"I…uh…it's not cologne. I don't wear it. Oh, by the way, I've decided to take the apartment," he said. "If it's still available."

Peaches sat up. "It's available. Will there be anyone else with you?"

"Anyone else?"

Peaches shrugged.

"No, just me."

"When did you plan to move in?"

"As soon as you leave to go speak to your clients. But first, here's another little beauty for you. It doesn't match your own, but it's gorgeous nonetheless." He handed her another rose.

"Lipstick and Lace," she said, and held it to her nose, noticing that her hands no longer trembled. "My other one just seemed to vanish. I couldn't find it this morning."

"Well then, you needed a replacement. They're delicate little things and they don't last long, but they're beautiful and fragrant for a little while."

"I dread what's ahead of me. The poor folks must be distraught by now."

"Or, perhaps your skills and talents will have won them over. Think positively."

Peaches walked back to the door and turned to wave goodbye to TuckerD, but he was already gone. "How does he do that?" she said to herself. "He just completely disappears. I need to investigate that man and find out exactly who he is."

And in her mind she heard Margaret-Ann's voice. *He's a loser. You can tell by looking. Same clothes all the time. What sort of man wears the same outlandish garb every day? I'm warning you, Peaches. This one is hiding something, and you'd best stay as far away as possible.*

Peaches sighed as she walked into the building, dreading having to deal with the distraught parents and the heartbroken girl. She brought the flower to her nose, inhaled the delicate scent, and took a deep breath. Then, she heard the girl's renewed sobs and squeezed her eyes shut.

A few more minutes. That's all I can take. If she doesn't choose The Dome, then —

"Peaches! Peaches!" Margaret-Ann called.

"I'm here, and I can hear the sobs," she said as she held up her trembling hands in front of her. "There's nothing more I can do, Margaret-Ann."

"Oh, no," Margaret-Ann said. "You won't believe what has happened."

"Let me guess. She's cancelled the order for the dress. She's choosing another designer and coordinator."

"Oh, Ms. Peaches," the girl cried, and grabbed her in a bear hug. "You did it. Somehow, you did it."

Peaches slipped out of the girl's grasp. "And what have I done this time?"

"You've worked a miracle, just like people always say you do. The White Castle is available for my wedding! Daddy got the call a few minutes ago. He's booked it and now, I'll be married just like my parents were, in The White Castle."

Peaches blinked twice as her lips slowly formed a questioning smile.

Chapter 11

In the dark, Peaches sat on a gilded chair at the head of the indoor wedding venue she'd created for her clients, The Dome. The spacious room could easily hold five hundred guests and a large wedding party, with plenty of walking and sitting space left over. She gazed at the gleaming cherry hardwoods, her eyes coming to rest occasionally on the reflections of light that shone from them. Then her eyes traveled upward to the dark cherry, hand-carved acanthus crown molding, a great contrast to the stark white of the walls. The right touch of elegance, perfect for formal or informal ceremonies.

But above it all was the centerpiece of the venue, the showpiece which attracted wedding parties from all over the world: the glass dome atop the building, its girders and supports all painted a brilliant gold. From its center hung one ten-tiered crystal chandelier. The cost, the time, the labor that went into this feat of engineering had cost Peaches almost a year's worth of profits, but she'd given tours once it was completed, and within a few months, she'd produced enough business and interest to recover the cost.

Peaches smiled to herself when she thought of all the effort that had gone into creating that particular vision. In front of each of the five large windows on each wall stood potted dwarf magnolias, a hybrid that grew to six feet and bloomed almost constantly. All the pots were highly decorated with an acanthus motif. White chiffon floor to ceiling draperies added another touch of elegance to the room, the soft drape of them reminding her of angel wings.

Peaches favored the architectural design of the acanthus, partly because it was rich and beautiful and partly because she loved its history. A Greek architect and sculptor in the second century was inspired by the sight of a woven basket that had been left on a young girl's grave. A few of her toys were in it, so a square tile had been placed over the basket to protect them from the weather. An acanthus plant had grown through the woven basket, mixing its leaves with the weave of the basket. The design he created from this vision became cherished throughout Greece as a most favored element of architectural interest.

Peaches had worked two years on the design of this space, and like the acanthus, she wanted it to be classic, elegant, and beautiful for all of her brides. She loved to see the looks of awe on the faces of clients when they saw it for the first time, fully decorated for their wedding.

So much of my life has gone into the weddings. The years, the time, the money, the thinking, the building…everything for the weddings.

"Margaret-Ann is right," she mumbled. "I'd be lost without the weddings. They've become my life."

Peaches shrugged and stood up, stretching her arms toward the sky. Her stomach growled, her whole body felt stiff and sore, and worst of all, her hands had begun to tremble again.

"I need a walk before bed," she mumbled to herself. "Then a yogurt, maybe with berries if we have any."

She couldn't remember the last time she'd been to the market. Margaret-Ann had probably gone to pick up a few things, and she was sure there would be berries in the fridge. Margaret-Ann knew how much she loved yogurt with fresh berries, her dietary staple.

Peaches slipped into her heavy coat, pulled a scarf around

her neck, and put on her wool knit cap. Though the tight knit cap flattened her hair, it kept her head and ears warm, and at this time of night and in the dark of the hour, she didn't have the time or the energy to care how she looked. All she wanted was a nice hot bath, a cup of yogurt, and the comfort of her saggy old bed.

As she hurried down the block toward the apartment, she hoped that Margaret-Ann had remembered to turn up the heat. Their usual winter-time sixty-two degrees just wouldn't be warm enough tonight. Not tonight. She was tired. She needed comfort from the warm bath, a warm room, and warm covers. A sudden memory flooded her mind, a memory of warmth, comfort, and safety.

"TuckerD," she whispered to the night air.

When he'd wrapped his blue coat around her in the garden, she'd never felt such…such peace. The warmth and comfort filled every fiber of her being. If she believed in Heaven, she'd swear she was closest to it at that very moment in her life.

The memory faded when Margaret-Ann opened the door. "Where on earth have you been, Peaches? I was worried sick."

Peaches stepped inside, removed her coat, hat, and scarf, and hung each one carefully on its hook. "I told you I'd be late," she said.

"You said eight," Margaret-Ann replied. "Eight. It's almost eleven! I made dinner. It's cold now."

"I'm sure I said 'late,' not 'eight.'"

Margaret-Ann shook her head. "I guess I'm getting old and my hearing's going. But you said eight. Are you hungry?"

Peaches nodded her head.

Margaret-Ann wrung her hands. "Honestly, Peaches, sometimes you worry me near to death," she said, with tears running down her cheeks.

"I'm sorry," Peaches said, and stepped beside her. "I don't mean to worry you. I just get carried away with my own thoughts."

Margaret-Ann sniffed.

65

"I'm sorry I worried you, but right now, I'm tired, I'm hungry, and I'm in need of a warm bath."

Margaret-Ann hugged her. "Well, there's food on the stove," she said. "Help yourself. I'm going to bed."

"Thank you," Peaches said, "for worrying and for making dinner. I know it will be delicious."

"It's not much," Margaret-Ann said. "Just a Cobb salad and some of your favorite cornbread."

Peaches giggled. "Only you, Margaret-Ann, would make a diet-friendly salad and pair it with cornbread."

Margaret-Ann smiled. "Oh, I took out all the calories as I was making it. Special recipe."

"Right," Peaches said. "I've had your special cornbread before. I couldn't zip my pants the next day."

"You've plenty of dresses," Margaret-Ann said. "Now goodnight, Peaches. Enjoy your salad."

Chapter 12

Just as she had put the finishing touches on her make-up and was about to leave the apartment, her phone rang. She swiped the screen and saw the caller I.D.

"Lily girl," she said in a perky voice. "What on earth have you been up to? We live in the very same town, and yet I haven't seen you in ages."

"Well, hey sweetie," Lily responded. "I've been trying to bring this case of mine to a close, and honestly, I've been overwhelmed with work. I've been out of town on several occasions, and I've missed our little outings. But the case is finally wrapped up now, thank goodness. Wanna meet me at the corner at O'Dells? Something I need to run by you. I've already ordered your breakfast."

"I'll be right there…and it better not be eggs and sausage. You know—"

"Relax. Far be it from me to get you to eat real food. See you in a bit."

Peaches grabbed her shoulder bag, tugged on her coat, and headed out. When she got to the corner, she saw Lily inside at a table nearest the front window.

"Well," she said as she entered, "I see you got my favorite spot."

Lily stood up and hugged her. "I've missed you, Peaches. Sit. Let's talk."

As soon as they sat, the waiter brought two cups of yogurt and a bowl of mixed berries, two steaming cups of coffee, and two glasses of water. Peaches nodded at him and smiled.

"So, how is Margaret-Ann?" Lily asked.

Peaches smiled. "You know Margaret-Ann, ever the faithful seamstress and my overbearing mom. She's fine. She still gets upset about my wanderings, but she looks fit and healthy—a bit overweight, but other than that, she's been a big help to me."

"Did you hear any more from the genealogist?"

Peaches shook her head. "No records exist of Frank Malone, my father, even though Margaret-Ann has their wedding certificate."

"You'll keep searching, won't you?"

"I don't think so, Lily. I've been searching for ten years now at no small cost. Whoever my father was, he doesn't want to be found or known. So, I'm done. I've spent a fortune only to find out that he can't be found."

"I think what you've found out is that Frankie Malone lied about his name and origins. But take heart, he gave you life, and by golly, look what you've done with it."

Peaches smiled. "It's a terrible feeling, Lily. I've no ties to anyone except Margaret-Ann. No aunts, uncles, no grandparents...no one. I feel like a drifter going through this world with no family connections at all to anyone. The famous Peaches Malone can't even claim a single relative other than her mom."

"Well, it's not for lack of trying. You've given it your best. Now cheer up, my friend. There are worse things."

"Worse things than being a drifter with no family?"

"You have a mother, Peaches. Margaret-Ann's a treasure. She loves you more than life. There are many who don't have that advantage."

Peaches nodded her head. "True," she said.

Lily held up her index finger as she swallowed her first bite of yogurt and berries. "She loves you dearly, you know."

Peaches nodded. "And she's the best at what she does. If it weren't for her skill as a seamstress, my business would be nowhere. You look wonderful, by the way. I envy that sleek black hair of yours. The bob cut is great. It's new, isn't it? And just look at that new suit, perfectly tailored, fitted in all the right places. Black and white really suits you."

"Well, of course, it's perfect," Lily said. "You made it! I got so many compliments on it, Peaches. But as you requested, I didn't tell anyone who the designer was."

Peaches chuckled. "Can't have my reputation as wedding guru ruined by a two-piece business suit."

Lily glanced around to see who else might be in the restaurant. The expression on her face was grim.

"Go ahead. Spit it out," Peaches said. "Tell me what's wrong."

"Do you remember when we both had just started out and we worked for Mayfield's? We both worked together designing wedding gowns, early on."

"Of course, I remember," Peaches said. "It was my first professional job as a designer. Gosh, we were both babies then!"

"Nineteen, if memory serves, and broke, living together in that dump of an apartment. We were desperate for work just to be able to eat."

Peaches shook her head. "Don't remind me," Peaches said, and took a sip of her coffee. "Those were hard times. And don't forget we were both newly divorced, too, which made matters even worse. Nineteen, divorced, broke, and desperate, but still clinging to our dreams. We must have been nuts."

"We ate lots of canned beans back then," Lily said. "And Vienna sausages with mustard."

Parris scrunched up her face. "And Spam," she said. "The thought of it makes me shudder."

"But you saved us, Peaches. You drew a wedding gown design on a white paper napkin, and as Fate would have it, none other than Mrs. Mayfield herself was sitting right across from you and was watching you like a hawk. She asked to see the design, and thanks to you, both of our lives changed that day. I've loved white paper napkins ever since."

"Me, too," Peaches said, and took a bite of yogurt. "I still do all of my designs on them, but I've moved up to those fancy premium ones now! They're bigger. Still paper, but bigger."

Both of them laughed.

"And you went on to law school," Peaches said. "I was so proud of you. Lily Buchanan, Attorney at Law."

Lily sipped her coffee. "Well, I graduated and got certified to practice here in Georgia, if you remember, but my private practice was a flop, and I really didn't care for it. It seemed so far away from what I really wanted to do. So, I just decided to give it up and concentrate on what I loved. I keep my certificate renewed every year though, as I still work for another practice."

Peaches sipped her coffee.

"Anyway," Lily said, "do you remember that there was a very young girl that was brought into our department shortly after we went to work there?"

Peaches narrowed her eyes. "I can barely remember what she looked like," she said.

"Well, let me refresh your memory. She was tall and skinny like me. She had curly red hair, and she wore some flowery perfume. You could smell her coming a mile away."

"Oh, the cheap perfume girl," Peaches said, and nodded. "What was her name?"

"Janet," Lily said. "Janet Mayfield. Ring any bells?"

"Oh," Peaches said, and put down her spoon. "She was Mrs. Mayfield's niece, right?"

Lily nodded. "She wanted to be a designer, but she had no skill for it. She used to use large pieces of paper with sketches on them, and was always summoning her aunt to look at them. But the girl had no drawing skills at all, and those designs…they were all copies of other gowns she'd seen."

"She wasn't there very long, was she?"

Lily shook her head. "Mrs. Mayfield promoted her to a desk job in accounting or something."

"Okay," Peaches said, "so why are we talking about Janet Mayfield?"

Lily leaned forward. "She's not Janet Mayfield anymore, Peaches. She went to art school then to a design academy in France, and several years later, with the backing of her wealthy French husband and her aunt, she opened her own boutique wedding shop."

Peaches said nothing as she took another sip of coffee. She just stared at Lily.

"Her husband's name is Etienne. She goes by the name *JLaRoche*."

Peaches went white, set her cup slowly down on the saucer, and dabbed at her mouth with her napkin. "My biggest competition," she muttered.

"Correction," Lily said. "Your *only* competition. The three of us have the only high-end wedding boutiques in the state. I'm certainly no threat since you and I work together. I help out with catering, flowers, venues. I'm only a consultant, and with *JLaRoche*, it's the same. *You* are a designer. She is not. She never learned how to design, so she sells other people's designs, with their permission."

"So," Peaches said as she finished her berries, "why is that important to me?"

"Because she's stolen one of your designs, Peaches."

Peaches nodded, then made a call on her cellphone. "Aileen?"

"Good morning, Peaches."

"Aileen, I'll be delayed this morning. I might not be back until noon or so. Can you handle things for me? And tell Margaret-Ann that I'm with Lily."

"No problem," Aileen responded.

"Done," she said to Lily as she dropped her phone in her purse.

The two of them left the restaurant and hailed a taxi. Lily gave instructions to the driver.

"I want you to see for yourself. If I'm wrong, I'll admit it and chalk it up to ageing, and we can forget about it."

Peaches nodded.

"Here's our stop," Lily said to the driver, who pulled over to the curb and let them out.

By the time Lily had signed the slip of paper for the credit card, Peaches was already standing in front of the store window at *JLaRoche*. They stood there together for a moment arm in arm.

"It's mine," Peaches said. "I did lace insets on the bodice and off-the shoulder styling long before they were popular." She pointed toward the mannequin. "And look at the lace intertwined with the satin on the sleeves, and the pearls perfectly placed beside each swirl. That's my signature style."

"Look at this," Lily said. "Her claim on the design. *JLaRoche.*"

Peaches said softly, "All of my designs are already copyrighted, patented, and filed with the government."

"You seem very calm about this," Lily said, pointing to the mannequin. "Aren't you furious? She's blatantly stolen one of your first designs, Peaches. Stolen it."

"My gut instinct is to smash in these windows, rip the dress off the mannequin, and beat Janet to a pulp," Peaches said, her arms folded across her chest. "But for some reason, I think there's more to this than meets the eye. I think she's doing this deliberately to get my attention. She wants a confrontation, but I don't know why."

Lily thought for a moment. "Peaches," she said in a barely audible voice, "Could this have anything to do with the award you won a few months ago? Fashion Designer of the Year?"

Peaches looked at her and nodded. "Could be. She was nominated, too. Do you think she's still angry about it?"

Lily chuckled. "Well, if she's not, I'm sure her sainted mother and adoring husband are. The prize money alone…."

"But they're wealthy already. Why would they bemoan losing $100,000 when they have millions?"

Lily held up her finger. "Ah, but it's those who *have* money who always want more."

"This is too far-fetched," Peaches said, and turned away from the window.

"What I want to know is how, when, and where she got the design for the precise knot work on the sleeves," Lily said. "Did she buy one of your gowns?"

Peaches shook her head. "Not that I know of. I certainly wouldn't have sold her one. That one in particular is an original. There was only one of them made, and it went to a client whose parents I'd known for years," she said as she fiddled with her cup. "They were Irish immigrants who'd done well. They requested that particular knot work and beading to remind them of their homeland."

"Then they probably wouldn't have sold it," Lily said.

"No, they didn't," Peaches said. "They all perished in a fire, but they bequeathed the dress back to me."

"What?"

Peaches nodded. "It's in a preservation box wrapped just so. It's in my apartment, Lily. It's been there for years."

Chapter 13

Lily and Peaches stood at the door of *JLaRoche Salon.*

"You ready?" Lily asked.

"Ready," Peaches said. "Let's find out what the former Miss Janet Mayfield is up to."

"Try not to lose your temper, okay?" Lily said.

"Me? A temper?"

"Just try to be calm. We'll get more information if we're both cool and calm."

"Okay," Peaches said.

As they walked in a bell chimed to signal their arrival. "Yes, may I help you?" the matronly woman behind the desk asked. Her gray hair was done in a tight bun pulled severely away from her face. She wore no makeup except for bright red lipstick.

"We'd like to see Janet, please. We're old friends. We'd just like to speak to her for a moment," Lily said.

The woman behind the desk flipped through an appointment book. "I'm sorry," she said. "She's very busy, and she's booked solid until this evening. Perhaps you could call and make an appointment." The woman slid a business card toward them. "She just doesn't have time to see anyone unless there's an appointment."

Peaches wandered over to the display window.

"Could you just buzz her and tell her that an old friend is here to say hello? This is such a gorgeous boutique. I've never seen anything quite like it, and the dresses are to die for," Lily said. "My daughter is getting married in a few months, so would you just tell Janet—"

"Mrs. LaRoche," the woman interrupted.

"Then please tell Mrs. LaRoche that Lily Buchanan would like to speak to her for a moment."

The matronly woman sighed but did as she was asked.

While the woman was occupied on the phone, Peaches deftly drew her cellphone out of her purse and took several photos of the dress—her dress—on display, with *JLaRoche* embroidered on it.

"I'm sorry," the woman said. "She's very busy."

"Remind her, if you will, that she and I worked together for a while."

The woman muttered something into the phone. "She'll be with you shortly," she said. "Just have a seat."

Lily walked over to Peaches. "Why don't you wait in the cab? Let me handle this right now. She might not even recognize me, but she'll know you instantly. Besides, I have a plan and a law degree!"

Peaches chuckled. "Okay, I'll go into Hadley's next door. I'll wait for you there."

"Oh, would you see if they have any of those packages of little gold stars?"

"Gold stars?"

"Don't ask," Lily said.

Peaches left *JLaRoche* still chuckling over the gold stars. But after she'd taken a few steps, she stopped, anger building inside her.

It's MY gown. She stole MY design.

Barely able to control the urge to scream, Peaches turned around and stormed into the salon. She found Lily and Janet seated beside one another having a rather heated conversation.

"How dare you?" Peaches yelled, and pointed a finger at the

girl. "How dare you steal my design and claim it as your own?! You're a phony, Janet, a no-talent phony who couldn't design a square box, much less a wedding gown. I'm suing you for copyright infringement and theft."

Janet gave a little chuckle. "Well, if it isn't the Fashion Designer of the Year, here and in person," she said. "How very nice to see you, Peaches. Oh, and by the way, that's not your design. I purchased that dress from Lady Vandermeer, who had no idea who'd designed it and didn't care for it in the least. Seems someone had thrown it into the garbage bin outside her house."

"That's hardly believable since all of my gowns are commissioned and each one embroidered with my logo. This is one of my originals. I'd know it anywhere. It has my signature knot work on it. My logo should be right under the cuff of the right sleeve."

"Well, I'm afraid you've no choice but to believe me, Peaches, since the gown has no logo anywhere except mine. Help yourself. Search for your logo. I can tell you it isn't anywhere on the gown."

Lily stood and grabbed Peaches by the arm. "We'll be going now, Janet, but I must tell you that I am an attorney, and I intend to pursue this case. Now, if you will be so kind as to remove the dress, I'll be happy to take if off your hands for the investigation — or you can allow the police to enter your shop and do it for you."

Janet sat for a moment and chewed on her bottom lip. She glanced at the woman behind the desk, then stood up. "You might as well take it. No one has expressed the slightest interest in it."

"Mrs. LaRoche," the woman behind the desk said, "perhaps you should consult your husband before you allow the dress to be removed. He is the owner of the salon, after all."

"By all means," Lily said. "I'll send the police around in a day or so to fetch it."

"The police need not be involved. I'll see that Etienne brings it to you himself."

Lily glanced from the woman behind the desk to Janet.

"She's right," Janet said. "My husband, Etienne, will be happy to deliver it to your office. The sooner this is settled, the better. Good day to you."

Janet LaRoche turned and walked down the long hall of the salon. She glanced back only once.

Chapter 14

At about ten o'clock that night, Peaches fixed two cups of hot tea with lemon and took them into Margaret-Ann's bedroom. Sitting propped on several fluffy pillows, covers drawn up over her, Margaret-Ann was watching her favorite show on TV.

"Oh," she said. "You've brought us tea. How sweet of you, Peaches. Pull up that folding chair and sit with me for a few minutes, won't you?"

Peaches put two napkins down on the nightstand and set the cups of tea on them, then slid back into the chair.

"Business was booming today, eh? You've so many new orders."

Peaches nodded.

"But that's a good thing, right? Having more orders than you can fill just ensures your business will continue to thrive."

"Oh, sure. Business has been great," Peaches said as she spread out her hands and checked her nail polish.

"So, why do you look so sad? Tell me, Peaches. What's bothering you?" Margaret-Ann said, blowing on her steaming tea.

Peaches took out her phone and found the photos she'd taken at *JLaRoche*. "Remember this dress?" she said as she handed the phone to Margaret-Ann.

"Oh, yes, how well I remember. This is one of your originals. Oh, my, I'll never forget the amount of time and effort that went into making those sleeves and that bodice. Took me an age to get that done, but that gown won hearts all over Georgia. Such a shame, though, about that family. Broke my heart." Margaret-Ann took a sip of tea. "When did you take this photo?"

"Today," Peaches said.

"But that's impossible. That gown has been stored here for a very long time."

"Do you remember a girl named Janet Mayfield?"

Margaret-Ann shook her head. "Name doesn't register... but wait, is she that tall, dark-haired girl that was always trailing after you like a puppy? Didn't she marry some rich guy?"

Peaches nodded. "Etienne LaRoche," Peaches said, "owner of *JLaroche*."

"Ah, the competition."

"Lily and I went there today, and I took that photo in her shop. It's displayed in the window." Peaches rubbed her forehead. "I need a cigarette."

"You don't smoke anymore, dear. Lace your tea with a bit of brandy. I think there's a bottle in the cabinet."

Peaches got up, found the bottle, and poured her almost-empty tea cup full of brandy. Then she gulped it down.

"Margaret-Ann," she said. "I can feel it in my bones. We've got a fight coming. That scrollwork and those knots on the sleeve of the dress, the laced bodice...those are mine, legally copyrighted, as all of my designs are. I won't let Janet—Ms. JLaroche—claim them as her own. No way is that going to happen. So, brace yourself for a court battle if that's what it comes to."

"What did Lily have to say about it?"

"Oh, she's bursting to get ahold of this and make a big case out of it. I'm sure she has every detail planned out, but I don't want to risk hurting the business. We're doing so well. This might cause a scandal. *JLaRoche* is highly respected."

"No worries," Margaret-Ann said. "A little scandal might be good for business. Besides, it wasn't *JLaRoche* who won Fashion

Designer of the Year, three years in a row. It was you, Peaches. And maybe that's at the heart of this. She's jealous and wants to shake you up. Anger and jealousy aren't good playmates."

"I don't want people digging into my personal life. Wouldn't it be grand if people found out I had no father? That will come out in a court case. No, this needs to be settled some other way."

"It won't come to that, dearie. Janet knows those designs are copyrighted. She must. No," she said, wagging a finger, "there's something else behind this. I just don't know what it is. Go to bed and get some rest. Things will be clearer in the morning. And Peaches, you do have a father. We just haven't been able to find him. Don't give up hope, honey."

Peaches went into the tiny bathroom and stared at her reflection in the mirror. She leaned in close to check for additional wrinkles or blemishes on her face. Satisfied that she didn't look any older tonight than she had that morning, she bent and brushed up her blonde hair into a ponytail high on her head. Then she washed her face and smoothed on the expensive Parisian night cream until her complexion appeared to have a healthy glow.

Don't give up hope.

Margaret-Ann's words filtered through her mind.

But I want to. I want to stop this endless searching. I want to relax and breathe.

Once in her pajamas, she crawled into her twin-sized bed and covered herself with a worn handmade quilt that she would have liked to claim as an heirloom, but which she'd picked up at Goodwill for five dollars years ago. The quilt was lightweight, the wedding ring pattern faded and, because of the weekly washings, loose at some of the seams, but Peaches liked its softness close to her skin.

Wedding ring pattern, she thought as she drifted into sleep. *I'm obsessed with weddings. Will I ever be normal?*

Chapter 15

The tall man in the blue velvet frock coat stood staring out the window of a luxurious office, complete with Persian rugs, a crystal chandelier, Tiffany lamps, and select pieces of Waterford crystal knick-knacks placed on antique cherry wood furnishings.

"It's not possible," his boss said from his executive leather chair. "Not possible."

"Why not?" TuckerD asked, his arms still crossed over the broad expanse of his chest, his gold and black ponytail hanging halfway down his back.

His boss chuckled. "You're kidding me, right?"

TuckerD turned to face him, searing him with his sea blue eyes. "I wouldn't be here if I were kidding. When was the last time I asked you for anything?"

His boss leaned forward and propped his elbows on the dark cherry wood desk. "If memory serves, you've never asked for anything."

TuckerD walked to the desk and took a seat in a soft navy blue leather chair. "Exactly, but today is different. I want a favor, a very special favor."

"You? A favor? You mean you want a break from your job? And what would you do on this break you need? You don't fit into society, TuckerD. You're a drifter. It's part of your job." The boss shuffled through some papers.

"I have a replacement worker," TuckerD said. "He'll handle things for me for a couple of days."

The boss laughed out loud. "Oh, that's rich, TuckerD. Rich. And who might this friend be? No, wait, let me guess. Gabe. Right?"

TuckerD nodded. "He can handle it just fine."

"Really?" the boss asked. "And who's going to cover for Gabe while he's covering for you?" The boss stood then and walked over to TuckerD. He leaned on the desk and he, too, crossed his arms over his chest. "Don't even say it," he said. "He is way too busy. No, he has enough work for dozens just like him."

"He said he would do it," TuckerD responded.

"Well of course, he did," the boss yelled, and spread his arms. "It's the woman, isn't it? This Peaches Malone?"

TuckerD's eyes widened.

His boss sighed again, this time very loudly. "Merciful heavens, TuckerD. You've been our agent for only God knows how long, and now you want to put all of that in jeopardy for... for a fashion designer? Well, the answer is no, absolutely not. I won't allow it, and my boss won't allow it. You've a job to do, and do it you will at precisely the right time." The boss sat back down at his desk. "If there's nothing else you want to talk about, you're free to leave."

TuckerD hauled himself out of the chair and headed for the door.

"Oh, and TuckerD," the boss said, "I'd caution you to remember just exactly who you are and what your job is. And more than that, remember who you work for. Good day."

Chapter 16

Peaches woke from a sound sleep to a loud banging.

BAMM BAMM BAMM

She bolted upright in the bed and looked around to get her bearings.

BAMM BAMM BAMM

She glanced at the alarm clock on her nightstand. The digital red numbers were clear: 5:15 a.m.

"Stop that banging!" she yelled as she crawled out of bed and put on a robe. "I'm coming." She slung the door open. "What is it? How dare you come banging on my door at—?"

"I apologize, Ms. Malone," the police officer said. "But there's an emergency situation, and I knew you want to be informed."

"Come in, Mickey," she said. "What sort of emergency? What's happened?"

The officer removed his hat and stepped inside the door. "There's been a burglary, ma'am," he said. "Seems someone broke into your studio. I'm not sure what was taken, if anything, but I'll need you to come with me to give it an inspection so that we can file a report."

"But I have an alarm system," Peaches said.

"Yes, ma'am. That's why I'm here. The alarm went off at the station. I got to the studio as fast as I could, but the damage was already done and there was no one around or inside. Would you mind coming with me to see if anything was stolen?"

"What sort of damage?"

Mickey looked at the floor. "The glass on your door is pretty well shattered."

Peaches covered her face with her hands and a little sob escaped her lips.

"Don't worry, Ms. Malone. Please don't worry."

"Mickey? What's wrong?" Margaret-Ann said from behind her.

"Good morning, Margaret-Ann. I was just telling your daughter that someone broke into the studio."

Margaret-Ann gasped. "No," she said. "We've never had a burglary, not in all these years."

"Mickey, I have a favor to ask of you before we go," Peaches said.

"Yes, Ms. Peaches. Anything."

"Come with me, please." Peaches walked across the small apartment and into her bedroom. Then she went to her closet and pointed up. "Will you get that big white box up there and hand it down to me? Be careful. It's heavy."

"What ever happened to that tall man with the blue coat?" asked Margaret-Ann. "He'd have no trouble reaching it."

"I don't know. He's gone, I guess," Peaches said with a little sting in her heart.

"Hmph," Margaret-Ann said. "No good, I told you. He's no good, just a poor drifter. Personally, I'm glad he's gone."

"Please, Margaret-Ann. I don't want to talk about him."

"Oh Lordy," Margaret-Ann said. Have you gone and fallen for him, Peaches? Tell me you haven't. He's no good, I tell you."

"Mickey, the box is right up there."

"No problem," he said, then grasped the box, grunted a bit, and held it.

"Just put it on the bed, please," Peaches said.

"Why are you getting that down?" Margaret-Ann asked.

"I'm just checking," Peaches said, "to make sure it's safe and sound. I haven't looked at it in a long time."

"Is there something you're not telling me?" Margaret-Ann asked.

But Peaches was absorbed in her task of carefully unwrapping the dress, her first, her original design, the one that propelled her to the top of the fashion world. She removed layer after layer of covering from linens and muslins to the final piece of acid-free paper.

Margaret-Ann stood beside her. "Oh, Peaches, it still looks beautiful."

A smile formed on her lips as Peaches gently lifted the top of the gown, the bodice studded with real pearls and a single emerald where the V-neck came together. She put the top of the dress back in the box, then delicately lifted out one satin sleeve embroidered in Celtic knot work studded with small round emeralds.

"That's sure pretty," Mickey said. "Those real?"

"The emeralds?" Peaches asked. "Yes, they're all real, as are the pearls."

Mickey whistled. "Don't you need to lock that up in a bank vault somewhere?"

Peaches shook her head. "No, it must be kept in perfect conditions. Wrapped in the correct materials, kept at precisely sixty-five degrees and in dry air. Moisture would ruin it."

"Ladies," Mickey said, "I really need to get back to the studio. A report needs to be filed."

"Forgive me. Let me wrap this, and if you'll be so kind, you can put it back for me. Then give me a moment to slip on some jeans and I'll be ready. Do you want to come with us, Margaret-Ann?"

"No, you go ahead. It'll take me a bit longer to get ready, and this is something that can't wait. I'll see you there in just a little while."

Thirty minutes later, the two of them stood inside the Peaches and Lace studio. After answering a barrage of questions, Peaches combed every inch of the place looking for anything that might be missing. She looked in every conceivable space, yet something nagged at her, something she'd forgotten.

She walked to her desk, and after a moment of recognition, her eyes fell on the one drawer she'd missed: the bottom right, the one that was always locked, her secret treasure trove. She searched in vain for the key, turning the usually organized top drawer into an unorganized mess.

No key.

She reached down and opened the drawer. The lock had been broken and the drawer slid out easily. Peaches felt her heart sink.

"No, no," she whimpered. "No...."

In the drawer were several stacks of solid white napkins. She'd drawn her first design on a white napkin for lack of anything else on which to do it. She'd handed that design to a woman who saw it and gave her her first job in fashion. She'd kept that original design, and from that time drew every new concept for a new gown on a plain white napkin, all of them stored in her bottom drawer. She'd just finished a new design and had put it, as usual, atop one of the stacks of napkins, and though the new napkins were there, the new design wasn't.

"What is it? What's wrong?" Mickey asked, and squatted next to her.

Peaches looked at him, a single tear falling down her cheek. "My new design has been stolen," she whispered. "It's gone."

Chapter 17

Peaches sat on the bench in the private garden. "That's enough of that," she mumbled as she wiped a tear from her face. "Crying is for babies."

"Not always," the deep familiar voice came from behind her.

Peaches turned around. "TuckerD," she said without smiling. "I haven't seen you lately. You have a habit of showing up when I least expect you. Do you do that on purpose?"

"I've been away."

"Ah," she said as she parked stray strands of blonde hair behind her ears.

"If I'm disturbing you, I'll—"

"Well, of course you're disturbing me." Peaches stood up and turned to face him. "I'm trying to find some peace out here, and now here you come sneaking up behind me."

TuckerD said nothing. He simply stared at her with a questioning look on his face.

"And when in the devil are you going to get some new clothes?" Peaches said. "I offered you a place to live. I offered you a job and some new clothes, but you disappeared."

"I'm sorry, Peaches. It was urgent business."

Peaches turned away from him. "You could have at least mentioned that you'd be leaving."

TuckerD took her by the arm and without effort, moved her gently closer to him. "Why are you upset?" he asked.

When Peaches looked up into those sincere sea-blue eyes, she started to cry all over again. TuckerD pulled her close and wrapped his huge arms around her, his orange and cedar scent wafting around them both.

"Please, Peaches, please don't be upset with me. I truly meant no harm to you. It didn't even occur to me that you'd be hurt or angry. I'm new at this. I don't really know how to act."

Peaches pulled away from him. "New at what?" she asked.

TuckerD lowered his head. "New at liking someone," he whispered.

Peaches chuckled and wiped a final tear from her cheek. "You've never had a girlfriend before? Is that what you're saying?"

"Why don't we sit down?" TuckerD said. "I'll try to explain."

The two of them sat on the bench, and Peaches turned to face him, her hands trembling now worse than ever. "Go ahead," she said, her eyes focused on his sea-blue ones.

"My job forces me to travel almost constantly," he said, and took both of her hands in his. "I've never been in one place very long, and I've never had a woman that I cared about the way I seem to care for you."

"You've never been in love?"

"Love?" TuckerD asked. "No, I don't think so."

"You've led a sheltered life, TuckerD," she said, and let her eyes travel to his broad shoulders, his massive hands, and his black and gold striped hair, gathered at the back of his neck in a long ponytail that hung halfway down his back. Then, it occurred to her. Her hands had stopped trembling.

TuckerD nodded. "Now," he said, "will you tell me what's wrong, why you were so upset?"

Peaches removed her hands from his. "They're not trembling," she said.

TuckerD smiled.

Peaches ran her hands through her hair and fluffed it.

"Someone broke into my studio," she said. "They broke out the glass door, the two glass display windows, and worse, stole my newest design."

For a few seconds, TuckerD put his hand to his temples and sat very still. "How could they steal your design?"

Peaches sighed. "I've always drawn my sketches for new designs on white paper napkins. It's a habit I developed as a young girl, and one I can't seem to break. I drew my latest design on a napkin and put it in the bottom drawer of the desk. Whoever broke in stole it."

"Then it's someone you know fairly well?"

"What?" Peaches shot him a questioning look.

"It had to be someone who's worked for you in the past or knows you pretty well. Otherwise, how would they know to look in the drawer?"

"I hadn't thought about that," Peaches said, and rubbed her temples.

TuckerD laid a hand on her shoulder. "In your position, you're sure to have enemies, or at least people who envy your designs and your talent. Can you think of anyone who — ?"

"Janet," Peaches said. "Janet LaRoche. She used to work for me. I saw her and her husband a few days ago at their bridal shop. Things didn't go well."

"She has her own bridal shop?" TuckerD asked.

"Oh yes, she's quite successful, but she doesn't design her own gowns. She sells designs by other people." Peaches ran a finger around her lips. "Why would she want mine? It just doesn't make sense. She can't make them and sell them because they're already copyrighted. If she tried to pass them off as hers, she knows I'd take her to court and fight her. So, she can't really do anything with them."

TuckerD leaned forward. "Do you think she knows they're already...what was the word?"

"Copyrighted?"

"Yes, would she know that?"

"I'm sure she would," Peaches said. "It's been my habit since I began working. I created a design, usually on a white napkin. I'd either copy it or later, scan it and send the design to a friend in the government. He'd get the copyright for me within a few days. I still do the same today, though it's easier and faster now. Everyone who works for me knows my habits where gowns are concerned."

TuckerD said nothing for a few seconds, but his deep rich voice soon broke the silence. "Perhaps it was someone in the studio who stole the design."

Peaches narrowed her eyes. "You think someone who works for me stole my design?"

TuckerD shrugged.

"My designs are like my babies," Peaches said as she hung her head. "This latest one was unique and beautiful, better than anything I've ever done. The thought of someone else having it… it…it breaks my heart."

TuckerD pulled her close to him. "It's all right," he said. "I promise you that things will be all right."

"But you can't promise that, TuckerD," she said as she pushed away. "You can't possibly know how this will turn out, or if I can recreate it exactly. When I'm making a new design, all the pieces just flow together. Afterwards, I look at it sometimes and wonder who did it."

TuckerD ran his hand down along her arm. Peaches felt the soothing warmth of his hand through her jacket. "I brought you something," he said, and pulled a rose blossom from his jacket.

Peaches managed a small smile. "Lipstick and Lace. Thank you. You know, it really does look like the rose has lipstick on. The petals are such a beautiful pink color topped with this sultry red edge, and then it draws my eye right to the pure white center. They're fascinating." Then her smile faded and she felt tears stinging her eyes.

TuckerD hugged her close again, his soothing voice somehow making her feel better. "Don't you worry, Peaches. You'll get the design back. I can feel it in my bones."

"TuckerD, do you have a father?"

Surprised, he cocked his head and narrowed his eyes. Then he nodded. "I do, yes," he said.

"I've never met mine," Peaches said. "I've been searching for over ten years, but the man who married my mother, Margaret-Ann, doesn't exist in any records."

"And that bothers you?"

Peaches nodded. "I'd like to know I had roots, connections to other families, but it's a small thing."

TuckerD hugged her close and kissed the top of her head. "Everyone has a father, Peaches. If he's out there, I'll help you find him."

Peaches sighed. "I'm tired, TuckerD. I'm tired of searching for him. I don't want to do it anymore, so now's the time for me to let it go. I have Margaret-Ann. I'll be content with that."

"You're a treasure, Peaches Malone," he said. "And one of these days I might surprise you with more information about your relatives than you can handle."

Chapter 18

TuckerD stood outside the entrance to the international airport in Georgia. He leaned against a wall and waited for his target.

He tugged at the tight collar of the shirt Peaches had loaned him and pulled on the cuffs of the sleeves to make them fit at his wrist. The khaki pants fit well enough, but the material itched. The tweed jacket strained across the expanse of his shoulders, and he feared the least movement might rip it in half. The loafers, though comfortable, gave him no footing, and were like mere strips of cloth over his feet.

The only thing she hadn't changed was his hair. The golden and black striped mass still gathered at his neck and hung down his back. However, the baseball cap he wore obscured his vision, and made his head feel as if it were in a vise.

Discomfort aside, he trained his eyes on the mass of people flooding into the airport. He was interested in only one of them, and as soon as he spied the elegant Etienne LaRoche, he bumped right into him and sent LaRoche down on his backside.

"Forgive me," TuckerD said. "I need to watch where I'm going. Here, let me help you up."

"You big oaf," Etienne said. "I don't need any help. Get away from me."

"But I insist," TuckerD said, and lifted him to his feet. "It was all my fault." He straightened the lapels on Etienne's jacket. "No harm done, I hope," TuckerD said.

"I said get away from me," Etienne mouthed as he swatted at TuckerD. "Take your hands off me, you lout. You could have killed me."

TuckerD backed away, put his hands together as if in prayer, and apologized again. "I'm very sorry to have caused you pain," he said.

Etienne swatted at him again and walked toward the entrance, turning back once.

TuckerD chuckled. "No, I'm not following you, buddy," he whispered. "I have what I want."

***

Peaches Malone sat at her desk trying to recall the design she'd created, the one that had been stolen. But try as she might, she couldn't recall the exact details. The shapes were correct, but the special qualities were missing.

She rubbed her temples and tried again, but the images just wouldn't come. She felt her eyes begin to tear but quickly gathered herself.

"Do not cry," she whispered to herself. "Do NOT cry."

When the door to the bridal shop flew open, Peaches looked up and gasped. "You!" she said, and came around her desk. "What are you doing in my shop? Leave this minute, or I'll have Jacob throw you out."

Janet LaRoche backed away. "Please, Peaches," she said with her palms outstretched. "Please, hear me out. I wouldn't be here if it weren't urgent."

"There's nothing you can say that I want to hear, you little thief. I'm calling the police."

"No! No, please. I can explain. I didn't steal it from you, Peaches. It wasn't me. Will you just listen before it's too late?" Janet grabbed the end of a desk to keep her balance. "Please, may I sit down and tell you what happened?"

Peaches walked out of the room and back into the fitting

station. She motioned to Margaret-Ann. The seamstress got up out of her chair and followed Peaches into the main area. When she saw Janet LaRoche sitting beside the desk in front, she stopped.

"What's *she* doing here?"

"That's what we're about to find out," Peaches said, and folded her arms across her chest. "You have five minutes. Then I want you out of here."

Janet nodded.

Peaches reached into the desk and took out her phone. She found the recording button and pushed it. Then she looked at Janet. "You don't mind, do you?"

Janet shook her head. "He's going to kill me anyway, so what does it matter? Please, Peaches, will you just hear me out?"

"Say what you want to say and then get out of my store!" Peaches said, arms folded across her chest."

"I didn't steal your design. I wouldn't, no matter what you think of me." Janet sniffed. "Etienne stole it, and he's on his way to the airport to get on a plane to Portugal, where he intends to sell it. He'll fetch a pretty penny from it, I imagine."

"What are you talking about?"

Janet sighed. "My marriage is a sham, Peaches. Etienne married me only because he thought I could lead him to you. When that didn't happen, he began to plan his escape. Through his connections, he divorced me. I signed, of course, but he arranged all of it. He adores your designs, and he knows how much they'd bring on the black market. He has connections, people you and I would avoid at all costs." Janet swallowed. "And now, he's stolen your latest design and is headed abroad with it."

Peaches chuckled. "He's a fool," she said. "That design is already copyrighted, both here and in many other countries, thanks to the genius of my lawyers. He won't be able to sell it to anyone."

"Legally, no," Janet said. "But you underestimate the power

of the connections he has. They'll buy your design from him, wait a while, and reproduce it, omitting a few of your trademark touches. They're not concerned with legalities." Janet brushed at her skirt. "My five minutes are up, I guess," she said as tears rolled down her cheeks.

"How long have you known?" Peaches asked.

"Only a day or so," she said. "I...I became suspicious of all his trips abroad. But before that, I already hated him because he did nothing but compare the designs I bought to yours. He said I was a no-talent dreamer who'd never be successful."

Peaches shook her head. "But you're already successful. Your business has been flourishing since the day you opened. You've won many awards in the fashion industry."

"No, no, you're wrong. I didn't win them. Etienne paid off some of those judges. I didn't know about the pay offs at the time, but he keeps good books of all his transactions, and I found one of those books hidden at the back of his closet. I went through it page by page just yesterday, Peaches. It seems I was married to a first-rate criminal."

Peaches turned off the recorder and scooted her chair closer to Janet's. "Look, Janet," she said softly. "You're not married to him anymore. You're not responsible for his actions."

"But your new design, Peaches. He has it."

"My lawyers had it first," she said. "I'll call them and tell them the story, and they'll be on it. They'll take any legal action against him that they can...if they can find him."

"I'll lose the business," Janet said, and covered her face with her hands.

"No, you won't," Margaret-Ann chimed in from across the room. She made her way to Janet and put a hand on her shoulder. "You won't lose your business, dear. It's yours. He can't touch it."

Janet cried even harder. "He...he...it's...it's his," she mumbled.

Margaret-Ann handed her a tissue. "Wipe your face, now."

"Etienne owns the business?" Peaches asked, and leaned forward.

"He owns everything," Janet whispered. "Everything. The apartment, the designs, the business, the cars, even the credit cards. It's all in his name. My name is nowhere to be found."

"Except on the divorce decree," Peaches said. "You do have that, don't you? And your name is on the store front and on the dresses, isn't it? JLaRoche? So, there are some things in your name."

Janet wiped a tear from her cheek and looked at Peaches. "His first name is Jacques. Jacques Etienne LaRoche. JLaRoche is *his*, lock, stock, and barrel."

Peaches glanced at Margaret-Ann, then nodded toward her cellphone. Margaret-Ann scurried over and handed the phone to Peaches.

"Wait here," Peaches said.

And with that, she got up and walked outside, cellphone at her ear.

Chapter 19

Peaches stuck her head in the door, cellphone still at her ear. "Janet, how tall is Etienne?"

"Six foot one, I think."

"Hair color?" Peaches asked.

"Dark brown, shoulder length. He has green eyes, dark brows, and a tan complexion. He's...he's quite handsome. And oh, he'd be wearing an expensive three-piece suit. He always wears them."

"Any scars or distinguishing marks?"

"A strawberry," Janet said. "He has a strawberry behind his right ear. He keeps his hair long to cover it up. It's a bad omen in his family in Portugal to be born with a strawberry mark. And one other thing, Peaches. He has a photographic memory."

"Do you have a picture of him, Janet?"

Janet fumbled in her wallet and drew out a small snapshot. "This is all I have," she said and handed it to Peaches.

"What city is his family from?"

"They're in Lisbon, the cultural center of the world, so Etienne says. They're descended from royalty."

Still on the phone relaying Janet's words, Peaches asked another question. "Do you think that's where he's going? Back to his family?"

Janet chuckled. "Not to his family, no," Janet smirked. "There's too much bad blood between them. He was going to

97

take me there to meet them, but they didn't want to see either of us."

"Or so he told you," Peaches said. "You don't know the truth of anything he said, Janet."

Janet lowered her head. "I've been such a fool."

"There's no time to think about that now. Do you have any idea where he'd be?"

Janet straightened. "There's a city listed in his book, a place called Anadia—I think that's right—where he spent a great deal of time with friends. It's circled in the book, so maybe he's going back there."

"Great," Peaches said. "That gives us a starting place at least."

Peaches walked over and whispered something to Margaret-Ann.

"No," Margaret-Ann whispered. "No, it's not safe. Let the police handle it."

Peaches whispered again, her hands on her hips.

"Not by yourself," Margaret-Ann said. "I'm going, too."

Peaches shook her head and blurted out. "Someone has to watch the shop. I can't close down for a week. We have a wedding this Wednesday, remember?"

"Peaches?" Janet's small voice called.

Peaches turned.

"If you and Margaret-Ann need help, I'd…I'd be glad to offer my services in whatever capacity they're needed. I know you don't trust me. Why should you? But I promise that I'd be a good worker—not for my own benefit, but for yours."

Peaches glanced at Margaret-Ann.

"Absolutely not," Margaret-Ann said. "After all these years of fighting and discord—and dishonesty—I'll not have you in our shop."

"I understand, Margaret-Ann. You have no reason to trust me."

***

Just then, a huge dark figure stood at the doorway and blotted out the sun. Peaches heard a tap tap tap, and opened the door.

"TuckerD! How nice to see you!"

"May I talk to you in the private garden for a moment? It's rather important."

"Of course. Come in. We'll go through here." Peaches looked at Margaret-Ann. "We'll just be a moment," she said.

"Hmph," Margaret-Ann replied. "It's the no-good model again. Probably needs money."

TuckerD nodded at her. "Pleasure to see you again, ma'am." Then he nodded at Janet. "Pleasure," he said.

As the two of them walked away and headed out into the garden, Janet responded. "He's the biggest man I think I've ever seen, but he's certainly handsome. You say he's a model?"

"He filled in at the last show," she said.

"I'll bet he got some swoons from the ladies," Janet said.

Margaret-Ann frowned. "I don't see why he would. He's just a big oaf. Can't even find clothes big enough to fit him."

"He doesn't look like an oaf," Janet said. "To me, he looks like a warrior."

Margaret-Ann laughed out loud. "Him? A warrior? He didn't seem much of a warrior when he came around begging for work and a place to live, but Peaches was taken in by his handsome face, I guess. She gave him a job and an apartment to live in. Imagine. A perfect stranger. Poor girl, she's always been a sucker for losers. She has a good heart, my Peaches does."

***

Out in the private garden, TuckerD and Peaches sat on the stone bench.

"So, what is so important?" Peaches asked. "You made it sound like an emergency."

"I hope I didn't upset you," he said. "It wasn't my intention."

Peaches turned and put a hand on his cheek. "I'm never upset when I see you, TuckerD."

TuckerD kissed the palm of her hand, then abruptly put her hand back in her lap. "On to business," he said.

Peaches looked down at her hand and felt as if she'd annoyed him. *When will I ever learn?*

"Are you okay?" TuckerD asked.

Peaches stared down at her hand without answering.

TuckerD gently took her face in his hands and turned it toward him. But Peaches avoided his eyes.

"Look at me, please. I've upset you somehow," he said. "Will you explain so that I won't make the mistake again?"

"It's silly," she said. "Let's get on with the business you're so eager to share."

"First of all," he said. "I've missed you, Peaches. But my job requires so much traveling. I don't want you to think that I'm ignoring you."

Peaches smiled. "I've missed you, too," she said.

"I have something for you. Now, close your eyes and hold out your hands."

Peaches did as she was told and quickly felt the pressure of what seemed like an envelope in her hands.

"Open it," TuckerD said. "I found it at an airport in Atlanta and thought you might want it."

Peaches opened the envelope and drew out a white napkin with her newest design on it. She looked at TuckerD. "My design!" she shouted. "You found it?"

TuckerD smiled.

"But…how did you…you just found it lying around? I don't understand."

"The details aren't important," TuckerD said, and leaned forward. "What's important is that you have your design back. I knew it was yours the moment I saw it. Your initials are right there in the corner."

"It seems impossible, TuckerD."

"Maybe it was meant to be. Maybe I was in the airport at the exact moment I was meant to be there. Maybe I was supposed to find it to help you."

"I don't believe in all that," Peaches said.

"Truly?" TuckerD said.

"If I can see it and touch it, it's real. If not, then no, I don't buy into the rest. One almighty ruler who controls everything? Then he fills the world with angels and demons? No, I can't for the life of me believe in any of it. Margaret-Ann took me to church all the time, but I never heard a single preacher who made sense."

"It happens to many people, I think."

"Oh, I believe in the forces of the universe, that great big universe out there. Yes, I believe there are powers somewhere that control many things, but natural powers, not supernatural ones. That's all nonsense."

TuckerD smiled. "You're right about the last part. There is power out there." TuckerD turned his head as though he were listening to something. "I'd better be going now," he said. "Duty calls."

"TuckerD," she said. "I…well…oh, never mind."

"I need to return these. I can't seem to fit into them well." He removed the tweed jacket, folded it, and laid it on the bench. Then he removed the too-tight shirt and did the same.

Peaches stared at his bare chest: tanned, smooth, rippling with muscles. The breadth of his shoulders made his waist seem small.

"I appreciate the use of the clothes, but they're just too small. I prefer my old ones." TuckerD stepped back a few paces. "I care for you, Peaches," he whispered.

"TuckerD, I…."

"Would you care to have dinner with me?"

"Dinner?"

TuckerD chuckled and nodded. "You know. That meal you eat in the evening."

Peaches laughed out loud. "Oh yes, I seem to remember."

TuckerD bent and kissed her lightly on the cheek. Immediately, Peaches inhaled his sweet aroma.

He was about to speak, so he opened his mouth, but no words came. Instead, his sea-blue eyes sparkled as a smile crossed his face. He touched her cheek. "I have to go now," he said softly.

"But what about your clothes? You can't run around shirtless in Georgia."

"Right," he said with a wink. "I'm stopping by the apartment to get a shirt and jacket now. No worries. I've enough sense not to go out in public half dressed."

TuckerD left and hurried around the corner. As he walked by the broken windows and door of the shop, he frowned. He looked behind and in front of him, and seeing no one, he snapped his fingers and lingered a moment, and as if he'd turned back time, the windows and door fell solidly into place, sparkling like new. With a smile on his face he disappeared down the street, his white shirt and blue frock coat sliding neatly into place on his body.

In the private garden, she heard her name being called.

"Peaches! Peaches!"

Peaches turned to see Margaret-Ann standing beside the open gate. "Yes, what is it?"

"The door and the windows are fixed. They look brand new. Can you believe it?"

"Who fixed them?"

"I saw a man leaving and tried to find him, but he was so fast, I didn't get a good look at him. Then, poof, he disappeared."

TuckerD? Could it have been him? No, no, he's not the type.

"The windows look wonderful, too. I don't think the insurance company has ever acted that fast."

"Our insurance company has never responded to a claim this quickly. There hasn't even been a legitimate notice filed. So, how would they know to fix the door and the windows?"

"It's a miracle, for sure. Oh, and the police are here to speak to you about the stolen design."

And then she remembered the white napkin in her pants pocket. *That man always seems to vanish into thin air. Where in the world did he go in such a short time?*

"Come in," Margaret-Ann said. "They're waiting."

Peaches stepped closer to Margaret-Ann. She reached into her pocket and pulled out the white napkin. "TuckerD, that no-good loser, as you call him, has saved the day. I don't know how he did it, but he brought this to me." She unfolded the napkin to reveal her latest design.

Margaret-Ann stared in disbelief. Her mouth dropped open, but then her eyes narrowed. "I don't understand. How did he find it?"

"I'll tell you the story. You might not believe it, but I'll tell you anyway. He must be some kind of guardian angel."

"But you don't believe in such things," Margaret-Ann said.

Peaches shrugged as they walked into the studio. "Is Janet still here?"

"Sitting in the very same chair," Margaret-Ann said. "I have a plan."

"A plan?"

Margaret-Ann nodded.

"So, don't keep me in suspense. Tell me about it."

"I will, as soon as you've told me about Mr. Whatever His Name Is."

Peaches frowned. "Now, just stop that. You know perfectly well what his name is."

"Hmph," Margaret-Ann huffed.

"TuckerD. His name is TuckerD," Peaches said as she tucked a strand of hair behind her ear.

"And where is he now? He's left again, I see."

Peaches took in a deep breath. "Yes," she said. "I suppose he has."

"But he likes you a lot," Margaret-Ann said. "He's not around much for someone who likes you. Did he ask you for money?"

Peaches held up her hands. "Don't go there again, Margaret-Ann."

"I'm only a mother trying to protect her daughter."

Peaches raised her voice. "Her thirty-nine year old daughter, who can very well take care of herself!"

"Hmph," came the sound. "We'll see."

Chapter 20

Two hours later when the police had completed their questioning and interrogation, Peaches felt somewhat relieved. She was filing charges against Etienne LaRoche, but not against Janet. The paperwork complete, she left her office and went into the main lobby.

Janet stood when she saw Peaches. "I've bothered you long enough," Janet said. "Thank you for listening, and I'm so very sorry about…well, about everything."

"What will you do now?" Peaches asked. "Do you have somewhere to go? Relatives, maybe?"

Janet shook her head. "My parents died when I was seven. My grandmother raised me, but she's passed on now."

Margaret-Ann cleared her throat. Peaches motioned her forward.

"Janet," Margaret-Ann said, her face stern. "I have a suggestion. Do you sew?"

"Sew?"

"Are you handy with a needle and thread?"

Janet nodded. "My grandmother was a seamstress. She taught me to sew when I was just a child."

Peaches narrowed her eyes. "What are you up to, Margaret-Ann?" she asked.

"Well, as you know, Peaches, Aileen is leaving us shortly for maternity leave, and Miss Cora, our assistant seamstress, has been gone for over a week. Work is building up, and with Aileen leaving...."

Janet's eyes widened. "I could do whatever needed to be done," she said softly.

"Wait!" Peaches said, and help up a hand. "Margaret-Ann, are you suggesting that we hire Janet, our biggest competitor? That's not going to happen."

"May I have a word, Peaches?" Margaret-Ann asked, and stepped toward the desk in the corner.

The two of them walked in silence until Peaches felt she would burst. "What are you thinking? Hiring Janet LaRoche? No, absolutely not."

"Hear me out, please," Margaret-Ann said, her hands clasped at her waist. "Remember what you used to say to me?"

Peaches shook her head. "I still can't believe you'd think of hiring our biggest competitor, and no, I don't remember. Enlighten me."

"Keep your friends close but your enemies closer," Margaret-Ann said. "The girl may be a competitor, but didn't you hear what she said? It's that sorry, no good husband...well, ex-husband now. It was all his doing. She was a victim of his ruthlessness. We're short-handed, and she knows the bridal industry. Maybe we can bring her over to our side. But she's got to have work and a place to live."

Peaches just stared at her.

"Put your fear aside, Peaches, and let your heart do the thinking right now. The girl's in trouble. She needs help. Perhaps we can kill her with kindness, so to speak."

"I don't trust her," Peaches said. "Who's to say she won't steal every new design I create? It's a terrible idea, Margaret-Ann."

"We need help right here in this shop. The Spring Collection is way behind. And you have more brides than you can handle right now. And don't forget about the Astons. That's a huge wedding, over a thousand guests. And the girl hasn't even decided on a dress yet."

Peaches sighed. "I guess you're right. I'll agree to it, but I need to call Lily so that she can begin to handle the legal issues involved."

Margaret-Ann smiled. Peaches dialed a number on the phone. "Lily, how are you? Yes, I'm doing well, but I need your help as soon as possible." Peaches listened. "An hour? Got it. Meet you at the coffee shop."

Peaches put her phone away and turned toward Margaret-Ann. Then she stepped forward and kissed her on the cheek.

"Okay," she said softly. "I'm meeting Lily in an hour. Until then, just take Janet on a tour of the studio, show her the sewing room, do whatever you want. But please, please, don't let her anywhere near my office. I'll go and deposit the new designs I've been working on, and then I'll lock up the desk drawers. Fair enough?"

Margaret-Ann hugged her back. "Thank you, dear. That's fair enough. No worries. I'll keep a close eye on her while you're gone."

***

In the coffee shop, Lily and Peaches sat at their favorite table by the window.

"So, what's going on in the world of high fashion? You look stunning as usual, by the way," Lily said, and blew on her hot coffee. "How you manage to stay so gorgeous is beyond me. But tell me what's wrong. You sounded worried on the phone. And what's with your hands, Peaches? They're shaking."

"It's nothing," Peaches said. "Does the name JLaRoche ring any bells?"

Lily chuckled. "I'll say it does," she said. "What's your competitor up to now?"

Peaches removed a white napkin from her pants pocket and slid it over to Lily. "Theft," she said.

107

Lily's eyes widened. "This is new, isn't it? I haven't seen it before. And theft? Explain, please."

Peaches parked stray hairs behind her ear. "Here it is in a nutshell," she said. "JLaRoche doesn't stand for Janet. It stands for Jacques. Her former husband's name is Jacque Etienne LaRoche. He owns everything—every design, the house, the car. He owns it all. Nothing is in Janet's name. And now, he's tried to steal the new design. Thankfully, it was recovered, but he broke into my shop and took it from my drawer. Then, he went to the airport and tried to leave the country with it."

"But he didn't get away with it, obviously."

"Right. And his former wife is sitting in my shop. She told me the whole story, and now, he's divorced her and left her with nothing."

"So all this time, Janet has been a fake."

"She had nothing to do with anything. It was only the name JLaRoche that made her rich and successful. Of course, she's not rich anymore, but her former husband certainly is."

"And where is he now?"

"Portugal, where he was born and raised, and also where he has some dark connections on the black market."

"But he couldn't sell something as your design because he doesn't have them," Lily said.

"No, he doesn't," Peaches replied, and took a sip of her coffee. "But what he does have is a photographic memory."

Lily's cup clanked as she set it back in the saucer. "Oh, my," she said. "There's really no such thing as international copyright that includes all foreign countries. With international dealings, the copyright must be requested in each country. I believe that Portugal is included, but I'll need to check."

"But what if it isn't?"

Lily leaned forward. "Then he's free to have your gown created and sold there."

"But that's still stealing."

"International laws are different, Peaches. We're covered in the UK and Ireland and in France, Italy, Spain, Germany, Russia, and Asia."

"But not Portugal?"

"I'm just not sure, but hang on, and I'll find out."

Peaches felt her stomach knotting up, bile rising in her throat. She watched as Lily punched a button on her phone and talked to someone, but she couldn't quite make out the words. She had a sinking feeling that almost overwhelmed her. She propped her elbows on the table and cradled her head with her trembling hands.

"I see," Lily said. "Then we need to get on that right away. We have some contacts, so it shouldn't be any trouble. And do remember to contact the prime minister as quickly as possible. He doesn't like criminals, especially thieves, but he does like me, and even better, his niece wore one of Peaches' designs at her wedding, so he'll help if he can."

Peaches perked up. "Yes," she whispered. "I'd almost forgotten. I designed gowns for her and her mother. They were beautiful."

"Okay, so it's not good news, but it could be much worse. The royal family still has those dresses you designed hanging in their museum. So, even though we have no copyright, we have the support of royalty who, in turn, have a deep hatred for criminals because they want Portugal to be a place of comfort and safety. They do a tremendous amount of international business that they don't want threatened by illegal activity. I've given all the pertinent details, so even if Etienne tries to sell one of your creations, our contacts will let us know."

Peaches sighed, then her cellphone rang. When she saw the name of the caller, she held out a hand to Lily. "I've got to take this. Give me a minute."

On the next ring, Peaches answered. "Yes, Mr. Bishop. How are you today?" She listened for a couple of minutes to what he had to say. A frown formed on her lips. "But I thought they were moving out? We had an agreement. They were to vacate the premises and leave two of the horses." Peaches listened again. "A slight chance? But what about the paperwork I signed? I trusted you to work out the deal, including the restorations. So, does that mean the deal is off or on? Give it to me straight. I'm tired of waiting for these people to make up their minds." Peaches glanced at Lily and rolled her eyes. "No, that's not acceptable to me. I won't wait another month for them to decide. Just tell them the deal is off the table for now. Find me another place, Mr. Bishop. A ranch with acreage and horses and room for a studio and workshop. That's my final word. Goodbye now. Sorry, Lily," Peaches said as she ended the call.

"Trouble?" Lily asked.

"According to Mr. Bishop, the former owners can't make up their minds. So, I told him to find me another place. But let's talk about my designs. I can house hunt later."

"We were speaking about the prime minister," Lily said as she took a last sip of coffee. "I have faith that the he and his staff will be vigilant and will act swiftly."

"But if Etienne's doing black market business, how will he know?"

Lily smiled. "They'll know. They're everywhere."

"Huh?"

"Spies, my dear. Or security agents, to use a better word."

Peaches cut her eyes at Lily.

"What is it?" Lily asked. "I know that look, but the answer is no. You're not hopping a flight to Portugal. Leave it to the people who know what they're doing."

"But—" Peaches said.

"No, absolutely not," Lily said, and put a hand on Peaches'. "Our little foray into England was nothing compared to this. This is black market. This is big government. This, my dear, is dangerous stuff, the sort that could get you killed."

"Over a wedding gown?"

"Over much less, I'm afraid."

Peaches said nothing for a moment. Then she glanced up at Lily with a smile on her face. "So, when do we leave?"

Chapter 21

"It's all settled," Peaches said to Margaret-Ann, exactly one week after the deal with the new house had fallen through. "Everything's in place."

"But Peaches, this could be dangerous." Margaret-Ann sat at the table. "And remember what happened the last time you tried to go after someone who'd stolen your designs? You remember, don't you?"

Peaches rubbed the scar on the side of her cheek. She could almost feel the jolt of pain when he'd bashed her in the face. The moon-shaped ring on his finger had cut a chunk out of her cheek. "I have a permanent reminder," she said.

"If that stranger hadn't intervened, I'm afraid the man would have killed you," Margaret-Ann said as her eyes filled with tears. "I couldn't stand to lose you, Peaches. I just couldn't take it."

"But I got the design back and had him arrested," Peaches said.

"You did, but only because you'd designed a wedding gown for the prime minister's wife and niece. I thank God for that every day."

"Lily's going with me this time," she said. "So, I think we'll be safe."

Margaret-Ann lowered her head.

"Look," Peaches said as she paced. "We've taken every precaution. Lily has some very good connections."

Margaret-Ann said softly. "It's just that...well...I have a really bad feeling about it. That's all."

Peaches let out a sigh, then walked over to her and hugged her. "Please don't worry," she said. "I promise to be very careful."

"Now, why would I worry about my only child running around Portugal chasing a member of a black market gang? Oh, honey, are you sure you'll be all right?"

Peaches smiled. "The prime minister and all of his agents are on this. I truly don't think I'll be in any danger. Otherwise, I wouldn't go."

Margaret-Ann rubbed her eyes. "Can't you just stay here where you're safe, and set your talents to work designing more gowns? You've plenty of business, plenty of clients who need you here. I haven't seen a single white napkin in at least a week."

"Now, Margaret-Ann, I've proven many times over that I know how to run my business. I've been doing a pretty good job for the last ten years."

"Hmph," Margaret-Ann said. "You have the best of everything: expensive perfumes, makeup, the finest money can buy. But why, Peaches, why do we still live in a pigsty?"

A tear trickled down Margaret-Ann's cheek. "I'm sorry, honey. I'm just afraid that if you go to Portugal, I'll never see you again."

Peaches put a hand on Margaret-Ann's cheek. "No worries, Mama. I'll be back safe and sound. You can count on it."

***

At breakfast a few mornings later, Peaches sat at the table and sipped her coffee. After an early call from Mr. Bishop, she felt good about the deal with another, even bigger, ranch house. The owners had accepted her offer, and even though no paperwork had been signed, her imagination ran rampant with redesigns of the spaces she needed. And though there weren't any horses involved, she could buy her own horses now. Choose the exact ones she wanted.

"Finally," she whispered. "Finally, we'll have a decent home."

"I want to talk about this trip," Margaret-Ann said from behind her.

"Geez, you startled me. What are you doing up so early?" Peaches asked.

"I don't want you to go," Margaret-Ann said. "I know you'll go anyway, but I don't want you to."

"I'm going. I have to," Peaches said as she drained the remains of her coffee.

Margaret-Ann stepped into the tiny kitchen and poured a cup of coffee, then busied herself with little kitchen tasks.

Peaches sighed. "I'll be perfectly okay."

Margaret-Ann turned around. "I worry about you, Peaches. Just look at your hands, dear. They never stop trembling. And, if I'm completely honest, I'll be lonely here without you."

Peaches got up and put her cup in the sink. As she headed out of the kitchen, she stopped. "My hands are just fine. I promise. And I know you'll be lonely, but I'll be back as soon as I can. I promise. I just don't want to turn down this opportunity. Lily and I will be guests at the royal palace with the prime minister and his family."

Margaret-Ann sighed. "I can't really blame you. I used to love to travel."

"He has organized a team of…a sort of SWAT team to guard and protect us. They'll be with us every step of the way. I have to know that Etienne is captured, and I want him to see me, too, to know that *I know* what scum he is."

"I see," Margaret-Ann said. "And how long will you be gone?"

"Five days. We'll leave tomorrow, Monday, and return late Friday night."

"Will you call me to let me know that you're okay?"

Peaches nodded and headed out of the kitchen.

"And one more thing," Margaret-Ann called to her.

Peaches walked to the kitchen, hands on hips.

"Will you promise me that you'll return safely?"

After a moment, Peaches replied. "I'll do my level best. And you'll be too busy to miss me."

"Why's that?"

"Everything we have needs to be packed up in boxes. On the day after I get back, you and I are moving."

"Oh, my God," Margaret-Ann said and rubbed her temples. "Another pig sty. No, I don't think I can take it anymore. I'll not live in squalor for the rest of my life, Peaches. No. If you want to move, go, but you go without me this time."

A big grin spread across Peaches' face.

"You're smiling. What's wrong? Oh, Lord, it must be worse than I thought."

Peaches stepped a little closer. "I'm smiling because you're going to be so surprised."

Margaret-Ann flopped down into one of the kitchen chairs and put her hands over her face. "Not again, Peaches. I've followed you from one dump to the other for ten years now. I'm done. I'm staying here. I can manage on my own just fine."

Peaches drew in a deep breath. "I will say one word that I want you to think about while I'm gone."

"And what might this magic word be?"

"Horses," Peaches said, and left the kitchen.

Chapter 22

Peaches munched on a pack of peanuts while Lily kept her phone pressed to her ear.

"I understand," Lily said to the caller. "We promise to obey all of the rules you provide, and we thank you for your trouble." With that, she ended the call.

"Well?" Peaches asked.

"The prime minister is sending his official car for us. It will be first in line as we leave the Portela Airport in Lisbon. The name of the residency is Sao Bento Mansion in Lisbon. That is where we will be staying. When we arrive at the palace, a greeting party will escort us to our rooms."

"Prime Minister Cosanto has come through for us, then," Peaches said.

Lily nodded. "Only a few more hours and we'll be there," Lily said as she fiddled with her watch. "I'm setting a timer so that we can change clothes. I don't think the prime minister will appreciate our arrival wearing jeans and T-shirts."

"He is a bit fussy about the way his court dresses, thank goodness. I think the gowns I sold him were the most expensive I've ever made, and the bridesmaids' dresses were almost as much. Even the flower girl's dress was over $10,000."

"But it was the most beautiful wedding I've ever seen. You did an excellent job of it, my friend."

Peaches nodded. "My career depended on it," she said as

she took another peanut from the tiny pack. "If I'd made any mistakes, my reputation would have suffered."

"You did a terrific job. I'd never been to a true cathedral wedding. It was stunning!"

"And I'd never made a gown with a cathedral train before! The thing was at least twelve feet long. Margaret-Ann worked day and night to finish it, and I must say that it was spectacular. Oh, there is one more thing, Lily."

"I'm all ears," Lily said.

"Are you familiar with Harmony House?"

"You mean the Salvation Army home for displaced women?" Peaches nodded.

"Go on," Lily said.

"If, for any reason at all, you get back to America before I do, would you arrange to go by my studio and into the workroom at the back? There's a large section blocked off, and inside it are three gowns and assorted veils and undergarments. All of it is labeled, and it all goes to Harmony House. You can ask for Marcus. He'll know what to do with it."

Lily just stared at her.

"Is something wrong?" Peaches asked.

"Wait," Lily said. "Don't tell me that you're donating those beautiful and expensive gowns to Harmony House. No, tell me it isn't true."

"What's wrong with donating?"

"Nothing, nothing at all, but I can't say that I've ever seen any sort of donation like that listed in your paperwork. And why would you donate those very expensive dresses to a charity organization when you could sell them and make money? Even if you sold them half-price, you'd still make gobs of money. I don't understand."

Peaches leaned close to her.

"It's just something I felt I needed to do, Lily. Something from my heart that has nothing to do with money, but everything to do with helping someone in need. I know that sounds strange coming from me, but I've been doing it for several years."

"I'd never have guessed," Lily said, and tucked her hair behind her ears. "So now, let me get this straight. You donate used gowns?"

Peaches shook her head.

"New ones?" Lily asked. "Don't tell me you donate brand new dresses."

Peaches nodded.

"These are dresses that clients ordered but never picked up for some reason. All of them were partially paid for. I don't take orders unless there's an initial payment."

"But that's half price, right? So you're still losing money."

Peaches nodded.

"And those dresses could be sold to someone else."

"Yep, they could, but in this case, they're donated to women who could otherwise never afford a Peaches and Lace gown. It's one small thing I can do."

"You're something else, Peaches Malone. Do the girls at Harmony House know who made those gowns?"

Peaches nodded.

"But they'll never tell. They're all sworn to secrecy. And trust me, if they wear one of them, they'll never tell a soul who made the gown. They'll wear it with pride knowing they have the finest gown available. It's good for the girls, and it makes me feel good, too."

"Well, then, I'm sworn to secrecy, too."

"Promise?"

Lily nodded. "My lips are sealed. "Well, to change the subject, how is Margaret-Ann?"

Peaches shrugged. "Not happy at the moment. But I hope all that will change if I can finalize the deal for the new house."

"Did you say you were moving your studio?"

"Let's just call it a second location. I don't want to lose my spot in downtown Atlanta, so I'll keep the shop open, but most of the work will be done at the new house if everything goes well. There's room for a wonderful studio and a wedding venue."

"Will your clients mind the drive?"

"It's only four miles away from the city, so if they mind that drive, then let them go somewhere else. It's all in my new brochures."

"You've put a lot of planning into this million-dollar utopia."

"Well, don't forget that the new studio and a wedding venue will be part of that, and those weren't cheap."

"No, I can imagine they weren't."

"Margaret-Ann deserves it," Peaches said. "If the deal goes through, she'll have every modern convenience, and she won't believe the new studio when it's finished. State of the art sewing machines that practically run themselves. But she'll still have her two old models. I doubt she'd work on anything else. Did you finish all your peanuts?"

Lily chuckled and handed over her unopened packet. "You know we'll have a big dinner at the palace," she said. "I was sort of saving room for the meal."

Peaches shrugged and fumbled with the package, her hands trembling more than ever. "I can't resist peanuts. I never buy them, of course, but when I find them on a plane, I claim those suckers for my own."

"When are you going to do something about that trembling, Peaches? It's gone on now for too long."

"It's just nervous energy, that's all. I mean, what else could it be? No worries."

"You're a mess, Peaches," Lily said with a laugh. "What would I do without you? So, the deal is done on the new house? You're ready to move in?"

"There's always more paperwork, you know. There's another couple interested in the property, but I keep up with it, and if I have my way, I'll get the ranch."

"When will you know for sure?"

"The realtor is supposed to call me the day we get back. He doesn't think the other couple will be able to arrange financing, and since I made a cash offer to pay in full, then he's almost certain I can get it. The current owners are almost desperate to sell."

"Really? Then why isn't it done already?"

"The other couple happens to be related to the current owners."

"Bummer," Lily said. "So, it's basically blood versus money."

"True. You'd think they'd be eager to sell and make the most money they could, but they just haven't taken the offer yet. And worse, the other couple already lives there. They're watching over the house and grounds for the owners."

"Double bummer."

"They were asking $550,000 for the entire property. I offered $600,000 cash."

"My gosh! Are they crazy?"

"Well, the husband jumped at the offer, but the wife didn't. It's her daughter who wants the house."

"Do you have any idea what the daughter offered?"

Peaches shook her head. "Mr. Bishop, my realtor, is doing all he can."

"Wait," Lily said and turned to her, maneuvering the seat belt. "Sam Bishop? Is he your realtor?"

Peaches nodded.

Lily smiled. "Sam and I go way back," Lily said, a blush forming on her cheeks. "Way, way back. Maybe I can find out something for you and speed up this process."

She winked at Peaches.

When the timer went off, Lily grabbed her purse and travel bag and got up. "Time for the pumpkin to turn into Cinderella," she said. "Be back shortly. And don't worry about the house. Now that I know who your realtor is, perhaps things will work out."

Peaches grinned. "Wait, I'll come, too. I'll grab the restroom when you're done before someone else claims it."

"Don't forget your purse," Lily said.

In thirty minutes, the two of them changed clothes, refreshed their makeup, and restyled their hair. As they walked back to their seats, Lily glanced at Peaches.

"I love your dress," she said. "It's very flattering. You're so gorgeous you make me sick. And the bad part is that you're gorgeous without much effort. That hair of yours amazes me, so long, blonde, and perfectly in place, but messy, if you know what I mean. I could hate you for that, you know."

"You have gorgeous hair, Lily. And I know for a fact that it takes very little care. It's naturally shiny, straight, and that beautiful blue-black. You look like a fashion model."

Lily shook her head as she sat down. "Maybe twenty years ago I could have passed for a model, but now, I'm too old to even think of such things."

"Me, too, but I try my best to think of being fashionable rather than thinking of my age."

"You're going to be a hit at the dinner. Honestly, Peaches, that dress is beautiful."

"It's one of my designs," Peaches said as she drew her compact out of her purse. "I had Margaret-Ann make it for me. She did an excellent job, don't you think?"

"The baby blue is stunning on you. I'd never have thought you'd look good in baby blue, but now that I take a closer look, the color matches your blue eyes perfectly. The knot work along the sleeves and the fine lace at the bodice are magnificent," Lily said and fingered one of the knots. "It looks so elegant."

Peaches checked her makeup, eyeliner, lashes, and lipstick.

"Stop that," Lily said. "You look perfect."

"Do I need more blush?"

Lily shook her head. "I told you. You look just perfect, so let it go and buckle your seat belt. We're about to land."

Peaches buckled up and looked out the window to watch as they descended into Portugal. She was struck at once by the vivid orange, gold, and green of the landscape, all seeming to float in the deep blue Atlantic.

"It's beautiful," she whispered, and then she saw the large golden dome of the palace not far from the white dome of a church.

"Isn't it?" Lily said.

"I might never leave here."

Lily frowned at her.

"Just look at it, Lily. All those sparkling white buildings of the town, the magnificent blue waters breaking at the shore. Imagine hearing those waves and being so close to the water all the time. Maybe I'd actually sleep once in a while. This, Lily, is the most gorgeous place I've ever seen."

"But it's not in the U.S., Peaches. We're in Portugal, remember? Your business is in Atlanta."

Peaches shrugged. "Give me a day or so to figure it out," she said. "But honestly, just from the beauty of it, I'd love to own a home here. And when I die, I want to be a very old woman watching from the balcony as the beautiful blue waters crash against the rocks."

Chapter 23

Pulling her rolling bag behind her, Peaches looked for a women's restroom. "Let's stop in here for a minute before we get in the car. Oh, did I tell you that Aileen took Missy home with her?"

"Missy?"

"The studio cat," Peaches said.

Lily, briefcase in hand, rolling bag behind, nodded. "That's good, I guess," she said. "I'm more of a dog person."

Peaches hurried to the wall of mirrors that lined the restroom. Then she unzipped her rolling bag and took out the item that lay wrapped in tissue paper on top.

"Oh, my word," Lily said. "You're wearing a fascinator? It's beautiful, Peaches. Gee, thanks for making me look like a plain Jane."

Peaches tilted the large-brimmed blue hat to just the right angle. She moved her head this way and that, adjusted the satin flowers, and secured the headband with bobby pins, concealing them carefully with her hair. After a final spritz of her favorite perfume, she stepped back and observed herself in the mirror.

"It's perfect," Lily said, looking sadly down at her two-piece navy business suit.

Peaches scrambled through her bag again. "Here," she said. "I brought this one for you."

"But how did you know what I'd be wearing?"

Peaches chuckled. "From our previous years as friends, I hazarded a guess that it would be a navy blue business suit. Now, put that thing on and let me see."

Lily adjusted the fascinator onto her head.

"Tilt it just a bit more," Peaches said.

"Like this?"

"Perfect. How do you like it?"

"Don't you think it's too big?" Lily asked. "It looks awfully big."

"Oh, darling, there's no such thing as too big when it comes to these fascinators. It's called The Charlotte, and is made from the softest Sinamay straw, so light it's almost see-thru. The wide brim disc shape is perfect with your outfit, and just look at the satin and straw loops. The bunch of tiny satin navy feathers will be absolutely show-stopping. Prepare to be ogled and whistled at!"

"I've never worn anything like this. I'll bet it cost a fortune."

"You look smashing," Peaches said as she made a final adjustment to her own hat. "That's what counts." Then she dug through her bag and brought out a pair of baby blue heels.

"Oh, my word," Lily said. "I should have known you'd have matching shoes."

"Do you like this fake snake print on them?"

"Any snake would be stunned to see his hide in a rich baby blue color, and yes, I think he'd approve. Peaches Malone, you are the very essence of fashion, my dear. Now, come on. The car's outside, I'm sure."

A chauffeur was waiting for them as they stepped outside and into the car.

"By the way," Lily said when they were safely belted in. "How's your love life?"

"Non-existent," Peaches said.

"But what about the tall man you told me about, the new one with the odd name."

"TuckerD?"

"Right. How are things between you two? Didn't he take the apartment above your studio?"

Peaches nodded. "But, there's something about him, Lily. Something I can't put my finger on. He's tall and gorgeous and kind and polite, a real gentleman, and his scent is magnetic. He smells like oranges and cedar. It's most pleasant."

"And the problem is?"

Peaches leaned toward her and whispered. "He's a bit mysterious."

"Explain, please."

"I really can't explain. He's not like any other man I've ever met. He's just…different."

"Is that a good thing or a bad thing?" Lily asked, smoothing her skirt.

"He gives a great backrub and a passionate kiss."

Lily's eyes widened. "So, the problem is?"

Peaches shrugged. "Okay, I like him. A lot. But he just disappears for days. I've no idea where he goes, and our contact is limited to a few minutes every now and then on the bench in my garden. That's it."

"Wait, you don't go out on dates?"

Peaches laughed. "Oh, sure, if you call fifteen minutes on a bench a date."

"I don't really understand," Lily said, and rubbed her temples.

"Nor do I," Peaches replied, and gazed out the window. "The strange thing is that I think he cares for me."

"Did he tell you that?"

Peaches nodded.

"What sort of job does he have that takes him out of town so much? Is he a salesman?"

"I don't have a clue."

"Drop him," Lily said, and looked her square in the eyes.

"Now. Before you *really* fall for him. The next time you see him, tell him to get out of your life. Be honest with him and tell him you don't want to see him anymore."

"Ladies," came the call from the front seat. "We'll arrive in two minutes."

"There's the palace," Peaches said. "Isn't it magnificent? Just look at that golden dome! Oh, I want to live here, Lily. I'm serious."

"Then you'd better call Mr. Bishop. But first, you'll need all sorts of paperwork about your finances, copies of legal documents. It's a complicated process. But perhaps if you speak with the prime minister, he can speed up the process. In the meantime, though, we need to see what's available in the housing market, don't we?"

Peaches smiled.

"Perhaps, Peaches, that's why we're really here. Not to find Etienne—we know the police will do that—but to find a home for you and Margaret-Ann. Maybe that is the real purpose of this trip."

Peaches felt a lightness in her soul that she'd never felt before. "Yes," she said. "Yes."

Chapter 24

Peaches sucked in a breath when she saw the palace. "It's the most beautiful place I've ever seen," she whispered.

The chauffeur, a short man with dark olive complexion, wearing a perfectly tailored suit, opened the door for them. "Allow me to be the first to introduce you to the world's most perfect city. Welcome to Lisbon!"

As she exited the car, Peaches felt as if her head were on a swivel. Everywhere she looked, she saw something spectacular: tall, round columns, high arches, classical sculptures, manicured gardens. "I can't believe how beautiful it all is," she said. "It's like paradise!"

"But of course it is! It's the royal palace," a man's voice said quite softly. "Warmest greetings from the prime minister and his family. I am Alberto, Head of Staff here at the palace. Allow me to escort you to your rooms."

Peaches and Lily glanced at each other and smiled.

"Lead on, Alberto," Peaches said.

"May I compliment you on your attire? You'll grace the palace with beauty and glamour."

"How kind of you, Alberto," Lily said. "Thank you."

"Considering that we have one of the world's most famous fashion designers with us, I expected nothing less," he said. "Your rooms are just up the stairs here." Alberto led them up the double winding staircase and off to the left. He opened the second door.

127

"This will be your room if it meets your approval, Ms. Malone." Alberto motioned her inside.

Peaches gasped. "It's gorgeous," she said.

"Very good," Alberto said, and walked down the hall to open the third door. "And this is yours, Ms. Buchanan—if it meets your approval, of course."

Peaches followed along.

"Just perfect, Alberto. Thank you."

"The buttons are on the wall just here," he said, and pointed. "Feel free to ring if you need anything. My personal one is the first button labeled 'Head of Staff.' But we've outfitted your rooms with all of the necessities."

"We appreciate your kindness, Alberto. Please give our regards to the prime minister."

"Indeed I shall," Alberto said. "Cocktails are served at 7:00."

"Would you happen to have any Maker's Mark? It's my favorite," Peaches said.

"But of course. Whatever you wish. Dinner is at 8:00. Evening attire. Oh, and no hats. The prime minister thinks it rude to wear hats at dinner. However, he does like tiaras."

Peaches and Lily looked a bit stricken.

"I'm afraid we didn't bring our tiaras," Peaches said. "We don't have occasion to wear them often."

"Do not worry yourselves," Alberto said, and walked toward the door. "I shall return momentarily."

"I don't even own one," Lily said. "Who'd have thought we would need a tiara? Of course, Alberto didn't say it was mandatory, just that the prime minister likes them."

"But he wouldn't have mentioned it if it weren't important," Peaches said. "Would we have time to go shopping before dinner?"

"I don't think you'll find a tiara shop anywhere around here," Lily said, and turned in a circle. "Just look at this room, Peaches. Isn't it lovely?"

"Both of the rooms are just stunning," Peaches said. "I've never seen architecture and buildings like this. They're just glorious, and just think of all the work that went into creating them."

"Ladies," Alberto said as he walked into the room. He carried a velvet pillow trimmed in gold. Atop it were two white boxes. "A gift for each of you."

"Gifts for us?" Lily asked.

"Yes, yes, help yourselves. Please, take a box."

Peaches took the one closest to her while Lily did the same.

"Open, please," Alberto said, his brown eyes sparkling against his olive complexion. As he smiled, his perfect white teeth gleamed like stars.

The women opened their boxes at the same time, their reactions to the gifts inside simultaneous. Their mouths dropped open, and they stared down at the gifts.

"These," Peaches said, "you can't mean they're gifts. They're...."

"Please try them on. There's a mirror here."

Gently, Peaches lifted out her tiara. It was covered in small diamonds and studded with emeralds, rubies, and sapphires. Lily's was exactly the same.

"Do you like them?" Alberto asked.

"They are beautiful, Alberto," Peaches said as she slipped hers into place. She admired the shape, rectangular with none of those silly points on it. It was simple, understated, and elegant. She fluffed her hair around it and smiled.

"Alberto, these are perfect, just perfect, for us both," Lily said. "This will be my first tiara, and my first time to wear one."

"You're pleased, then," Alberto said. "The prime minister will be happy. His wife will be even happier, since it was she who chose them for you. You are the first to whom the prime minister's wife has made such a gift."

"We don't know what to say, Alberto. We're honored and

humbled by such an act of kindness," Peaches said as she folded her trembling hands as if in prayer and bowed slightly.

Alberto bowed in return and left them.

Chapter 25

Peaches stood in front of the cheval glass mirror and turned this way and that, then leaned in closer to check her make up. Finally, she reached for the jewel-encrusted headband...or tiara...so graciously bestowed on her by Mrs. Cosanto. Though her hands still trembled, she managed to pick it up.

She placed it carefully on her head. With her blonde hair pulled back into an elegant chignon, the tiara sparkled. A few tendrils of hair draped her cheeks precisely as she'd wanted. The long sleeves of her red satin and lace formal gown fit snugly at her wrists, while the mermaid shape hugged her slim body, the back of it falling into a two-foot train. The red soles of her black Louboutin heels added a final touch of elegance. She'd chosen small ruby and gold studs as earrings.

With one last swirl of sparkling blush on her cheeks, she smiled and let out a deep breath, and turned when the door to her suite opened.

"I can't do anything with my hair," Lily said as she walked toward her, then stopped abruptly. "Can...oh, Peaches, you look stunning! I don't think I've ever seen you in that gown. Is it new?"

Peaches nodded her head. "Margaret-Ann's handiwork," she said.

"She's a genius," Lily said. "Now, help me please with this tiara."

"Sit," Peaches said, pointing to the vanity chair. "Let's see what we can do."

Peaches brushed the top and sides of Lily's hair straight back away from her face. "Give me a few of those bobby pins on the vanity."

Peaches parted the back of Lily's hair and swooped it all into a curl on top of her head. Securing it with several pins, she moved on until all of Lily's hair was pinned in long loose curls. Then she placed the tiara gently on the top, pulled out a few strands of dark hair on each side, and stood back.

"Voila!" she said.

"Wow," Lily said, "I look like a princess. How did you do that so quickly?"

Peaches shrugged. "I could see it in my mind, and it just made its way to your hair."

Lily stood. "Well?"

"The gown is lovely, Lily. Blue is your color, and it matches almost perfectly with the sapphires."

"What about my earrings?"

Peaches scrunched up her face. "They're a bit too much. The large gold hoops detract from the tiara, and heaven forbid we do that. Here," she said as she walked to her jewelry case. "Try these. Just plain blue studs, but they'll work."

Lily swapped out the earrings and glanced into the mirror. "You're always right about fashion, Peaches. Always. If you weren't rich already, I'd hire you as my personal assistant."

Peaches chuckled.

"Oh, and I made a call for you," Lily said. "I talked to Mr. Bishop. He wasn't happy, but I convinced him to hold off on any offers on the property for a month. He finally agreed."

"Thank you. When is dinner? I need to call Margaret-Ann."

"You have fifteen whole minutes before they come for us."

Peaches grabbed her phone, her hands trembling. "Oh, I'd forgotten the time difference. What time is it in the U.S.?"

"They're six hours ahead of us, so it's roughly 1:00 in the

morning there."

"I might scare her if I call now."

"But have you talked to her at all since we arrived this morning?"

Peaches shook her head.

Lily frowned. "Call her. Even you wake her, what does it matter? I'll wait for you out in the hall. There are some interesting pieces under glass out there. I'm too nosy not to go and take a look."

Peaches nodded and made the call.

A sleepy voice said, "Hello?"

"I'm so sorry to wake you, Margaret-Ann, but I wanted to let you know that I'm in Portugal safe and sound."

"Oh, Peaches!" came the excited voice on the phone. "Peaches!"

Peaches hated it when she gushed. "Remember that red gown you made for me?"

"Oh, yes, I remember," Margaret-Ann said, and yawned. "It showed off your figure to a T. But that was a while ago."

"I'm wearing it now," Peaches said. "Lily says it looks stunning."

"Well, Peaches, if anyone could pull off a mermaid gown, it's you. What did you do with your hair?"

"A chignon. The prime minister's wife gifted us with tiaras encrusted with jewels. I wanted to show it off, so I had to think of a way to pull my hair back."

"You're having a lovely time, aren't you?"

"It's only my first day, but so far, I'm captured by this place. There is something I want to tell you."

"Go ahead."

"I'm going to extend my stay for a few days."

Margaret-Ann remained silent.

"But I'd also like for you to come and see Portugal for yourself."

"You want me there with you?" Margaret-Ann asked.

"I want you to see Portugal."

"I don't know what to say, Peaches."

"Lily, the prime minister and I will make all the arrangements. Janet can watch the shop."

After a few seconds of silence, Margaret-Ann said, "I've never seen Portugal."

"I'll make all the arrangements. In the meantime, you continue to pack up our things. And don't take any new orders right now. How are you coming on the gowns?"

"They're just beautiful, and Janet was right. She can sew up a storm."

A knock sounded at the door.

"I'll call tomorrow with details for the trip. Good night, Margaret-Ann."

"Sweet dreams, Peaches."

Chapter 26

"Alberto is here for us," Lily said as she opened the door.

"Coming," Peaches called as she took one last look in the mirror.

Alberto walked in front of the two of them as he escorted them down the stairs and into an ornately-decorated drawing room, where he stopped and turned to them.

"May I take this opportunity to tell you that both of you look absolutely beautiful. The prime minister and his wife will be enthralled by you."

Peaches nodded her head. "Would you mind if I took a moment to look around in this room?"

Alberto motioned her forward.

Peaches was drawn immediately to a glass case which held only a man's shirt. She looked at the notes inside. *King Ferdinand of Spain, 1828. Gift from Hibernians.* "Alberto?" she asked.

He walked to her side.

"The lace on this shirt. I know it. I know this pattern," she said.

"The lace is from Ireland," he said, "a gift to King Ferdinand."

"Ireland?"

"Oh yes, there were great relations between Spain and Ireland, Ms. Peaches. And Portugal is in alignment, as well. At times there has been turmoil, but now, our great country is prospering."

135

"But Alberto, I told you that I know this pattern. I've seen it only recently on a man's shirt."

Alberto shook his head. "I don't doubt your word. But that pattern was made specifically for Ferdinand. It was an arrangement between Spain, Portugal, and Ireland. The pattern was unique to his wardrobe, and hasn't been reproduced since the early 1800s."

Peaches folded her hands at her waist. "I see," she said.

"Shall we?" Alberto asked and motioned toward the door.

When she reached Lily, she whispered. "I'll explain later."

Alberto led them down another flight of stairs and into a room the size of a football field, centered with a table that could easily seat a hundred people.

Peaches stood transfixed at the beauty of the room. Six tall arched stained glass windows graced the right side, lit magnificently with ten enormous crystal chandeliers down the center of the room. The ceiling looked to be thirty feet tall, and on the left side stood five enormous white columns. The corners of the room were ornately dressed with carved golden corbels, the back wall covered with a floor to ceiling mural depicting the city of Lisbon, the buildings bumping up against one another, the roofs in bright orange tile, the ocean a glorious sea blue.

"This is our formal dining hall," Alberto said.

"It's quite lovely," Peaches said. "Full of majesty."

Alberto smiled. "This way," he said.

They followed him into a smaller room, also ornately decorated, the terra cotta floors gleaming, the carved wooden table large enough to seat fifty. Red brocade draperies hung in three floor to ceiling windows on the outer wall, pooling at the bottom in a brilliant red and gold cluster of gorgeous material. Three crystal chandeliers, smaller than those in the formal dining room, hung above the great table, already set with several crystal vases of fresh and aromatic flowers, along with fine porcelain china and gold tableware.

"I've never seen anything as beautiful," Peaches said softly.

"The grandeur of it is almost overwhelming," Lily responded.

"You will find cards with your names on them," Alberto said. "I believe you are to be seated to the right and left of Prime Minister Cosanto." Alberto walked to the head of the table. "Ah, yes, your places," he said. "Please remain standing until the prime minister and his wife are seated."

"Where are all the other people?" Peaches asked.

"This is the private dining room," Alberto said. "Only the royal family and four heads of staff will be present."

"Will you be joining us, Alberto?" Lily asked.

"I shall," he said with a smile.

Alberto clapped his hands and the double doors opposite the grand table opened. Three finely dressed staff members entered and stood at their seats. Behind them came Prime Minister Cosanto, just as Peaches remembered him from the one visit he'd made to her shop a few years ago when she was commissioned to create a gown for his niece. He was dressed in a most elegant Italian suit. His graying hair was thick and parted to the side, while his tanned skin made the white of his shirt even whiter. He wore a serious expression as he took his seat. Behind him came Mrs. Cosanto, a short but slim beauty of a woman with black hair piled atop her head in a beautiful arrangement of curls, highlighted by a diamond tiara similar to the ones she'd given her guests. She wore a gown of turquoise, which complemented her olive skin and slim figure. A long string of pearls, draped several times, gave her a look of royalty. To Peaches, she hadn't aged a day.

Alberto nodded his head as a staff member helped seat Mrs. Cosanto and a beautiful young woman with jet black hair pulled back with a thin but expensive looking headband. She had thick dark brows, olive skin, and a complexion as smooth as silk. Her baby blue evening gown served as the perfect vehicle to highlight her dark features.

137

"Please be seated," Alberto called to the other diners.

Two staff members helped Peaches and Lily with the chairs.

The prime minister spoke. "We would like to welcome our guests, Ms. Peaches Malone and Ms. Lily Buchanan from America. We are delighted to have them in residence." He lifted a glass of champagne. "To our guests," he said. "Portugal is honored to have you. Thank you for gracing our table. And allow me to present our daughter, Bella. She is the young beauty sitting next to her equally beautiful mother."

Bella held up a hand and offered a big smile.

"She is stunning," Peaches said, and elbowed Lily.

"Isn't she gorgeous?" she whispered. "She's a fashion plate if I've ever seen one."

After the toast, the meal proceeded nicely. An appetizer of clams in white wine sauce with butter and cilantro on toasted bread was followed by more dishes than Peaches had ever seen. As each dish was served, its name was called out.

"It is so very nice to see you both again," Peaches said. "I never dreamed I'd be in Portugal, but I am so very grateful that you asked me here."

"But of course. You did such a beautiful job when my niece married. Marietta and I want the very best for our daughter, and you, my dear, are the very best. Alberto," the prime minister said. "Please bring a cocktail for Peaches. Maker's Mark is her preference. Is that correct, Peaches?"

Peaches blushed. "Yes," she said. "It's my favorite."

"Good," he said, "and just in time for the meal."

Shrimp *acorda* came first, a thick soup topped with fried shrimp, followed by *alheira*, a meat sausage topped with a poached egg, then *arroz de pato*, a fried duck rice. The favorite dish of the night was something called *bolinhas*, fried cod fritters served with rice and a sumptuous salad, and as a final dish was *bras*, salted cod with onion, potatoes, parsley, and a sprinkling of black olives. Tiny chili peppers called *piri piri* soaked in saffron, garlic oil, and parsley served as a topping for each course.

Peaches and Lily would glance at each other occasionally, both fearing they would pop wide open if they had to eat another bite, but then another tempting dish would make its way to the table, and they couldn't be rude, so they tried every dish. But then the pastries made their way to the table. Delicious dishes called *cavacas*, similar to American cupcakes, and éclairs provided all the delicate sweetness anyone could want.

There was little conversation during the meal, but after dessert and espresso, Alberto clapped his hands and the heads of staff went into action clearing the table, while Alberto helped the ladies out of their seats and led them into a cozy room off the dining room.

"Please," the prime minister said as he seated himself in a large overstuffed navy leather chair and puffed away on a pipe.

"Mrs. Cosanto," Lily said. "Peaches and I are so honored to have these beautiful tiaras."

"They really are exquisite," Peaches said.

"Please," she said in a heavy accent, "call me Marietta, and it was my honor to gift you with them."

The prime minister cleared his throat. "May I say that all of you, including my lovely wife, look quite stunning tonight. Such a privilege to dine with beautiful women. But then, I have the pleasure of dining with one beautiful woman every night," he said, and winked at Marietta. "Now, shall we discuss our business? Would you care for an after-dinner cocktail?"

Both Peaches and Lily nodded, then Peaches leaned forward in the leather chair. "Have you had any news about Etienne LaRoche?"

"He is in custody as we speak. I took the liberty of sending my best team to locate and capture him. There was little struggle. It was an easy task. Several others are imprisoned, as well."

Peaches put a hand to her chest. "I'm relieved," she said. "Even though I managed to get the design back, he might have had time to copy the design and sell it as his own. Is there a chance that I might question him to find out the truth?"

"No need. I doubt that you would get the truth from him. Besides, his accomplice is in custody with him. It was a…how do you say? Mafia-style gang. They are all in our jail awaiting trial, and the judgment will be swift and severe. They will all spend many years in jail."

Peaches glanced at Lily.

"And you will testify at the hearing, no? It will be your word that will allow justice to be carried out swiftly. The people of Portugal respect you greatly, Ms. Malone. They will expect an appearance at court."

Lily nodded. "Of course, we'll be there," she said.

Alberto came in with the drinks and distributed them quietly.

"There is another point of business we should discuss," the prime minister said. He glanced at Marietta and smiled. "Our daughter, Bella, will be married soon. We'd be most grateful if you would take over the wedding preparations, and perhaps use one of your new designs for her. It means that you will have to extend your stay, and of course, your room in the palace will be yours for as long as you need it."

"And for the wedding," Marietta interjected, "there is no budget, Peaches. I have already hired a wedding planner. The wedding will be here in the palace, of course, but the most important thing is the dress. And for that dress, for one of your new designs, the budget is unlimited."

"Indeed," the prime minister said.

Peaches thought for a moment. "You want me to design a dress for your daughter. I'm very pleased. However, I would have to go back home where the studio is so that Margaret-Ann, my seamstress, can help me create the dress. But then there are fittings, so I'm a bit confused."

The prime minister chuckled. "But of course you are. Our most fervent desire is that you remain here with us until after the wedding. We have two wonderful sewing studios. You'll have all the help you need."

Peaches said nothing for a minute or so. "Prime Minister, Marietta, might I ask a favor of you?"

"Of course, dear," Marietta replied. "What is it you need?"

"A home," Peaches said. "Here, here in Portugal. A cliff top home where I can look out over the ocean and hear the waves breaking on the rocks."

Marietta and the prime minister smiled. "I have just the place for you," Marietta said. "It is a gorgeous home located atop a craggy cliff that overlooks the Atlantic."

"Is it for sale? Is it large enough for a makeshift studio and for Margaret-Ann to set up a fitting room? Oh, and there might be a young woman named Janet coming, as well."

Marietta looked at her husband. He nodded at her. "Well, I'm afraid that technically, it is not for sale," she said in her heavily-accented voice. "However, it is perhaps a home that could be given in exchange for services — a trade, so to speak."

Peaches crinkled her brow. "I don't understand," she said.

"The home," Marietta said, "is ours, mine and my husband's. It is a property which we have never occupied. We bought it, along with another, when they first came on the market a year ago. Sadly, they've both been vacant all that time, though I check them once a week and have them both cleaned and inspected regularly to make sure they are in excellent repair."

"If you will stay and help us with this wedding, Ms. Malone, we will gladly offer you and your party the house on the cliff, perhaps as partial payment. But first, I think you should see it. Do you agree?"

Peaches was stunned. She couldn't form the words to say how she felt.

"I think her silence indicates that she agrees to your terms, Prime Minister Cosanto," Lily said.

Chapter 27

"Good night, Alberto. We appreciate your help today," Lily said.

Alberto bowed, opened the doors for them, and left.

"Meet me back here once we've changed," Lily said. "I'm dying to hear about the lace on the shirt." A few minutes later, the knock sounded. "Come on in," Lily called. "Want a hot toddy?"

Peaches shook her head. "I've had enough."

"Go ahead, take a seat. Wasn't it nice of them to put us in such wonderful rooms? You could live in these rooms for a week without ever stepping foot out the door. They're so well stocked I can hardly believe it." Lily opened the small fridge. "Just look at all that food! I've never seen so many types of cheese. The wine fridge is full, and the baskets are filled with fruit. They really know how to treat their guests."

"I hadn't even looked," Peaches said.

"Maybe because you don't eat enough to keep a bird alive," Lily said, and chuckled. "Although…you did some damage at dinner tonight."

"Their food is so good," Peaches said. "I probably haven't eaten that much in a full week."

Lily sighed.

"What's wrong?" Peaches asked, fiddling with her pajama pants.

"You love everything about Portugal, don't you? The food.

The homes. The people."

Peaches got up and started pacing the room. "It's the strangest thing, Lily. I've never felt as at home as I feel here. Could I have Portuguese ancestors, anything to explain why this place makes me feel as if I belong here?"

"We could search the archives," Lily said, "to see if we can find a connection. But maybe it's just the beauty of the place that has you in its grip."

"Maybe so."

"You made a quick and rash decision asking about a home here. Are you sure? Have you thought it through?"

"I have this vision, Lily," Peaches said. "I'm not sure where it came from, but I've had it since we first boarded the plane."

"So, tell me."

"I can see a compound, a castle, studios, horses. And I see all of us living there together. You, Margaret-Ann, Janet, all of us living and working together."

"Me?"

Peaches nodded.

"But I work in Atlanta," Lily said.

"So do I," Peaches responded. "But I can see it, Lily. All of us here together, all of us working. I know it seems like a rash decision, but I've seen it, and I believe in my heart that it will happen."

"I don't know how you're going to pull this one off, Peaches, but if anyone can, you can. Now, aren't you going to tell me about this mysterious lace?"

Peaches took a deep breath. "It could all be in my imagination," she said. "But I would swear that TuckerD has the very same lace pattern on his shirt sleeves."

"A copy, of course," Lily said, and took a sip of her toddy. "Just because Alberto said there were no replicas, that doesn't mean that someone didn't make one. For all we know, there could be hundreds of these patterns scattered all over the world."

"But isn't it a little strange that here I am all the way in Portugal, and what do I find? A lace pattern that exactly matches the one on TuckerD's shirts. Doesn't that seem odd?"

Lily raised her eyebrows. "Truthfully, it does."

"And I just keep wondering why," Peaches said, and propped one side of her hair behind her ear. "Why would I find something that reminds me of him? If it were across the street or in a lace factory, I could deal with it a little better, but here? In Portugal? At the palace of the prime minister?"

"What do you know about the lace pattern on his sleeves?"

"I recognized it, I thought, as Carrickmacross lace. The lace, I know, is from Ireland. He said his grandmother gave him the shirt."

"So the pattern may or may not be the same?" Lily asked as she got a refill.

Peaches twirled a strand of hair that hung below her shoulder, her trembling hands relaxing as she did. "It certainly looks like the same one, but I must be mistaken."

"As I said, it could be a replica. That's my guess. Once it's seen, anything can be duplicated."

"Like my dresses," Peaches said, and lowered her head.

"We've taken every precaution," Lily said, "and so has the prime minister. But I think the person who will be most helpful is Marietta."

"Marietta?"

"She's a fashion fanatic! She'll keep her eye on every new wedding gown that appears. Didn't you see the stack of bridal magazines in the den? There must have been fifty of them. It looked from the spines as if they were all in different languages, from all over the world, Peaches. You have an ally in Marietta."

"That's good to know."

"And just think of the connections she has! I can assure you that she will be your very own watchdog."

"I'm almost sure that Etienne sold the design before he was

144

arrested, so there's no telling who has access to it now, even though he and his cohorts are in jail. That's what bothers me the most. Who got that design between the time he stole it and the time it was taken from him?"

"It will all come out in court. They will see to it that your design is safe from being copied."

Peaches yawned. "I think it's bedtime," she said. "All of a sudden, I'm exhausted."

"Me, too. Can you find your way back to your room?"

Peaches chuckled. "Since it's just next door, I think I can manage."

"Well, I know how you are about directions," Lily said, and laughed. "Just be careful not to go into anyone else's room, especially if it's a man. You'd give him a heart attack."

"That bad, huh?"

"Oh, Peaches, you're a stunner even in your jammies and without makeup. You make me sick. And congratulations on your newest commission, by the way. Bella will make a stunning bride."

Peaches smiled. "I can hardly believe it. Just as I'm thinking I'd like to live here, I get an offer of a home AND a studio and a new dress to make. It's almost unbelievable, but almost as if it were meant to be," she said as she opened the door.

"Good night, old friend. Get some rest," Lily said.

As Peaches went to step through the door, Lily called out to her. "You know I'm staying, too, don't you? The prime minister gave me a commission as well. He wants to hire me as part of his legal team."

"And why didn't you tell me?"

"I haven't agreed to it yet. I didn't really want to be here without anyone close to me. I guess I didn't want to start a new life by myself."

"Coward," Peaches said. "Then I'll arrange a room for you at my house. That way, we can start new lives together. Deal?"

Peaches waved and walked out of the room. Then she went down two flights of steps and into the den, and stood beside the glass case that held the shirt. She reached into the pocket of her pajamas and pulled out a tiny notepad and pencil. Then, she began to sketch, grateful that her hands had calmed enough for her to draw her design.

Chapter 28

At the bridal shop in Atlanta, Janet LaRoche opened the first letter in the stack that awaited her. Seeing that it was another invitation, she set it aside. Two more followed, both set aside for Margaret-Ann to look at.

But the third one looked different. No return address was written, and the sloppy handwriting on the regular address lines looked familiar. The longer she looked at it, the more familiar it became. Janet sucked in a breath as she felt her stomach knot.

"Etienne," she whispered.

With trembling fingers, she opened the envelope and drew out the single half-sheet of paper inside. Scrawled across it in red ink was a message.

You aren't safe and neither is she. I will kill you both, and laugh when I do it.

Janet sat stone-still while the message became fixed in her mind. She read it again and again and again.

"Janet, can you come back here for a moment, dear?"

Margaret-Ann. No, no, she can't see this.

Janet folded the note, stuck it back in the envelope, and stashed it in the drawer. "Coming," she called back, hearing the tremors in her voice. She cleared her throat and called again. "Just one second, Margaret-Ann."

She stood on wobbly knees and braced herself on the desk, taking a deep breath to calm herself. In through the nose, out through the mouth. And again. In through the nose…hold, hold, hold…out through the mouth…slowly. She shook out her hands and as she did, it occurred to her that she would have to leave the shop to protect Margaret-Ann. The thought made her nauseous. She loved it here, and loved Margaret-Ann like a mother.

As she walked down the hall, she put a smile on her face, even though what she wanted to do was collapse into a ball on the floor and cry her heart out. A tear escaped from her left eye.

No, no crying. No. You must protect Margaret-Ann.

"How can I help?" she asked brightly.

"Oh, there you are, dear," Margaret-Ann said as she fiddled with the dress while instructing the model to stand still. "What do you think of the fit of this gown? Isn't it too low cut in the front for a church wedding?"

"Where's the drawing of it?"

"On my table."

Janet picked up the white napkin, but her hands shook so badly that she put it back on the table. "It's exactly as Peaches drew it, except that the V is filled in with lace. What if you put a skin-colored mesh underneath the lace?"

"I could, but still, it seems too low cut for a church wedding, especially since our bride is rather buxom."

"But she chose it, right?"

Margaret-Ann nodded. "Poor choice for someone with her build. Our Peaches should have been here to steer her to the correct one. I'm not very persuasive, but Peaches can handle the brides and get them to purchase the dress that makes them look like royalty. This one, though, will look like a giant pair of bosoms walking down the aisle."

"Oh," Janet said and took out her cellphone. "Why don't you take a photo and send it to her for a suggestion?"

Margaret-Ann stepped close beside her. "You look pale, Janet, and your poor hands are trembling. What's wrong, dear?"

After a moment of silence, Janet spoke up. "I'll be leaving

soon. I've decided to…to go back to my hometown and try to re-establish my business."

"Oh, I see," Margaret-Ann said. "So the trip to Portugal?"

Janet shook her head. "I can't."

Margaret-Ann put her hand on Janet's cheek. "I'll miss you terribly, dear," she said. "But, you know, you really don't have to go."

Janet narrowed her eyes.

"Whatever problem you have, we can work it out. Peaches knows a lot of people, and so do I. Why don't you tell me the truth, and we can try to fix whatever's wrong."

Janet tried to speak but couldn't manage to say a word.

"Let me guess," Margaret-Ann said. "You've heard from that no-good ex-husband of yours."

Janet nodded, and then crumpled into a chair, sobbing.

When a knock sounded at the door, Margaret-Ann ignored it. But when the bell rang to signal that someone had come in, she patted Janet on the shoulder. "I'll be right back, dear. You stay right here."

Margaret-Ann hurried down the hall as fast as she could. "Yes? How may I…?" When she saw TuckerD standing inside the shop, she stopped. "What are *you* doing here?" she said. "I see you still haven't changed clothes yet. Nasty, just nasty."

TuckerD said very quietly, "Might I find Janet LaRoche here?"

"You certainly may not," Margaret-Ann said. "You've no business with her, and Peaches is away, as well. I'd prefer it if you left both of them alone." As TuckerD walked toward her, Margaret-Ann backed away. "Go away," she said. "You're not welcome here."

"I know," he said softly, and put his hand on her shoulder. "But I can't leave just yet."

Margaret-Ann felt a sudden warmth spread through her body, a nice relaxing warmth that brought to mind the days when she would lounge by the side of the pool and let the sun warm her. She took in a deep breath and sighed with pleasure.

"I'll only be a minute," TuckerD said.

Margaret-Ann nodded as he walked down the long hallway.

"Janet," he called softly.

Janet looked up, first at his feet then up and up until she saw his face.

TuckerD knelt beside her. "Janet," he said.

She nodded at him.

"You must go with Margaret-Ann to Portugal."

"But…Etienne," she said. "He wants to kill me."

TuckerD smiled and nodded.

"And….and he wants to kill Peaches, too," she said, and began sobbing again.

"You must go to Portugal with Margaret-Ann," he said, and put his hand on her shoulder.

Janet took a deep breath. "I don't…never mind."

"Everything is already paid for." TuckerD stood and held his hand out to Janet. "Be brave," he said.

Janet straightened her skirt and smoothed her silk blouse, then ran a hand over her hair. "Thank you," she said, but when she looked up, he'd already gone.

Chapter 29

TuckerD sat across the desk from his boss.

"I've considered your request," the boss said. "You asked for an additional week."

"Yes," TuckerD said, "but I'd prefer a month if that's possible."

The boss leaned back in his chair and twirled a pencil in his fingers. "This must be a matter of importance to you," the boss said. "In all these years, you've never requested a change in schedule."

TuckerD leaned forward in his chair. "Sir, it is a matter of the utmost importance, such an urgency as I've never felt before."

The boss stood and walked over to the massive window. "Atlanta is a bustling city, isn't it?"

TuckerD got up and stood beside the man. The two of them, one tall and broad, the other short and slim, stared down at the busy roads, congested with traffic and people.

"Have you spent much time in Portugal?"

"Many years ago, during the civil battles, I was there for a week or so. Other than that, no. I haven't been back since then."

"It's quite a different place than it was two hundred years ago," the boss said. "It is a thriving country, economically sound, with a prime minister who rules strictly but fairly. He's done a remarkable job of keeping his country virtually crime free and quite stable in its economy. He's also responsible for the rejuvenation of the village houses in his home base of Lisbon. And his refurbished palace is a sight to behold. Word has it that he paid for all of the renovations himself."

"Commendable," TuckerD said.

"And the whole world knows of his great respect for Ms. Peaches Malone. He sings her praises whenever he can, and now I understand that there's to be an upcoming wedding."

TuckerD's heart skipped a beat when he heard her name. "A wedding?"

His boss nodded. "His daughter is getting married. And guess who will be designing her wedding gown?"

"But how do you know about it?"

"Actually, I've known the prime minister since he was a young boy. He had a bout of pneumonia when he was only six years old. It almost claimed his life. Thankfully, he survived to become the great man he is today and to lead his country into prosperity. I check in with him every now and again."

"I see," TuckerD said.

"In spite of what I told you earlier, my own superiors have granted your request. In fact, it's extended. You will have a full year. I expect you to make good use of it. Since this is your first request, you've been very kindly given more time than you asked for."

TuckerD lowered his head. "I'm both humbled and honored."

"I'll contact you again. No delays after that time. Understood?"

TuckerD nodded. "Understood."

"Here, these are for you," he said as he handed TuckerD a bundle. "If you're going to be in Portugal, you must dress a little differently."

"But—"

"No buts. These will fit you and will allow you to blend in when necessary. There are three complete and very classy three-piece suits, shirts, ties, with appropriate shoes. If you are seen in Portugal, you must look like you haven't just stepped out of a

Victorian-era catalog. Your hair can remain as it is."

"But I've worn these clothes for centuries. They're my sort of signature look. I like them. They're comfortable."

"Comfort won't serve you well in Portugal, my friend. The look must match a typical Portuguese man of some rank and quality."

TuckerD sighed. "Very well," he said.

"Fine. Now, step into the bathroom and change into one of them. Leave your blue frock coat and the shirt, britches, and boots here."

After a few minutes, TuckerD emerged from the bathroom wearing a sleek gray suit with a gray and navy blue tie and matching vest, and a crisp white shirt with no lace on the cuffs. His shoes were black dressy loafers.

"Well, well," his boss said. "You look rather dapper. Everything fits, I see."

"At least there's that," TuckerD said.

"And remember," the boss said, "the world, all of it, can be a dangerous place. Even in a peaceful modern city like Lisbon, upheaval and violence are present. There was an assassination attempt on the prime minister and his wife only two years ago. The culprit was caught, thank goodness. Just don't deceive yourself into thinking that Portugal is without its own problems."

TuckerD bowed. "Thank you for your wisdom and insight. It's information that I will put to good use."

The boss chuckled. "You've always wanted to be a warrior. I think you might get your chance."

Chapter 30

"Margaret-Ann?" Peaches said.

"Oh, Peaches! I'm so glad you called."

"You sound a little frazzled. Is everything okay?"

"Yes, yes. We're fine. Janet and I are coming to see you. When I called the airline this morning, there was already a reservation, paid in full, for two tickets to Portugal. We even fly first class, compliments of the prime minister. He must be a very kind man."

Peaches pointed at Lily and covered the phone. "Did you know about the tickets?"

Lily shrugged and shook her head.

"So when do you leave?"

"We're almost packed," Margaret-Ann said, "because we leave in three days. Isn't it exciting? I've never even thought of flying first class. I can't wait to see the little luxuries."

"Has everything been okay in the shop?"

"Oh, it's fine. We have only one booking, though. I've been struggling with one of your designs for a way to make it fit a rather buxom bride."

"Oh," Peaches said, and took a sip of coffee. "The V-neck? It wasn't exactly designed for someone who's buxom."

"Tell me about it. Anyway, Janet came up with the idea of inserting a thin layer of flesh-colored tight mesh about halfway the length of the V, and then putting the white lace over it. It offers a bit more, uh, cover up."

154

"Good idea. Are there any other new orders?"

"You know, we don't have a single one. Odd, isn't it? We're usually booked solid, but not now. I'm working to finish this deep V dress. I should have it done by tonight. But when that's done, there's nothing else waiting."

Peaches frowned and fiddled with the tie on her robe. "There are no new orders?"

"Not a single one, Peaches."

"Well, I have one here in Portugal. The prime minister's daughter, Bella, is getting married in a few months. I've been asked to make her dress...with no budget restrictions."

"Wonderful," Margaret-Ann said. "You know, Peaches, that there are rumors swirling around here about Etienne LaRoche. Janet said she got a note from him, but honestly, we've searched all over and can't find it."

"What did the note say?"

"Poor Janet," Margaret-Ann said. "She was so upset. The note said something about...well, never you mind. Janet really can't remember, and neither can I, so it's best forgotten. Besides, we'll be with you in Portugal, so what can he do?"

"He's in jail here, you know, along with several of his cronies. He was accused of international fraud and theft. I have to testify against him in court."

Margaret-Ann was silent.

"Are you there?" Peaches asked as she paced Lily's room.

"Oh, yes, dear. I'm here, but I'll be there with you in just a few days. Don't bother yourself about the court thing. I'm sure it will be fine."

"So, you're going to close up the shop then? Is Aileen upset?"

"Not at all. She seemed happy to have a break. Besides, that husband of hers is pressuring her to stop working and concentrate on having a baby. She told me to tell you that the cat was doing just fine."

"Oh, good. Well, you have plenty to do to get ready," Peaches said. "Don't forget that the movers are coming. Our things, such as they are, will be shipped here. And please don't forget the wedding dress in the top of my closet."

"No, no I won't," Margaret-Ann said.

"Good. It will be odd at first, but I think you'll love it here, and the three of us can run the business in Portugal."

"You'll be proud of me, Peaches. I put a notice in the paper saying that Peaches and Lace would be closed for renovations, and that any inquiries should be directed to an email address that Janet created on G-mail. Now, wasn't that smart? She's bringing her laptop so she can keep up with any questions."

Peaches smiled. "I'm proud of you, Margaret-Ann. Of you and Janet both. Excellent work. Now, just get that buxom bride taken care of and we'll be fine. Did she pay you?"

"Twenty thousand in full," Margaret-Ann said. "I'm bringing the cash with me, along with your own cash box. Yes, I know where you keep it. I purchased a brand new travel bag, one of those that slips under the seat in front, so the money will be with me at all times. And I've very carefully hidden all of it in several pieces of underwear and clothing, all separated into different plastic bags. The new travel bag even has a lock and a chain that can be clipped securely to my belt."

Peaches shook her head. "You've done well, Margaret-Ann. I want you to keep the twenty thousand as your own. Consider it a nest egg, of sorts. I need to ask a favor of you."

"What is it?"

"I need you to unpack the money, all of it, and put it into a suitcase of its own. You can keep it in the plastic zippy bags, that's fine. But the bag needs to be labeled Peaches Malone, a suitcase all its own. You can put in a few of my articles of clothing, but basically, it's just the money."

"But why?" Margaret-Ann asked.

"The prime minister has arranged for a special member of his secret team to transport the money from Atlanta to Portugal.

He'll come by the shop to get it."

"But...no...I can't hand over our money to some strange man. Speaking of which, that boyfriend of yours dropped by yesterday. He's not such a bad guy. Still had on those same old clothes, though."

"TuckerD? He came by the shop?"

"He did, but he didn't stay long. He just came by to talk to Janet for a minute."

"Janet? What did he need to see Janet about?"

"Odd, isn't it? She said he wanted her to agree to come to Portugal. Then he left, as always. But, he's okay."

Peaches walked over to where Lily was standing and pointed to her phone. "Wait...TuckerD came to the bridal shop to speak to Janet about coming here?"

Lily's eyes widened.

"Yes, that's what I said, dear. It's odd, but it wasn't an unpleasant thing at all. I rather like him. He's very...uh... comforting to have around, but I do wish he'd change those clothes."

"I'll miss that guy," Peaches said. "There's something about him...but never mind. Nothing to be done now."

"I'm sorry, dear," Margaret-Ann said.

"No matter. Now, Margaret-Ann, this is very important. The money must be given to the security agent."

"How will I recognize him?"

"He will arrive the day before you leave. He'll seem a well-to-do businessman, except that he'll be wearing a sort of sash over his shoulder of red and green, with the Portuguese coat of arms in between the bright colors. He's a special envoy. He's also a member of an elite security team. Just look for the banner he's wearing underneath his suit coat. He'll leave his coat unbuttoned."

"It just doesn't seem right," Margaret-Ann said, "to hand over your entire life savings to some stranger. What if he runs off with it?"

"He won't. If I have faith in the prime minister and his team, then you should, as well."

Lily motioned for the phone. "Hello, Margaret-Ann, this is Lily."

"Oh, Lily, dear, how are you?"

"Just fine, thank you. Now, we have this money situation all in hand. Your job is just to give it to the agent. He'll make sure it arrives here safely. And he'll be using the private jet, so he'll be back here in Portugal long before you are. We'll send you a text when he arrives."

"But it's all the money we have, Lily. I think it'd be safe enough in my bag. I'll watch it like a hawk."

"I know you will, but there's no need for you to be under that sort of pressure. When he arrives, he'll expect you to take a photo of him with your cellphone and send it to Peaches immediately. Peaches will forward it to the prime minister for proper identification, and once we have that, you are to give him the bag."

"It all sounds very complicated and it makes me nervous. I don't like it at all."

"We're just trying to keep both you and the money safe. It's a long flight with two layovers, so you'll be probably fifteen hours on and off the plane. That's a lot of time to be responsible for a bag. This is the best way."

After a moment of silence, Margaret-Ann spoke up. "All right," she said, "but I'm not giving him all of it. I can't. I'll give him what is in Peaches' box, but my money stays with me."

Lily chuckled. "Good enough, Margaret-Ann. We're counting on you. Consider this an official mission."

"An official mission?"

"Indeed. What is more important than getting you and your money safely to Portugal?"

"I'll do my best," Margaret-Ann said. "My level best. Take

care of Peaches, and give her a hug for me."

"Consider it done," Lily said.

Margaret-Ann hung up, but not with a smile on her face.

Chapter 31

At 4:00 a.m., TuckerD stood outside the Peaches and Lace Bridal Salon. Except for a homeless man snoring inside a large but open cardboard box, the streets were deserted.

TuckerD slipped quietly past him and into the private garden at the back of the shop. His heart felt heavy as he realized just how empty the stone bench looked without Peaches sitting on it. It was her bench, her private space, her retreat. He could feel her presence, smell the perfume she wore. He ached with longing for her, and he knew that for the first time in his life, he was in love. But he shook his head and carried on, chiding himself.

An absurd notion, an impossibility. Peaches Malone is mortal, human, forbidden.

He walked to the edge of the garden and opened the gate which led to the apartment in back. As he surveyed the small space, he noticed that it seemed too dark and quiet. He flipped the light switch but nothing happened. He heard no sound from the refrigerator humming, and saw no indication of light or life.

With a snap of his fingers, he set it all right. The refrigerator hummed to life and a light came on in the kitchen. He checked the cabinets. Empty. So with a mere thought, the cabinets filled themselves with a variety of canned goods. He peeked inside the refrigerator and found it empty, too.

As he walked into the bedroom, he saw it change from a dark and dreary space to a bright room with a new double bed, a

160

dresser, several art works on the wall, and a new overhead light. He moved to the small bathroom, renovated it with just a look, and turned the new faucet to make sure that water came flowing out.

He stood at the door and smiled at his handiwork. He'd created a perfect space. Once he was settled in, he'd have access to both the salon and the private garden. And that was what he wanted. In particular, he wanted to be able to come and sit on the stone bench, savor his images of Peaches, and most of all, keep her birds fed. Besides, someone needed to protect the place while the women were gone.

Now, he just had to get word to Peaches. But he settled instead on a meeting with Margaret-Ann.

***

Precisely at 8:00, Margaret-Ann and Janet walked down the street to open the door to the shop. They were both shocked to see TuckerD — was that TuckerD? He looked different.

"He's finally changed clothes," Margaret-Ann said to Janet. "He looks like a man about town."

"Do you think he wants to model for Peaches again? Maybe he's looking for work."

"Well, he'll be in for a shock, won't he, when I tell him we're closing the shop for a month. And who is that other man standing next to him? Another no-good...." But she stopped and remembered how comfortable she'd felt the last time TuckerD visited. "Let's see what he wants," Margaret-Ann said.

"Good morning, Margaret-Ann. Good morning, Janet," TuckerD said.

They both smiled at him and nodded.

"Peaches told me I could live there. She gave me the key, and because I thought it was a good idea, I took the liberty of making it perfectly suitable."

"She didn't mention a thing about it to me," Margaret-Ann said.

161

"Of course," TuckerD said. "Perhaps you'd like to call her now."

"What time is it in Portugal?"

"About 2:00 in the afternoon."

Margaret-Ann dialed the number and put it on speaker.

"Hello?"

"Peaches," Margaret-Ann said. "I hate to bother you, but I need to ask you something."

"Hello, Peaches," TuckerD said quite loudly.

"TuckerD, is that you?" Peaches asked.

Margaret-Ann handed him the phone.

"It's me, yes," he said. "I've missed you."

Peaches was silent for a moment. "So, what is the problem there?"

"I wondered if it would be all right if I moved into the apartment out back."

Peaches hesitated. "Of course," she said at last. "But Margaret-Ann will be leaving in a few days." Something about hearing TuckerD's voice, so soothing and reassuring, convinced Peaches that he was telling the truth, and before she could stop them, the words tumbled out of her mouth. "I trust you, TuckerD."

He rubbed his forehead with two fingers. "Thank you, Peaches. Thank you. It means a great deal to me to hear you say that."

"I have a runway show coming up in a few months. Is there any way you could get to Portugal and be one of the models? You were a big hit at the last one."

"When is the show?"

"February," she said. "Is it possible for you to be here?" Peaches held her breath.

"Peaches, I'm not sure, but I'd love to be there if it's possible."

Peaches let out a breath. "I'll spring for your ticket if—"

"Not necessary, but thank you. I can take care of transportation myself."

"So you'll come then? I can put you on the roster as a model? It would be a great help to me."

"February, you say?"

"Yes, February 5th. Can you be here?"

"I'll need to check with my boss before I can give you a definite answer." TuckerD rubbed his forehead. "That's the best I can offer now."

Peaches bit at her bottom lip. "Very well," she said, making her voice sound as professional as possible. "Margaret-Ann has all the contact information. Please be sure to get it from her and let me know something as soon as you can. If you can't make it, I'll need to find another model."

"I'd like to take Margaret-Ann to see the changes I've made in the apartment. Is that all right?"

"Yes, please, I'd like for her to see it. That thing's been a mess for so long. Any changes you made will surely be an improvement."

Margaret-Ann took the phone. "I miss you, Peaches, but I'll see you soon."

"And you're all right with TuckerD moving into the apartment?"

"I am, dear, as long as you say it's all right."

"Let me know what changes he's made."

Margaret-Ann chuckled. "I'll watch him like a hawk while I'm here, and I'll keep you informed about his every move."

"Yes, I'm sure of it. Bye now."

"Well, Margaret-Ann," TuckerD said. "Would you like to see the apartment?"

Margaret-Ann nodded and followed him up the stairs. When he opened the door for her, he stood back and ushered her in.

"Oh, my word," she said as she stepped in and looked around, her hands trailing lightly over each surface. "Everything's so new and so clean. It must have taken a whole crew to renovate to such an extent. The place is beautiful. It's like a miracle."

"You approve, then?"

"First let me see that horrid old bathroom," she said.

TuckerD nodded.

Margaret-Ann walked back to the bathroom, stuck her head in, and gasped at the shiny new space, even with a glassed in, stand up shower."

"You did this?"

TuckerD nodded. "Are you displeased?" he asked.

Margaret-Ann shook her head. "Who knew you had this kind of talent!" she said, and laughed. "You've done a wonderful job here."

TuckerD put his hand over his heart. "Thank you," he said and bowed slightly. "I hoped you'd like it."

"You can bring your things any time," she said. "Peaches would be amazed to see the difference you've made here."

"I'll need the keys," he said, "if that's all right. While you and Janet are gone, I can check on the salon and make sure it's safe and secure."

Margaret-Ann smiled. "We need a good security guard," she said. "Here are the keys. If you'll give me a sheet of paper, I'll write down the contact number for Peaches."

TuckerD bowed and handed her a pen and paper.

Margaret-Ann wrote down the number and turned to walk outside, but stopped. "Do you work?" she asked and narrowed her eyes.

TuckerD nodded. "Yes, but I travel a great deal with my company," he said, and put his hands behind his back. "I might be gone for days at a time, but the apartment and the salon will be safe."

"I want Peaches to find a man who can make her happy, but who can well afford to give her everything her heart desires. If you can't do that, I'd ask you to leave her alone. Good day to you, TuckerD."

Chapter 32

The three of them cut a fine figure as they walked out of the palace. The one, tall with long dark hair and a two-piece, finely-cut pantsuit; the other, shorter with luxurious blonde hair, wearing Givenchy jeans and a silk blouse; and the third, the shortest, her long black hair in an elegant chignon, wearing a floral sheath dress and sandals.

"Thank you, Alberto," Marietta said as she climbed into the passenger seat of the royal traveling car, an armored Jaguar.

Two staff members, one on each side, opened the door for Peaches and Lily. "Thank you," they replied in unison, and climbed into the back seat.

"Nice car," Peaches said, as she ran a hand over the soft black leather. "Very nice."

"We have beautiful weather today, so your search should not be hampered by wind or rain.

Marietta smiled. "I've chosen two wonderful places for you to see," she said. "Both face the sea and have outstanding views. Both are 18th century castles which have been renovated, and both are reasonably priced. I didn't think you'd be interested in the modern apartments. They're everywhere now."

"Exactly right, Marietta. Thank you," Peaches said, and smiled at Lily.

"I chose the castles because they would allow you room for a studio and a shop on the premises."

"That's even better," Peaches said. "I wondered where I might open a shop here."

Marietta handed Alberto a small piece of paper. "The addresses are here. I think we'll see the Alamenda first. It's the longest distance away."

"Tell me about it," Peaches said.

Marietta nodded to Alberto.

"The Alamenda is a restored late 18th century castle on the coastal side of our fair city. It is high up among the cliff tops, and from certain points, you can see both the Atlantic Ocean and the Tagus River. If it's a view that you want, Alamenda is perfect."

"Will there be room for Margaret-Ann and Janet?"

Alberto chuckled. "I believe there are six bedrooms and seven bathrooms."

"So, why is it vacant?" Lily asked, leaning forward.

"Technically," Marietta said, "it isn't for sale yet. The owner passed away only a month ago. He was a very good friend to us. He lost his wife many years ago and never had children, so his one living brother would stand to inherit. I spoke with the brother on the phone. He is interested in selling the property since he's very well established in Sintra. He owns a resort villa there and doesn't want to leave."

"I see," Lily said.

"I wouldn't show you a place that you couldn't purchase," Marietta said, "or that wasn't big enough for you to have your family and your studio. All of Portugal would be thrilled to have you in residence here, Peaches. You're very well-known and admired."

"Thank you, Marietta," Peaches said. "I have fallen in love with your country, and I hope your husband can arrange for me to live here."

"He can arrange practically anything," Marietta said and smiled. "I believe he intends to have you move here as the palace's designer in residence—though of course, you'd be in your own home. But do not worry yourself. He'll make everything legal. That's part of his job."

While they drove, Peaches contented herself with admiring the pristine homes, all painted brightly and topped with tile roofs and all side by side, touching each other as if they were old friends.

"What is that gorgeous domed building?" Peaches asked.

"That is called the Church of Santa Engracia," Alberto said. "It was destroyed in the 1500s. Reconstruction took three hundred years. But she's beautiful, no?"

Peaches sighed. "Beautiful, yes," she said. "Will I be able to see the city from the Alamenda Castle?"

"Oh, yes," Marietta said. "Not only the city, but the ocean as well."

Peaches smiled and patted Lily's arm. "I'm so excited," she said. "I feel like a whole new me is emerging."

"Our ancestors tell us that everyone has a '*casa do coracao*' — a home of the heart, a place where they feel they are meant to be. Perhaps Portugal is your heart's home," Marietta said.

"Pronounce it again, please, Marietta."

"Casa…dough…cor a SAY o."

Peaches repeated it slowly.

"Perfect," Marietta said. "You'll be speaking Portuguese before you know it."

"Ah, we're close now," Alberto said. "It's just up this hill."

Marietta pointed. "There it is, Peaches. Castle Alamenda. You'll notice that it is built in a U shape so that the view is the greatest and the outside area is protected."

Peaches sucked in a breath. "Oh, my," she said. "It's magnificent. Are you sure that this is within my budget, Marietta?"

Marietta smiled. "Let's take a look, shall we?"

Alberto opened the doors and ushered them forward.

"Just look at this place, Lily," Peaches said. "Just look."

"Everything you see comes with the home," Marietta said.

They walked up several steps before they came to the stone structure.

"It's just like a medieval castle," Peaches said as she walked.

"It's huge, Peaches," Lily said. "And magnificent."

Marietta laughed. "Come," she said, "we'll show you around."

Once inside, Lily and Peaches stood silent and perfectly still, both of them vaguely aware that Marietta was talking, but neither of them hearing anything she said.

"Come, come," Marietta said, raising her voice. "There is much to see. This is the entrance hall. It rises to a height of three floors. The red, blue, and gold tapestries, hanging from the balustrades on the stairs on each side of us, signify the House of Alamenda. Those should be left in place, as one of them dates back to the 15th century. Straight ahead is the formal dining room, and beyond that is the kitchen."

They walked on stone floors that led them to a grand space filled with an enormous, richly decorated formal dining area with a massive walnut table.

"Thirty people could easily sit around that table," Peaches exclaimed. "And just look at the buffet and the china cabinet. I've never seen furniture so ornamented. It must have taken years to do all that carving."

"Furniture makers were the pride of the Gothic era," Marietta said. "These pieces were all hand carved with meticulous detail. Did you notice the gargoyles atop the...what did you call it? The china cabinet?"

Peaches tapped Lily's arm and then pointed up.

"Oh, I see them now," she said. "Why would they want gargoyles?"

"They were ancient symbols of protection. You'll find them...and cherubs...on many of the older pieces among the intricate carvings. The Gothic period is most noted for its heavily ornamented dark walnut furniture here in Portugal. Much of the

168

furniture is stained almost black. Now, follow me to the informal dining area."

They walked down the long corridor, all of them surrounded by stone.

"How do you control the temperature?" Lily asked. "I expected it to be freezing cold, but it's comfortable."

"The joys of modern electricity and heating and cooling units," Alberto said. "I believe this castle requires five different units. Am I correct?"

"Yes," Marietta said.

"Cha Ching!" said Lily. "The cost must be enormous."

"Thankfully," Marietta said, "Mr. Alamenda installed something that has been in use in Portugal for several years now. Though you cannot see them, two of the tiled roofs are entirely covered with solar panels."

Peaches smiled. "Solar panels. I'd never have dreamed it. Marietta, is there a space on this lower level for a bedroom and bath for Margaret-Ann? I don't think she'd want to climb those stairs."

"Mr. Alamenda was a man of practicality. When he refurbished the castle, he made use of the most modern advances in construction and design. Come with me. I'll show you what I had in mind for Margaret-Ann."

Off to the right, large double doors caught Peaches' attention.

Marietta nodded. "Through those doors," she said.

Peaches opened the double doors. Her mouth dropped open when she saw the enormous Gothic bed, matching dressers, and bureau. The room was awash in sunlight coming from the enormous ceiling-high window at the side of the room.

"It's beautiful," she said.

"There's more," Marietta replied. "That door to the right leads to a bathroom. Try it."

"Go ahead, Lily. See what you think," Peaches said.

Lily opened the door and said only one word. "Wow."

Peaches looked inside as well and saw a brightly tiled floor, toilet, bathtub, shower, and vanity. Another door led to a large closet.

"There are safety rails in the shower," Marietta said. "This area was Mr. Alamenda's, and he installed every sort of safety precaution. Do you think Margaret-Ann would like this?"

"With all these rich colors, the bright sunlight, and this gorgeous bathroom, I think she'd feel like a queen."

"I thought it would be perfect for her," Marietta said. "What do you think, Lily? Is there anything you can think of that might need to be redone?"

"Not a single thing," Lily said. "It's just perfect for her. And all of this furniture stays?"

Marietta nodded.

"I can't get over how high the ceilings are," Peaches said.

"Well, it is a castle, after all."

"Come," Marietta said. "I want you to see the studio space and workshop area. Afterwards, we'll take a look at the five bedrooms upstairs. The upstairs is divided into the north and south wings, so there are actually two separate living spaces. I thought that Lily might want to use one of them. But first—ah, here it is…the kitchen."

"Modern appliances?" Peaches asked as she took in the great space. "How wonderful. Margaret-Ann would be so pleased."

Marietta smiled. "The great stone hearth, where most of the cooking was done in old times, is as it was. It needs a bit of cleaning, but otherwise, it is fully functional. I doubt that you would have need of it, but occasionally, we can get some cold winds, especially on the mountain top. Shall we go outside?"

They walked out onto the veranda which overlooked an enormous pool and was surrounded by lush gardens.

"This is beautiful," Peaches said.

"The studio and workshop are there," Marietta said, pointing to high-walled structure made of stone. "I envision a sign on the outside that says, 'Peaches and Lace Boutique.' You can see that it is joined to the castle proper on the top level. See the walkway?"

Peaches nodded.

"The bottom level is separate and would be a perfect studio space. Let's go inside."

"Oh," Peaches said, "there's already an office."

Marietta nodded. "Would it work for you?"

Peaches looked around the large space occupied by two ornamented bookcases, a large desk, and four armchairs. She sat in the soft leather desk chair and imagined herself talking to brides and their families, showing her latest creations, and planning dates and venues. "What do you think of it, Lily?"

"It seems perfectly functional and appropriate for what you need. But are there any issues with electricity? You'll use a lot of it with the workshop."

"Well, there are three separate outlets in here. Let's check the workshop."

"I see only two outlets."

"You can add as many as you need," Marietta said.

"And I'm surprised at how comfortable and light it is. I thought it would be dark and cold, but those large windows along the back let in so much light, and the temperature seems fine. Don't you agree, Lily?"

"I've no complaints at all," Lily said.

"Where does this door lead?"

"Open it," Marietta said.

Peaches opened the door, Lily right behind her, to find an enclosed structure of about two hundred square feet. Inside it was an ornate stone bench, and toward the back wall stood two trees.

"Orange trees," Marietta said. "Mr. Alamenda was quite famous for his oranges. They're juicy and sweet, with just the right amount of acidity."

Peaches frowned. "But I know nothing of how to care for

orange trees."

Marietta chuckled and dismissed her with a wave of her hand. "Nothing to worry about. These trees are more than fifty years old, and their caretaker lives nearby. He and his sons do all the work in exchange for fruit for themselves. He's also the full-time gardener. Because of his family, the gardens flourish."

"But of course I'd pay them," Peaches said. "I can't expect them to work for nothing."

"They take what they want and need in food, dear. It was a bargain struck many years ago. If you like this castle, you must respect its traditions."

"I love this castle," Peaches said. "I don't even want to look at another one. This is the one I want."

"But Peaches," Lily said, "shouldn't we at least *see* the other one?"

Peaches shook her head. "I understand your concerns, Lily. Rationally, I know that looking at only once place doesn't make sense, but I also know that the moment I stepped foot on this property, it felt like home. Home."

"Well, I can't argue with that," Lily said. "And I have to admit that it does rather suit you, though I'd never in a million years have pictured you living in an old castle…in Portugal! You've been a city girl in Atlanta for so long. And what about Margaret-Ann? And your clients? Oh, and one more thing: your boyfriend."

Peaches was silent for a moment. "Sadly, the boyfriend isn't in the picture anymore. I talked to him about coming to the runway show. He couldn't give me a straight answer. However, Margaret-Ann wants to be with me, and as much grief as I give her most of the time, I want her here, too. When I first mentioned this to Marietta, I told her I must have a place that would be perfect for Margaret-Ann, Janet, you, and me."

"And how did I do?" Marietta asked.

"I'd like to make an offer," Peaches said. "What is the asking price?" Peaches had a moment of nervousness, and her hands trembled. *What if I can't afford it?*

Marietta took out a folded slip of paper and handed it to Peaches.

Peaches moved closer to Lily and opened the note. The paper was blank.

"What?" Lily said. "That can't be right. For all of this space? No, there must be some mistake."

"It is a very special price for a special person," Marietta said. "An arrangement, so to speak. And remember that we offered you space in return for Bella's gown."

"Arrangement?" Lily asked. "On what terms?"

Marietta looked at Peaches.

"Please," Peaches said. "I'd like to know the terms."

"Peaches, this is payment for Bella's gown. You owe nothing for the property, my dear, but there are a few stipulations. The former owner insists that the gardener and his family must be allowed to keep their jobs and to tend the gardens as they always have. And the household staff must remain, as well."

"The household staff?" Peaches asked. "What do you mean?"

"They are not here now, of course, but when occupied, the house has a butler, a housemaid, a cook, and a young man to tend the livery stables."

"You never mentioned there'd be staff, Marietta. And livery stables? There are horses here?"

"Of course," Marietta said. "This is Lisbon. Everyone has at least one horse. You happen to have two very fine ones."

"So, if I take the castle, I must pay the wages of all the staff members?"

"Correct," Marietta said.

"But that's a lot of people to support, Marietta," Peaches said as she paced. "But if, as you said, the castle comes to me as payment for Bella's gown, then I can handle the wages."

"You are accustomed to American prices. Here in Lisbon,

wages are much different, especially when you're providing them with a home."

"A home?"

"Yes, didn't you notice the buildings at the far end of the property? There are several, and they are homes for the staff. Remember, Peaches, that the way of life here is different. These families have lived and worked on this property for most of their lives."

Peaches let out a sigh. "And how much are the salaries?"

"The cost would be four hundred dollars per month per family."

"And how many families?"

"Two, including the gardener."

"What do you think, Lily?"

"I don't think you can turn this down," Lily said.

Peaches walked to the large window and stared out across the property. With the window open, she could hear the splashing of the waves against the rocks far below. The sound soothed her.

"I agree to the terms," she said. "Staff and all."

Marietta smiled. "You've made a wise choice," she said, and hugged Peaches. "You'll be happy here."

Peaches glanced at Lily. "What do you think, Lily?"

"I think you should consider the work that needs to be done in the workshop and the studio."

Marietta held up a hand. "Excuse me for a moment," she said as she walked a few steps away from them.

"Oh, gosh, do you think something's wrong?" Peaches asked Lily.

"If there's anything wrong, you can afford to fix it. She's giving you this castle! With all this antique furniture? The furniture itself must be worth double that much. And you have servants, for goodness sakes!"

Marietta walked toward them with a frown on her face. Peaches felt as if her stomach had turned upside down. She had to hold to Lily to keep her balance.

"We're in luck," Marietta said. "The former owner is in construction. He agreed to offer his services and to send his own construction crew to help with any changes you might need...at no charge."

"No charge?"

Marietta nodded.

Peaches clasped her hands tightly together and looked at Lily. "Well? What should I do?"

"Are you sure you don't want to look at the other place?" Lily asked, parking her hair behind her ears.

Peaches reached into her purse and brought out her checkbook and calculator. After a moment, she cocked her head and looked at the figure. Then she filled in the check. "Here, Marietta."

Marietta looked at the check. "But this is too much, Peaches."

"Yes, but the staff must be paid. So the check covers their wages for five full years, if my calculations are correct."

"Are you quite sure?"

Peaches nodded. "If you will agree to this arrangement, then I'm pleased with it. And it will take the worry off me for having to remember to pay the families. I can't do that when I'm designing and having runway shows. In fact, I'd prefer that you arranged for someone else to pay them. You can do it however you wish."

"But we haven't seen the upstairs yet. So, before I take this, I want to show you the sleeping and living quarters upstairs. Agreed?"

On their tour of the upstairs, Peaches saw five beautifully furnished bedrooms, all done in Gothic, hand-carved furniture with four-poster beds, chairs, dressers, and enormous arched windows.

"There are no closets up here, but you see that each bedroom has at least one wardrobe for hanging clothes, though this larger master bedroom has two. Each bedroom has its own bathroom, as well."

"I feel as if I'm walking around in a dream," Peaches said. "All of this could belong to me. I can't even comprehend it."

"It is the most beautiful castle I've ever seen," Lily said. "And there's even a space for me!"

"Well, of course there is. That's part of the deal. You'll go back to Atlanta to finish your work, get everything in order, and then you, my friend, will come back to Portugal as my personal attorney, with a bonus of having your own south wing to live in! Deal?"

"Agreed," Lily said.

"Ladies, you'll notice an abundance of large tapestries and paintings. Those must stay with the castle."

"Most certainly. I wouldn't change a thing," Peaches said.

"Down this hall is the library," Marietta said. "Shall we take a look?"

Peaches saw Marietta scurry ahead with her phone pressed to her ear. "No, she wants it all," Marietta said softly. "Everything just as it is." She turned to Peaches. "Forgive me. Mr. Alamenda was concerned that he'd have to find new homes for the furniture. Of course, we own the castle, but our terms with its former owner were that if we sold it, the furniture must either come back to him or stay with the castle. Some of these pieces are priceless antiques dating back hundreds, even thousands of years."

"But you said the castle came just as it was, fully furnished," Peaches said, tucking her silk blouse more tightly into her jeans.

"Well, you're American, Peaches. He was concerned that you'd think the furnishings too old, maybe not modern enough for your tastes." Marietta opened the double doors. "The library," she said.

Peaches and Lily walked into a room that was filled floor to ceiling with books in beautifully ornate soaring bookcases. In the center of the room, atop a thick, brightly colored rug, sat an enormous desk and a leather chair.

Peaches sat in the chair, examined the desk, and then turned around to gaze out the one large arched window. In the distance, she could see a deep blue spreading out to the horizon. "The ocean?" she asked.

"Yes," Marietta said. "The Atlantic. Sometimes, when it's quiet and the window is open, you can hear the waves crashing against the rocks."

"I think I'll claim this as my very own sitting room," Peaches said.

Marietta's phone rang. "Yes?" Marietta listened but did not speak. Then she took a deep breath. "There is one more thing I need to show you," she said. "We'll go back downstairs if that suits you."

They followed along behind her and stopped in the entrance hall at the bottom of the stairs. When the double doors to the front entrance of the castle opened, a crowd of people came in.

"This is your staff," Marietta said. "Your gardener, your cook, your housemaid, your butler, and his son, the man responsible for the horses."

Each one bowed in turn.

"They've brought a gift for you," Marietta said.

"A gift?"

Marietta nodded.

"But they didn't even know I'd buy the castle. How could they have a gift for me?"

"It isn't often that someone new comes to Castle Alamenda. Consider it a welcome gift."

The gardener stepped forward and bowed. "I am Rafael, the gardener," he said in a thick accent. "This is your cook, my sister, Carla. And this is my daughter, your housemaid, Linda. This is my oldest son, your butler, Javier. And this is my youngest son, your horse keeper, Maximo."

Peaches nodded to each one.

"Papa," Javier said. "*Adona.*"

Rafael held up a finger. "*Momento,*" he said, and came back holding a small, fluffy black and white…dog with a pink ribbon tied around her neck.

Lily sucked in a breath.

Peaches stepped back and shook her head.

"I, uh, I wasn't prepared for an animal," she said. "I've never had a dog before. I'm just not sure about this."

Rafael looked at Marietta, his face full of concern. Marietta motioned to Peaches and Lily. "Let's step into the living room," she said quietly.

"Why on earth would they bring a dog?" Peaches said, her voice tinged with anger.

"Peaches," Marietta said, and put a hand on her arm. "The puppy is a gift to you. She is a Portuguese water dog, a special and rare breed. She is friendly and loves people. She doesn't bite, and won't be a moment's trouble. The puppy's mother and father are both international champions. These people have spent a small fortune buying her for you. I beg of you not to offend your staff with words of anger and displeasure."

Lily nudged her. "Say something."

"I don't know anything about dogs. Nothing."

Marietta tried one last time. "Javier will train her. She will have her own quarters, so she'll be no bother to you at all. In Portugal, every castle needs an 'adona,' a lady of the castle who will guard and protect the owner. Please, I beg you not to offend these good people."

"I can't. I just can't. I don't mean to offend them, but what would I do with a dog? I'm sorry, Marietta, but I haven't even moved in yet. Couldn't they give me a little time to get used to the idea? Right now, I'll be covered up with designing, moving, getting things in order. I can't see how I'd also take care of a dog."

Just as the three of them were about to leave, the puppy bounded into the room and sat at Peaches' feet. Peaches backed away. Adona sat where she was and whimpered.

"She's adorable," Lily said. "Not a single speck of dirt on

her."

"Oh, no," Marietta said. "Javier treats her like a little princess."

Adona whimpered again.

"She wants you to pick her up," Lily said, and poked Peaches in the arm. When she did, Adona looked at her and growled.

Marietta gasped. Adona whimpered. Lily poked Peaches again. Adona growled and turned toward her.

"Well," Lily said, "it seems she's already decided to protect her mistress."

Peaches poked at the puppy with her foot. "You'll have to take care of yourself. I don't know anything about dogs."

Adona got up, lowered her head, and walked slowly away, glancing back at Peaches as she left.

Peaches' heart almost melted when she saw the puppy looking so sad. She knelt down and called her. "Come here, Adona," she said.

The puppy slowly walked toward her and sat in front of her, as if for inspection.

"Aren't you a lovely pup!" Peaches said, and stroked Adona's fur.

Faces lit up all over the room.

"I've never owned a pet of any kind," Peaches said. "I've had only one encounter with a dog, and that was when I was a little girl. The neighbor's dog bit me, and I ended up in the hospital. I've had nothing to do with dogs since that time. But this pretty pup makes me want to give it a chance."

Adona wiggled and wagged her tail. Gently, Peaches picked her up and smiled at her. "So, Adona, I guess we're stuck with each other." Adona licked the side of Peaches' face. "You smell so good," Peaches said. "You're a beautiful little pup. I think we can work things out." Adona snuggled down into her arms. "Her fur is soft like silk," Peaches said as she brushed a hand across the puppy's back.

Lily stepped forward to pet the puppy, but as soon as her

hand went out, the puppy came instantly awake and growled.

"It's okay, Adona," Peaches said. "Lily is our friend. She won't hurt us."

Adona looked up at Peaches and then to Lily. She stuck out her tiny pink tongue and panted.

"Try again," Peaches said.

Lily patted the little dog on its head, then ran her hand along its back. "My God," she said. "She already obeys you, Peaches."

Peaches smiled. "Thank you, Javier," she said. "You've done an excellent job with our Adona, but from now on, I'll take over the training."

"But you've never had—"

"I can learn if you'll help me," Peaches said. "She must learn how to act around expensive fabrics, wedding gowns, and runway shows. Can you help me teach her?"

Javier bowed. "As you wish, Ms. Peaches. Shall I take her now?"

Peaches held Adona up to her face. "Be a good girl and listen to Javier. If you're going to be my dog, you must learn your manners." And with that, she handed her back to Javier. "I'll be signing those papers now, Marietta," Peaches said. "Let's do it so that I can move in and begin my new life."

Chapter 33

The next few weeks seemed so much a blur of events that Peaches could hardly remember what happened from one day to the next. Had it not been for the help given by Marietta and the prime minister, she would still be living at the royal palace, making no progress at all with the new Peaches and Lace Studio. Even with Margaret-Ann and Janet safely in Lisbon, Peaches missed Lily, who had gone back to the States. She missed their nightly talks and giggles, but like her, Lily had a job to do.

The prime minister, through his plethora of connections, had not only managed to approve her request for residential and business applications, but had also arranged for a meeting with both the American and Portuguese Embassies, and had accompanied her to both. Without those meetings, Peaches would have had to go back to the States herself.

But Marietta had been right. Peaches found that she was much admired in Portugal, and the citizens of Lisbon, especially, had donated their own good time to making sure that the Peaches and Lace Studio would be outfitted with the very latest in technology. They had remodeled, renovated, and reconstructed the studio to the exact specifications Peaches had requested, and now, only days after moving into Castle Malone — Mr. Alamenda had graciously consented to have the name legally changed, and had even seen to it himself — Peaches admired the handiwork of everyone involved.

"It's just beautiful," Margaret-Ann said. "Oh, Peaches, I never dreamed we'd live in a place like this. A castle, our very own castle!"

"It's yours now, Margaret-Ann," Peaches said, admiring her mother's slim new figure and trendy hairstyle. The gray hair had been retouched and highlighted and cut in a stylish bob. With the recent weight loss, she'd dropped two dress sizes. Peaches felt, for the first time in a very long time, that Margaret-Ann had come into her own. "Adona and I are just living here with you." Peaches picked up the puppy and nuzzled her. "You're a very good girl, aren't you?"

Adona licked her on the chin and propped her head on Peaches' shoulder.

"But why would you put it in my name? Why not in yours?"

Peaches shrugged. "I have the sign on the studio," she said as she savored the sweet melon. "That seems quite enough. It's so large and ornate that no one in Lisbon could miss it. Every time I see it, my heart flutters. *Peaches and Lace Studio* done in lovely script and lit from behind. It's lovelier than I ever dreamed. Do you like it?"

"That studio and the sign are more than I could ever have imagined," Margaret-Ann said. "The new sewing machines, the mirrored fitting room with that raised platform for the brides to stand on. The storage area with more room than we'd ever need. And that beautiful meeting room facing the pool and gardens. It's almost beyond belief. Are you absolutely sure that all of this belongs to us?"

"I told you, Margaret-Ann," she said, and put Adona back down on the floor. "Sit," she said softly. Adona did as she was told. Hands trembling only slightly, Peaches took a small treat from her pocket and gave it to her. "I've explained it all. All of this belongs to you. It's signed, sealed, and paid for in your name, and the staff members are paid in full for the next five years. But you don't have to worry about it since Alberto has agreed to oversee them and disburse funds."

Margaret-Ann sat down in one of the leather chairs in her bedroom. "I want to ask you a couple of things," she said.

"Okay," Peaches said, and reached down to rub Adona's head.

"First of all, please tell me whether or not you're feeling all right. Are you ill?"

Peaches held out her hands. They trembled, but not as badly as usual these days. "Do I look ill?"

"You look wonderful, but with all of this planning and paying in advance, I wondered if you might have…well, a deadly disease that you've not told me about. Your shaking hands worry me, Peaches."

"I'm fine, really."

"And you're not planning on going back to the States? Why would you sacrifice all of the business contacts you have there? You've made your money in America. How do you know you can do the same in a foreign country? I guess I just don't understand why you'd take that chance."

Peaches reached into her pants pocket and brought out a folded sheet of paper. "Read this," she said, and handed the paper to Margaret-Ann. "Aloud, if you don't mind."

Margaret-Ann read. "Portugal is a developed country with a high-income advanced economy and high living standards, being the 20th most advanced country in terms of social progress and the 25th most prosperous one. It also is the fourth most peaceful country in the world, and is one of the fifteen most sustainable states. Additionally, the country is ranked highly in terms of press freedom, moral freedom, and ease of doing business."

"And besides all that, just look around you," Peaches said. "It's the most beautiful place I've ever seen. The moment I stepped off the plane, I felt as if I were home, really home," Peaches said. "And since I've been here, I've changed. I feel as if a new me is emerging. Are you unhappy here?"

"No, of course not. It's just that…well, I was born and raised and have lived all of my years in America. Now, don't get me wrong," Margaret-Ann said, and leaned forward. "It is beautiful here, and you've done a mighty fine job of taking care of everything. But I worry, Peaches. I worry about the business that you spent years and years building from nothing. It seems that you're throwing it all away."

Peaches sighed. She scooted back in the chair and rested her head on the back of the fine leather. "We have Bella's wedding and three others scheduled in just a few months. Bella has chosen a beautiful gown, one of my newest designs. Since there was no budget for the gown, I've made it spectacular. I hope she'll love it. She'll come for her fitting tomorrow."

"Bella is the daughter, right?"

"Yes, the wedding venue — which we can offer our wealthiest clients — was created by the good citizens of Lisbon, and it is like paradise, surrounded by the pool, the gardens, and a view of the Atlantic. It's the venue I've always seen in my head, but until I came to Portugal, I had no idea where it was. I truly believe that we are where we need to be."

Margaret-Ann sat back in her chair and smiled. "But some will want a church wedding," she said.

"There are plenty of cathedrals in Lisbon, and the prime minister has agreed to intervene on my behalf, since I'm not a citizen, to help make arrangements with the churches if they are required."

"You seem to have thought of everything," Margaret-Ann said.

"Oh, I had plenty of help from Lily, Marietta, and the prime minister. Believe me, it isn't all my doing."

"One more question?" Margaret-Ann said.

Peaches reached down and picked up Adona and put her in her lap. "What do you think, Adona? Should we entertain one more question?" Adona gave a soft yelp then licked Peaches' hand. "Adona says yes."

"What about TuckerD? I know you liked him."

Peaches closed her eyes and said nothing for a moment.

"I'm sorry, Peaches. Do you miss him?"

Tears welled in her eyes. "Terribly," she said, and sniffed. "I miss the little beautifully-scented roses. I even miss that blue Victorian frock coat. He'll be back, though. I just feel it in my heart, but I have some questions for him. Do you remember that white shirt with the lace cuffs he always wore?"

"How could I forget? I thought he didn't own another change of clothes."

Peaches got up, went to the bureau, and grabbed a white napkin. "Take a look at the lace. Is it the same?" she asked as she handed it to Margaret-Ann.

"It certainly looks like the same pattern."

"I thought so, too, but there's a slight problem."

"What sort of problem?"

"Well, let's just call it a problem of provenance," Peaches said, and sat down again.

"Provenance?"

"The lace you see on the pad is a pattern I sketched from the den in the palace."

"The royal palace?"

Peaches nodded. "Downstairs in the den is a glass case, and inside it is a man's shirt with lace cuffs. The note with the shirt has these words: *King Ferdinand of Spain, 1828. Gift from Hibernians.* Look at the bottom of the napkin. You can see the inscription."

Margaret-Ann looked puzzled.

"Alberto told me that this pattern was exclusively for King Ferdinand, and that it was never made again once it was made for him," Peaches said. "Yet, it is an almost exact match to the lace pattern on TuckerD's shirts. How do you explain that?"

"Well, obviously, Alberto is wrong."

"I don't think so," Peaches said. "There is a letter explaining

185

that this pattern was solely for the king, and would not be made in Carrickmacross or any part of Ireland. Imagine King Ferdinand seeing his lace cuffs worn by commoners!"

"I'm confused now," Margaret-Ann said.

"When I see TuckerD again, I'm going to ask him how he came to be wearing a shirt with cuffs made exclusively for the King of Spain in 1828. Even with all his charm and—well, all his charm, I don't think he'll be able to answer to my satisfaction."

"Didn't you tell me that the shirt was a gift from his grandmother?"

Peaches nodded and stroked Adona's head.

"Was his grandmother from Ireland?"

"I don't know," Peaches said. "All he said was that the shirt was handed down to him by his grandmother."

"Well, perhaps, Peaches, your TuckerD might be much older than he appears, and just maybe his grandmother didn't make his shirt, but rather it was a family heirloom and could have been made around that time. Maybe his great grandmother was a lace maker from Ireland, or maybe his great great grandmother made it and wanted a replica for her family."

Peaches didn't respond.

"In any case," Margaret-Ann said, "I think this TuckerD is much too old for you."

"You haven't seen him without his shirt on," Peaches said, and lifted her eyebrows.

"Peaches, shame on you. You've been fooling around with him?" Margaret-Ann leaned forward. "Tell me you haven't. It can't lead to anything. He's broke, no job, nothing. He has only one change of clothes, for goodness sakes. I'm glad we moved away. You've no business with a man with no future."

Peaches stared out the large window before her. *I wanted him to be my future,* she thought. *I wanted him.* Then she sat up straight and shook her head. *Nonsense. Think with your head, girl, not your heart.*

"I don't think you have to worry about that," she said to Margaret-Ann. "If he's as broke as you say he is—and who knows?—then I doubt very much he'll find his way to Portugal. He was a good model, though."

"Hmph," Margaret-Ann said. "He's handsome, that's for sure, but he's a nobody with nothing. You're Peaches Malone, the most beautiful woman I've ever seen. The right man is out there just waiting to sweep you off your feet."

"At my age? I don't think so," she said, focusing her deep blue eyes on a painting of the Portuguese landscape hanging above the mantle. She tucked a stray blonde hair behind her ear. "I'm too old for such nonsense."

"Age doesn't matter, my dear, when a woman looks like you do. You're only thirty-nine, Peaches. You're not ancient by any means. Besides, your beauty could win any man's heart, just at the sight of you."

"Oh, Margaret-Ann, those are dreams for young women. Be realistic."

"Then I guess I have no hope, either."

Peaches was taken aback.

"I think about it. Sometimes," Margaret-Ann said. "Yes, I see that look on your face. I might be in my sixties, but I'm not dead, Peaches. Occasionally, I think about romance. It's just an old woman's fantasy, I guess."

Peaches crossed her legs and put Adona in her lap. She stroked the silky fur. "I make my living off fantasies, beautiful gowns and gorgeous weddings that girls have been dreaming of since they were little. Without those visions and dreams in their heads, where would I be?"

Margaret-Ann chuckled. "And my biggest dream of all is for you to design a wedding gown for the most beautiful wedding ever held in Portugal. Your own."

"Oh, Margaret-Ann, how silly. I hardly think a wedding gown is in my future—not one for me, anyway."

Margaret-Ann fiddled with the buttons on her dress. "One thing I've learned about life, Peaches, is that you can never tell what mysteries and miracles are ahead. I believe in my heart that there's a wonderful one waiting for you."

Peaches planted a kiss on Adona's silky head and stood up. "My time's come and gone," she said. "I'm too hard-headed, too independent for any man out there. Now, come along. We have a meeting with our newest client, the prime minister's cousin. Beautiful girl. We don't want to disappoint her."

"If she has a gown and a venue designed by Peaches Malone, she couldn't possibly be disappointed."

Peaches laid a hand on Margaret-Ann's shoulder. "Thank you," she said. "Peaches and Lace couldn't exist without your hard work."

Margaret-Ann smiled. "Nah," she said. "I'm just another horse in the stable. You're the genius."

"Only with white napkins," she said. "You bring the designs to life. Without your skills at sewing, no one would ever have seen a Peaches Malone gown."

Margaret-Ann chuckled. "Well, then, I'd better get this old horse back to her stable. We've another gown to make, another wedding to plan, and that's what we're all about. Bringing dreams to life."

Chapter 34

He had a fondness for horses.

TuckerD ran his hand along the smooth back of the chestnut-colored horse beside him. At nineteen hands high, with flowing light chestnut mane and a tail that reached almost to the ground, the horse was one of the largest and most beautiful he'd ever seen. The brilliant green eyes gave him an almost-human quality.

"You're a big fella," he said, and stroked the horse. "A Lusitano, yes? And a champion, as well."

The chestnut whinnied.

"Yes, I know. Your owner is gone. He didn't want to leave you, Galahad, but he was very ill. There's nothing to fear. I know someone who'd love to have you. Shall we go and meet her?"

The chestnut whinnied again and moved away.

"There's no need to be afraid," TuckerD said, and moved closer. He stroked the horse again. "Shh, everything is all right," he whispered, and laid his head on the horse's forehead. "Close your eyes. You'll be just fine."

He felt the horse shudder then calm, and finally close his eyes.

"That's good," he whispered. "Good. You're safe with me."

TuckerD reached into his pocket and pulled out a tiny rose blossom, which he tucked carefully into an envelope, and then into a stringed pouch that he put around Galahad's neck. He patted the horse again.

"Just relax," he said. "I've got you."

And in an instant, the two of them disappeared from the horse farm in Atlanta and stood on the grassy fields of Castle Alamenda.

***

Peaches looked up from her work when she heard a knock on the door of the office.

"Yes," she said. "Come in."

Two very Portuguese looking men stepped just inside the office.

"Javier, Maximo," Peaches said, and put down her pencil. "I'm very busy. I've asked you to take your concerns to your father. By the way, did you fill all the birdfeeders?"

"Yes, they're all filled," Javier said. "I thought you might want to see the new horse."

"I haven't bought a new horse," Peaches said.

"But he's here," Javier explained. "We were working and he just...he appeared out of nowhere, wearing a leather pouch around his neck."

"I don't understand."

"The horse is right outside, very close to the back of your office. He has a pouch. I...we...just thought you might want to see him."

Peaches gave them a questioning look, but got up and followed. As she stepped outside, she saw him, the largest horse she'd ever seen.

"He's enormous," she said, and shielded her eyes with one hand. "A chestnut. Just look at that beautiful flowing blond mane and the light withers around his hooves. He's a beauty. What do those two pouches contain?"

Javier walked slowly up to the magnificent beast, but as he did, a whinny made him take a step back. He reached out a hand to stroke its forehead, but the horse bucked slightly and moved away. His eyes were trained on Peaches.

190

"He's looking right at you," Javier said. "Perhaps he'll allow you to get close to him."

She and her mother had cared for many horses, but none this big and none she hadn't raised from foals, or at least young colts. But she felt no fear of this giant animal, so she took a few steps closer. The horse stood still until she was right in front of him. She bent her head back and looked him in the eyes.

"You, sir, are a magnificent giant," she said.

As if in agreement, the horse nodded.

Peaches chuckled. "And what do you have around your neck? Javier," she said, "come and get these pouches for me. I can't reach that high."

This time, when Javier got close to the horse, he didn't back away. He gently lifted the two pouches from the horse's neck and handed them to Peaches.

She opened the largest pouch first. Inside she found several different papers about the horse.

"His name is Galahad," she said. "He is four years old and already a champion. Where is Ms. Margaret-Ann? I want her to see this horse. She won't believe her eyes. Rafael, go and get her quickly."

At the bottom of the page, written in a beautiful old script, were these words: *A gift to you for Castle Alamenda.*

"It seems that Galahad is a gift for the castle grounds. This horse has to be worth a fortune. Was anyone with him when he arrived?

Javier shook his head. "No, my lady, he just seemed to appear in the field."

"What is it?" Margaret-Ann called as she emerged from the studio with Janet trailing behind her. "Is something wrong?"

"Come and look," Peaches said.

Margaret-Ann gasped as she beheld the enormous horse. Then a smile crossed her face. "He's magnificent."

"Isn't he?" Peaches said. "I'll bet he's at least nineteen hands, don't you?"

"But where did he come from?"

Peaches handed her the note. She read it and looked at Peaches. "Do you think the prime minister had something to do with this? I've heard him mention horse racing several times."

"I don't know," Peaches said. "Wait, there's another pouch. Let's see what's in it."

She opened the smaller pouch and sucked in a breath. Inside it was a miniature Lipstick and Lace rose blossom.

"TuckerD," she whispered as she lifted it gently. "You haven't forgotten me."

"What is it?" Margaret-Ann asked.

Peaches held out the delicate blossom in the palm of her hand. "A rose blossom called Lipstick and Lace."

"Wait a minute," Margaret-Ann said. "TuckerD gave you several of those, didn't he?"

Peaches nodded.

"Is he here, then?"

"I don't think so, but…I don't know."

"I must get back to my sewing," Margaret-Ann said as she walked away. "We're on a tight deadline."

Peaches nodded. Then she sniffed the little blossom. "Heavenly," she said.

The bottom of the envelope was entirely covered in tiny seeds no bigger than the head of a pin. Written above them was, "Lipstick and Lace."

She handed it to Javier. "I'd like these planted around the fence at the outdoor wedding venue."

Javier looked inside and frowned. "Ms. Peaches," he said, "I'm afraid these roses won't grow in this climate. Only bigger, much heartier roses grow well here."

"Plant them anyway," she said. "It's worth a try."

Javier shrugged.

"They'll need to be watered if they grow, and we have some

special rose food with nutrients. That should help give them a boost. You have enough seeds there to surround the outside wedding venue, and if you have seeds left over, plant those along interior sides of the courtyard. Imagine how beautiful the castle and the venue will be with these roses all around them."

Javier lowered his head.

"Get your father to help you with the planting, and do it right away while the weather is cool."

Javier nodded but didn't move. "I don't want you to be disappointed if the plants don't grow."

Peaches felt a pang of guilt in her heart. "Don't worry, Javier. I believe they will eventually grow and flourish here. If they don't, then there's no one to blame. I'm counting on Mother Nature to make these grounds and your hard work perfect for them."

Galahad whinnied.

"See, Galahad agrees with us, so it must be right."

Peaches stepped closer to Galahad and stood as tall as she could to rub his muzzle. "Would you like to go and meet your new horse friends?" she asked. "I think you'll like them."

The horse stared directly into her eyes for a few seconds, then turned and galloped down the field toward the stables. He stopped once and looked back at her.

Peaches nodded at him. "We're glad to have you with us, Galahad," she called. When she was sure the horse had made it to the stables, she whispered, "You're a gift, a precious gift from a very special man." And her heart was filled with gladness as she admired her new home. "It's almost paradise," she said.

Chapter 35

Peaches bent close to the desk, her eyes focused on the new wedding gown design she was drawing on a white paper napkin. It was unlike anything she'd designed before. She could imagine the dress in her mind. White satin skirt, white lace bodice and sleeves, long satin train, all embroidered with satin Lipstick and Lace roses in a diagonal shape that ran from the tip of the right shoulder down to the waist, and then all the way down and around the long train. It would take months of work, but she thought it might be one of her most beautiful gowns to date. The knock on her office door startled her.

"Come," she said.

Janet appeared at the door.

"I'm frightened," Janet said. "Really frightened. You see, I got a letter from Etienne. It was delivered here, and it's the second one I've gotten."

"What did it say?"

Janet was quiet for a few seconds.

"What did it say, Janet? Tell me," Peaches said as the paced across the room.

"It was short, just two sentences," Janet said, and began to cry. "I don't know what to do anymore, Peaches. I'm terrified."

Peaches took a long soothing deep breath. "Now, tell me what the letter said, Janet."

"Word for word it said, 'I will kill you. I will kill her.'"

194

Peaches stopped her pacing. "And you know for sure it was from Etienne?"

"He signed it with a fancy letter E, which is his sort of signature."

Peaches put her hand on her forehead.

"Here's what I want you to do, Janet. Do you still have the letters?"

"Yes, I have both of them."

"Good," Peaches said. "I want you to give them to me. I'll, in turn, give them to the prime minister. Clear?"

"Yes," she said, and sniffed.

"Now, go back to the office and get those letters. Then bring them to me immediately. It's critical, Janet, that we have that evidence."

"Thank you, Peaches. And be careful. Remember, he wants to kill both of us."

Peaches felt a little shiver run up her spine, and her hands trembled worse than ever.

"You're a life-saver, Peaches," Janet said. "Etienne is in jail. This is just one of his scare tactics. He's tried this before, but I'm still here."

"I'm proud of you, Janet," Peaches said, and flopped down in a chair next to her desk.

***

"Margaret-Ann," Peaches called. "Don't forget that we have dinner tonight with the royal family."

The pup, Adona, lay at her feet sound asleep.

"I remember," Margaret-Ann said, and stuck her head around the door. "It's a shame Janet can't go, but we're so far behind. She said she'd rather stay here and work."

"I'm proud of the progress she's made here in Portugal, and I'll make sure that she can go with us next time," Peaches said. "Alberto has already called and said he'd be here for us at 6:00. "

Peaches looked at her watch. "That's only a couple of hours

from now. Do you know what you're wearing? You'll have to make yourself a whole new wardrobe since you've lost so much weight. But your new hair color and cut — I'm so glad you decided to let it grow — that and your weight loss — fifty pounds, mercy — you look like a very classy lady."

"Oh, thank you, dear. There should be more than one classy lady for a castle this big. Now, I have to get back to my sewing. This wedding gown isn't going to make itself."

"Only for an hour. We want to look gorgeous for our dinner. I'll be right back. I need to go up to my room for a moment," Peaches said, and picked up the white napkin. "Come, my sweet Adona," she said. "You're getting so big."

As she opened the door, she heard a whinny.

"Galahad! What are you doing way up here? Adona, look who's come to visit." The horse bent his head down. "Ah, do you want a tickle?" Peaches asked as she reached up and rubbed his muzzle.

Adona whimpered and Galahad lowered his head and licked her right on the face. The pup scurried behind Peaches' leg.

"Now, Adona," she said, and pulled the pup back onto her arm. "This is Galahad. He seems to like you, so you must be friendly." Peaches picked up the gangly pup and held her close to Galahad's muzzle. "Galahad, meet Adona," she said. "I trust you'll be the best of friends."

After the introductory sniffing, Adona jumped out of Peaches' arms, ran up under Galahad, and then took off down the field, barking as she ran as if she wanted the gigantic horse to play with her. Galahad whinnied and ran after her.

Peaches watched as the two of them run around the fields, Adona barking, Galahad prancing and whinnying.

"Be careful," Peaches shouted.

Adona sat immediately, and Galahad halted. Both of them stared back at her. Peaches was taken aback.

"Galahad, how did you know what I said?"

Neither animal moved, each one's eyes trained on Peaches.

I'll see how smart you are, Peaches thought. "Galahad," she called. "Would you like to see the castle?"

The enormous horse half reared, and when his hooves again met the ground, he nodded that huge chestnut head, his long blond mane almost reaching to the ground and his feathery withers aglow in the bright sunshine.

Peaches laughed out loud. "Come along then, my beauties," she said with a bit of trepidation, since Galahad wore no saddle and had no reins. She walked around the courtyard and opened the huge double doors leading into the castle proper.

"Ms. Peaches," Javier said when she came in. His eyes widened as he looked behind her and saw the great horse and the small puppy. "You…surely you cannot bring Galahad into the castle."

"It's my castle," she said. "I can do whatever I want. Besides, he came to the studio door with no saddle and no reins. He could have gone anywhere and we'd be none the wiser."

"We had no saddle large enough for him. My father is seeing to it, though," Javier said.

Suddenly, Linda, the housekeeper and sister to Rafael, and Carla, the cook, Rafael's daughter, along with her brother, Maximo, came running toward the door.

"*Dios mio!*" Maximo said.

Peaches chuckled. "I'm taking him for a short walk through the front room. He will not harm anything. Come, Galahad."

Adona ran alongside as the massive horse stepped carefully into the front room. He walked very slowly around, taking time to sniff each piece of furniture as if he were a man sizing up the place. Then he looked up and his eyes went to the formal dining room. He looked back at Peaches.

"Go ahead," she said.

Galahad went slowly up the stairs to the formal dining room and stood for a moment, his eyes taking in all of his surroundings.

Then his nose lifted and he sniffed rather loudly.

"I think he smells that delightful scent coming from the kitchen. Carla, do we have a carrot?"

Carla nodded and disappeared into the kitchen. She returned quickly with several raw carrots in her hands.

"Thank you, Carla. Now, come along, Galahad, and you can have a carrot for your outstanding behavior."

Galahad turned slowly around and went down the stairs, following Peaches out the door.

"Ms. Peaches," Javier said and ran after her, putting his arm on hers.

Galahad made a snorting sound and pushed him away from Peaches so forcefully that Javier fell on his backside.

"Did you want to say something, Javier?"

"The horse does not belong inside the castle, ma'am," he said as he got to his feet and brushed himself off.

"One look around didn't hurt anything. He did no damage, and his curiosity is satisfied. But I do appreciate your concern for the castle, so thank you."

Javier nodded.

Still holding the white napkin, she turned and walked toward the courtyard.

Chapter 36

Peaches checked her lipstick again in the full length mirror in her dressing room. She drew back her lips to make sure there was none on her teeth.

She stepped back from the mirror to get one last look at her gown. She'd designed it herself, and was quite pleased with the peach-colored satin of the long mermaid-style skirt and the peach-colored netting underneath the white lace of the bodice and long sleeves. She fingered the boat neck design of the bodice and then turned to make sure that the backless gown draped as it was supposed to, with two layers of peach satin at her waist.

"Ah, now, don't you look beautiful," Margaret-Ann said from behind her. "You're a glittering jewel, my dear. Marietta and the prime minister will be impressed. Let's put your hair in a chignon."

"I'm terrible at fixing my hair, which is why I leave it long and let it do what it wants. Good idea, and I love your dress, by the way. You look stunning. The black is elegant and sophisticated. You look like a whole new person. I'd only change one thing."

"Somehow, I knew it was coming."

Peaches picked up a large, glittering silver bow. "Just be still for a minute," she said. "Let me see if I can get this…ah, now. Take a look."

"Oh, mercy, Peaches, I'm too old to wear bows!"

"But you're not too old to be classy and elegant. That bow

adds sparkle to your black crepe sheath. It's the touch of life that it needed."

Margaret-Ann turned as far as she could to see the big silver bow attached to the back of her gown exactly at her waistline.

"Well, what do you think?" Peaches asked.

"If you think it looks good, then so be it. You're the one with the fashion sense, not me."

Peaches put her hands on Margaret-Ann's shoulders. "I'm only a designer. I think up designs in my head. You, on the other hand, bring them to life on the sewing machine. I could never do that. I'd be nowhere without your help."

"Oh, now, don't embarrass me, Peaches. Let's get that hair fixed. We don't have long before Alberto will be here."

Peaches sat at her vanity and watched her mother bring her long blonde hair up and fashion it in a perfect chignon. Then she fitted the tiara in place and pulled a few strands of hair to fall precisely around her face and neck.

"Done," Margaret-Ann said. "How do you like it?"

"It's beautiful," Peaches said. "It lacks only one thing. Can you guess?"

Margaret-Ann chuckled. "I know you too well, Peaches," she said, and handed her the bottle of JOY perfume. "Want me to give it a spritz?"

Peaches nodded and inhaled as Margaret-Ann sprayed.

"I just adore that fragrance," Peaches said. "And what perfume are you wearing?"

"Nothing right now. I'd forgotten about it, but I have plenty of my old stand-by, Beautiful by Estee Lauder."

"Well, perhaps it's time for the new you to have a new fragrance," Peaches said. "Try this. You might like it.

Margaret-Ann took the gold box that Peaches handed her and stared at it.

"Go ahead. Open it."

She carefully untied the black and gold ribbon and opened

the box. Then she looked at Peaches with a frown of confusion on her face.

"Try it," Peaches said. "It's Chanel No. 5, the latest version called Parfum Grand Extrait."

"But it looks so expensive, Peaches."

Peaches chuckled. "A whole new you deserves a whole new perfume. This is one of the best. Go ahead. Try it. And remember, spritz and step into it twice. Don't spray it directly on you."

Margaret-Ann held up the bottle and sprayed, then stepped into the mist of fragrance. She repeated the action and then closed her eyes. "I love it," she said.

"Good," Peaches said. "I bought an extra bottle of it, so you'll have to start wearing a bit of it every day."

"I'd feel guilty wearing this every day. I know it cost a fortune. I don't need such a fine fragrance, Peaches."

"Well," Peaches said, and reached for the bottle. "I guess I should send it back then."

Margaret-Ann put her hands on her now-slender hips. "I'll keep it, thank you very much," she said, and turned so that Peaches couldn't reach the bottle. "No sending back needed."

Peaches smiled. "One more thing," Peaches said, and reached inside her dresser drawer. She took out a long slim box and handed it to Margaret-Ann.

"Now, what's this?"

"Go ahead. Open it. It's a gift from me to you."

Margaret-Ann opened the box and gasped. "Your Rolex! I've always admired it."

"Well, now you can have it to wear as much as you like." Peaches patted her chignon and leaned closer to the mirror.

"But why?" Margaret-Ann asked.

Peaches simply held up her arm.

"Oh my goodness! Where did that one come from?"

"Father of our newest bride," she said. "I could hardly believe it."

"Merciful heavens," Margaret-Ann said as she fastened the watch to her wrist.

Peaches chuckled. "Well, you certainly can't wear two of them," she said.

"Ah, I think I hear Alberto driving up."

"Good, he's early. I need some time with the prime minister before dinner. You can listen to Marietta tell you how gorgeous you look."

As they headed down the castle stairs, Peaches thought about Etienne LaRoche and his threat to kill her. It made her shiver, but then her thoughts turned to TuckerD.

"Where are you when I need you?" she whispered so quietly that no one else could hear. "Where are you?"

Chapter 37

"Is there a problem, Peaches?" Marietta asked as they sipped their after-dinner coffee.

Peaches lowered her head. "I'm afraid so," she said very quietly.

Marietta looked at Margaret-Ann and then back at Peaches. She summoned Alberto. "Alberto," she said, "is the meeting still in session?"

"No, madam, it is ending as we speak," Alberto said. "The party is moving to the formal den for more discussion, I believe."

"And a drink or two," Marietta said with a smile. "Be a dear, then, and ask the prime minister if he can spare a few moments to speak with us before the discussion. Please convey that it is a matter of some urgency."

Only a few moments later, the prime minister entered the room.

"Ah, there you are, dear," Marietta said. "Care to sit with us for a while? I know you have the meeting to attend to, but Peaches has an important issue to discuss with you. Would you spare her a moment of your time?"

"If there is no time for you and our friends, then there is no time at all, my dearest," he said, and sat beside Peaches. "Now, tell me what's wrong."

"I don't want to be an alarmist," Peaches said, and pushed a stray hair behind her ear, "but something has happened, and it frightens me."

"Frightens you? Well, then, tell me. We can't have out most famous resident feeling afraid."

"My friend, Janet--Janet LaRoche, former wife of Etienne LaRoche."

The prime minister leaned forward. "Etienne LaRoche? But he is in prison. She has nothing to fear from him."

Peaches scooted up in her chair. "You don't understand. Someone brought a letter to Janet. She's here with us, of course, but she found the letter slipped under the door of the salon."

Peaches reached into her bag and pulled out the two letters and handed them to the prime minister.

Carefully, he opened the letters and read aloud.

'I will kill you. I will kill her,' and it was signed with his signature E. Janet is sure he wrote it because the handwriting matches his exactly. Alberto, may I have a coffee please?"

"Of course, Your Excellency. Right away, sir."

"But he could not have written it and secreted it out of the jail. I would have been informed of such activities, and any letters would have been taken directly to the warden, who would have immediately brought them to me. This case has been highly publicized because of your popularity. Etienne is very closely watched."

"Then either someone else forged his handwriting, or...the staff...." Peaches stopped.

Prime Minister Cosanto looked shocked.

"Your coffee, sir," Alberto said, and put a cup and saucer on the table. "May I bring coffee for anyone else?"

"Thank you, Alberto," the prime minister said with a smile. "If we need you, we will call. Please close the doors on your way out. Oh, and do check on the men in the discussion room to see if they need anything. Tell them that I am delayed, but will join them as soon as possible."

Peaches couldn't help but smile as she listened to his thick

Portuguese accent. "I do not mean to imply that your staff is responsible, Prime Minister. But that sort of frightening message has me deeply concerned. Etienne wants it known that he plans to kill me."

"Oh, Peaches," Margaret-Ann said, then put hands to her face. "My beautiful Peaches."

Marietta got up and sat beside Margaret-Ann and put an arm around her shoulders. "There, there, dear. I promise you that we will take care of this. Do not worry yourself."

"I should have told you, Margaret-Ann," Peaches said, "but I didn't want you worried. Besides, I wanted a chance to speak privately with the prime minister. He's been such a help and comfort to us."

"Peaches, please, call me Paulo. You address Marietta by her name, so feel free to address me with mine. You're almost like a family member."

Peaches nodded and smiled.

"Now," he said, "we must get to the bottom of this frightful mystery. I won't have the three most beautiful women in Lisbon distressed." He took a sip of his coffee.

Folding the letters, he said, "I will consult with the security team and the Minister of Justice before I speak to the warden. Please don't be alarmed if several workers come to Castle Alamenda and begin to work in the gardens."

"Workers?"

"There will be three additional workers on the grounds at all times, Peaches. Javier can assign them tasks. They will all be members of our Elite Strategies Team, trained to protect our citizens, yet they will be disguised as ordinary workers. In effect, they are guards, a special team sent to make sure that you are protected against harm at all times. Does that meet with your approval?"

Peaches nodded.

"Margaret-Ann, how does that sound to you?"

"It will make me feel much better," she said. "Thank you for caring so much about her welfare."

"It is my responsibility to ensure the safety of all our residents. Our crime rate here is very low, and I want to keep it that way."

A knock on the door sounded. "Yes?" the prime minister called.

Alberto came in and walked directly to him, then bent down and whispered something in his ear. The prime minister looked at his watch.

"Please tell the gentlemen that we will reconvene tomorrow at luncheon since there is an urgent matter I must see to. Thank you, Alberto—and will you please bring the gifts I showed you this afternoon?"

Peaches glanced at Margaret-Ann.

Only a few moments later, Alberto entered and set two packages down on the table.

"As you requested, Your Excellency."

"Thank you, Alberto. Please join us," he said, and pointed to a chair.

"Me, sir?"

"Well, certainly. You were, after all, responsible in part for the gifts."

Alberto smiled and took a seat.

"Marietta, will you do the honors?"

Marietta smiled and picked up the two small packages, one of which she handed to Peaches, the other to Margaret-Ann.

"Oh, mercy," Margaret-Ann said, her new dark bob bouncing as she talked. "I never expected such a surprise."

"Open it," Peaches said. "Let's see what it is."

Margaret-Ann carefully unwrapped the small box and gasped. "Oh, oh, it's so beautiful," she said. "It's for me? Are you sure?"

Marietta smiled. "Yes, it is, as a complement to your new look. Do you like it?"

Margaret-Ann held up the gift, a silver and gold brooch studded with blue jewels. "It's the most beautiful brooch I've ever seen," she said.

"It is an old sailing ship," Marietta said, "one of the great symbols of Lisbon as a harbor city. The blue jewels along the bottom are sapphires that represent the ocean. The gold, of course, forms a circle around the silver and diamond sailing ship."

"It's breath-taking," Margaret-Ann said. "I've never owned anything as fine as this. How can I ever thank you, Marietta?"

"I'm afraid the credit goes to our own Alberto. He had the piece designed especially for you."

"You, Alberto?"

He smiled and nodded.

"Thank you," Margaret-Ann said, and wiped a tear from her eye. "I shall wear it every day."

"I am happy it pleases you," Alberto said in his thick accent.

"Go ahead, Peaches, open yours," Marietta said.

Carefully she unwrapped the small box, and when she opened the lid, she gasped. "A rose," she said. "Just look at all the jewels! Marietta, you shouldn't have. It's magnificent."

"Alberto, too, had this designed for you, with our approval, of course. It is a Lipstick and Lace rose, red and yellow petals with green stem."

"Oh, my, are those emeralds that form the stem?"

Marietta nodded.

"Rubies and yellow diamonds form the petals. Do you like it?"

Peaches got up and hugged Marietta. "With the exception of this tiara and Margaret-Ann's brooch, I've never seen anything so lovely."

"I wish you much success with your roses, Peaches. It would be such a lovely sight for our city if they grew and flourished, and I admire your courage in planting them. We'll be watching to see how they fare."

"We'll have another wedding to plan soon, won't we?" Peaches asked. "Your…is it your cousin?"

"My first cousin's daughter, yes," the prime minister said. "She'll be here in a day or so, and she insists that she must have an exclusive Peaches and Lace wedding gown."

"She's only eighteen," Marietta said, "but she's a force to be reckoned with. Mila is quite outspoken, and she knows what she wants."

Margaret-Ann smiled. "Sounds like Peaches. They should get along famously."

Thirty minutes or so later, as Peaches and Margaret-Ann waited for Alberto to bring the car, the prime minister showed her to a grand round table near the front of the palace.

"One last gift for now," he said. "For you, Peaches, locally grown."

Peaches admired the large fruit basket.

"All the berries you could want, and a few small melons, as well. There are seeds to plant so that you can pluck your own berries off your bushes eventually. Alberto knows where and how to plant them for the best yields. At the bottom of the basket is some of our own yogurt. I hope you'll enjoy them all."

"Yogurt and berries," Peaches said. "My ideal breakfast. Thank you so much, all of you. I feel as if it's Christmas morning."

The prime minister and Marietta helped load Peaches, Margaret-Ann, and the gifts into the back seat of the limousine.

"Please call me as soon as your friend arrives with the letter."

"Yes, I will," Peaches said, "and thank you so much. You're spoiling us, you know."

"Our exact intentions," he said, "for our most famous resident."

Chapter 38

The pounding on the door startled Peaches so much that her pen slipped out of her hand and dropped to the floor.

"Please, not now. I'm working," she called.

The pounding stopped momentarily, but started again.

Peaches got up and stormed over to the door, but then she calmed herself, took a deep breath, and rotated her shoulders.

"Who is it?"

"I am sorry, Ms. Peaches, but—"

Peaches opened the door to see Javier and Maximo standing just outside. She said not a word.

"Forgive the interruption," Javier said softly. "Please."

Peaches said nothing.

"I...it's...it's...."

Peaches folded her arms across her chest.

"Galahad," he managed. "Galahad is...."

She cocked her head.

"He's out of control," Maximo said. "He does not like the new workers. You are—"

Without a word, Peaches stepped out of the studio and locked the door behind her. Then she nodded at Javier and Maximo.

She followed them across the field, not minding at all that the wet grass was ruining her leather pumps and staining the hem of her white silk pants. She reached up and ran her fingers through the long tendrils that fell onto her face. When she worked nowadays, she kept her hair in a high elegant ponytail that hung to her shoulders. Even with the new air conditioning units, the heat outside still seeped in, so at times, the office space in the studio was warmer than she liked. But in another week, the problem would be solved when the small unit for her studio space arrived.

She heard the snorting before she saw the horse. "He's in distress," she said. Peaches picked up her pace and soon passed three workers sitting in the grass.

"That beast tried to run us over," the workers said almost in unison.

Peaches chuckled. "If that magnificent beast had tried to run you over, you wouldn't be sitting up right now."

When she approached the horse, she spoke in a soft voice and stood on a stool to rub his muzzle and forehead. "Galahad, my darling giant," she said as she rubbed him. "These men are workers sent by His Excellency to protect me."

Galahad whinnied, then turned his great head and looked at her.

Peaches smiled. "I know," she said. "You, my majestic beast, are my protector, and I couldn't ask for a better or brighter one." Galahad moved his head up and down as if to agree with her. "So, just between the two of us," she whispered close to his ear, "can we just pretend to let them do their jobs? Can you put up with them for a few days?" When Galahad made no response, Peaches sighed. "I've been threatened, Galahad. Someone wants to kill me."

Galahad let out an alarmingly loud snort and pawed at the ground. The men seated on the grass immediately scooted back.

"It's all right," Peaches said, and rubbed his forehead. "Will you let these men help you to guard me? They might not do much good, but their job, like yours, is to protect me." Galahad nodded his huge head. "There's a good boy," Peaches said, and put her cheek on his muzzle. "My great good boy, my protector and guardian." She wrapped her arms as far around his neck as she could and gave him a squeeze. Then she kissed his muzzle and jumped down off the stool.

As she walked back to her studio, she shuddered just a bit. Someone was watching her. She turned to look at Galahad, but he seemed busy being brushed by Javier. The workers were all up on their feet turned away from her, so Peaches shrugged and just kept on walking. Every now and then she glanced back, but saw nothing out of the ordinary. Still, she couldn't shake the feeling.

Someone was watching her.

She didn't see the man standing behind the large oak tree.

Chapter 39

After the incident with Galahad, Peaches felt the nerves prickling all over her body. She knew, she just knew, that someone had been watching her. Her hands trembled. Her knees felt like rubber, and her heartbeat hammered in her chest. She could barely stand, so she sat on one of the shaded sofas in the courtyard.

Peaches focused her attention on the beautiful vistas surrounding this highest point of the castle grounds. Her eyes traveled from house to house beside and below, the first row built only one hundred feet beyond the enormous expanse of the Tagus River, as deep blue and beautiful as the Atlantic Ocean into which it flowed. Each segment of homes rose higher and higher toward the highest point in Lisbon, the Hill of the Three Churches, capped by Lisbon's grandest and largest monastery, St. Vincent de Fora. Directly beside it rose the golden-domed Church of Saint Engracia, and beyond that stood St. Stephen Church, a smaller but older and richly adorned paragon of Baroque architecture built in the 12th century.

Focusing on the gorgeous architecture, enmeshed in the historical significance of this beautiful city, Peaches rested her head on the back of the sofa, her troubles vanishing. She took a deep breath and felt such gratitude that she could live in Lisbon surrounded by thousands of years of ancient history. She shut out all other sounds around her and listened for the rushing waves of the Atlantic as they crashed against the mighty rocks along the coast. Her heavy-lidded eyes closed, and the only sound she could hear was the crashing of the waves far below.

As she drifted to sleep, she was vaguely aware that someone was sitting next to her, but the pull of much-needed rest wrapped its arms around her and stole her away.

***

In the dream, she saw herself in a grand ballroom dancing with a giant of a man who held her closely and tenderly as romantic classical music played in the background. The two of them swayed back and forth, arms wrapped around each other.

She wore one of her latest wedding gown designs, an all-satin baby blue, form-fitting creation with a long blue satin train embroidered with tiny white roses. Her hair was carefully drawn into an elegant chignon that showed off the tiara Marietta had given her. She felt the warmth and closeness of his tuxedoed body next to hers, the power in his muscular arms, the grace of his steps, the protection of his broad shoulders. She smiled as she looked up briefly and saw two white doves fly overhead, a symbol of two people beginning a new journey together, a new life. As the dancing slowed, she saw his handsome face, his sea blue eyes sparkling as he looked down at her, a faint smile playing on his lips.

"I love you, Peaches," he mouthed. "For eternity."

His soft words made her heart feel as if it would burst from utter joy, and when he ran a hand through her hair, she felt overwhelmed.

"And I love you, TuckerD," she whispered.

He scooped her into his arms and walked to the arches in the wedding venue. With her head on his shoulder, she smelled the heavenly aroma of oranges and cedar. She heard the ground beneath them begin to give way, heard the snapping and crumbling, but still, she smiled.

"Are you ready?" he asked.

"For you, I'm always ready," she said, and tightened her hold on him.

"Peaches, Peaches, are you ready?"

The voice was not his. The harsh sound of it interrupted her dream.

"Peaches, wake up," she heard as someone shook her shoulder.

"I'm tired," she said.

"You have to get up," Margaret-Ann said. "Go fix your hair and your make up. You look a fright."

Peaches opened her eyes.

"Get up from there and get ready," Margaret-Ann said, her hands folded in her lap. "Your hair's a mess—just look at the way it sticks out all over your head—your makeup is nearly gone, and your clothes are wrinkled beyond recognition. What on earth have you been doing out here?"

"Well, I was having a nap."

"A nap? You look more like you've been rolling down a hill. You have a reputation to think of. No one wants to see an ugly Peaches Malone."

Peaches pulled herself up, glared at Margaret-Ann, and walked back into the castle. As she made her way up to her bedroom, she heard the words again, as she'd heard them from her mother so many times as a girl.

No one wants to see an ugly Peaches Malone.

Peaches winced at the comment, one she'd heard since she was a young girl. She'd stayed awake at night wondering if she would ever be beautiful. Even at twelve, she knew in her heart that in order for people to like her, she had to be pretty... no, beautiful. Using what nature had given her even then, she became obsessed with finding the perfect make-up, the perfect hair style, clothes, jewelry. She remembered a time when she was fourteen and Margaret-Ann worked two jobs just to be able to afford to buy her an expensive make-up kit with a booklet on how to use each product. It must have cost her a fortune, but all she'd said was the mantra:

"No one wants an ugly Peaches Malone."

Margaret-Ann had insisted that she study that booklet and memorize each step, the purpose of each of the cosmetics and how to use them properly. And it was as she studied the booklet that the truth hit her and hit her hard. It was the day her hands first began to tremble.

"I'm nothing," she said, "unless I'm beautiful. My beauty is all I have."

Chapter 40

"Surprise!" Lily said as she stepped into the great doorway of the castle. "Surprise!"

Peaches ran to her and held her in a bear hug, almost lifting her off the ground. "Oh, Lily, I'm so happy to see you," she said as she released her captive and stepped back. Then she hugged her one more time.

"Are you okay, Peaches? I've never known you to be much of a hugger," Lily said as she deposited her suitcase and duffle bag onto the floor.

"I'm fine," Peaches said with a smile.

"I just had to come," Lily said, and straightened her dress. "I've missed you so, Peaches. Atlanta is just not the same without you."

"Oh, Lily, you made it, dear," Margaret-Ann said. "I was so worried you wouldn't be able to get away."

Lily stared at the lovely older woman in front of her. "Margaret-Ann? You...you look gorgeous. I'd never have recognized you."

"She does look lovely, doesn't she?"

Lily nodded her head. "It's a complete transformation. My goodness, when did this happen?"

Margaret-Ann blushed. "Well, to be honest, when I found out I was moving to Lisbon, I went on a diet, and I stuck to it. I was determined not to be pudgy in this new city. And then,

I went to a salon and got my hair cut and colored. And then, when I got here, the whole look seemed to come together. I can't explain it. Maybe it's a magic castle."

"Whatever it is, you look fabulous," Lily said, and hugged her.

"Uh, hello, Lily," a soft voice came from behind Margaret-Ann.

Janet stepped out of the shadows.

Lily looked at Peaches. Peaches arched her brows.

"Janet came over with Margaret-Ann, Lily," Peaches said. "She's going to be helping in the workshop. Janet needed a home, and Margaret-Ann needed the help. Our business has really blossomed here."

"I think it's wonderful the way things have worked out for you here, for all of you," Lily said. "Now, may I please sit and take off these shoes? They're killing me!"

"Feel free to sit anywhere you'd like, my sweet friend. "Oh, and just one more little introduction before you get settled." Peaches stuck her head out, put two fingers in her mouth, and whistled. Adona barked and came running into the castle, where she immediately sat at Peaches' feet, panting loudly.

"Oh my goodness, is that our little Adona?" Lily asked. "Just look how she's grown."

"She's almost twenty pounds now," Peaches said, and knelt to rub the dog under the chin.

Adona got up and went to inspect Lily. "Hello there, Adona," Lily said. "You are a beautiful girl."

Adona sat and panted, her mouth forming what Lily thought was a smile.

"She likes compliments," Peaches said.

"May I pet her?"

"In a bit," Peaches said, and called Adona to her. "Now, Adona, if you'd like to stay inside with us, go tell Linda to give you a quick bath. And be sure to get dried off."

217

Adona looked at Lily, as if weighing the trouble of a bath against being able to visit and get a head rub. Then she turned and headed toward the laundry room where her doggie bath was.

"She's really smart," Peaches said. "Uncommonly so."

"I'll say she is. It's...well, maybe Margaret-Ann is right. Maybe this really IS a magic castle."

"We have to get back to work, I'm afraid," Margaret-Ann said. "Brides wait for no man. Come along, Janet. We'll see you later at dinner."

Lily and Peaches waved as they left.

"Feel like a little walk?" Peaches asked. "I want you to meet someone. Why don't you put on some good walking shoes and we'll walk down the fields together?"

"Give me a minute to change out of this suit," Lily said. "A nice walk is just what I need after all those hours on the plane."

"No, this time you'll have an entire wing to yourself, with enough space for a separate office. You can arrange it however you like since it's huge! Your bags are already there. Go up the stairs and turn right. Go through the double doors. That's your space."

"My goodness, a wing to myself? Peaches, that's way too much."

"You'll adjust," Peaches said, and chuckled.

"I can't wait to see it," Lily said.

"I think you saw it when we first looked at the house, didn't you?"

Lily opened her mouth in surprise. "Oh, that beautiful wing with the large windows? Oh, my."

"That's it," Peaches said. "Mine's on the opposite side."

"Give me a few minutes," Lily said as she walked up the stairs. "Then I have something to talk to you about."

Lily hurried up the stairs and disappeared down the hall. When thirty minutes passed, she stood at the balcony.

"Ready," she called down to Peaches.

"Well, then, get down here and let's go," Peaches said, and chuckled. "How you manage to change in that time is beyond me — but then, you've always been good at it. It takes me an hour after all the makeup enhancements and trying to decide what to wear, not to mention this mass of blonde hair that never ever does what I want it to do."

"Yes, I'm a quick-change artist, while you, my dear, are simply an artistic genius. Just look at us and you'll see that I'm right. Here I stand in jeans and a T-shirt, and there you are in your fine Prada trousers and blouse, your casual day-time wear. And then there's that face, that incomparable face."

"Pish tosh," Peaches said. "You were a model once upon a time. Don't downgrade your own beauty. Now, let's get walking."

As soon as the two of them started across the field, Galahad whinnied.

"He knows we're coming," Peaches said.

"Who?"

"It's a surprise," Peaches said, and took a small device from her pocket. She stopped walking, pushed a button and spoke. "Javier, Maximo," she said. "Let him out."

"Yes, ma'am," came the reply.

"Just wait here," Peaches said to Lily. Within only a couple of minutes, Peaches heard the great hoof beats on the ground. "Here he comes," she said. "My Galahad."

Lily watched as the gigantic horse ran straight toward her. She grabbed Peaches' arm.

"Don't worry. He's very smart."

Galahad stopped when he was about five feet away. He snorted and nodded his head up and down.

"Come and meet Lily," she said to the horse.

Galahad advanced slowly and stopped when he was about a foot away.

"Galahad, this is Lily. Lily, this is Galahad."

Taller than Peaches by several inches, Lily reached up and put her hand out to him. Galahad sniffed and whinnied softly.

"Lily is my most cherished friend, Galahad."

Galahad stepped closer and bent his head to nuzzle Lily.

"You're a beautiful boy," she said, and stroked his forehead.

"Now, Galahad, go and show Lily what a magnificent animal you are."

The horse nuzzled Peaches, then lifted his head and trotted off down the field. He reared up and whinnied loudly. He reared again, his front feet moving as if in a dance. Then he bolted toward the end of the field. He stopped, his back legs kicked out, he snorted, then pawed the ground with his front hooves.

"He's putting on a show for you," Peaches said.

He dropped his head and sniffed along the ground. Then, he stopped and reared up, snorted, and his hooves barreled down on his target.

"I'd hate to be on his bad side," Lily said, and chuckled.

Peaches snapped her fingers. From far down in the field, Galahad heard and came galloping back to her.

"Where on earth did you find such a horse?" Lily asked. "He must have been someone's prized champion."

"He found me, Lily. Javier called me in a dither and said there was a new horse in the field. He had leather pouches around his neck. In one of them were his papers. He is a champion."

"So, what was in the other pouch?"

"Only an envelope."

Lily looked at her. "And?"

"And…," Peaches said. "Inside there was a Lipstick and Lace rosebud and a lot of seeds."

"I must be missing something," Lily said. "Who'd give you seeds?"

Peaches clasped her hands in front of her and cleared her throat. "Well, TuckerD used to give me rose blossoms—Lipstick and Lace—when I'd see him. He sent Galahad and the envelope.

I've had Javier plant the seeds all around the wedding venue."

"So he's here, then?"

Peaches shook her head. "I don't know. I wish I did, but I know he sent Galahad, and I know he was the one who sent the rose blossom and the seeds. No one else could have known about the seeds."

"And why the horse?"

"He knows I love horses. I think Galahad's former owner must have passed away and the horse needed a home. But I don't know anything else."

"He's an odd man, Peaches," Lily said as they turned to walk back to the castle. "I don't mean he's a bad man, just odd, very odd. He has to be hiding something."

"Like what?"

Lily shrugged. "How should I know? He sends you this horse as a guardian, I'm sure, but he doesn't deliver it himself — or if he does, he hides so you won't see him."

"Why would I need a guardian, Lily? I have a whole staff, and the prime minister has workers all around the farm."

"Etienne, of course," Lily said. "He might be in jail, but he's a vengeful man. I have no doubt he'd get a few of his associates to try to harm you."

"But the case is over and done with. I got the designs back. The court case is over."

"You weren't listening," Lily said, and stopped outside in the courtyard. "Etienne and his bunch are like the Mafia. They deal in vengeance. That's really why I came to visit. I've had word that his gang is back together and planning something deadly."

Peaches gave her a wide-eyed stare. "Are you serious?" she asked, and hugged her arms close to her side.

"Word is that he's planning a hit, Peaches, and it has your name on it."

Chapter 41

Peaches tried to focus on a new design, but her thoughts were on Etienne.

"Are you having any luck?" Lily asked.

The two of them were seated on the brocade sofa in the informal living room, Peaches with her white napkin on a small table in front of her; Lily with a stack of papers that needed signatures.

Peaches put down her pen. "I can't seem to think of anything except Etienne. Why would he order me killed?"

"It's not just you. It's Janet, as well. You're both in grave danger from him and his gang."

"Did you notice how many workers were out in the fields?"

"Seven or eight," Lily said, and put aside her papers. "Many more than I thought you'd need."

"And there are three working alongside the gardener in the wedding venue, one in the courtyard."

"You certainly have enough workers," Lily said. "Their paychecks must be astronomical."

"I wouldn't know," Peaches said, and got out her compact. She flipped open the lid and checked her makeup.

"You don't pay them?" Lily asked. "You look perfect. No need for the compact. There's not a hair out of place, your lipstick is shiny, and your mascara is, as always, lush and gorgeous."

Peaches closed the compact with a click. "They don't work

for me," she said. "They work for the prime minister. It's his equivalent of our SWAT team."

"You're kidding!"

Peaches shook her head. "Nope. He sent them here when I told him about the letter Janet received. We also have an extra housemaid, the tall one with the short brown hair. She's on his team, too. And cameras. They're all over the place, inside and out. You can't see them, but they're there."

"So your magic castle is also a fortress," Lily said.

"I'm under a sort of house arrest," Peaches said. "Well, not an arrest, but an order not to leave unless I'm accompanied by Alberto and a guard."

Lily turned to face Peaches. "I can hardly believe he's gone to so much trouble for you—not that you don't deserve it, but that he would take such an interest in keeping you safe."

"He says it's for Portugal," Peaches said. "He wants to keep me safe because I'm loved and admired here for some reason. My designs have always sold well here, but I thought it was only because of his niece and the gown I made for her. But apparently, the people of Portugal think I'm special."

Lily smiled. "Of course you are. The Portuguese are famous for their love of beauty. You, your gowns...you're beyond compare."

Peaches dismissed the comment with a wave of her hand. "Don't be silly," she said. "I'm a thirty-nine-year-old woman who works night and day and leads a boring life. That the people of Portugal seem to like me is a wonder in itself. I'm no one special, Lily, just an ordinary designer."

"You're hardly ordinary," Lily said. "Ordinary designers don't have their designs featured in the fanciest magazines, nor do they win awards."

"Oh," Peaches said, "I need to talk to Margaret-Ann. We have a runway show in a few days, but I'm not sure we have enough models. I'll have to speak to Marietta to see if she can help."

"How many new designs do you have?"

"The same as usual, about ten," Peaches said, and brushed at her pants. "I'll be back in an hour or so. If you need me, just buzz me. I hate to work while you're here, but...."

Lily laughed out loud. "You're always working, Peaches. Even when you're not working, your mind is designing new gowns. Besides, I'm waiting for a call," she said and held up her latest technical marvel. "It's an iPad with phone. I'll be fine. Plenty to keep me busy."

As Peaches walked toward the door, Lily called to her. "You should really learn how to use one of these, you know. You could do your drawings and save all of them right here. And if the phone rang for the business, you just click a button and answer it."

"My white napkins will do just fine."

Lily shook her head. "We need to bring you into the twenty-first century."

"No problem," Peaches said with a grin. "My designs do that for me. Buzz if you need anything."

***

Bella, the prime minister's daughter, stood before Peaches in a magnificent wedding gown, a unique creation just for her. The petite dark-haired beauty seemed nervous.

"Relax, dear," Peaches said. "If you want to be Portugal's most beautiful bride, we'll have to make sure this dress fits perfectly."

Peaches ran her hands along the fitted waistline, smoothing out the seams. Then she stood back and surveyed the dress from top to bottom. The pure white satin fairly glowed. The round neck and long sleeves fitted perfectly. The full white skirt ended just at the tops of her heels, and swept into a six-foot train embroidered around the edges in baby blue lace. A baby blue thin satin belt at her waist tied in back and fell the full length of her train in baby blue ribbons.

"I didn't want long sleeves," Bella said softly, "but Mother said that since it's a Catholic wedding, I must be covered. No skin showing. I know she's right, but it's not what I wanted."

"So, you don't like the dress?" Peaches asked.

Bella shook her head, her long silky black hair, which fell to her waist, shining like a beacon. "It was my mother's choice, not mine," she said, and lowered her head. "It's beautiful, really, but it's just not what I wanted."

Peaches paced back and forth in the room. "And what was it that you wanted?"

"If you'll be so kind as to give me my purse, I'll show you, but you have to promise that you won't show Mother or Father. They wouldn't approve. I had a hard enough time convincing them to let me have a baby blue belt. My mother said it was too unconventional for the prime minister's only daughter. I'm representing all of Portugal."

Peaches gave the nineteen-year-old her purse, and from it the girl withdrew a photograph. "This," she said as she showed it to Peaches, "is the most beautiful gown I've ever seen. It's my dream dress."

Peaches smiled. "It's one of mine," she said. "The strapless peach colored tulle and satin embroidered with flowered lace. I remember exactly who wore it."

Bella nodded. "My cousin Mila," she said.

"And this is the dress you really wanted?" Peaches asked.

Bella's eyes filled with tears. "Yes, ma'am," she said, and sniffed. "When I saw her come down the aisle, my heart skipped a beat."

"But she was married outside, right?"

Bella nodded. "Mila is not Catholic. She could have her wedding anywhere."

Peaches stuck her head out of the door of the fitting room. "Margaret-Ann," she called. "Come here for a moment, will you?"

When Margaret-Ann came in, she looked at Bella. "You look lovely, my dear," she said.

Bella covered her face with her hands and sobbed.

Peaches squeezed her eyes shut.

"Whatever is wrong here?" Margaret-Ann asked.

"She doesn't like the dress," Peaches said. "It's not her dream wedding gown."

"But, what's wrong with it? I made it exactly to—"

"To her mother's specifications," Peaches said. "That's the problem. Bella doesn't like the dress, but her mother insists that she wear something conventional. She was the one who gave us a description of what she wanted. But this is the gown Bella really wants."

Peaches handed the photo to Margaret-Ann.

"But I've already made this dress. I remember it well."

"Yes, so does Bella. It's the gown she wants."

"Oh, dear. What do we do now?"

Peaches paced the floor again. "Bella, will you have a separate wedding feast before the wedding? Isn't that a custom here?"

Bella nodded. "The week before the wedding, the two families get together for a wedding feast, but normally, we wear traditional Portuguese clothing. They look more like costumes. I can't stand them, but I have to do what my parents want."

"Oh," Peaches said, and began her pacing again.

"Knock, knock," Lily called from the doorway. "May I come in? Oh, Bella," she said as she walked around the young bride. "You look beautiful."

A tear rolled down the young girl's cheek.

"We have a bit of a problem," Peaches said. "She doesn't like the dress."

"But didn't she pick it out herself?"

Peaches put her finger to her lips.

Lily got the message instantly. "Well, then, we must think of a solution to the problem, right? Does she have another in mind?"

Peaches handed her the photo.

"Oh," Lily said, "I remember this one."

Margaret-Ann chimed in. "You know, Bella, this dress could be slightly altered to become a brand new gown. It would keep the long tulle skirt and train, but we could modify the strapless top with long sleeves and a higher neckline. I think it would be stunning. Instead of the peach color, we could use your baby blue trim. I think I could make something you'd love."

"That's an excellent idea," Peaches said, and stood beside Bella. "What do you think? Should we go for it?"

Bella shook her head. "I don't think Father will pay for two dresses, especially against Mother's wishes. He'd never go against her. In our country, the bride wears the same gown for the wedding and the reception afterwards. My parents will both expect me to wear this dress."

"Peaches," Margaret-Ann said, and moved closer to her. She whispered in her ear. "What about the runway show? Could she be a model? At least she'd be able to wear the dress."

Peaches smiled. "Lily, will you get in touch with Marietta on your gadget there?"

Lily tapped her iPad and soon the phone at the royal palace was ringing. "Alberto, this is Lily. Is Marietta available to speak with me?" She nodded at Peaches. "Oh, hello Marietta. How are you today?" I need your advice on something if you have a moment. Here's the problem," Lily said.

Peaches opened her mouth. "No," she mouthed.

Lily held up a hand. "It seems that Peaches needs another model for her runway show next month. Bella is here for her fitting, and we wondered if there's any chance that she could model a design for Peaches." Lily listened. "Yes, that's right. Peaches and I just wondered. She would have to rehearse and wear one of the new wedding gowns, but other than that, it's a safe and easy job. Since you're coming to the show yourself, you could watch her." Lily frowned.

Bella spoke up. "Mama, please. I'd love to do it. Imagine being a model for Peaches Malone. It's—" Bella lowered her head. "Yes, Mother, I know. We are not working class."

"Marietta," Peaches said. "I'd consider this a personal favor. I'm without a model for this very special gown. Bella would not be paid. She would simply be volunteering her services for a worthy cause. This is a charity show, Marietta, my very first in Portugal. The proceeds from the entrance fees will all go to the AOC organization. I know it's one of your favorites. Or if you want, you can choose another."

Peaches glanced at Margaret-Ann, whose mouth gaped open, and at Lily, who had a look of shock on her face.

"Yes, that's right. Charity." For the first time, Peaches saw Bella smile. "For the abandoned babies, Mama," she said into the phone. "Just think how much money Peaches could raise for them." There was silence on the other end of the phone. Suddenly, tears streamed down Bella's face.

Peaches glanced at Lily and Margaret-Ann. Three pairs of shoulders slumped.

"Thank you, Mama. Thank you so much," Bella said, and sat up a little straighter. "I'll represent all of Portugal with pride and dignity. And yes, I'll tell her."

Lily ended the call by tapping a button.

Margaret-Ann leaned in close to Peaches and whispered, "You'll be losing a lot of money, dear. We're sending out five hundred invitations, and at two hundred dollars for admission...."

Peaches patted her on the arm. "We'll be fine," she said. "I've never done anything like this before, but it felt right."

"My mother wanted me to tell you that your donation to AOC—that's Abandoned or Orphaned Children—might just save hundreds of babies from dying, and that you're doing a good and noble thing."

"How is that?" Lily asked.

"My mother is head of this charity. It's designed to help babies who've been abandoned in baby hatches all over Portugal."

"Baby hatches?" Peaches asked.

Bella nodded. "Many babies are abandoned every year. Most of them are put in boxes or baby hatches in local clinics and churches. The weight of the baby sets off a bell so that the workers will know to come and get the child. Then, they're taken in and often raised by a staff member or a church group. Some are adopted out to good homes. Some aren't, but they are safe and protected. Otherwise, they would have been killed."

Peaches sat down. "I had no idea," she said, and rubbed her forehead.

Margaret-Ann moved next to her and hugged her. "You can help them, Peaches. That's what counts. Today counts, not what happened ages ago. This is your second chance, and I think it might be one more reason why we are here in Portugal."

Chapter 42

Toward nightfall, around eight-thirty, Peaches walked out to the enclosed cabana and took her favorite seat, the sofa placed just right to allow her a magnificent view of the ocean. With Lily away at the royal palace and Margaret-Ann and Janet enjoying one of Clara's home-cooked Portuguese dishes and special desserts, Peaches finally had some alone time. She opened her container of yogurt, sprinkled a few strawberries in it, and took a big bite. The yogurt was tangy and tart, the strawberries sweet and luscious.

Given to bouts of stomach trouble, Peaches knew the heavy Portuguese food wouldn't agree with her after today's emotional meeting with Bella. But the yogurt was the balm she needed. She'd eaten it for years to keep her problems at bay. It never made her stomach cramp until it bent her double, never caused any sort of pain, and never gave her indigestion. The true Greek yogurt that the prime minister had given her not only left her free of pain, but also seemed to calm her.

When she'd finished the last of it, she sipped some water and leaned her head back on the plush, brightly colored sofa cushion. She closed her eyes and listened to the waves crashing against the craggy cliffs below. She inhaled then exhaled. Inhaled then exhaled.

For an instant, she thought she heard footsteps nearby and remembered that she was not to be alone. But she felt no fear, and her need for solitude outweighed the need for safety at the moment. Besides, who could see her tucked away inside this cabana? It was enclosed on three sides and left only the front open. A heavy curtain could be drawn over it for total privacy.

So, she settled back and savored the sounds of the water and the solitude of the moment. But when she heard the footsteps again, she felt a vague sense of alarm.

"Don't be afraid, Peaches. It's just me," he said.

She wanted to jump up and throw her arms around him, but instead, she barely opened her eyes and said, "I'm not afraid of you, TuckerD, but I am quite angry at you."

"May I sit down?" he asked.

Peaches opened her eyes and stared at him. He'd changed. He wore modern clothing, an expensive suit, white shirt, and tie. Gone were the blue frock coat and the lacy cuffs of his shirt.

"I liked your other clothes better," she said. "You don't look like my TuckerD."

"I'm trying to blend in."

"Hmph," she said, thinking that no matter what he wore, women would fall all over themselves for him, this giant of a man with the face of a Greek god and the physique of an Olympic champion. And those shoulders. Dear me, those shoulders!

"Please, may I sit with you?"

Peaches sat up and glared at him. "You think you can just waltz back into my life after all these months of no contact, and I'll just say, 'Sure, sit beside me. Then do what you always do. Leave.'" She folded her arms across her chest.

"Am I mistaken," he asked, "or was it you who moved away?"

"Don't be smart with me, TuckerD. I had no way to contact you, no address, no phone...don't you think that's a bit strange? If you'd wanted to stay in touch, you'd have given me a way to contact you."

"Please, may I sit?"

Peaches nodded.

He sat down beside her and ran his hand along her cheek. "I've missed you so, Peaches."

"I'd never have known it, TuckerD. You didn't care enough to try to get in touch with me." She ran her fingers through her hair and frowned.

"Ah, now you're wrong there."

"Really?" she said, and removed his hand from her cheek.

"I sent you gifts, my dear, to let you know I was thinking about you."

Peaches thought for a moment. "The roses and seeds," she said.

TuckerD nodded. "And?" he asked.

Peaches smiled. "My Galahad, the most magnificent horse I've ever seen...and the smartest. But why didn't you deliver them yourself?"

"I was working," he said, and ran a hand across his black and gold hair.

Peaches reached out and touched the long fall of his hair down his back. "It feels like silk," she said. "It's softer than anything I've ever felt."

"Nothing about me can compare to your beauty, Peaches. It radiates around you like the sun." He put his lips lightly to hers. Her skin tingled where he kissed her, and she felt herself relax, her anger floating away on the breeze. Then he kissed her full on the lips. "I've missed you," he whispered against her lips as his hands traveled up and down her back. He kissed her again and again, then pulled her onto his lap. "Will you have me, Peaches? Will you show me how to give myself to you?"

She got up off his lap and pulled the heavy curtains closed, then secured them on each side so that no one could enter. As she walked, she removed her long nightshirt to reveal that she wore nothing underneath. She stood naked in front of him.

TuckerD towered over her when he stood. "You are the most

beautiful woman I've ever seen," he said, and touched her cheek.

"Take off your clothes," she said. "Let me look at you."

Piece by piece the clothes came off.

"My magnificent TuckerD," she said. She walked around him. "You have two scars on your back up by your shoulders."

TuckerD nodded.

"Were you beaten? What sorts of scars are they?"

"It's been so many years ago," he said. "Nothing for you to worry about."

When she was standing in front of him again, she reached up to put her arms around his neck.

"Will you have me, Peaches?" he asked. "Will you?"

She sat on the sofa and patted a spot next to her. He sat and pulled her into his lap as if she weighed nothing, and kissed her neck ever so gently. With only one kiss, the two of them were carried away. They gave of themselves with an almost violent passion. Afterwards, after the crying out, the sounds of exquisite satisfaction, Peaches slipped out of his lap and lay on her side on the sofa. TuckerD scrunched in beside her, covered them both with a blanket, and began to hum.

"What is that song?" Peaches asked in a sleepy voice.

"An Irish ballad called, 'I'll Love You Every Time.'"

"Rest now, TuckerD."

He moved and kissed her neck. "I don't want to rest, my dearest. Time moves so quickly. I don't want to waste a second of it."

He turned her over gently. Before she could respond, they were rocking and swaying to each other's rhythms. And afterwards, each time TuckerD touched her, it led to more lovemaking, time after time, each more intense than the last.

"Peaches," he whispered. "Peaches."

Hours later, when she woke from an exhausted sleep, she reached for him beside her on the sofa. He was gone. As her anger and hurt grew at a fever pitch, she put her nightshirt back on and then heard a voice.

"Care for some yogurt with strawberries?" he asked. "It's almost morning."

"Oh, you!" she said. "I thought you'd disappeared again."

TuckerD smiled at her. "Peaches," he said. "I don't leave because I want to. I leave because I have to. My time is not my own. If it were, I'd never leave your side. I know how hard you work at your designs and the weddings. You know all about time constraints, yes?"

She nodded and took a bit of yogurt. "Are you in the Mafia? Is that it?"

He chuckled as he told her no. "Nothing like that," he said. "The company is global, and right now, I'm an integral part of it. I've some work yet to do, but then I'm certain I'll be granted the leave of absence."

"Leave of absence?"

TuckerD nodded. "I'd like to spend some time with you here."

Peaches put down her yogurt and kissed him on the cheek. "Really? You're taking a leave of absence?"

"Yes," he said.

"TuckerD, couldn't you just get another job? I mean, surely, you're not bound to one job forever. If it's money, you could model for me. I'd pay you well," she said, and winked.

He sat back on the sofa and hugged her close to him. "I don't need your money, Peaches. I've plenty of my own. And besides, I don't need much money where I live."

Peaches snuggled against him. "Then quit," she said. "Quit your job and come work for me."

"I can't quit permanently, my love, but I'm looking forward to the leave."

"May I change the subject for a moment?" she asked, and sat up.

TuckerD nodded.

"I'd like to know a little more about that lace, the lace on the shirt you wear with your frock coat."

"Ah," he said. "It was a gift, a family heirloom passed down to the oldest son. That's me." TuckerD sat forward, his elbows on his knees.

"You don't know where it came from?"

He shook his head. "All I know is that it's been in my family since…well, since before my great great grandmother was born. It passed down from generation to generation until a little while ago, when it was gifted to me."

"But Alberto told me that no other lace pattern like that was made. It was forbidden because it was for a king."

"I can't answer your question, Peaches. It is an inheritance that I treasure. But the woman who made that lace is long gone, and she kept no records of its creation. But I might ask her the next time I…."

Peaches's eyes widened.

TuckerD chuckled.

"You were going to say the next time you saw her? But how is that possible?"

"I do a lot of meditating," he said softly. "Sometimes, in deep meditation, I feel as if…well, let's put it this way. Deep meditation sort of takes me out of this world and into another. That's the best I can do, Peaches."

"I see," she said.

TuckerD stood and dressed. "Now, give me a nice kiss, please, my lovely one," he said as he straightened his tie. "I must go for a short time, but remember what I said. I've been approved for a leave of absence so that I can be here with you."

Peaches stood on her tiptoes and kissed him goodbye.

"I love you, Peaches," he said. "With whatever sort of heart I have, I love you with all of it."

Peaches bent to get her pen and napkin, and when she stood again, TuckerD was gone.

Chapter 43

"Don't say a word," Peaches said to Lily as she quietly came back into the castle.

Lily chuckled. "Someone's been…uh…frolicking, I see. You've been gone all night. I can see the sun beginning to rise. Must have been quite the night."

Peaches put her hands on her hips. "I told you not to say anything."

"Sorry, babe. I couldn't resist. The woman standing in front of me is not Peaches Malone. She looks more like some bedraggled homeless person. Maybe I should call the security guards to check you out."

"Oh, you," Peaches said, and then she laughed out loud. "I'm sure I look a fright. I need to run upstairs and do a makeover before Margaret-Ann sees me. She's usually up by 5:30 or 6, so I don't have much time."

"No worries. I haven't heard a peep out of her or Janet. If you hurry, you can…uh…straighten up, and then come back down here and fill me in on all the details." Lily winked.

Peaches ran up the stairs as fast as her tired legs could carry her, and ducked into her room. Thirty-five minutes later, she appeared at the top of the stairs wearing jeans and a silk blouse, her hair and makeup perfect.

"I think you've just beaten your own record for quick-change," Lily called up to her.

When Peaches took a seat next to Lily, she let out a breath.

"Tell me everything," Lily said. "Spare no details."

"Well, it all started with yogurt and strawberries," Peaches said. "I was eating, and then there he was in the cabana. I was furious at him."

Lily arched an eyebrow.

"At first," Peaches said. "Then we talked a long time, and one thing led to another, and somehow we ended up naked."

"How do you figure that happened?" Lily said, and chuckled.

"He's magnificent, Lily, like no other man I've ever seen. He's a giant, a massive man, tanned and built like a tank. His shoulders are so broad I can't reach around them. His chest is full, and yep, he has a six-pack. Visually, he's stunning, except for those scars."

"What scars?"

"On each shoulder blade, he has a really big scar. Whatever caused it must have been painful."

"Did you ask him about it?"

"He said it was long ago and nothing for me to worry about."

"Hmm," Lily said.

"And that ponytail. Black and gold striped hair worn in a long ponytail. You'd think it would be off-putting, but it's soft and silky."

"The man has a ponytail?"

"Oh, that's right," Peaches said. "You've never seen him, have you?"

"I've never had that pleasure."

"When he comes back, I'll introduce you to him."

"Promise?"

"I swear I will. I want you to see him for yourself."

"So, what is he doing in Portugal? Did he come all this way just to see you?"

Peaches poured some coffee from the pot on the table and added a dash of cream and sugar. "I'm not sure. He said he had work to do here."

"Well," Lily said as she refilled her own cup, "how convenient is that?"

"Oh, I know you hate him, but—"

"How could I hate him when I've never even met him? I don't hate him, Peaches. I hate what he does to you. When he's gone, which is 99% of the time, you mourn him, you grieve for him," she said, and took a sip of her coffee. "He disappears for months on end and you have no idea where he is. That's not good. No matter *who* he really is—and we don't know for sure just *who* he is—he's using you, and I hate that."

"And you think I should—"

"You should dump him immediately. Find a normal person who will be around when you need him, or just when you want him. What good is TuckerD to you if you only see him once every few months? That's not a relationship, Peaches."

"I love him, Lily."

Lily took another sip of coffee. "When you meet a man who will treat you right, you can begin to un-love him. I'm not trying to tear you away from your true love. I'm just trying to make you see reason," she said, and leaned forward. "This man is not a man you can trust or depend on for anything. He shows up when and where he pleases. He leaves just as quickly, and then you don't see him again for months. Doesn't it make you furious?"

"I'm furious until I see him or until he touches my cheek. Then, I'm like wet noodle," Peaches said, and grabbed a scone filled with strawberries. "We have some sort of special connection. I can't explain it, but I just feel as if he and I will be together forever. Does that sound strange?"

"I felt the same way about Anthony in the beginning. We had a special bond that only people in love can have, and I was certain we'd always be each other's one and only love. Then, poof. He found another true love and vanished."

Peaches got up and hugged her friend. "I'm so sorry, Lily. I know how it hurt you."

"Well, my point is that everyone who falls in love thinks their love is special and that it will last forever. But, it doesn't, Peaches. It just doesn't. Not for many people. For some, yes. But for most, no. It doesn't last. Just look at the divorce rate."

Peaches sat back, sipped her coffee, and took a bite of her scone. "Carla's a good cook," she said. "Have you had one of these?"

Lily smiled. "I've had two already."

Peaches chuckled. "TuckerD fed me yogurt with strawberries this morning, so I don't know why I'm hungry."

"He fed you yogurt?"

Peaches nodded. "I thought he'd disappeared again, but he came walking in with a carton of yogurt with strawberries on top."

"Okay," Lily said. "A point in his favor then."

"How many does he need to get your approval?"

"You'll be able to tell just by the smile on my face."

"It was the most glorious night of my life, Lily. I've never felt such passion. And at my age! But he makes me feel young and sexy, vibrant and alive."

Lily sighed. "Well, that's something, at least—two points then."

Peaches took the last bite of her scone, wiping the dripping strawberry juice from her fingers. "I won't let him go, Lily. I can't. Not now. Not ever, if I have my way."

Adona, who'd grown considerably in the last months, jumped up on the sofa and whined.

"There you are, my pet," Peaches said, and rubbed the dog's silky coat. "Coming after a scone, eh?" Peaches picked up the last scone and broke off a bite of it. "Here ya go," she said. "Now, hop down off the leather sofa. You might tear it."

Adona hopped down, but sat at Peaches' feet and whined.

"Do you think I've spoiled her?" she asked Lily.

Lily laughed out loud. "That dog has it made," she said. "She sleeps on your bed. She eats whatever you eat. She watches you like a hawk, and she stands outside the bathroom when you shower. Oh, and lest we forget, she won't let anyone she doesn't know get within shouting distance of you. So, yes, she's spoiled, but in a good way. She's quite the little guardian."

Peaches rubbed Adona's head. "You're a good girl. Yes, you are," she said. "One of these days, I might need a guardian."

Chapter 44

Lily finished her coffee. "Can we talk about something else besides your love life and your dog? I have some business news."

Peaches wiped her hands and scooted back on the sofa, Adona still at her feet. "I'm all ears," she said.

"We have an offer on the apartment and the studio," Lily said as she rifled through some papers. "You had the price for both listed at $900,000."

"It's a prime location," Peaches said, "in the heart of downtown Atlanta."

"Yes, I know that, but you didn't tell me that you'd had the studio and the apartment renovated."

"What are you talking about?" Peaches asked with a frown. "I haven't done anything to the apartment, and the only thing I know about the studio is that the windows were fixed after the robbery."

Lily handed her five photographs. "Take a look."

Peaches thumbed through each photograph, a questioning look on her face. "I don't get it. Whose place is this?"

"Yours," Lily said. "The entire complex has been completely renovated. The apartment and the studio and the workshop all look brand new. If I'd known, I'd have made a different starting price."

"But who did this?"

Lily shrugged. "I thought you'd hired someone to do it, but I wondered why you didn't mention it."

"Who took these photos?"

"The security guard, of course. My firm contacted him and asked him for photos."

Peaches leaned forward toward Lily. "He must have photographed the wrong place, then, because I've done nothing to it. I haven't even been there for months."

"No, it's the right place. He has a key and he checks front to back every day, Peaches."

"It's just not possible."

"Possible or not, we have a sound offer on the table."

"From whom?"

Lily shifted her place on the sofa. "That's the only catch. I have a name and a credit check, but I don't know the buyer personally. My firm investigated but found nothing suspicious about him. He has the money, and apparently, he's a well-known realtor in the area. He's trying to buy up the whole block bit by bit, starting with your place."

Peaches stood up and opened the door. "There ya go, my sweet Adona. Go find Javier and have a good run."

Adona dashed out the door.

Peaches folded her arms across her chest and sighed.

"What's wrong?" Lily asked.

"Nothing, really. It's just that something about all of this doesn't feel right. I don't know who renovated the place. Who would do that? And I don't have a clue about the potential buyer. It worries me, that's all."

"Wanna hear the offer?"

Peaches looked at her and then turned away and stared out the window. "Go ahead," she said.

"The man has offered $1.5 million."

"What?"

"The only catch," Lily said, and got up off the sofa, "is that he wants a quick close. Thirty days." She handed the paperwork to Peaches. "It's all there in black and white. $1.5 million with a thirty-day close."

"But what about inspections? Titles? How can we do that in thirty days?"

Lily waved a hand. "No problem. Read the papers. He's a well-to-do realtor. He doesn't want an inspection. He's seen the property twice, hasn't asked about anything it except whether or not he could close out quickly. Seems he has other business offers to make if he's going to buy up the block."

"And why would he want the whole block?"

"He says he wants to own some of the historic places in downtown. He plans to buy them one at a time until he owns all the historic homes on that block."

Peaches turned toward Lily. "If he'll go to $1.8, I'll sign."

Lily shook her head. "I don't think he'll go for it. He's already given you well over the asking price."

"Tell him I'm having second thoughts, thinking of moving back. Just make up something."

"Believe it or not, Peaches, I know how to negotiate. All I can do is tell my firm about your counter offer, but I warn you now. The man has offered you $600,000 over asking. I doubt he'll go any higher."

"I have faith in you. If he goes for the deal, I'll sign it quickly. If not, then maybe there will be another buyer."

Lily walked to where Peaches stood at the window. "What's all of this about? You're turning down that much money? Why?"

"With that extra money, I can build a domed wedding venue for indoor weddings. That's my big dream, Lily, and I can see to it that Margaret-Ann will be covered in case anything happens to me. The profit from this sale will go directly to the prime minister for safe keeping."

"It's all profit, Peaches. You owe nothing on the studio or the apartment, and you've paid cash for this gorgeous castle."

Peaches shrugged. "That's my final word, Lily. If he agrees

to it, then —"

"Fine," Lily said in a huff. "I'll call the office. But I think you're making a big mistake, just for the record."

For some reason that she couldn't understand, Peaches smiled.

Thirty minutes later, she smiled even bigger as Lily told her the news. The buyer had agreed to her price.

Chapter 45

Around five that afternoon, Margaret-Ann walked into the informal living room. "Well?" she asked. "How do I look?"

"Margaret-Ann," Lily said, "you are absolutely stunning. Careful now, or the prime minister might set his sights on you."

Margaret-Ann laughed. "Oh, don't be silly. He has his beautiful Marietta. What would he want with an old woman like me?"

"This must be a magic castle," Lily said. "The longer I stay, the younger you look. Honestly, Margaret-Ann, you're beautiful. That blue dress highlights your hair and eyes. The length is perfect—not dragging the floor, but just right at your heels. And those see-thru lace sleeves are very flattering, my dear."

"Don't forget about the brooch Marietta gave her," Peaches said. "Even though it's encrusted with rubies, it's perfect with your dress and those heels. I've never seen you wear them before, and if I'm not mistaken, those are Louboutin, right? The signature red sole matches the rubies exactly."

"I splurged," Margaret-Ann said. "Marietta said I needed a beautiful pair of heels. She picked these out for me. I've never spent that much money on a pair of shoes before."

"The purchase was well worth it," Lily said. "They will go with anything."

"You two look gorgeous," Margaret-Ann said. "I see that Peaches is wearing blue, too. How nice the dress looks with your tiara, and Lily, you're all decked out in emerald green. It's a lovely gown."

"We're planning to take the palace by storm," Lily said, and laughed.

"I think we can take it just by beauty alone," Margaret-Ann said, and patted her hair. "I can't wait to see Bella again. She's such a beautiful young girl. I do hope we can work out some arrangement about the dresses. Marietta has already given her approval for the runway show, right?"

"Yes, but it's the prime minister's approval that we need," Peaches said, and glanced at herself in the ornate mirror just beyond her. "I hope we can get that tonight. The runway show is only two months away. There's so much to do."

"What time will Alberto be here?" Margaret-Ann asked.

"He said about 5:30, so we don't have long to wait."

A rapping on the door startled them.

"Is that Alberto already?" Margaret-Ann asked.

Lily opened the door.

"I need to speak to Miss Peaches," Javier said.

"Javier," Peaches said. "What's wrong? You seem out of breath."

"Please step outside if you will."

Peaches followed Javier outside only to see Galahad standing in the center of the driveway.

"Galahad, my love," she said, and reached up to touch the tip of his muzzle. "Now, what are you doing in the driveway?"

"I apologize, Miss Peaches," Javier said. "He broke away from me before I knew what was happening, and he ran like wildfire up here."

"Is something wrong?" Lily called from the doorway, Margaret-Ann close beside her.

"Lily, something is wrong with Galahad," Peaches said and reached up again, but this time, Galahad bent his head and pushed her backwards. Then he pushed her again so hard that she fell off the driveway and into the small front garden. She cried out when she landed on her backside in the mulched garden. She'd fallen on a decorative stone, and as she did, she heard a rip.

"My dress!" she cried. "My dress! Galahad, what is wrong with you?"

The horse reared and snorted, but he would not move away from Peaches.

Javier pulled at the reins and tried to get the great horse to move, but it was no use. The animal would not budge.

"I'm sorry," Javier said. "I can't seem to move him." Javier turned and yelled for his brother and father. "Maximo, Papa, come quickly." Then he turned back to Peaches. "Here, let me help you up," he said.

But Galahad reared up again, backing Javier away from Peaches.

"What's gotten into you, Galahad?" Peaches asked. "Just look what he did to my new gown. Enough now, enough."

"It might have been the man," Javier said. "That's all I can think of."

"What man?" Peaches said. "Just look at my dress! My new dress."

"The one in the blue frock coat. I saw him earlier talking to Galahad."

Javier held out a hand to help Peaches out of the garden, but once again, Galahad reared and drove him away.

"TuckerD," she muttered. "Galahad, move away so that I can get up, please," Peaches said to him in a firm voice. "Move away."

Instead, Galahad moved even closer to her, his head lowered in front of her. Just then, Peaches heard a sound that made her heart race: squealing tires. She looked up as a small black car sped through the circular driveway. Her heart skipped a beat. Her hands shook worse than ever.

Two gunshots rang out.

Peaches screamed.

Then the car burned rubber and sped away. Only a few seconds later, a second car sped out of the driveway in pursuit.

"Call the police!" Peaches cried. "Is anyone hurt?"

Lily checked Margaret-Ann, then raced to where Peaches sat in the garden. "Galahad's been hit, Peaches. He's bleeding."

"Javier!" Peaches yelled. "Galahad's been shot."

"Did you see anyone, Peaches?" Lily asked. "Could you see who was driving?"

Peaches shook her head. "I didn't see anything. It happened so fast. Margaret-Ann, are you okay?" she called. "Is everyone okay?"

"Only Galahad was hit," Lily said. "But there were two shots. We need to find that other bullet."

"Lily," Peaches said as a trickle of blood oozed onto her shoulder. "My head."

"Oh my God, Peaches. Margaret-Ann, I need a piece of cloth," she yelled, but by the time the words came from her mouth, the entire staff had gathered.

Maximo was seeing to Galahad. Carla had a handful of small towels, and Javier placed himself next to Peaches.

"Miss Peaches," he said. "Please allow me to escort you inside."

"Is everyone all right, Javier? Was anyone hurt?"

"Just you and Galahad. He saved your life by pushing you out of the way."

Peaches smiled. "He's a good boy, my Galahad." Peaches leaned on Javier as he helped her, and she took a step forward. "I can't seem to get my balance," she said. "Maybe it's the shoes."

Javier scooped her up into his arms and carried her into the castle, depositing her gently on the sofa. He removed her shoes and helped her find a comfortable spot.

"Thank you," Peaches said, her voice a bit hoarse. "What about your father and Carla? Are they safe?"

248

"They are fine, Miss Peaches. My father and Maximo are taking care of Galahad. Carla is tending to your mother."

"How is Galahad? How bad is his wound?"

"Not too bad," Javier said. "Maximo says he'll be just fine in a few days."

Peaches sighed. "Tell Maximo I appreciate him."

Javier nodded.

"I'm fine now, too," Margaret-Ann called from across the room. "Just my nerves got the best of me, but Carla gave me some tea that calmed me down."

"Lily?"

"I'm right here, Peaches," she said. "The prime minister and Marietta are on their way."

Javier examined the wound on Peaches' head. "It's minor," he said, "just above the ear. The skin is broken, but it's not a deep wound and should heal in a few days. This bandage will keep it from bleeding, but...."

"But what?"

"I might need to cut your hair so that I can put medication and a bandage on it."

"No," Peaches said. "Do not put scissors to my hair, Javier. Do the best you can. If it's only a minor wound, it will heal just fine."

After a few minutes of applying ointment and struggling to get a bandage in place, Javier stood up. "I think that will be sufficient."

"Javier, will you call the rest of the staff together as quickly as possible?"

Javier cocked his head. "All of the staff?"

"Yes, please. And the extra workers, too, if you don't mind."

Peaches let her head fall back onto the soft cushions of the sofa. When Adona clamored into her lap, she ran her fingers through the dog's silky fur. She patted the space beside her, and Adona curled up next to her.

249

"How are you feeling?" Lily asked. "Does it hurt terribly?"

Peaches turned her head, winced, and then smiled. "I'm okay," she said. "I think it's the shock of it more than anything else. Someone tried to kill me, right?"

Lily put a hand on Peaches' arm. "That was a close call," she said.

"Is there any blood on this gown?" Peaches responded, tears running down her cheeks. "I don't know why I'm worrying about a little blood when the thing is almost ripped in half."

Lily got up and looked at the top of the gown. "Just a smidge on the shoulder."

"I can get it out. Don't you worry, Peaches," Margaret-Ann called. "I've a solution that will get out anything. And I'll fix that beautiful gown for you. The most important thing is getting that wound looked after."

"Someone tried to kill me, Lily."

And at that, Peaches burst into tears. Adona whined in sympathy.

Chapter 46

Peaches calmed herself and got up off the sofa. The wound made her head throb, but she ignored that pain. There was work to do.

"How dare he?" she said to Lily as she paced the floor. "How dare he come to my home and try to destroy me."

"You don't even know who it was, Peaches," Lily said as she straightened the cushions.

"No, I don't, but I will. I will find whoever was responsible for this outrage and put him behind bars."

"Peaches, please sit down. You have a head wound. It's not healthy for you to be pacing in such a state. You need to rest to give your body time to heal."

"Rest?" she said as she paced, the hem of her tattered gown dragging along behind her. "You think I can rest? Someone tried to kill me, Lily. How can I sit back and do nothing?"

When the doors opened, Alberto rushed to her. "Oh, Miss Peaches," he said, and hugged her. "We came as soon as we heard."

The prime minister and Marietta stood in the doorway. "Ahem," said the prime minister.

"Oh, forgive me," Alberto said.

The prime minister dismissed him with a wave of his hand.

"Paulo, Marietta," Peaches said. "Please, come in."

"We have the shooter in custody, Peaches. He is a member of

one of Etienne's gangs, but he is safely locked away."

"Etienne's gang? How did you get him so fast?"

"Special forces," he said, but didn't elaborate. "Fear not. You will be protected around the clock against any sort of event like this. It simply will not happen."

Peaches nodded.

"I've brought the palace doctor and the veterinarian to see about you and Galahad, Peaches. Kindly allow the doctor to examine your wound."

"It's nothing, really," Peaches insisted.

Marietta took her by the arm. "Come, dear. Sit down and let the doctor make sure there's no room for infection. You can never be too careful."

Peaches sighed but sat on the sofa. "No cutting my hair, please," she said.

After the doctor had finished examining and re-dressing the wound, he gave her three shots. "One to stave off infection; the other to keep inflammation down, and the last for pain," he said to her in a thick accent.

"Thank you," she said, though the wound now throbbed even worse.

"I would advise a day's rest at least," the doctor said. "Complete rest."

"And you have witnesses," Lily said. "Margaret-Ann and I have heard the doctor's orders. You and Adona can rest on the sofa for the remainder of the day."

"Too much movement will reopen the wound," the doctor said. "It must stay closed in order to heal. Is that understood?" The doctor gently laid a hand on her arm and spoke in a softer tone. "I am only a physician, Miss Peaches. I cannot tell you what to do. I can only advise to the best of my ability."

"It's very painful," she said, and touched the side of her head.

"If you consider bed rest for just a little while, the medicines will do their job and you will feel relief."

Peaches looked at him but said nothing.

"Trust me," he said. "The medicines will help the pain, and I have brought the prescriptions with me so that they may be administered as directed."

Lily held out her hand. "I'll put them in the cabinet," she said.

"Marietta," Paulo said, "I think it would be appropriate for the ladies to change into something more comfortable. Do you agree? I have much business to attend to before I can sit and talk."

Marietta nodded. "Come on, Peaches, let's get you out of that gown. Lily, Margaret-Ann? As you can see, I'm not dressed for a formal occasion, so please change into something more informal. Paulo and I have brought a wonderful dinner for later. Come, Alberto."

Alberto took Peaches' arm and held it snuggly against him. "Lean on me if you need to," he said.

Peaches smiled. "Thank you, Alberto, but I'm perfectly fine."

***

Below them, the prime minister gathered the staff and summoned them all outside, each one walking with their heads bowed in honor of him.

"Raise your heads," he said. "We have much work to do, and I will need your help."

Once they were outside, Javier spoke, his back straight, his head held high. "May I speak, Excellency?"

The prime minister nodded. "Speak your peace, Javier."

Javier laid a hand on his father's arm and then nodded to Maximo. "Are we all to be terminated, Excellency?"

"Terminated?"

"Yes, Excellency," Javier said. "Will we all lose our jobs here? We failed to protect the lady of the castle."

"No one will lose a job, Javier," the prime minister said, and stepped closer to him. "What happened today could not have been foreseen. But, in order to ensure that it never happens again, you must all agree," he waved his hand over the gathered staff, "to help me and the security team to make the castle safer. Does everyone agree?"

A collective "Yes, sir," sounded from the staff.

"We will do whatever you wish of us, Excellency," Javier said.

The prime minster stepped back. "Very good," he said. "Now, on to our business." As he spoke, a large truck pulled into the driveway. "Ah, sooner than I expected. That's good. Javier, you and Maximo will see to it that these gates will be managed, patrolled, and maintained at all times. It will take some time to get them installed, and there will be a code to be entered in order to come in, but they are to be kept locked and patrolled at all times. Is that clear?"

"Yes, Excellency."

"There will be no more opportunity for anyone to speed through this driveway. Two other gates will be installed as well. One will be outside the studio where it enters the house. A larger one will be installed at the side of the house so that no one will have access to the back lot and the fields without a code."

Javier nodded. "And who will have the codes, sir?"

"Only four people. You, Maximo, Alberto, and myself."

"And Miss Peaches, of course," Javier said.

The prime minister gave him a cold stare.

Javier shook his head. "Oh, Excellency, forgive me, but surely you cannot mean that Miss Peaches won't have the code to her own castle!"

"That is exactly what I mean, Javier. Miss Peaches is to be accompanied at all times. If she is with Lily and her mother, then someone from the team must accompany them. If she leaves the property, someone must be with her. And if she's here, then again, someone must be vigilant. I've taken the liberty of assigning that task to you, Javier."

"Me? Oh, no. Miss Peaches barely tolerates me," Javier said, and ran his hand through his thick black hair. "She won't be pleased. She won't be happy about this at all."

"Javier, you are well suited for this job. You have plenty of military background, and you know the household well."

"Miss Peaches will complain, Excellency. She is going to be very upset."

"Then you will have to learn the fine art of discretion, Javier. I want her protected. Is that clear? Now, please ask Marietta if she is ready to go."

With that, the prime minister turned toward his car while Javier hung his head.

Chapter 47

In three days' time, the doctor announced that Peaches had fully recovered. She'd also learned that the prime minister was preparing the palace auditorium for the runway show, the date of which had been changed to three months away. Marietta and Alberto had taken the liberty of creating and mailing four hundred invitations to royals and their families across the surrounding countries, and expected, according to the responses, a show of at least five hundred people.

Peaches and Margaret-Ann ruled the workshop and studio like task masters, working together to make sure that things ran smoothly. Peaches designed eight new gowns, and with the arrival of Janet LaRoche, Margaret-Ann felt a little less overwhelmed. Janet had proven herself a wonderful seamstress.

With ten gowns expected for the runway show, Peaches had work to do. The shop, by order of the prime minister, would remain closed to new customers until after the show. But best of all, Bella would be allowed to model the beautiful dress that her mother didn't approve of for her formal wedding. Instead, she would be allowed to wear it at the wedding feast the week before the wedding. Peaches didn't understand why Marietta had changed her mind about only traditional Portuguese dress being allowed, but as long as Bella was able to wear the dress, she was happy.

The last three days had brought changes to Castle Malone,

even though sometimes Peaches slipped and still called it Castle Alamenda. The truth was, she liked the old name better than the new one, and had even thought about having it changed back, but ditched the notion because she didn't want to seem ungrateful. Still, she had mentioned it to Marietta on several occasions and hoped by some miracle that it would happen.

Now, she looked up at the backlit sign at her castle's entrance. It read: Castle Alamenda. She'd had the new sign removed and the original put back in place. It took the workers only two hours to make the change. She held in her hand the box of new business cards. The slogan on each one read: *Peaches and Lace Studios at Castle Alamenda.*

Peaches smiled. "Much better," she mumbled.

She walked to the cabana, closed all the curtains, and sat on the sofa. She breathed in the calming solitude, then picked up her pen and a white napkin, along with the lap desk that Margaret-Ann had arranged to have designed. The white desk sported a pen holder, a small curved lamp, a square napkin holder, and a clip in the center to hold her white napkins in place.

At 4:00, there was not enough natural light at all, so Peaches turned on the small lamp on her lap desk. It shone a single bright beam onto the napkin, the napkin with the design of a very special wedding gown, the best she'd ever done. It was white satin and crepe, an A-line style, simple but elegant.

Like a queen, she thought.

A rounded neck and bodice in sheer white lace with peach colored mesh beneath and matching white long sheer sleeves completed the look. The front panel from bodice to floor was embroidered with a delicate design that mimicked lace. From just above her knees, the skirt bloomed out in peach colored tulle that fell to the floor. It would take months to do all the detail, but Peaches didn't care about that now. This design she would hide away. Eventually, Margaret-Ann would make it, but not for show and not for sale. A special dress for a special person. She had no idea who it was, but she had faith that time would reveal the answer.

She examined the design again, made a few changes, and began to draw the completed masterpiece on a fresh napkin. Absorbed in her work, she didn't hear the curtain open.

"Peaches," came the familiar voice.

Startled, she dropped her pen.

"I didn't mean to frighten you," he said.

"I hate the way you sneak up on me like that," she said, and reached to get her pen.

TuckerD lowered his head. "May I sit down?" he asked softly.

"I see you've again abandoned your blue frock coat and opted for the modern suit," she said, and put her napkin and pen away. "Now, I want you to listen carefully. I'm tired of staying hidden whenever you're around. If you want to go inside, that's fine." Peaches cocked her head and waited for his answer.

"All right," he said, "but only if we can have some private time. There is something I need to talk to you about."

As they stepped out of the cabana, Javier cocked his head.

"Javier, this is TuckerD," Peaches said. "Have no worries. He is safe. I want to introduce him to Lily."

"I will accompany you, yes?"

Peaches nodded.

When they walked through the doors, they found Lily on the sofa working on her laptop, and Margaret-Ann sitting in a chair not far away, her sewing in hand.

Peaches cleared her throat. "Margaret-Ann, you remember TuckerD, don't you?"

"Hello," she said, but her face didn't light up. "You look different in those clothes."

"Lily, this is TuckerD."

Lily got up and came to stand beside them. "Ah," she said, "the elusive TuckerD. It's nice to meet you, at last. Won't you sit and visit for a little while, or must you be going now?"

Peaches gave Lily a look.

Adona ran in and sat at Peaches' feet. "Adona, this is TuckerD. What do you think?"

Adona looked at him, cocked her head, and moved to sit beside him.

TuckerD knelt and rubbed the silky coat. "You are a beauty," he said softly. "And I hear you're quite a good guard dog."

Adona wagged her tail and gave a soft bark.

TuckerD reached into his pocket and drew out a dog treat. "Here ya go. You're a good girl, but you'd better eat in the kitchen. You don't want to get crumbs on the furniture."

Adona took her treat and ran to the kitchen.

Peaches' eyes widened. Margaret-Ann sucked in a breath, and Lily gaped with her mouth open.

"Did that dog just do what you told her to do?" Lily asked. "Peaches is usually the only person she listens to."

TuckerD shrugged. "I, uh, I've always had a way with animals," he said, and stood up.

"We could use your help right here at the castle," Lily said.

TuckerD smiled. "Unfortunately, I'm already employed, but should I have an opening, I'll consider it."

"What are you doing here in Portugal, TuckerD?" Margaret-Ann asked.

"Business matters," he said.

"Hmph," she replied. "That must be some company you work for to send you here so many miles away from Atlanta."

"Well," he said, "we're global, so I often travel."

"And what is the name of the company?" Lily said. "Perhaps I know of it. I do a lot of traveling in my job, as well."

"I don't think you'd know of it," he said. "May I sit for a moment, Peaches?"

Javier led him to an overstuffed leather chair. "Please," he said. "Make yourself comfortable."

"Thank you," he said, and gave a slight bow to Javier.

"Did you know that someone tried to kill Peaches?" Margaret-Ann said. "Too bad you weren't around for that."

"Yes, I have reliable contacts," he said. "But she and Galahad have recovered. I am thankful for that, and I see all the work that's going on to further ensure her safety. She has a good friend in the prime minister."

Margaret-Ann went back to her stitching.

"Did you know, TuckerD, that I can't find you listed anywhere on the Internet?" Lily said. "It's as if you don't exist."

"You've been searching the Internet for him?" Peaches said, and held out her arms. "Why on earth would you do that?"

"Habit," Lily said. "I have to check out clients and buyers all the time. It's what I do, remember?"

TuckerD stood up. "Well, I'd better be going now," he said.

"So soon?" Peaches asked.

Lily glared at him. "You're ignoring my statement, TuckerD?" Lily asked. "Can you explain why you're not listed anywhere?"

"Perhaps, Miss Lily, it is because I am of little importance."

"Or perhaps you're hiding a very dark secret," Lily said, her eyes locked on his. "You haven't even told us the name of the company yet."

TuckerD bent and kissed Peaches on the cheek. "I'm sorry, Lily," he said. "I'm not at liberty to divulge that information."

"Stay a while longer," Peaches said.

TuckerD shook his head. "I really must be going, but remember what I told you. I'll be back before you know it."

"And you'll model for me in the runway show?"

He smiled down at her. "If I can arrange it, I'll be here for the show. Trust me?"

Peaches nodded.

Just as he got to the door, TuckerD stopped and turned to face Margaret-Ann and Lily, who both glared at him and sat with their arms crossed over their chests.

"It was a pleasure to see you both," he said. "I look forward to speaking with you again soon." Then he snapped his fingers.

Peaches, Lily, Margaret-Ann, and Javier stood motionless. They didn't even blink their eyes. It was as if they'd frozen in place.

"I'm sorry, my love," he said, and kissed Peaches on the top of her head. "There are some things I just can't tell you right now, but I will be back very soon, and then, I will tell you anything you want to know. Just trust me, Peaches. Trust me."

He walked out of the doors and closed them behind him. Once outside, TuckerD snapped his fingers again.

Peaches blinked her eyes and looked around to get her bearings. Margaret-Ann sat working on her stitching. Lily stood by the sofa. Adona whimpered at the door, and Javier stood right beside her.

Peaches put her hand to her temple on the spot where she'd been wounded. The place was still a bit tender, and now it throbbed. *Work through the pain, girl, just work through the pain.*

She clapped her hands. "Okay, let's get to work. The runway show is fast approaching, so we have plenty to do. Where's Janet? Anyone seen her?"

"She's in the workshop," Margaret-Ann said, "sewing her little heart out."

"Am I the only one who feels a bit odd, like I've missed something? And Adona, why do you keep whimpering at the door?"

"I'll take her outside," Javier said.

"Lily, do you have a strange feeling?"

Lily nodded. "It's almost as if I fell asleep for a minute then woke up again. Odd."

"Margaret-Ann, you?"

She nodded. "Most unusual," she said.

"What's the last thing you remember?" Lily asked.

"I was out in the cabana working on a new design."

"Oh, good," Margaret-Ann said. "Be quick about it so that

we can get it made for the show."

"This one's special," she said. "It's not for the show. I'll just save it until I know the right time for it."

"Well," Margaret-Ann said, "we'd better get out there and help Janet."

As the two of them left, Lily called to them. "Remember, dinner at eight. Alberto will pick us up. I can't imagine why the prime minister wants us to be there again. But I guess we'll find out."

"I hope there's nothing wrong," Peaches said. "And I really hope that Bella hasn't changed her mind about her dresses. That would be disastrous."

"Okay, let's get back to work," Margaret-Ann said. "We've so much to do."

On their way to the workshop, Peaches turned to Margaret-Ann. "I can't get rid of this feeling that I missed something."

Margaret-Ann said and patted her arm. "It couldn't have been anything important or one of us would have remembered."

"I suppose you're right," Peaches said, convinced that something had happened that she just couldn't remember.

Chapter 48

TuckerD sat with his arms folded across his chest, a scowl on his face. He wore the executive three-piece suit instead of his blue frock coat.

His supervisor, Nathan, shook his head.

"I want to marry her if she'll have me. She has my heart, something I thought was impossible."

"It's unheard of, TuckerD, and you know it. Marriage to a mortal? Impossible."

Nathan got up and stood in front of his desk. "Unheard of," he said again. "And, I might add, impossible. Your heart is not yours to give away, nor is it available for anyone else."

TuckerD stood up. "But it's happened. Can't you see that? Maybe it's impossible. Maybe it's forbidden, but it's happened. I have fallen head over heels in love with Peaches Malone. I want her to be my wife."

"Romantic love has no place in your job, TuckerD," Nathan said, and rubbed his forehead. "You *must* understand that. You can no more marry than you can father a child. It won't happen, not now, not ever."

"You're wrong. I've given her my body and my heart."

"Your body? What are you talking about?"

TuckerD walked to the window and stared out. "You know what I'm talking about."

Nathan stepped beside him. "That's impossible," he said.

"You do not have the power to function that way. You're simply not capable."

"I am and I did," he said.

Nathan slumped into a chair. "Oh, God," he said. "What have you done, TuckerD? What have you done?"

For a long while, TuckerD stood in silence. "I had the most wonderful experience of my life," he said finally.

The man jumped up out of the chair, his face reddening. "Can you hear yourself?" he yelled, and waved his arms. "Can you hear your own words? What you want is impossible, and what you're doing is forbidden. Forbidden. Do you understand, or must I spell out the word for you?" Nathan shook his head.

"Please, Nathan," TuckerD said as he leaned on the desk. "If you allow me to marry her, I'll keep doing my job. I promise you that."

Nathan chuckled. "And what about Miss Malone? This is not about you, TuckerD. It's about her. What sorts of consequences can you foresee in stalling for a year? You can't just pick a person at random and say, "'Oh, well, we'll take her out of the prescribed timeline. No problem.'"

TuckerD banged a fist on Nathan's desk. "You can fix this, Nathan. I know you can. You've done it before. Why won't you do it for me?"

Nathan leaned back in his chair and said nothing for a few seconds. "And what, may I ask, will you offer in return?"

TuckerD stared down at him. "In return?" he asked.

"Yes. If I arrange for you to marry this woman, what will you offer us? What could you possibly offer us?"

Tucker D rubbed his forehead. "I've told you. Partial service during the year. Full service afterwards."

"You're telling me that when you're wrapped in the arms of your true love, you'll still answer the call if you hear it? And just how will you explain it to your wife?"

TuckerD shook his head. "I don't know, but I'll think of

something."

Nathan got up and stood at the window. "Remarkable views here," he said. "Come, see for yourself."

TuckerD walked to the window and stared out at the grand mountains, green with forest; the glittering lake beneath the bright blue sky, the cottony white clouds. "It's beautiful," he said.

"Does it make you homesick?"

TuckerD didn't answer.

"Take this, my friend," Nathan said, and handed him a short gold rod that glittered in the sun streaming in through the window.

"What is it?"

"Your passport, so to speak. It's powerful, so use it wisely. Keep it near you at all times, because unless you can touch this, you'll never survive."

"But I don't know how to use it."

"Yes, I know," Nathan said. "But that is something only you can discover."

"You want me to go now?"

"Go, my friend, and enjoy your life.

"Nathan," TuckerD said, "I—"

"Go," Nathan interrupted. "You're wasting time."

As TuckerD headed for the door, Nathan said, "Don't dare ignore the calls, TuckerD. Otherwise the deal is off. If I hear of even one person you've ignored, I'll have you back here so fast it will make your head spin. Understood?"

"Understood," TuckerD said, and walked out.

As he ventured out the door and onto the sidewalk, he wondered about many things. Would Peaches want him? Would she marry him? And what about her mother and the others? Would they be willing to accept him?

He had no answers, but at least, for a while, he'd have a mortal coil—he'd be partially human. Then the biggest question of all came to his mind.

Will I be able to survive among them?

Chapter 49

The castle was at last secured, or considered so by the prime minister. Large black electric iron gates stood at the entrance and exit points of the driveway, the breezeway that separated the studio from the castle, the front double doors, and the front entrance to the back yard. High security fencing, reaching seven feet tall, wove around the entire property in the back.

The only open and unprotected space was the courtyard and the garden wedding venue. In truth, though, they were surrounded by the tall iron gates as well, but the wealth of trees hid the fencing entirely. Peaches insisted that her courtyard and the garden wedding space be free of any encumbrance.

By the time all the work was done, Castle Alamenda had become a fortress. When the prime minister's spies discovered that Etienne's gang of retailers were selling her designs, that was bad enough, but when they found out that Etienne was designing gowns using her name and selling those designs as Peaches and Lace Originals, Etienne's sentence was lengthened and he was shipped off to another country to serve time in its prison. Most of the retailers had been found, tried, and imprisoned as well, but there was one that remained elusive. And it was that one that the prime minister was fixated on finding. It was that one who had put into play a second attempt on her life, a failed attempt stopped before it even got started, thanks to the security team.

Peaches went about her daily routine of designing gowns

and holding gorgeous weddings for her brides, but her creative juices were dampened by the knowledge that someone was still trying to kill her. Her presence endangered everyone at the castle. She knew that these were fairly clever criminals, and that one day, they would succeed in their task, even with all the security measures in place.

But she realized, too, that she had a top-notch security team, and that her ever-present shadows, Javier and Maximo, kept her shielded for the most part. Galahad and Adona had grown into animal warriors and protectors, with Galahad making daily rounds to her studio, and Adona hardly ever leaving her side. And though she knew she was protected, she also knew that her main concern was not for herself, but for Margaret-Ann and Lily, the two people she loved most in the world.

It was amidst this perpetual worry that Peaches felt her creativity wane. Accustomed to designing new gowns every day, she found herself creating perhaps one every week, if that. Continuing in this vein would destroy the business she'd worked so hard to establish. Her last client, a royal cousin to the king of Spain, had virtually designed her own gown. Had it not been for Margaret-Ann's talent and the young girl's delight, it could have been disastrous.

And now, she wanted her genius back. She just didn't know how to make it happen. She put her head in her hands, but when tears threatened to form in her eyes, she inhaled and stopped them. She thought about tomorrow's rehearsal for the runway show.

"You'll do this, Peaches Malone," she said to herself, her hands still trembling. "And it will be the best show Portugal has ever seen. Fight this fear. Fight it."

"Did you say something?" Margaret-Ann said from the doorway leading to the workshop.

Peaches smiled. "I swear, Margaret-Ann, you heard that all the way back in the shop?"

Margaret-Ann chuckled. "I was just outside the door. I needed to ask you a question." Margaret-Ann stepped up beside her and held a sketch in her hand. "Instead of pure satin all the way down on the skirt, what do you think of adding a bit of tulle, maybe peach colored?"

"What?"

"Well, we make the satin a sort of half skirt, with tulle beneath it falling to the floor, not all the way around. Just in front."

Peaches shook her head. "This is a traditional satin gown for a traditional bride. Tulle is nice, but not for a traditional gown that many of our royals demand. But, you could try that idea with taffeta, maybe. It's not so heavy. I think a modern bride might like it."

"I like that idea," Margaret-Ann said.

"Is everything ready for the rehearsal tomorrow?"

"I hope so," she said. "The dresses are all sublime, but the models aren't my first choice. We need professionals. I wish you'd paid our regulars to come for the show. This is our first here in Portugal, and I don't want it ruined by models who don't know how to stand and turn."

"Hang on. Let me make a call." She punched the buttons on her cellphone and waited. "Marietta? I need a favor that only you can help me with." After listening, Peaches spoke again, pacing as she talked. "I'm in desperate need of experienced models, about nine of them. Do you have any idea where I could find them? The rehearsal is tomorrow night." She listened again. "Oh yes, of course, Bella is still in the show. She's actually a very good model. She has the stance just perfect. But I have ten new dresses to show, and very few models who know what they're doing." Marietta talked for a few minutes. "Oh, and I might need you to help with the show if possible." Peaches smiled. "Thank you, Marietta. You're a jewel."

"Well?" Margaret-Ann asked.

"I don't know exactly what she's planning," Peaches said,

and parked a stray hair behind her ear, "but she said she'd take care of it."

Margaret-Ann smiled. "She's very good at taking care of things. Let's hope she can find us some models, good ones. Don't worry yourself so, Peaches. Everything will be all right."

And with that, Margaret-Ann turned and walked back down the hallway.

"After all these years, she still knows when something's bothering me," Peaches whispered to herself.

A knock on the door startled her. Her hands trembled more than ever. "Yes?" she called. Then Javier's words echoed in her ears. *Allow no one entrance unless I clear them.* But surely Javier was outside. "Javier, is that you?" she called. Her heart began to beat a little faster. Had she remembered to lock the door? Then she stomped her foot. *Quit being such a baby. Where is your bravery, your courage, your spunk? What is wrong with you?*

Peaches squared her shoulders. "I'm done with being afraid," she whispered to herself. "Done. Over it. Finished."

When a second knock sounded, she smiled and went to the door, flinging it open without a care. Her eyes widened and her mouth hung open.

"I...I came to see if you needed help with the rehearsal," he said, his blue frock coat the deepest blue she'd ever seen. "I do have a little experience."

Peaches smiled. "TuckerD, what on earth are you doing here?"

"I came to help," he said. "I told you I'd be back, and here I am, ready to help with the show. Is that all right?"

A strange sense of power washed over Peaches, like a river, an ephemeral flow that trickled throughout her body, took away all of her fear, and nourished her soul. She inhaled and felt like her old self for the first time in months.

"All right?" she asked as she motioned for him to come in. "Of course, it's all right. I didn't expect to see you again for a while. Did you lose your job?"

"No, I didn't lose it," he said, and lowered his head slightly. "I'm…I'm just taking a short leave of absence, sort of. I'll need to check in pretty regularly, but I'll have a little more free time now."

"Sit," Peaches said. "Make yourself comfortable."

He sat in a chair by her desk, the scent of him drifting into her nostrils.

"Where on earth do you find that cologne? Orange and cedar wood is such an odd combination, but it smells quite heavenly."

"I don't wear any kind of perfume. A man shouldn't do that." He squirmed in the small chair, trying to find a comfortable spot to hold his tall frame. "Peaches," he said, "there's something I want to talk to you about. Would you like to go to lunch?"

Peaches shook her head. "It's such a hassle trying to leave the grounds, but Carla would be glad to make something. I'm sure she's already working on lunch. That woman loves to cook. By the way, how did you get past Javier? He stands guard here until I leave, but I didn't see him when I opened the door."

TuckerD shrugged. "I didn't see him," he said. "Perhaps he was called away."

"Hmph," Peaches said. "That's odd. He's always out there."

"Peaches, there's something I need to talk to you about."

Peaches got up and hugged him. "Why the long face? Is something bothering you?"

"Yes," he said. "I've been trying to tell you that we need to talk. Is there any place where we can have some time together alone?"

Peaches raised an eyebrow. "Oh," she said with a smile. "I see. Alone as in…." She raised both eyebrows quickly. "A little rendezvous?"

TuckerD rubbed his forehead. "No. Well yes, but no, not that kind of alone. For talking," he said. "Is that possible?"

The cell phone rang. "Ah, Marietta, that was quick," Peaches said.

Margaret-Ann poked her head around the hallway door, but her eyes went immediately to the man sitting next to Peaches. "TuckerD!" she said softly. "What is *he* doing here?" Margaret-Ann trotted back down the hall and motioned to Janet. "I want you to see someone," she said. "You'll never believe who's shown up."

Janet followed her and both of them peeked around the corner of the hallway door. "Oh, I remember him," Janet said. "He helped me when Etienne's men tried to hurt me. I don't remember his name, though."

"One second if you please, Marietta," Peaches said as she got up and walked to the hallway door. "Yes, is there something you two need?"

"He's back?" Margaret-Ann asked. "I'm sure he needs work. His type always does. We can use him tonight in the rehearsal."

Peaches motioned to Margaret-Ann. "I'm talking to Marietta. I think she has some models lined up for us."

TuckerD sat with his elbows on his knees trying to get comfortable, but for some reason, his stomach felt queasy, a feeling he'd never known before. So, he got up and walked back outside, where he found Javier leaning against one of the iron gates, Adona at his feet.

TuckerD nodded and watched Javier's eyes widen. Adona ran to him and sat. Then she whined and rolled over onto her back.

"Ah, you want a rub, eh?" TuckerD said as he knelt. "How's your friend, Galahad?"

Javier walked toward him, a scowl on his face. "How did you get in here?" Javier asked. "This is a restricted area, so I must ask you to leave. I'll show you out."

But TuckerD didn't move except to rub Adona's stomach. "I'm here to speak with Peaches on an urgent matter," he said. "If you'll check with her, she'll vouch for me."

Javier knocked on the door to the studio.

"What is it?" Peaches said. "Javier," she said when she opened the door.

TuckerD stepped up beside him. "I'm afraid this is my fault. He doesn't know who I am."

Peaches stared in surprise. "You? I thought you'd left again."

"No, you were quite busy," he said, and locked his hands behind his back. "I came out here so as not to disturb you."

"Oh, really?"

"It's the truth," TuckerD said. "I could see how hectic things are in the workshop, and I know that the runway show is—"

She turned to Javier. "This is my friend TuckerD. You've no need to worry about him, but I appreciate your vigilance. And TuckerD, this is Javier. He is my security guard and the manager of the estate."

Javier gave a slight bow. Following his lead, TuckerD did the same.

Peaches chuckled. "Now, if you two can occupy yourselves for a little while, I have work to do. The runway show is tomorrow. I've no time to waste. And Javier, are there workers in the courtyard?"

"No, ma'am, not today."

"Then please arrange for a private luncheon at noon for me and TuckerD at the cabana."

"Certainly," Javier said.

"Thank you," she said, and disappeared into the studio.

Chapter 50

"Margaret-Ann," Peaches called as she walked down the hall. "Did our models show up?"

"See for yourself," Margaret-Ann replied.

Peaches looked at the sixteen young Portuguese men and women who stood in the sewing room—eight females, eight males, all of them good looking.

"Where are the others?" Peaches said, and waved her arms about.

"Marietta said she would send ten. I've ten new gowns to show. How can I show ten gowns with only eight female models?"

Peaches walked back into her office and got Marietta on the phone.

"Marietta, thank you for sending the models, but I don't have enough. I've ten new gowns to show." Peaches nodded. "Yes, Bella will model one. But that still leaves me short." Peaches listened. "Oh, yes, that would be very nice. Mila is a beautiful girl. Do you think she'll do it?" Again, she listened to Marietta. "Just do the best you can. I'm two male models short if Bella and Mila can model the gowns. Bella's young man will be fine, but I need one more…. Wait…perhaps I don't," she said, and parked a stray strand behind her ear. "I think I can find one replacement right here in my own backyard. Just please send the girls as soon as possible, and make sure they know that the show is tomorrow night."

After another moment of listening, Peaches said, "How many?" Peaches' eyes grew wide. "I've never given a show in front of three thousand people. This will definitely be a first, and thank you for taking care of the tickets. This wouldn't have happened without the help of you. I'm very grateful. See you tomorrow at around 3:30?"

Peaches smiled and leaned back in her chair. "Margaret-Ann!" she called. Peaches could hear the sounds of her stacked heels knocking against the floor, and when she walked in, Peaches said nothing. She simply smiled at her.

"What?" Margaret-Ann said. "Why are you looking at me like that? What's gone wrong?"

"Nothing's wrong," Peaches said. "I…I just wanted to tell you that I think we'll have enough models. And I wanted to say that I love your new hairdo. The silver shines like stars and is becoming on you. Much better than the brunette. And I like the long shaggy style. It's very flattering. You really do look beautiful."

Margaret-Ann fingered the long silver hair that fell below her shoulders. "Well, I'll never be a Peaches Malone, but I do like my new look. At least now I can pass for a professional instead of a dowdy old seamstress. Sometimes, when I walk by the mirror, I'm taken aback by the change. I hardly recognize myself."

Peaches chuckled. "You're definitely not dowdy," she said. "You're slim and quite elegant now, and your new wardrobe just enhances the look."

"None of this would be possible without your hard work, Peaches. You've given me the means to become a new person, and I am grateful."

Peaches waved her hand in dismissal.

"Now, tell me how many models we'll have for the runway show. Who else do I need to fit?"

"Bella and Mila, and Bella's boyfriend. And I have someone in mind for another."

Margaret-Ann raised an eyebrow. "How long will he be here

this time? A day? An hour? How do you know he'll be around for the show tomorrow night?"

"He said he'd come back to help with the show, and I believe him."

Margaret-Ann walked to the desk and hugged Peaches. "I know you want to believe him, Peaches. But he disappears. He's a loser. That's not good, and it's certainly not good enough for Europe's most esteemed designer. You deserve so much better than an out-of-work, unreliable man like him."

"How do you know he's a loser, Margaret-Ann?" Peaches said, and cocked her head. "I mean, really, how do you know? What is it about him that says he's no good?"

"Just what I said, Peaches. He's here one minute, gone the next. If he doesn't stay around to be with the woman he claims to love, what makes you think he'll stay around for the show? I think you're so enamored with him that you're blind to his faults. Besides, there's something about him that is just...weird."

"Like what?"

"Well, his clothes, for one," Margaret-Ann said, and stepped closer to Peaches. "Why would he wear that old Victorian frock coat? He's had it on every time I've seen him. Doesn't he have more clothes?"

Peaches leaned back in her chair. "Is that it? His clothes?"

"No, Peaches, that's not it," Margaret-Ann said, and squared her shoulders. "There are lots of things about him that put up warning signals. He doesn't have a job," she said, and held up one finger. "He wears the same clothes all the time." Another finger went up. "He's almost like...like a ghost or something. He just suddenly appears. Then he's suddenly gone," she continued, and put up another finger. "He just doesn't act like a normal human being. I hate to say it, Peaches, but there's something terribly wrong with that man."

Five fingers told Peaches that Margaret-Ann was quite serious.

Peaches held up her index finger. "I think I'm in love with him."

Margaret-Ann turned to go back to the workshop. "Well, at least you're not certain. There's time to change your mind. I love you, Peaches, and I want the very best for you. He's a far cry from the very best. All he wants is your body and your money." Margaret-Ann held up a hand. "I can't talk about this anymore, except to say that you can learn to un-love him just as easily as you can think you love him."

When Margaret-Ann had left, Peaches got up and opened the door. She stepped outside. "Where is TuckerD?" she asked Javier.

Javier frowned and motioned to the courtyard.

"You opened the gate for him?"

Javier nodded. "You said he was fine, and he asked to see the roses."

Peaches smiled. "I'll just go and speak to him," she said, motioning for Javier to open the gate.

Peaches walked out onto the courtyard and found him kneeling down beside some of the rose plants. She watched as he touched them, and the roses grew at least two feet and were filled with blooms.

Peaches gasped, then covered her mouth.

TuckerD wandered around the courtyard bringing the seedlings to grown plants, each bursting with pink and yellow blooms. He didn't stop until he'd come to the last set of seedlings. Then he reached into his pocket and brought out something gold. Peaches couldn't tell what it was, but she watched him hold it over the plants, and in turn, stared in wonder as they grew tall and bloomed.

Her knees began to shake, so she went back through the gate and into her studio. She plopped down in her chair and put her head in her hands.

I must be hallucinating, she thought. *What I just saw is impossible.*

Margaret-Ann's words echoed in her brain. *He's weird. He just doesn't act like a normal human being.*

Who is this man? What have I gotten myself into?

A knock on the door startled her and she jumped, her heart beating so fast and so loudly that she could hear it in her ears, her hands wiggling like two worms on hot rocks.

Instead of getting up, she called, "Yes, who is it?"

"It's me, Javier."

Peaches let out the breath she'd been holding.

"The luncheon is ready and waiting for you and your friend in the cabana. Carla fixed something special."

Peaches stared down at the paperwork on her desk. The knock came again.

"Miss Peaches," Javier said. "Luncheon is ready when you are."

Peaches swallowed hard. To soothe herself, she opened the desk drawer, took out her hand-held mirror, and surveyed her face and hair. She fluffed her hair, put on fresh lipstick, thickened her mascara, smoothed on a dot of her La Mer foundation, and spritzed on her favorite perfume: Joy. She used a bit of mineral blush to add some sparkly highlights to her cheeks.

Peaches took a deep breath, smiled back at the image in the mirror, then leaned in close. *What is this?* She thought she saw the beginnings of crow's feet around her eyes, but as she ran her fingers softly under each eye, the little lines disappeared.

"A little smoothing was all it needed." She indulged herself in another spritz of her perfume. "All better," she whispered.

Before she left, she glanced into the full-length mirror on the opposite wall. Lipstick and Lace roses patterned the silk sundress she wore. She spun around and watched the cascade of roses settle in a silken swirl around her. A tuck here, a pat there, a perfect drape of cool summer elegance. Spaghetti straps showed off her tanned skin and toned arms.

She shook her head until her hair fell in a flowing drape and

278

settled below each shoulder.

Perfect.

She slipped tanned feet — toenails painted bright pink — into her Louboutin open-toed heels.

No one wants an ugly Peaches Malone.

She tried to banish the thought, to keep it away from her mind, to keep it from playing like a broken record every minute, but it was always there, always.

A knock sounded again at the door.

"Coming."

She brushed at her skirt, then turned sideways to check herself in the mirror.

Then she walked to the door and opened it. Instead of Javier, she found TuckerD standing there, his hand raised again as if to knock.

Chapter 51

Peaches and TuckerD sat in the shade of the cabana, the aromas of Carla's luncheon menu wafting around them. Broiled salted cod, hot bread fresh from the oven, two wedges of fine cheese, and a salad of grilled broccoli, carrots, and tomatoes lined the small table before them.

"You look beautiful, Peaches," he said. "I think you're more beautiful every time I see you."

Peaches smiled. "Thank you," she said with a hint of a smile. She broke off the end of a wedge of sharp cheese. "Would you like a bite?" she asked TuckerD.

"Is it good?"

Peaches shrugged. "You'll have to determine that for yourself. Open your mouth."

TuckerD did as he was told, and Peaches popped the small bite into his mouth. He chewed and swallowed and screwed up his face. "What do you call this?" he asked.

Peaches laughed out loud. "Oh, that's a good one, TuckerD." He cocked his head.

"Oh, the type of cheese, you mean? Carla calls it Nisa," she said, and took a bite. "It's made here in Portugal, and I just love the taste of it. For a minute there, I thought you didn't know it was cheese."

TuckerD sat with his elbows on his knees. "There is much I do not know about human—I mean, your life, Peaches."

"Well," she said, and took a bite of the cod, "if you ever stayed around long enough, you might learn a thing or two. Here, try a bite of the cod. It's really good."

He leaned back and opened his mouth. As soon as he closed it again, he coughed. Then he shook his head and pointed to a napkin.

"You don't like the cod?"

He put the napkin to his mouth and spit out the fish. "It's foul tasting," he said, and coughed again. "What did you call it?"

"Salted codfish. Here, try this," she said, and popped a small cold piece of watermelon in his mouth. "How's that?"

TuckerD nodded and smiled. "I like it," he said. "What is it called?"

Peaches stared at him for a moment. Then she sat forward to face him. "You act as if you've never eaten food before. How could you not know what watermelon is?"

"It's not common where I come from," he said, and leaned closer to her.

Instantly, she caught his familiar scent and inhaled: oranges and cedar. She felt she could live the rest of her life breathing in that delicious aroma.

"Look, Peaches, there is something I need to talk to you about."

She gazed into his deep blue eyes, the deepest blue she'd ever seen. She took in, once again, the long hair tied at his neck, the craggy but handsome features of his face, the broad width of those shoulders. He was the man of her dreams: strong, tall, ruggedly handsome, kind and loving.

She smiled and put her hands on his cheeks. "I adore you, TuckerD."

He smiled and removed her hands, then kissed the palm of each one. The kisses sent tingles down her spine.

"Peaches," he said, "I want to be with you." He reached into his breast pocket and pulled out a small blue velvet bag, then withdrew its contents. "This once belonged to a queen," he said as he fastened the emerald and diamond necklace around her neck. "And now it belongs to you, my queen."

She gasped and fingered the exquisite piece. "Give me that mirror behind you," she said. "Yes, that." When she gazed at the sparkling stones, her mind raced back to the time when queens were treasures of their territories, worshipped and adored. "It's magnificent, TuckerD, but I am no queen. I don't even have a father. I'm afraid my lineage is not anything worthy of being called a queen."

He took both of her hands in his and kissed her fingers. "You are my queen," he said, "and I want to be with you forever. Be my wife, Peaches. Please."

Peaches swallowed hard.

"Marry me, Peaches," he said, and kissed her hands again. "With all of my heart, my body, and my soul, I love you. Say you'll be my wife, Peaches."

"Your wife?"

TuckerD smiled. "You're my heart, Peaches, the only woman I've ever loved," he said, and put a hand on her cheek. "I'm asking you to spend the rest of your life with me. I'll do whatever you want, go wherever you want to go. Or stay right here. Your life, your family, and your work are all here. I'd never pull you away from that."

Tears welled in Peaches' eyes, but she wiped them away quickly. She took his hand from her cheek and kissed his palm. TuckerD smiled.

"I'm sorry," she said. "I'm so sorry, but I can't marry you, TuckerD. It wouldn't be fair to either of us."

"I...I don't understand," he said. "You love me, right?"

She nodded. "Love doesn't conquer all," she said. "I have no time or room for a husband. My life is all about my gowns, my work, my shows. Marriage would make me feel tied down, trapped."

"Trapped?" he asked. "You'd feel trapped with me, caught in something that you couldn't get out of?"

Peaches nodded.

"But how do you know that?"

Peaches stood up. "I've been married before, TuckerD. I'm not a good wife, and that won't change. My life is my work." Peaches reached up and took off the necklace. "Keep this," she said as she handed it to him, "for someone who deserves it."

"You deserve it, Peaches," he said, and stood. He placed his hands on her shoulders. "Can't you at least give me a chance to prove that to you?"

Peaches stared at him for a moment. "I love you," she said, "but marriage right now is...it just wouldn't work. Can't we remain as we are?"

TuckerD smiled. "If you will wear the necklace, then I agree," he said as he fastened it around her neck again.

Peaches chuckled. "Oh, TuckerD, whatever would I do with you if we were married!"

TuckerD kissed her lightly on the cheek. "There's only one thing I'd ask of you, Peaches. Just one thing."

Peaches cocked her head. "And what is that one thing?"

TuckerD kissed her softly on the lips. "That you love me with all your heart."

Peaches smiled. "Done," she said. "Now, the rehearsal is tonight. Will you be there?"

"I've taken a short leave of absence, so you might find that I'll be around more than you want."

"I don't think that's possible," she said, and touched his cheek.

"Peaches, may I stay here with you? At the castle?"

Peaches rubbed her arms and noticed that her hands had stopped trembling. "If you stay here, you'll have to interact with Lily and Margaret-Ann. Can you do that? Won't that be unpleasant for you?"

TuckerD shook his head. "I think I can manage it."

"Oh, I've got it," she said, and clapped her hands. "I have the perfect place for you to stay. It's called the Suegra Suite. It's a private suite on the back of the castle. It has its own entrance, its own kitchenette, and is completely private. Oh, and it has beautiful views. How does that sound?"

"Perfect," he said. "Like you, Peaches."

Peaches shook her head. "And can you deal with all of the security in place?"

"Certainly. Sometimes, they probably won't even see me. I'll be discreet."

She stood on her tiptoes to hug him. "Good, then it's all taken care of. And you can help Maximo with Galahad. He's a magnificent animal, but he still has some problems with training and obedience."

"I'm good with animals," he said. "I'd be honored to help Maximo."

"And you can help in the garden, as well." Peaches smiled. "I think it will work out beautifully."

Chapter 52

Margaret-Ann and Lily stood by the window in the great room, Adona wiggling at their feet.

"I just don't understand," Margaret-Ann said, wringing her hands. "How is it possible?"

"I don't have a clue," Lily said. "Yesterday, they'd barely sprouted out of the ground. Now, they're all at least three feet tall and covered in blooms."

"They're gorgeous roses—Lipstick and Lace, I think they're called—but how on earth could they have grown so quickly?"

"Has Janet seen them?" Lily asked, and went back to the large table where she'd set up a makeshift office.

"Oh, no," Margaret-Ann said. "She was up before dawn this morning and went out to the studio to work on the dresses for the runway show. Everything needs to be perfect for the rehearsal tonight."

"She's turned out to be quite the helper, hasn't she?"

"She's been a God-send," Margaret-Ann said. "She might not be a designer, but she certainly is a fine seamstress, with the delicate touch needed for the gowns. And she's a fast worker, as well."

Margaret-Ann glanced out the window again. This time, she saw TuckerD and Peaches walking around the courtyard admiring the roses.

"Oh, come look," she said to Lily. "It's that man again."

285

Lily came in a flash.

"He's showing Peaches the roses. She's smiling like she's seen the queen of England."

"Didn't he give her the seeds?"

Margaret-Ann nodded.

"Perhaps they're some kind of fast-growing hybrids," Lily said as she watched the two of them stroll around the courtyard. She wished she could hear what they were talking about. From the looks on their faces and the gestures they made, the topic of conversation seemed to be important.

"I wonder what they're saying?" Margaret-Ann said. "They don't look too happy."

"Maybe he doesn't want to be in the show," Lily said. "He's certainly handsome enough."

Margaret-Ann shook her head. "A handsome loser," she said. "He seems to have had his hair trimmed more neatly. But he's still a loser."

Lily chuckled. "And why do you say that?"

"Well, for one thing, he's unreliable. Here one minute, gone the next. And it hurts Peaches when he disappears and she has no idea when or if he'll come back."

Lily pushed a stray hair out of her face. "But she seems to deal with it, Margaret-Ann."

"He doesn't work. If he did, he couldn't run around Portugal at a moment's notice. It's plain as day to me that all he wants from Peaches is her body and her money."

"And do you know a man alive who wouldn't want Peaches' body? She's a beautiful woman, Margaret-Ann. Any living, breathing male would want her. You can't fault him for that."

Margaret-Ann slumped into a large leather chair beside the window.

Lily walked to her and knelt beside the chair. "What is it, Margaret-Ann? What's bothering you so?"

Margaret-Ann wiped a tear from the corner of her eye.

"Peaches thinks she loves him," she said softly.

"And what is so wrong with that? Peaches falls in love easily, but she falls out of love quicker than anyone I've ever seen. You know it's true. So what if she does love him today? By the end of the week, he'll be just another throwaway."

Margaret-Ann smiled. "Oh, I'd forgotten all about that, Lily," she said, and rubbed her hands together. "Thank you for reminding me. She's gotten mixed up with so many losers. She married one of them, you know."

Lily chuckled. "I remember. I was there," she said. "But one thing about Peaches is that when she says she's had enough, she fixes it quicker than anyone I know. Married one week. Divorced the next. Never a thought given to the latest ex. Well, you know what I mean."

"That's Peaches," Margaret-Ann said, and smiled. "But this time it's different, Lily. There's something about him that's gotten hold of her. I can tell. Just look at her face when she smiles at him. Her entire countenance changes."

"Trust me, Margaret-Ann. It's temporary. Men are always temporary with Peaches."

"I'm not so sure about this one. There's something unique going on with the two of them."

"She told me they had a special bond," Lily said. "I've never heard her say that before."

Margaret-Ann rubbed her temples. "I'm worried. What if he asks her to marry him? And what if she says yes?"

Lily leaned forward and patted Margaret-Ann's knee. "And give up all that she's worked for? Give up this castle, her gowns, her place here in Portugal, her family? Nope, it ain't gonna happen, Margaret-Ann. It just will not happen."

"I wish he'd go away and never come back. He scares me."

"Scares you?"

Margaret-Ann nodded. "He's got a hold on her, and that scares me. And it scares me that she might fall for his lies like she has before, chuck everything to run after him."

Lily leaned back in her chair. "You're confusing the young Peaches with the older one, Margaret-Ann. Ten years ago, maybe you'd have had to worry. But now, Peaches is a woman of substance, a woman of means," she said, and leaned forward again. "She beautiful, she's rich, she's powerful, and even better, she's beloved. Her designs are considered valuable treasures, and they are snapped up by royal families all over the world. She doesn't need a man to give her anything."

"But…but don't you think she longs for a man? Most women do. It's only natural. And she did tell me that she loves him."

Lily shook her head. "I'm afraid our Peaches is a woman who changes her mind quickly. She can be totally in love one day and totally unconcerned the next. My prediction is that within a month's time, the man will be out of her life for good."

Margaret-Ann smiled a thin smile. "This one has been coming around for a while now. He just doesn't seem to want to let go. And Peaches doesn't seem to want him to go, either. I keep expecting her to walk through the door and announce that she's having a wedding of her own."

Lily laughed out loud. "And how many times have you heard her say she'd never, ever get married again? It's practically her mantra."

"Okay," Margaret-Ann said. "I'll try to stop worrying. But that guy's up to something. I can guarantee you that."

"And if he is," Lily said, and tucked her legs up under her, "our Peaches already knows about it."

Chapter 53

Peaches walked in the door with her hands clasped at her waist and a sad expression on her face.

"There she is," Margaret-Ann said, and stood up. "What's wrong, dear? You look so sad. Has something happened?"

Peaches rubbed the back of her neck with her trembling hands and forced a smile. "No, runway jitters. That's all."

"But that's not like you," Lily piped in. "You're confidence personified during your runway shows. You shine like a beacon that mesmerizes everyone in the room."

Peaches sat in one of the overstuffed chairs. "Maybe it's just that this is the first one in Portugal. I don't really know what to expect. I don't even know the language."

"Oh, don't be silly," Lily said. "For goodness sakes, you're already famous here. You're loved and considered a treasure. People will be falling all over themselves to buy your dresses. Think of the cost of the tickets for the show! And they were sold out in a couple of days. No, my dear, you've nothing to worry about."

"So you think they'll like the new gowns? Two of them are quite unusual for a Peaches original."

"All the better," Lily said, and stood. "Want some tea or coffee?"

"Coffee for me," Peaches said. "Margaret-Ann?"

"Yes, tea would be lovely."

"I'll just tell—" But before she could finish the sentence, she saw Carla walking toward them carrying a silver tray.

"Carla, how did you know we'd want coffee and tea?"

Carla just smiled. "You are the lady of this fine castle. It is up to me to predict what you will want."

Peaches nodded in her direction. "You're a jewel, Carla. I'm honored to have you."

Carla blushed and bowed. "Thank you, Ms. Peaches."

Javier came through the door. "The perimeter is secure, Ms. Peaches," he said. "All is well."

Peaches nodded at him. "That's good to know," she said. "Javier, I want you to remain here while we're at the rehearsal for the runway show. This is your castle to protect now. So, you must not abandon your post."

"Very well," he said. "Shall I send Maximo to escort you?"

"Oh no," she said, and took a sip of coffee. "Maximo is to guard his area, especially Galahad. I won't take a chance on the horse being hurt again. Alberto and two of the prime minister's guards will be with us tonight."

***

At four o'clock, Alberto waited in the driveway for Peaches, Lily, and Margaret-Ann. Peaches came out wearing jeans and a T-shirt and carrying a garment bag, while Margaret-Ann wore a stylish two-piece pantsuit, and Lily shone in her two-piece suit.

"Ready?" he asked in his thick accent.

Peaches nodded. "Did the models arrive on time?" she asked.

He glanced at Peaches but didn't respond.

"Alberto, what's wrong? Who's not at rehearsal?"

"A slight problem with the male models."

Peaches frowned. "Which one?" she said.

Instantly, Peaches' thoughts went to TuckerD. Would he abandon her now? On the night of the rehearsal for her first show in Portugal?

"Who's missing?"

Alberto held up two fingers.

"Two models aren't there?"

Alberto nodded. "Marietta is beside herself."

"Oh, mercy," Margaret-Ann said.

"I'll take care of it," Peaches said. "There are two other male models on stand-by. No problem."

Peaches smiled, but her heart felt as if it had dropped into her stomach. *He's abandoned me. How could he? Just because I wouldn't marry him?*

As they parked at the auditorium's entrance, Peaches got out in a huff and headed in to see Marietta. She walked down the long corridor, peeking in at each room to make sure the girls were being dressed and fitted properly.

"Any problems?" she asked when she saw Janet.

"None so far with the girls, but two of the male models—"

"I know," she interrupted. "Alberto's already told me. Let me know if you need anything."

She walked back to the large fitting room, where Marietta sat in a chair with her hands over her face.

"Marietta, are you all right?"

"I'm afraid I've let you down, Peaches," she said, her face wrapped in sadness.

Peaches pulled up a chair and sat close beside her. "You've done nothing to let me down, Marietta."

"But two models are missing. Lorenzo, that very handsome one, and Tucker, your friend."

Peaches waved a hand at her. "Don't worry," she said. "This happens all the time. I always have models on standby, both male and female."

"You do?"

"Of course, Marietta. You can't be a successful designer with superior runway shows if you're not prepared for the problems that crop up. On my first few shows as a new designer, I ended up being a model a few times, so I learned pretty quickly that things happen. Sometimes people just can't make it, so I have to be prepared with substitutes."

"You modeled your own dresses?"

Peaches chuckled and nodded her head. "More than once, I'm afraid, and it wouldn't have been bad except that the gowns weren't fitted for me. My models are usually tall and thin with long arms and legs, so I sort of disappeared beneath the fabrics of the gowns."

Marietta chuckled. "I wish I could have seen it," she said. "But not in a mean way, of course."

"Well, I did my best to look as 'model-ish' as I could, though it was evident I wasn't cut out for the job. Now, let's go check to see how the models are doing."

As Marietta and Peaches walked toward the fitting room, Peaches called to Alberto to check the microphones and the stage mirrors. "Oh, and be sure to contact the stage manager to make sure he doesn't forget about the show tomorrow night."

Peaches and Marietta walked into the enormous fitting room and surveyed the models, then went to each one, called their name, and checked them on the list.

"Where is Lorenzo?" No one responded. Peaches cleared her throat. "Where. Is. Lorenzo?" She glanced at Marietta, leaned in, and whispered something to her.

Marietta clapped her hands so that all the models would focus their attention on her. "We must help Peaches find Lorenzo," she said. "Now, if you know where he is, speak up. If he fails to show up for rehearsal, then he forfeits his place in the show."

"He's supposed to be my partner," one of the girls called from the back. "I haven't seen him for several days."

Peaches sighed and put her hands on her hips, then paced in a circle. "He's our best looking male model," she said. "I wanted him to be the one to escort the model wearing the new featured gown. With his good looks and the surprise of the new gown, I was sure it would be a big seller. Perhaps some young girl has given him refuge. In any case, we can't wait. We have to get all the models fitted and on stage."

Peaches raised her voice and directed it to the stage. "We know the rules, right? No drinking, no smoking, no being late to rehearsal, but most importantly, no being late to one of the shows. I have replacements ready to step in, and if you have to be replaced for a single show, that's it. You can't model for me again. Simple and easy rules to follow. Understood?"

The models nodded in unison, their eyes wide with fear.

Peaches smiled at them. "Don't worry. You'll all do just fine. I'm proud of all of you."

Smiles beamed all around.

"It's time to take your places with the seamstresses. Each gown, each tuxedo must be perfect." she said. "In one hour, we'll assemble back here on stage for the rehearsal."

Someone tapped her on the shoulder.

"Peaches?" Janet said. "May I have a word?"

Peaches stepped down from the staging area and walked toward her office, motioning for Janet to follow. "What's wrong, Janet?" she asked. "Any problems so far with the fittings?"

"Oh, no," Janet said. "The dresses are simply gorgeous, and these models are beautiful. So far we haven't had a single mishap. No tears or rips or smudges. Nothing. The buttons have been very successful with this new batch of gowns, and those with zippers have done well, too."

"So, what's the problem?" Peaches asked as she took a seat behind her desk.

Janet pulled out a small envelope and gave it to Peaches. "This was on my station when I came in today."

Peaches looked at the plain white envelope, opened it, and drew out a small piece of paper. *You will all be destroyed by the end of the show.*

Her eyes widened as she read the message, and her hands shook as she fumbled to dial a number. "Get me the prime minister," she said to the voice on the other end. "Tell him it's Peaches and it's an emergency. I need him and his security team here in the auditorium immediately."

Chapter 54

As TuckerD walked past, Peaches put a hand on his arm. "Thank you," she said, "for coming back."

"I didn't want to leave you without a model. I know how much stress that puts on you, Peaches."

Peaches sighed. She felt her heartbeat quicken and her face redden. "Thank you. Can we talk after the show?"

"If you'd like, of course. I'll be here."

Peaches smiled up at him, her heart pounding at the mere sight of this man.

The double doors swung open as the prime minister and his team walked in.

"What's this about?" TuckerD asked.

Peaches removed the piece of paper from her pocket and showed it to him. "I called for the prime minister," she said, and brushed her hair back from her face.

"Where did you find this?" TuckerD asked.

"Janet found it on her desk when she came in this morning."

Peaches suddenly felt as if her knees would collapse. She steadied herself on the seat back. Instantly, TuckerD's hand was on her elbow. "It's been going on for months now, and I want to brush it off as nothing, but he's tried once. He'll try again. I keep looking over my shoulder and wondering which of the men around me might be an assassin."

TuckerD pulled her close to him and wrapped his arms

around her. "Don't worry," he whispered. "Everything will be all right. You have the palace guards, the security team, and me. No one's going to hurt you." TuckerD closed his eyes for a few seconds and kissed the top of Peaches' head. "Better?"

Peaches blinked a few times and smiled. "Better."

"I'll go check with the seamstress," he said. "Rehearsal's fast approaching."

"Peaches," the prime minister called. "I received your message. Now, tell me what this is all about."

"Thank you for coming," she said, and handed him the piece of paper. "I could be overreacting, but this has happened enough that it's beginning to worry me. Someone could be there at the castle right now wreaking all sorts of havoc. And why? All over a silly design. I just can't understand why that would be worth killing me for."

"Come," he said softly. "Let's go into your office." When they were seated, he spoke. "Peaches," he said in a quiet voice. "We're not dealing with rational people. These are thieves, killers, hardened criminals. Life is not sacred to them. Only revenge is worth seeking."

"I testified against them, and so now, I must watch while they try to kill me. The castle is like a fortress, I have security with me at all times, but still—still I know that somehow, they will break through the barriers and kill me. I don't worry so much for myself, Prime Minister, but for Margaret-Ann and Lily and Janet."

"All you need to worry about, dear lady, are your designs and your shows. Everything else is well in hand. I promise you that. You have a team around you the likes of which you can't even imagine." The prime minister stood. "I must leave you now," he said, "but I want you to relax. Your very first show in Portugal is tomorrow night. Alberto and Marietta have put their hearts and souls into making sure that this is the catalyst you need to make you the most sought after designer in all of Europe, and Portugal will become the wedding gown capital of the world." A big smile spread across his face. "The world will be at your feet, Peaches, so I encourage you to enjoy every minute of it."

"Thank you," she said, and smiled. "I'm deeply honored to be living and working here, Prime Minister, and I will do as you say and enjoy every moment."

Chapter 55

The models lined up one by one for inspection. Margaret-Ann went around to each one checking for tiny smudges, rips, or tears, Peaches following close behind with her own sort of examination. She ran her hands along the sleeves of the latest showpiece, a peach-colored tulle and satin ball gown delicately embroidered with rosettes of white lace around the hem and the cuffs. The bodice was cut in a sweetheart neckline also embroidered with rosettes of white lace. The back of the dress, however, was the star of this show. It plunged to the waist in a deep V enhanced by a large white satin bow, with satin streamers that fell to the bottom of the dress.

"Turn, please," Peaches said.

The young model held out her arms and twirled around, and Peaches smiled as the sound of satin brushing lightly against the floor filled not only her ears but her senses. There was something about the sound that made her heart flutter with joy.

"Again," she said, and smiled. "A little slower this time. We want the audience to be able to see each fine feature of this gown."

The model did as she was told, but in the middle of her turn, Peaches cried out.

"Stop! Stop right there. Don't move."

The young model froze, a look of absolute terror on her face.

"Margaret-Ann," Peaches said, and put down her clipboard. "The bow isn't sewn properly. It should be stationary, but it flops when she turns."

"Oh, dear," Margaret-Ann said as she examined the bow. "Oh, here's the problem. The stitching has come loose."

"The stitching is loose? Who sewed this on?"

Margaret-Ann wrung her hands. "Well, I did, of course," she said. "It won't take any time to fix."

"She's not telling the truth, Peaches," Janet said, and stepped onto the stage. "I'm the one who sewed on the bow. I thought it was tight enough."

"Ah, well," Peaches said, and grinned. "So, let's get it fixed, shall we? I'll leave it in your capable hands."

Peaches walked off the stage and went to the first row of seats. From her handbag, she pulled out her compact, flipped it open, and checked her face in the mirror. "A Peaches Malone gown must be perfect," she said loudly enough for everyone to hear.

No one wants an ugly Peaches Malone.

She shook off the thought, then ran her little finger across her bottom lip, and wiped beneath each eye. She blinked to check her mascara, turned her head to check the bronze blush, and held out a hand to check her nail polish. Finally, she reached into her bag and removed a small bottle of perfume. She spritzed twice, inhaled the wonderful aroma of Joy by Jean Patou, and closed her eyes.

"Perfect," she whispered.

The floral notes of the perfume relaxed her. She flexed her trembling fingers and grabbed her clipboard. This time, she started with the male models, each outfitted in black tuxedos with satin lapels and crisp white shirts.

"Check your sleeve lengths," she said, her voice soft and calm. "One inch of shirtsleeve should be showing. And check your pocket squares. Each one is designed to match your partner's gown, so make sure you have the one with your name on it. Oh, and don't forget about your shoes, guys. They need to gleam!"

She went around to each model, and paused when she came to TuckerD. She looked him over, then arched an eyebrow. "That's not the right shirt," she said.

He didn't respond.

"Will you please answer me? You really need another shirt, so let Margaret-Ann help you find another."

"I can't do that," he said softly.

"Why?" She brushed at her silk blouse and straightened the buttons.

TuckerD sighed. "There wasn't one big enough to fit me, Ms. Malone," he said without looking at her. "I tried on several, but none of them would even button."

Peaches tapped her pen on the clapboard. "Perhaps you could wear the one you wear with your business suit."

He nodded and left the stage.

Peaches turned her back to the models and closed her eyes. They stung from stress and fatigue, and her skin prickled as if ants crawled all over her. She rubbed the back of her neck and smelled the sweet fragrance of her perfume when she lifted her arm.

She felt an arm slide across her shoulders.

"Peaches," Margaret-Ann whispered. "Calm yourself, dear. Everything will be all right. Janet has fixed the problem with the bow, and your gowns are all just magnificent. The man will find the right shirt, and all will be well. Please, please try to relax. You look so pale and drawn. Please don't let this make you sick."

She hugged Margaret-Ann. "You know me," she said. "I'm never sick. It's just the pressure of the show. That's all. I'll be fine. I promise."

But in her heart she knew two things.

First, she had to make amends somehow with TuckerD for refusing his proposal.

And second, someone was trying to kill her.

Chapter 56

The curtains came up to reveal an audience of so many people that some of them were standing in the aisles.

Peaches took one last look in the mirror. With her hair in an elegant chignon topped with the tiara Marietta had given her, she turned her head this way and that. She stepped closer to the mirror, checked her makeup, lipstick, mascara, lashes, and blush, and smiled. She thought it might be the best makeup work she'd ever done—fitting for this, her very first runway show in Portugal.

The gown of blue sequins and lace with a five-foot train and chiffon overlay fit her perfectly. The bodice hugged her closely, while the sequins shimmered in the light. The floor-length skirt hugged every curve as it cascaded to the floor, while the chiffon overlay, alight with sequins, shining pearls, and brilliant diamonds, gave the outfit the look of royalty. She made one full turn, and her eyes lit up as she watched the shimmering skirt billow behind her.

With a final spritz of her perfume, she leaned in to the mirror. "I am Peaches Malone," she whispered, "and this will be my best show ever." Adona whimpered behind her, the big pink bow on her neck a little wobbly. "Come, my little love," she said. "We're about to make history."

Head held high, Adona's leash in her hand, she walked out onto the stage and immediately the world turned black.

Blinded by flash bulbs from below, some not a foot away, and stage lights from above, she momentarily lost her way, but she felt the pull of Adona's leash and followed the dog to the podium, where she balanced herself and put on a smile. She felt Adona's weight on her feet, and somehow, it made her feel more grounded. She held up a hand — her signal to stop taking photos — and waited for the world to return into her sight lines. And then the chanting started.

"Peaches! Peaches! Peaches!"

The words roared through her brain, so she held up a hand again as the audience quieted. She balanced herself another time, looked out into the audience, and smiled.

"Thank you all so much for attending my first runway show in this lovely country of Portugal, my home as well as yours."

The audience whistled and clapped.

"Tonight I'm premiering ten new gowns, and I hope that you will love them all. They're modern, unique, and just the thing for today's young brides. Some of them are inspired by the rich colors found here in Portugal, the earthy beige, caramel, and sand, and one brilliant gold to represent the sun."

Peaches walked to the center of the stage and spread her arms. A second set of curtains went up to reveal ten bridal couples.

"Behold," she said. "Spring's Delights."

The audience gave a collective gasp.

Peaches made her way back to the podium and waited while Adona settled on her feet. As she glanced back at the first couple, she noticed the couples in the wings and wondered why Lorenzo, who had finally shown up, had switched places. He was to accompany model number two, but he had moved, and each time she glanced back again, he moved further down the line.

"Dress number one is called A Hint of Spring. If you like it, please jot down the name so that we can discuss details later."

The first couple paraded down the runway, the model wearing the wedding gown superb in her carriage and expression. The

302

billowing layered dress fit her perfectly, and in its peach tones with overlays of white chiffon, the young woman drew ooohs and aaahs from the audience.

"Dress number two is called A Taste of Spring," she said, and looked back at the bridal couple.

Where is Lorenzo?

Then suddenly, Lorenzo ran back into place and stood beside the bride.

Peaches let out the breath she'd been holding. But as they walked down the runway, a group of young girls began to chant.

"Lorenzo. Lorenzo. Lorenzo!"

Lorenzo lowered his head and glanced back at Peaches.

"Stop this," she mouthed, and glared as if she could shoot him with her eyes. Though she abhorred the thought of stopping one of her shows, she felt the time had come, the one and only time she'd ever done such a thing. But stop it she did.

"Security," she said into the microphone. "Please remove these girls from the auditorium. I'll not tolerate such interruptions." She held up a hand. "Please, forgive me, my friends, but I'll return quickly." And with that she left the podium and walked to the back stage out of view of her audience.

She found her target. "Lorenzo," she said, and motioned to him.

He hurried over to her. "Yes, Miss Peaches?"

"Get your things. You're fired. Not after the show, but right now. Go."

Her face was like an ancient stone mask.

"I'll say it only one more time before I have you escorted out by the guards. Get your things and go. You're fired."

Lorenzo's face contorted with rage. He turned to walk off the stage, but turned back to face Peaches. Peaches suddenly felt two large hands on her shoulders, and she glanced up to see TuckerD's tall frame looming behind her. She patted his hand.

"You'll pay for this," Lorenzo shouted. "Yes, ma'am, you'll

pay for this."

Peaches arched her brows. "You're no threat to me, Lorenzo. You have only yourself to blame. Now, get out and don't come back."

When Lorenzo left the stage, the audience stood up and cheered while Peaches watched the prime minister issue orders to his security team. They fanned out and left the building within minutes. Then the prime minister turned and looked toward her. He gave a simple nod of his head. That little nod was all it took to bring Peaches back to her confident self.

The remainder of the runway show went so smoothly that it felt like only minutes until it was over and the crowd descended on her. Adona was allowed out of her place at Peaches' feet, and welcomed the reprieve as she licked everyone in sight.

In an uncharacteristic move, Margaret-Ann, attired in an elegant two-piece white linen suit and white Louboutin heels, came to the front and began to help take orders for the gowns. Peaches nodded at her and smiled.

Margaret-Ann raised her hand. "You may place orders with me," she said, and soon a crowd gathered around her. At first, she struggled with all of the required information. In addition to names and phone numbers, she needed to know the name and style of the gown, the date of the wedding, and the venue for the wedding. She also had to schedule fitting times and dates. By the time she'd finished the first three, the process became easier, and by the end of the night, she said everything from rote memory.

When everyone but the prime minister and Marietta had left, Peaches and Margaret-Ann collapsed in two of the auditorium chairs.

"You were such a good girl, Adona. You made me very proud."

Adona put her paws in Peaches' lap and whined.

Peaches stroked her head. "Such a good girl," she said as she grabbed a treat out of a small plastic bag in her purse. "Sit,"

Peaches said, and the dog obeyed. "Easy," she said, and the dog gently took the treat from her hand, and was content to sit at her feet and chew on the doggie bone. "Who would ever guess that I would develop a love for dogs?" Peaches said.

Margaret-Ann chuckled. "Not me, that's for sure. But you have the best dog in Portugal. Adona is a wonder."

When the prime minister saw them, he chuckled. "Now, surely, we can find more comfortable accommodations for Portugal's premier wedding gown designer and her assistant. Why don't you join us for a light meal? Alberto will drive us and return you to the castle. Adona is welcomed to join us as well."

Peaches glanced at Margaret-Ann.

"I'm game," she said. "It will be good for Peaches to relax. She's looking a bit pale these days."

Peaches shook her head and sighed. "I keep telling you I'm fine, just fine."

Janet, who had just walked in, nodded at everyone.

"Yes, but you forget that you're talking to your mother," Margaret-Ann said, and stood up. "Mothers know these things. Don't you agree, Marietta?"

"Indeed I do," Marietta said.

"I rest my case," Margaret-Ann said.

"You look wonderful, Margaret-Ann. I simply adore that two-piece suit. I've never seen a design like that." Marietta lowered her head. "Peaches, did you design your mother's suit?"

Peaches shook her head.

Janet nudged Margaret-Ann. "Go ahead," she said. "Tell them."

"I designed it myself," Margaret-Ann said so softly that no one heard her.

"I didn't hear you," Marietta said.

Then Margaret-Ann straightened her shoulders and held her head high. "I...I designed it myself," she said.

"And I'm a witness to it," Janet said. "She did it all herself."

"Mother!" Peaches almost shouted. "You did this yourself? Why, it's beautiful. When did you become interested in design?"

"On the day I saw your first design on that white paper napkin."

Peaches' mouth dropped open. "But you discouraged me for years," Peaches said, and leaned forward. "Why?"

"Because I was a stupid old woman who thought that the only good jobs for women were as either wife or secretary. I couldn't imagine you making a living by drawing dresses. And we were in Atlanta, where there were so many brilliant designers. I wanted you to be successful, honey," she said, and folded her hands in her lap. "But I was so afraid that you'd be swallowed up by all the competition."

Peaches just stared at her.

"I didn't realize the extent of your talent, Peaches. I wish I could change my early behavior, but—"

"Come now," the prime minister said. "There isn't one of us who hasn't had a rocky start in this life. Besides, look at you now. You're the most famous wedding gown designer in all of Europe."

Peaches smiled. "We've come a long way from those ratty little apartments, haven't we? Thank goodness we'll never have to live that way again."

Margaret-Ann got up and took Peaches' hand. "I'm so proud of what you've accomplished, Peaches. You've exceeded my every expectation, and you've made yourself a star in the designer world."

Peaches put her hand over Margaret-Ann's. "No, no, it wasn't just me. If you hadn't been an expert seamstress able to bring the gowns to life—"

"Alberto!" the prime minister said. "Come, come. Let us feast and make merry."

As they walked to the car, Peaches glanced across the narrow street and stopped dead still. Her heart hammered in her chest.

Her fingers trembled. Her stomach felt tied in knots.

There, standing in an open doorway, stood Lorenzo, his fingers mimicking the shape of a gun.

Chapter 57

After the banquet, Peaches stood before the mirror in her bedroom and did a twirl. The runway show had proven so successful that she and Margaret-Ann would be busy filling orders for the next eight months. For the first time in her career, she thought seriously about putting a sign outside that said, "No new orders," but then her business sense took over.

After the current orders were filled, the next bit of business would be to build an addition to the studio, a space where Margaret-Ann could create and bring to life her own line of women's elegant two-piece suits. Excited about this venture, Peaches did one last twirl and leaned closer to the mirror. She turned her face this way and that.

"Not too shabby for thirty-nine," she whispered, though forty was fast approaching.

Adona whimpered.

"Go to sleep, dear one," Peaches said, and walked over to her. "I'll be along shortly."

Adona curled beside one of the pillows, her usual spot, and went to sleep.

Peaches went into her enormous dressing room, carefully removed her blue dress, hung it in a space created for her long gowns, and grabbed her pajama pants and T-shirt. Once she'd washed her face, brushed her teeth, and smoothed on her expensive night-time moisturizer, she headed to bed. But just as she settled in and got comfortable, a knock sounded at her door.

Peaches narrowed her eyes and listened. Another knock came. Adona whimpered. Peaches reached over and rubbed her head. With a sigh, she got up and went to the door.

"Yes?" she asked. "Who is it?"

"It's me, Peaches. Janet. I must talk to you."

Peaches opened the door. "What's wrong?"

"May I come in for a moment?" Janet asked, her hair a mess, her gown lopsided on her shoulders.

"You haven't even changed clothes yet?" Peaches asked.

Janet wrung her hands. "Peaches, I have something important to tell you. May I sit down?"

Peaches pointed to two overstuffed leather chairs. "Go ahead," Peaches said, and parked a stray strand of hair behind her ear. "Tell me what's wrong."

Janet still wrung her hands, but now she looked down at her lap.

"Janet," Peaches said. "What is wrong? Are you ill? You look pale."

"I'm not ill," Janet said, and smoothed her mess of a skirt.

"Then, please, Janet, tell me what's bothering you. It's late and I'm exhausted."

"Yes," Janet said. "I know you must be, but I didn't think this could wait. Peaches," Janet finally said, her voice cracking slightly, "I know Lorenzo. I recognized him, or thought I did, the very first time he showed up to model. But I wasn't sure, you see, because when I knew him, he was bald. He kept his head shaved."

Peaches leaned forward.

"But his name is not Lorenzo," Janet said. "It's Bacci, or that's what I knew him as. Mal Bacci is his nickname. Bad Bacci."

"And how did you know him?" Peaches asked as she stood and walked to the mantle.

"Mal Bacci is in Etienne's gang. They were like brothers,

grew up together, lived next door to each other. Tight friends. Mal Bacci is just as feared as Etienne. He controls the gang with an iron fist."

Peaches paced back and forth in front of the large mantel. Then she got her phone and punched a button.

"Don't call Javier," Janet fairly shouted.

Peaches narrowed her eyes and put her hands on her hips. "What are you talking about? Javier is in charge of my security team."

Janet nodded. "Mistake number one," she whispered. "He's friends with Etienne and with Mal Bacci."

"What?" Peaches shouted. "That's not possible. He's been thoroughly checked out."

Janet arched a brow.

Peaches knelt beside her. "What does *that* look mean? What are you trying to tell me?"

"All I know is that for some reason, Mal Bacci has changed his appearance, grown back his hair, changed his style, and then suddenly shows up here to apply as a model. He's a criminal. Why would he want to be a model?"

Peaches sat down and fiddled with the thick rug on the floor. Then she looked up at Janet, her eyes alight. "I've got it. Don't you see?" she asked.

Janet shook her head and wrung her hands again. "I don't see, but I'm afraid," she said.

Peaches picked up her phone again and pushed a button. A sleepy voice answered.

"Alberto," she said. "This is Peaches. Please forgive me for waking you, but something's come up here that I think the prime minister should know about right now." Peaches listened to the now more alert Alberto. "Thank you," she said. "And Alberto, enter as secretly as you can. Let no one stop you."

Peaches looked at Janet. "I think Lorenzo—Mal Bacci—planned it perfectly. He didn't want to be a model. He wanted to be a model for *me*," she said, and pointed to her chest. "If he works for Etienne, then being one of my models puts him in direct contact with me. Don't you see?"

"Oh, Peaches," Janet said, and lowered her head. "What have I done? I should have told you as soon as I remembered him. This is all my fault."

Peaches stood and waved her arms about. "Yes, you should have come to me immediately, Janet," her voice raised slightly. "You should have told me everything. I don't know why you didn't."

Janet stood up, too. "I was afraid, Peaches," Janet said, her hands hugging her shoulders. "He wants to kill me, too. I was afraid he'd know and come after me. I'm a coward, a selfish coward."

Peaches sat in one of the chairs. "The important thing to remember is that you found the courage to tell me." Peaches picked up her phone again and was about to dial, then stopped. "What about Maximo? Is he in on this, too?"

"Maximo, no. He hates Javier and Etienne. He thinks they're cruel, and besides, Javier once kicked Galahad, but the horse wouldn't stand for it and kicked back. Hurt him pretty badly. Javier won't go near him now. You've nothing to fear from Maximo. He's one of the good guys."

"Thank goodness," Peaches said, and tapped a spot on her phone. "Maximo," she said when he finally answered. "Forgive me for waking you, but I need your help. Can you come up to the castle?" Peaches listened. "I don't care what you wear, Maximo. This is a matter of urgency. I need your help right now."

Peaches fixed herself a coffee with a touch of Bailey's Irish Crème. "Care for a cup?" she asked Janet. "I won't sleep tonight, but then, it's almost morning anyway."

Janet stood beside her. "I'd love a cup."

Within minutes, a knock sounded at the door.

"Come in, Maximo," Peaches called.

The door opened slowly. "It's me, Miss Peaches. Javier," he said as the door opened wider. "I take it you were expecting my brother. A bit unusual for Maximo to be inside the castle. Is our Galahad ill?"

"Javier," Peaches said, and put on a fake smile. "How can I help you? Please be quick about it. I'm not dressed for company."

"I was merely making sure all was well. I heard voices, and seeing the time, I worried that you were ill."

"Nonsense," she said. "I'm doing fine. Is there anything else you need?"

Javier hesitated.

"Good night to you, then," Peaches said, and closed the door. "Janet," she said. "Guard this door while I change."

After only a few moments, Peaches reappeared looking radiant. Dressed in jeans and T-shirt, her face done up perfectly, hair piled elegantly on top of her head, she looked as if she were headed to work.

"Wow, that was fast. And just look at you. Like you just stepped off a magazine cover. How do you do it?"

"Years and years of practice. A swipe or two of foundation, a little mascara, eyelashes, and a brush of blush. One must maintain an image," she said in response, and patted her hair. "No one wants to see Peaches Malone without stylish hair and beautifully applied makeup. It's just the way things are."

Another knock sounded at the door. This time, Peaches opened it herself. "Maximo, please come in," she said.

The tall, blond, dark-eyed stable hand walked past her, his shoulders hunched.

"Stand up straight," Peaches said. "You've nothing to be ashamed of here. You guard one of my dearest treasures, so you occupy a very important place at the castle."

Maximo stood to his full height.

"Better," Peaches said. "I don't want to see you slouching around here again, Maximo. You're an important part of the family, and you need to claim that for yourself. We couldn't function without you."

For the first time since she'd met him, Maximo smiled. "As you wish, Miss Peaches."

"Please, take a seat," she said, "and then, tell me what you know about Lorenzo and Javier."

Maximo's eyes widened.

"You heard me plainly. I need information about them both."

Maximo stood up. "But I don't know anything," he said. "I'm not in their gang. I can't run with that crowd."

Peaches glared at him until he sat down again. "Now, answer me this. Are Lorenzo and Javier simply low-life criminals, or are they capable of killing?"

"Killing? They're thieves, I know that. But killing?" Maximo rubbed his temples.

"Have you known of a time they've killed anyone?" Peaches asked.

Maximo rubbed his hands. "Once," he said, "a man died during one of their robberies, but it was an accident. It's Lorenzo you have to watch out for. He has a mean streak. Etienne is never involved, just from a distance, so Javier and Lorenzo do his dirty work for him, but Lorenzo is unpredictable, so Etienne has barred him from the gang…or that's what I've heard anyway."

Peaches leaned toward him. "So, Lorenzo is working on his own now?"

Maximo shook his head.

Peaches curled the end of her hair around her finger as she waited for an explanation. Finally, she spoke up. "If he's not working on his own, who backs him? Who is he working for?"

A third knock sounded at the door.

"Who is he working for, Maximo?"

"Miss Peaches," Alberto called, "may I come in?"

Peaches smiled and went to the door. "Of course, Alberto, please come in," she said. "You're always welcome."

Maximo got up and walked to the door. "I'll go back to the stables now," he said as he eyed Alberto. "Our Galahad doesn't like to be left alone for too long. He's as spoiled as Adona."

"Please come for breakfast in the morning at seven. Carla will be delighted to see you."

Maximo nodded to her and left.

"I've brought the prime minister," Alberto said in a booming voice. "He's stationed extra guards around the perimeter."

"You're both so thoughtful," Peaches said.

Adona stood in front of Peaches, wagging her tail at Alberto.

"Animals love me," Alberto said as he reached down to pat the top of her head.

"Janet," Peaches called, but when she looked back, she saw that Janet had fallen asleep on the sofa.

The Bailey's, Peaches thought, and chuckled.

She shooed Alberto out and closed the door behind her.

Chapter 58

TuckerD stood behind a pillar on the brick-paved entrance to the Lisbon National Museum. A few feet below him two men talked and gestured, shouted and waved their arms.

"It has to be tomorrow," the one said loudly. "We can't afford to wait any longer. Tomorrow morning at ten, just as we've planned."

"No," the other said. "We're not ready. It's just you and me. We have no back up, and there are a thousand things that could go wrong."

"What does it matter if things go wrong? As long as we do the job, we'll be paid. It's about the money, man. Can't you see that?"

"And what if we get caught? Are you ready to be executed?"

"No problem. I'll make sure we get in and that we don't get caught."

TuckerD came out from behind the pillar and walked slowly down the stairs that led to the street. When he reached the bottom, he turned toward the two men. "Lorenzo, isn't it?" he said. "I was in the runway show."

Lorenzo turned around and recognized him. "Yeah, I remember you. What brings you here at this hour?"

"Couldn't sleep," TuckerD said. "A walk always helps, and I'm staying only a block away. I was just trying to get a peek inside the museum when I heard voices."

Lorenzo chuckled. "Hey, a couple of blocks down there's a house that offers a lot more to see than antiques. Right, boys? But you might not be into women."

One punched the other on the shoulder and laughed.

TuckerD yawned. "I'll be on my way now," he said. "Oh, and it was nice to see you, Javier. I assumed you'd be at your guard post tonight. Is the area left unguarded then?"

"Only for a few minutes," Javier said. "I'm on my way back right now."

"Does Ms. Peaches know there's no guard on duty?"

Javier nodded. "Maximo is covering for me."

"Interesting," TuckerD said, and walked away.

***

Peaches found herself in the throes of a disturbing dream.

She perched on the edge of a cliff with a straight drop of many hundred feet into the rocky shores of the sea. Ahead of her, just beyond reach, a piece of lace matching TuckerD's hovered, occasionally floating upwards with the wind, but returning to the spot just beyond her reach. She couldn't reach out for fear that she would plummet from the cliff to her death. Beyond the piece of lace opened a portal, and inside the portal an old woman dressed in regal attire from the 18th century held a tray. Atop the tray lay a piece of the lace. The old woman bent forward and presented the lace to…a king? Yes, he looked like a king. But just as the king reached for the tray, the old woman turned around, her face wrinkled, time-worn, and haggard, but her sea blue eyes shone like bright jewels, and for the first time, Peaches saw the stunning necklace she wore.

"This belonged to a queen," *TuckerD's voice rang in her ears.*

The old woman held out the tray.

"Touch the lace, darling," *she said to Peaches.* "Touch the lace and the necklace. They're magic, and they will protect and heal you. Take them, darling."

Peaches reached to touch the lace, but feared she would fall from the cliff and withdrew her hand.

The old woman smiled a toothless smile. "You must take the lace, darling. You must. It will save you."

Peaches reached again, grabbed the lace and the necklace, and felt her foot slip. She tumbled from the cliff toward the water below.

"No, no," she said. "I can't swim."

"Peaches," she heard. "Wake up, Peaches. You're dreaming. Open your eyes, dear. You're safe."

Peaches opened her eyes, sat up, and looked around. Then she flopped back down on the pillow.

Margaret-Ann squeezed her hand. "You're fine. That must have been some dream."

"I fell off a cliff into the sea trying to get a piece of lace. You're already dressed. What time is it?"

"A few minutes after eight," Margaret-Ann said.

"Eight! Why didn't you wake me? I'll be late to work."

Peaches threw back the covers and swung her legs off the bed. She parked her hair behind her ears and popped a mint into her mouth.

"It's Sunday, dear," Margaret-Ann said, "and except for this notation about TuckerD, your day is free."

"Free?" Peaches asked. "No consults, no meetings, no engagements?"

"Not a single one," Margaret-Ann said. She stood up and clasped her hands at her waist. "And that makes me glad. I want you to rest, please. Make your old mum happy and spend the day relaxing. You can wear that new outfit I bought you, the one made just for lounging around." Margaret-Ann walked into the closet and grabbed the shirt and pants off a hanger. "Look at this," she said, and held it up for inspection. "Soft fluffy cotton top with a bateau neck and a built-in bra! Matching soft wide-leg pants. Nice pale shade of blue. Perfect for a Sunday spent lounging in Portugal."

"I like it," Peaches said. "Okay, that's my outfit for the day. And you're a hundred percent positive that there is nothing on my schedule?"

Margaret-Ann picked up the day planner that Peaches always kept nearby and showed it to her. Except for the name TuckerD written above one of the lines, the page was empty.

Peaches smiled and sighed. "Good," she said. "I might be forced to relax. Has Lily gotten in yet?"

Margaret-Ann shook her head. "Her plane arrives at 10:00. Alberto has agreed to fetch her and bring her here. That Alberto. He's such a dear."

"Yes, he truly is. I don't know what we'd do without him. Well, I need to get up and make myself presentable. Can't lounge around if I don't look good. You never know when some handsome stranger might come calling."

Margaret-Ann waved a hand in dismissal. "Perish the thought," she said. "We don't want any strangers, handsome or otherwise, to come calling today."

They both chuckled.

As Margaret-Ann opened the door to leave, Peaches called to her. "Mother," she said.

Shocked at the sound of the word, Margaret-Ann stopped and turned towards her with a smile on her face.

"It just slipped out," Peaches said. "Would you ask Carla to make some biscuits—Lily loves them—and tell her I'm on my way down for coffee?"

"My pleasure," she said. "Oh, and you might want to hurry it up. TuckerD is waiting for you outside in the cabana. He didn't want me to wake you."

Chapter 59

At a few minutes before nine, Peaches strolled out to the cabana to find TuckerD, Adona at his heels. She smiled when he appeared and leaned on the column closest to her. Peaches saw that he wore his regular TuckerD outfit—blue frock coat, black breeches, and black boots—and frowned.

He won't be staying long.

But she managed a smile.

He walked to her and hugged her so tightly she almost lost her breath. Then he kissed her hard on the lips, and her world swirled around her. His lips were smooth and soft, yet hungry and demanding, as if they would devour her. The scent of cedar and citrus wafted through the air.

"Oh, how I've missed you, Peaches," he said, and set her gently on the ground. "How I've missed you." Then he pulled her to him again. "I love you so much, Peaches. I don't even have words to describe how I feel. Come, let's sit down. I have a surprise for you."

Peaches dropped his hand. "I didn't particularly like the last surprise you brought for me," she said. "Surprises with strings aren't really surprises, are they? They're more like bribery and traps."

"I made a mistake," he said softly. "I won't make it again. But one of these days, Peaches Malone, you will marry me of your own free will. You will come to me all on your own."

Peaches adjusted her sunglasses. "You sound quite sure of yourself," she said.

Adona whimpered and put her head on Peaches' leg.

TuckerD smiled. "Perhaps it's just wishful thinking," he said, "but it's what I believe in my heart."

"Aren't you hot, TuckerD? It must be ninety degrees out here, and you with that heavy coat."

"The weather doesn't have much effect on me," he said. "Never has. Hot, cold, snowing, raining, freezing, or burning hot, it just doesn't register with me somehow. I know that's odd, but it's the truth."

Peaches stared at him and took in his handsome face. "There is much about you that is odd, TuckerD. When you add them all up, it leads to some interesting conclusions."

TuckerD waved a hand at her. "Don't waste your time, Peaches. I'm just a man—an odd one, but a man nonetheless."

"My man," she corrected, and winked at him.

"Not until you put a ring on it, baby," he said, and laughed again.

Peaches shook her head. "You made a joke! That's the first time I've ever heard you joke about anything. It's delightful." She took his face in her hands and kissed him on the lips. "Well done, TuckerD. Well done."

Carla opened the curtains and carried a tray to the table next to them. "A little refreshment," she said. "It's so hot today."

Peaches could see the line of perspiration dotting her upper lip. "Thank you," she said, "for coming out in the heat to bring this to us."

Carla shrugged, her dark hair bouncing on her shoulders. "I'm Portuguese," she said, and wiped her brow. "I'm used to the heat, but today something about the air doesn't feel right to me."

"What do you mean?" Peaches asked, and gathered up her hair into a ponytail which she held with a rubber band.

"There's something heavy and dark about it," she said.

"Something ominous."

"Oh," Peaches said, and frowned. "That's not good."

But Carla smiled at her and shrugged. "No worries, Miss Peaches. We are all protected here, aren't we?"

"Yes," she said. "We most certainly are. Now, will you take Adona inside with you? I know she'd love to be in the lake, but there's really no one to watch her. Maybe Maximo can let her swim later."

Carla nodded and called to Adona. Adona pricked up her ears.

"Come along, Adona. Carla will give you a nice treat."

But Adona didn't follow. She stayed where she was with her head on Peaches' leg.

"It's okay," Peaches said. "She can stay out here."

"So, about the surprise," TuckerD said, and reached into his breast pocket, a wicked smile on his face.

"Oh yes, I'd forgotten," Peaches said, then got up and flipped on the overhead fan. "Ah," she said and fanned the front of her blouse. "Much better. Now, proceed."

He opened the pouch and pulled out a necklace, the same one he'd tried to give her before, and now, the one she'd seen the old woman wearing in her dream.

She gasped when she saw it again. Its beauty left her speechless, almost as if she'd never seen it before. The diamonds sparkled, the emeralds glowed, and Peaches swore she could hear the old woman speaking to her again.

"You must take it, darling. It will save you."

TuckerD watched her reaction. "Peaches," he said, "the old woman you saw in your dream was my great great grandmother. A dowager queen gifted her this necklace when she was just a young girl. Many family members have worn it since then, but it is always my great great grandmother's choice, and she has chosen you to wear it next."

Peaches shook her head. "But I'm not your family, TuckerD,

and the only thing I know about your great great grandmother is that she gifted the lace and the necklace to a king."

"Peaches," he said, and touched the sides of her face, "that king ruled a minor territory in what is now Spain. His rule was short and not noteworthy, but nonetheless, he held the title of king for five years. King Julian. Years later, his heirs and their families would carry the names of Julian, Carolo, and Malone.

"And you, Peaches, are his seven great granddaughter. This necklace is your rightful inheritance."

Peaches blinked. "What did you say?"

"You, my dear, are the great granddaughter of King Julian."

"I…I…I am the granddaughter of a…king?"

TuckerD fastened the necklace into place. "Now, it has finally found its rightful owner," he said, and kissed her cheek. "And you, my darling Peaches, no longer have to question your roots."

"So, I'm not some cast-away kid whose father left her when she was a little girl?"

"Frank Malone didn't leave you intentionally, Peaches. He passed away a year after he left. He knew he was dying, and he didn't want you or your mother to watch that. It was a selfish move on his part, but he had what he thought was your best in his heart."

Peaches cocked her head. "He passed away? We never knew," she said. "I thought…I thought I just wasn't good enough, that he left because I was too much trouble."

"He left because in his own warped way, he loved you and your mother."

A tear rolled down Peaches' cheek.

"Peaches," TuckerD said, "now, my dear, you know who you truly are. You don't have to worry about your father. You don't have to worry about the relatives you never met because YOU, my sweet, are royalty. I have the papers to prove it. You, Peaches Malone, you are the granddaughter of King Julian of Spain."

Peaches crawled into his lap and wept.

Chapter 60

At 9:30 the next morning, Lily, Margaret-Ann, Janet, and Peaches watched as the preliminary construction of Margaret-Ann's studio and shop began. They stood outside near the cabana.

"No, I don't agree, Peaches," Margaret-Ann said. "It should be your name on the outside, not mine. No one knows who I am."

"But by the time this is finished, people will know who you are and what you do," Peaches said. "Marietta has already told us that. All we have to do is get it built and get you to work. Your business will skyrocket."

"And what about *our* business, Peaches? We make wedding gowns, not two-piece suits. How will we ever get everything done?"

"Marietta is already interviewing candidates for seamstress positions for both of us. I think if we each hire three more assistants, we'll be okay. And we'll coordinate the weddings the way we've always done. It won't be so drastic a change."

Margaret-Ann shook her head. "But I don't want to stop making your wedding gowns, Peaches. I've done it for the last twenty years. It's all I know, and I don't trust new girls to do it. No, it's not a good idea."

Peaches shielded her eyes from the sun. "Don't worry about that. No one can make my gowns the way you can, so the assistants will take up the slack. Really, Margaret-Ann, you're worrying for nothing. It will all work out."

323

"She's right," Lily said. "You and Peaches are a team…except that now, you are both designers. Just think how wonderful it will be to see women wearing your suits, Margaret-Ann. It will make you so proud, and probably very rich."

"But I already feel that way every time I see one of our brides. Peaches designs, I bring them to life. That's what we've done for as long as I can remember. I'm old now, and I'm scared of change."

"You're not old," Peaches said. "You've turned sixty, a time when many women are coming into their own, so this is perfect timing for you."

"But I'll be here, too," Lily said. "And Janet. The four of us will make this work. I promise you."

Peaches smiled at Lily. "I know you still have your job with the prime minister, and I worry that you'll miss being in the royal palace."

Lily chuckled. "How could I refuse such an offer? That glorious suite you outfitted for me? I'd be silly to turn that down. The prime minister has given me leave to help get the business off the ground. My place at the palace will always be ready for me. But right now, I'll be concentrating on this new business while my assistants at the royal palace keep things running smoothly there."

"Well, we're delighted to have you as a temporary resident," Margaret-Ann said.

"And you won't mind my being around all the time?"

"Mind?" Peaches said. "It was my idea, remember?" Peaches heard barking. "Here she comes," she said as Adona rounded the corner. Peaches knelt and rubbed Adona all over. "You're such a good dog," she said. "My little Adona."

Adona flopped on her back so that Peaches could rub her belly.

"And spoiled rotten," Lily said.

Then they heard a sound they hadn't heard in several weeks:

hooves. When Peaches looked up, she saw Galahad.

"Ah, there you are, my jewel," she said, and walked over to pet the horse. "What a magnificent animal you are."

Galahad moved his head up and down.

"See?" Lily said. "He agrees with you. That's one smart horse."

"He is majestic, isn't he?" Peaches asked. "A gentle giant." Peaches bowed in front of him. "You, Sir Galahad, are one of nature's wonders."

Galahad responded by extending a leg and dipping low in front of Peaches.

She rubbed his muzzle and forehead. "I treasure you, my Galahad, my lovely giant beast."

Suddenly, Galahad righted himself and stared toward the entrance gates. He whinnied and took off in a full gallop. Peaches looked around to see what had disturbed him.

"What's wrong, Galahad? I've seen that stance once before, when—"

Peaches heard two gunshots and watched as Galahad fell.

"Galahad! My Galahad! No!" she screamed, and bolted toward the gate, Adona beside her. As she ran toward Galahad, she heard another shot and Adona fell. Peaches screamed. "Adona! My precious, my precious." Tears welled in both eyes, blurring her vision. "Adona, my darling. My sweet Adona. Wake up, honey. Mama loves you." When Adona twitched, Peaches kissed her on the nose and whispered, "I'll be right back, my sweet pup. Hang on for Mama."

Four more shots rang out, but Peaches had no idea where they came from or where they landed. All she could think about was her precious giant, her magnificent Galahad, and her wonderful Adona.

"Galahad!" she screamed over and over.

Lily and Margaret-Ann both screamed. Lily took off and ran to Adona.

"Call Maximo," Peaches screamed. "Get Maximo here immediately."

Peaches reached Galahad and bent down across him, the life draining from the two of them. Far away, she heard the wail of sirens and a sound she didn't recognize. An explosion? Flames rose high into the air, the wooden interior of her workshop crackling.

"Fire!" Maximo yelled. "The workshop is on fire!"

The gunshots stopped, but the building blazed.

Then Margaret-Ann fell to her knees. "Oh, God. Dear God."

Lily watched as TuckerD bounded up from the stables, his blue coat flapping at the sides, his face contorted in pain and fury. He moved so quickly that he seemed but a blur to her.

Though Peaches was stretched over Galahad, she raised her head. Her life's work now ablaze, she screamed. "Save the workshop! Please, please, save my workshop! My whole life is in there."

Suddenly, she saw a crowd of firefighters doing their best to put out the fire. And in her delusion, each firefighter became a gown that she'd designed. She watched as each one of them shriveled and disappeared, replaced by the fireman.

"My gowns," she screamed one last time. "My life's work of gowns!" Tears coursed down her cheeks. "My whole life's work," she sobbed over and over again. "I'm ruined." The grief was almost more than she could bear. The gunshots, the fire. The message was right.

You will all be destroyed.

But then some giant shape appeared before her. Then she felt the two familiar arms around her, arms that lifted her off Galahad and enfolded her.

"I've got you, Peaches," the voice said.

TuckerD.

"No, you must get Galahad and Adona. Go to them first, and the fire. It's destroyed my workshop."

326

"Adona will recover," he said. "You, however, have been shot three times."

"Galahad, my magnificent Galahad."

"Maximo is with him," TuckerD said.

She let herself pitch forward right onto his chest, and when she did, she heard herself moan then cry out, overcome by the intense pain in her back and shoulders. Each time TuckerD pulled her closer and ran his hands over her body, the pain shot through her again and again, like a million fire ants biting and stinging. She cried out again.

Then a tiny sound drew her attention from the pain: metal hitting concrete. It came a second and third time.

Bing. Bing. Bing.

"Sleep now, Peaches," TuckerD said. "Adona will be fine. The fireman have put out the fire. Most of your gowns are saved. Rest easy, my love."

Then she heard a ripping sound — material being torn?

TuckerD pried her fingers apart, put something in her palm, and closed her fingers around it. And then, the old woman's voice came back to her. *Touch the lace, my darling. It will save you.*

Peaches closed her eyes. But then, she flew away into a bright world and squeezed her eyes shut against the radiant light.

Chapter 61

Three days after the shooting and the tragedy of the great fire, Peaches woke up for the first time, immediately aware of several things: the heavy lump across her feet, her fingers tightly wrapped around a piece of material, and TuckerD sitting beside her bed.

"Well, hello, my love," TuckerD said. "Don't try to talk. You've some healing to do yet."

She mouthed something that he couldn't decipher, so he handed her a tablet and pen. "Hang on," he said. "I'll get Margaret-Ann and Lily. Stay, Adona."

Peaches moved her head and saw that the heavy lump at her feet was Adona. She wiggled her fingers under the dog's chin, and as she did, the piece of material fell out of her hand. She gathered it up and brought it to her face.

"The lace," she whispered.

Touch the lace, my darling. It will heal you.

An image of the old woman crept into her mind, and heeding her words, she bunched up the lace and kept it in her palm. "I'll never be without it," she whispered.

But then she squeezed her eyes shut against the visions of her workshop burning. She imagined each of her new designs, and many of her older ones, blackened and turned to ash. All those years, all that work, gone within minutes.

She sobbed so heavily that she could barely breathe. To her, the gunshots were nothing, the gowns, everything—and now, everything was lost. She saw no way to recover. Her life, as she had known and lived it for twenty years, was over. Sorrow and hopelessness settled around her like heavy blankets threatening to smother her under their weight.

Of a sudden, Margaret-Ann and Lily tiptoed into the room. "Peaches, Peaches," Margaret-Ann said, and sobbed.

Peaches held out a hand to her. "Mother," she said so softly it was barely audible.

Lily stood behind her, tears coursing down her cheeks. "It will be all right, honey. I promise. You just need to get well. The workshop can be rebuilt."

Peaches turned her head away from them.

"We're just grateful to have you alive, Peaches," Lily said. "You were shot three times, but your man over here, by a miracle we still can't understand, removed the bullets, stopped the bleeding, and saved your life right in front of us."

"TuckerD," she whispered.

"One thing's for sure," Lily said. "He's a keeper."

Peaches whispered, "The gunshots are nothing. My workshop was everything to me. My designs. My designs, all lost. All gone. My life is over."

TuckerD took Peaches' hand and kissed it gently. "I have a little gift for you," he said, "something salvaged from the fire."

Peaches turned to him.

TuckerD held up a rather large stack of white paper napkins. Peaches' eyes widened.

"Your designs, my love, all here where you first drew them."

Peaches took one, then another, then another, and slowly, a smile spread across her face.

"The fire wasn't as destructive as we had first thought," he said. "It blazed, burned for only a few minutes, then was out quickly thanks to the excellent efforts of the fire marshal and his team."

329

"The gowns?" Peaches asked.

"Some were saved, Peaches. They'll need cleaning, but you have a fair supply, and all the ones you stored in the very back room are in perfect condition."

"The back room," she whispered. "It's where I keep the gowns for upcoming weddings." Tears coursed down her cheeks.

"Oh, honey, don't cry," Margaret-Ann said. "We don't have to start over. We just have to begin again with the stock that we have. The prime minister has already sent his crew to rebuild the workshop. It's a blessing, a real blessing. I know you don't believe in such things, but I do, and I know in my heart that we are truly blessed."

Peaches smiled.

TuckerD looked at the clock on the wall. "Time for your meds," he said. "The doctor says you need to be on antibiotics and pain pills for a couple of weeks, just to make sure there's no infection in the tissue. And that trembling in your hands...it's called Essential Tremor. There's no known cure, but no danger either. So, you're going to be all right. Everything will be all right."

Peaches held the designs close to her bosom. Then she glanced around the room and saw Margaret-Ann, Lily, and TuckerD. She felt her precious Adona on her feet. She realized, maybe for the first time, how much she truly loved each of them, and how fortunate she was to have them with her. Her heart swelled with love.

"Peaches, dear," Margaret-Ann said, and sat next to her. "May I change the subject and ask where you got the beautiful necklace on the bureau? It must be worth a fortune. Those emeralds and diamonds are magnificent."

Peaches glanced at TuckerD and nodded.

"I...well, it's been in my family for generations. I gave it to Peaches as a sort of wedding gift. But, she, we...we decided that marriage wasn't feasible."

Lily glanced at Margaret-Ann, then back at Peaches. "Feasible?"

"Maybe practical is a better word," he said. "I travel a great deal, and Peaches is busy, and to be honest, I knew you and Margaret-Ann didn't trust me and wouldn't want me hanging around all the time. Margaret-Ann thinks I'm a loser, and you think I'm a shyster."

Peaches whimpered and a tear rolled down her cheek.

"Now, look what you did," Margaret-Ann said. "You've made Peaches cry. Shame on you."

"Forgive me, my love," TuckerD said, and kissed her hand.

Peaches shook her head. Peaches looked at them but did not speak.

"TuckerD," Lily said, "why don't you take a short break? Margaret-Ann and I will give her the meds. You've been here all night, and you must be weary." Lily walked to his chair by the bed. Then she bent down and kissed his cheek. "I can never thank you enough for saving our Peaches. In my book, you're a definite keeper, and I want to be matron of honor at your wedding."

"Thank you, Lily," he said, "but it's Peaches who makes the call here. Now, I really need to work for a while if you don't mind taking over. I'll be back later." He leaned over and kissed Peaches' forehead. "I'll be back," he said.

Peaches grabbed his arm. "Galahad," she said.

TuckerD bowed his head.

Peaches began to sob. "My Galahad."

"Peaches, stop your crying. Galahad is not dead, my love. He has merely gone back to his heavenly home."

"What?"

"Galahad was…was…your guardian angel, Peaches. His job is done, and he's with other angels now. Someone else will need him soon."

Peaches closed her eyes and shook her head. "I don't believe you. He's dead, isn't he?"

TuckerD took her hand and held it to his cheek. "The magnificent Galahad is not dead, my love. He thrives."

"But I don't believe in all that heaven stuff," she said. "Angels and God…they just don't make sense."

TuckerD laughed. "You're surrounded by them now, just as you have been throughout your life."

From the air, TuckerD plucked a beautiful Lipstick and Lace bloom. Lily and Margaret-Ann gasped. But Peaches smiled.

TuckerD handed the rose to Peaches. Then he closed his eyes and said one word. "Sing." The room took on a golden glow as the glorious sound of voices filled the room. "Look," he said to Peaches.

As she watched the corner of her bedroom, several diaphanous figures clad in white appeared, their mouths moving in song. Beside them, she thought she saw—for only a second—her Galahad, huge, magnificent, his eyes focused on her.

"I love you, my Galahad," she whispered.

Galahad nodded and gave a soft whinny, then vanished.

Peaches felt tears of loss sting her eyes as she closed them. She felt her chest heaving.

"Peaches," TuckerD called. "Open your eyes, my love. All is well."

Peaches slowly opened her eyes to see Margaret-Ann and Lily standing beside the bed, TuckerD seated in a chair beside her. She glanced to the corner of the room, and was aware only of the large tapestry hanging on the wall and the fireplace glowing with flame.

"I don't understand," she whispered.

TuckerD leaned close, his breath on her ear. "Ah, but you do, my love, you do. The angels came to sing to you. Keep that image in your mind always."

Chapter 62

Lily sat in the chair next to the bed and handed Peaches a small cup and two tiny pills. "Here ya go, hon. Take your meds. If you're a very good girl today, we might just go outside for a little while."

Peaches shook her head. "No. Not outside. I want to see the prime minister and Alberto. Where is Javier? He hasn't been around."

Lily frowned. "I fired him," she said. "He opened the gate for our intruders. He'll never work anywhere near here again. The prime minister has already arrested him. Javier, Lorenzo, and Etienne's gang planned this attack on you. They'll never get out of jail."

"Why?"

"Simply put," Lily said, "money. Your lawsuit made their actions known, and also made sales of any of their supplies, including your stolen wedding gowns, illegal. With you out of the way, they could go back to stealing and selling illegal goods, and Javier and Lorenzo were involved in it the whole time."

"How did you find out?"

"We have friends here, Peaches. Janet clued us in. Then Maximo filled in the gaps. When he saw what his brother had done to you, he went wild and almost beat him half to death before the security guards could stop him, and thankfully, Maximo was never involved in their gangs. As it turns out, he's hated Javier for years and was waiting for an opportunity to turn him in. You, my dear, gave him that opportunity."

"I should thank him."

"Thank him and trust him, because he is one of us now. I gave him Javier's job as butler."

Peaches smiled. "He probably doesn't like that very much," she said.

"It's only temporary. I have another butler recommended by the prime minister. He'll be here in a few days. His name is Enzo."

"What about Maximo?"

"Ah, Maximo, I'm afraid, will have his hands full. The prime minister has arranged a bit of a surprise for you, with TuckerD's help."

"Oh mercy," Peaches said, and tucked her hair behind her ears. "What kind of surprise?"

"Would you like to see a photo?" Lily asked as she rummaged through her bag and brought out an 8x10 glossy. "Here they are."

Peaches took the photo and her eyes widened. "Margaret-Ann, look at this," she exclaimed. "Aren't they beautiful?"

Margaret-Ann smiled. "A prize-winning black stallion and his mate…who happens to be with foal."

"I can hardly believe it," Peaches said. "I'm so very grateful."

"They won't replace your Galahad, but at least they'll provide you some comfort," Lily said, and wiped a tear from her eye.

"And TuckerD had a hand in this?"

Lily nodded. "He's an angel, Peaches. He insisted on finding the perfect horses for you. He loves you, hon. He truly does."

"That man. Whatever will I do with him?"

"I have a suggestion," Lily said. "But it isn't one you'll like."

"I have a suggestion, too," Margaret-Ann said. "I'll be right back. Don't say anything, not one word, until I come back. Swear?"

Peaches glanced at Lily and they joined pinky fingers. "We

swear," they said together.

After only a couple of minutes, Margaret-Ann came through the door carrying a large box.

"Here, let me help," Lily said, and got up to hold the door for her. "Good grief, this is heavy. What's in here? Buried treasure?"

Margaret-Ann smiled. "You might call it that," she said as she and Lily placed the box carefully at the foot of the enormous bed.

"Think you'd be all right propped up on some pillows?" Lily asked Peaches.

When the maneuvering was done and Peaches lay pain-free on the pillows, Margaret-Ann opened the box.

"Peaches," she said as she lifted the gown from the box, "this is one of your own designs, but one that I secreted away because it was the most magnificent gown I'd ever seen, one so beautiful that only its creator should wear it. So over the years, I worked on it little by little, and when I finished it, I thought it was the most wonderful gown I'd ever made."

Lily walked over to help Margaret-Ann hold up the dress. Made almost entirely of pure white satin, the dress had a simple long-sleeved bodice, tucked in at the waist, and a full white satin mermaid-style skirt with a long kick pleat of white tulle. Attached at the shoulders in back, a white satin train spilled nearly six feet onto the floor.

"It's a dress a queen would wear," Margaret-Ann said. "And you and only you are meant to wear it."

Tears rolled down Peaches' cheeks. "I…it's stunning, Margaret-Ann. I don't know what to say."

"I have a suggestion," Lily said, and chuckled. "Tell TuckerD you'll marry him. You can live here with all of us, and when he's gone on his jobs, you'll have us as company. It's high time for this dress to be worn. By you."

"And just think how it will look with your new necklace," Margaret-Ann said. "I cut the neckline just right, and I didn't even know about it then!"

Peaches smiled, and when TuckerD walked through the door, she held out a hand to him. "Come, sit beside me," she said.

TuckerD did as he was told. "Have I done something wrong?" he asked, glancing back at Lily and Margaret-Ann.

"Wrong? No, you saved my Adona. You saved me. And you gifted me with those stunning horses. I'd say you've done everything right, TuckerD."

TuckerD smiled and kissed her forehead. "Just doin' my job, lady," he said.

"Oh yes, about that job," Peaches said. "I'd like to offer you a permanent position here at Castle Alamenda."

TuckerD smiled again. "You know that I will always be here for you, Peaches. Always."

"And do you remember...?" Peaches said, and winced when she moved to stroke his cheek.

"Easy now. You're supposed to be resting. Can't this wait?"

In unison, Margaret-Ann and Lily said, "No, it can't wait."

TuckerD arched his eyebrows and looked over at them. "Am I in trouble?"

"Remember the in-law suite I suggested?" Peaches asked. "Well, I've changed my mind."

TuckerD lowered his head. "Oh," he said. "So I should find accommodations somewhere else?"

Peaches nodded.

"I see," he said, and moved to get up. "I understand."

Peaches touched his arm. "Look at me, TuckerD," she said softly. Once he looked at her, she smiled. "I think you should take up your rightful position right in here."

"But this is your bedroom suite," he said.

Margaret-Ann cleared her throat. When TuckerD looked at her, she held up the wedding gown. "I made this for my daughter," she said. "She'll be glorious in it."

Lily chimed in. "And I'll be matron of honor."

Peaches stroked his cheek again. "And I, my dear, will be the bride. Now, if I could only find a groom, the picture would be complete."

TuckerD stood up and looked from Margaret-Ann to Lily to Peaches. "Yes?" he asked.

Peaches smiled. "The granddaughter of King Julian of Spain invites you to join her royal family."

Margaret-Ann and Lily applauded, and a single tear of joy rolled down TuckerD's cheek.

The End

About the Author

Joy Ross Davis is a student of the romance, lore, and magic of the back hills of Tennessee. She writes imaginative fiction featuring unusual angels as main characters. Her novel, Countenance, won a Silver Medal of Excellence in an international readers' awards contest while her novella, Emalyn's Treasure won a coveted Gold Medal from Readers' Favorites. She has lived and worked in Alabama for most of her life. She has a Ph.D in Creative Writing, and for many years, taught English at a local community college. She retired to become a caregiver for her mother who suffered from dementia. She wrote her first novel shortly after her mother's death. For several months in 2007, she lived in Ireland and worked as a travel writer and photographer. She lives in Alabama with her son and three rescue dogs.

Published works available on Amazon and Barnes and Noble:
Countenance
Emalyn's Treasure
The Transformation of Bitty Brown
The Sutler of Petersburg

Sisters Divided
Mother, Can You Hear Me?
The Witch of Blacklion

Find her on FB (jdavisangelwriter) and Twitter (@joyrossdavis)

www.ingramcontent.com/pod-product-compliance
Lightning Source LLC
Chambersburg PA
CBHW020245200626
46816CB00001BA/139